Shallow Grave

*Also by Cynthia Harrod-Eagles
in Large Print:*

Grave Music
Death to Go
Death Watch
Orchestrated Death
Deadfall
Hollow Night

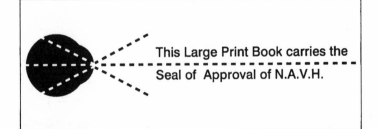

Shallow
Grave

A Bill Slider Mystery #7

Cynthia Harrod-Eagles

Thorndike Press • Thorndike, Maine

Published in 2000 by arrangement with Scribner, an imprint of Simon & Schuster, Inc.

Thorndike Large Print ® Mystery Series.

The tree indicium is a trademark of Thorndike Press.

The text of this Large Print edition is unabridged.
Other aspects of the book may vary from the original edition.

Set in 16 pt. Plantin.

The text of this Large Print edition is unabridged.
Other aspects of the book may vary from the original edition.

Set in 16 pt. Plantin.

Printed in the United States on permanent paper.

Library of Congress Cataloging-in-Publication Data

Harrod-Eagles, Cynthia.
    Shallow grave an Inspector Bill Slider mystery /
Cynthia Harrod-Eagles.
        p. cm.
    ISBN 0-7862-2342-1 (lg. print : hc : alk. paper)
    1. Slider, Bill (Fictitious character) — Fiction. 2. Police
— England — London — Fiction. 3. London (England) —
Fiction. 4. Large type books. I. Title.
PR6058.A6945 S5   2000
    823'.914—dc21   99-055053

For Tony, my accessory before and after

Chapter One

Eheu Fugaces, Postume

The Old Rectory, St Michael Square, on the Mimpriss Estate, was the sort of house Slider would have given anything to own.

'On a copper's pay? Your anything wouldn't even make a down payment,' Atherton said.

Slider shrugged. 'What's a man without a dream?'

'Solvent,' said Atherton.

It was a long house, built of stone, whose façade reflected three different periods. The middle section had the perfect proportions of classical Georgian domestic, with a fanlighted door and small-paned sash windows disposed harmoniously about it. To the right was an early-Victorian addition, very plain, with tall, large-paned sashes. The section to the left seemed much older: the stone was undressed and uneven, the windows casements, and at the far end were two pairs of double wooden doors like those of an old-fashioned garage. But despite, or even because of, its oddities, Slider coveted it. Whoever had altered and added to it over the ages, they had had a sense of proportion. As with a beautiful woman, he thought, the character in its face only made it more beautiful.

The Mimpriss Estate was itself an oddity. In the middle of the west London sprawl of Victorian-Edwardian terraces, it was a small area of large and desirable houses, built in the Arts-and-Crafts style at the turn of the century by a wealthy man with a bee in his bonnet. Given the proximity to central London, houses on the estate were now worth small fortunes. For the Old Rectory you were talking a three-quarter-million touch, minimum, Slider reckoned. Atherton was perfectly right, though it was unnecessarily cruel of him to have pointed it out.

The estate comprised half a dozen streets, with St Michael Square in the middle and the railway running along the back. The church in the centre of the square was dedicated with nice inclusiveness to St Michael and All Angels. Slider turned to look at it as Atherton locked the car, and was mildly surprised. This was no painstaking 1890s copy. It stood in its own small, railed churchyard with all the grave, reserved beauty of the fifteenth century, its grey stone tower rising serenely above the tombstones to dwell among the clouds. 'There should be rooks,' Slider said. 'Or jackdaws.'

'Settle for magpies,' Atherton said, as one of them went off like a football rattle in a tree overhead. He turned to look at the church as well. 'It's old, isn't it? Not just Victorian?'

'Early Perp,' Slider said. So, there must have been a village here once. 'He built the estate round it.'

'He who?'

'Sir Henry Mimpriss. Industrialist and amateur architect.'

'The things you know!'

'I read,' Slider said with dignity.

'*Si monumentum requiris*,' Atherton remarked admiringly. 'Wren only had a cathedral, and even that had some other bloke's name on it.'

It was one of the nice things about London, Slider thought, looking round, that you never knew when you would come across the good bones of an ancient settlement visible under the accumulated flesh of urban development. In this square, as

9

well as the church and the Old Rectory, there was a row of cottages whose Victorian tidying-up couldn't fool the trained eye, and a pub called the the Goat In Boots whose wavy roof and muddle of rear buildings dated it along with the church. Inn, church, rectory and a few houses: all you needed for a country village — set, in those days, amid the rolling hayfields and market gardens of Middlesex. And then the railway came, and life was never the same again.

Atherton was reading the church notice-board. 'Rev. Alan Tennyson. Tennyson's a nice sonorous name, but I think the Alan's a mistake. Lacks gravitas.'

'Make a note to tell his mother.'

'And they only get a service every second Sunday,' Atherton said. They started across the road towards the house. 'If this is the Old Rectory, where's the new one? Or does "old" just mean "former"?'

'Pass,' said Slider.

'It looks like three houses in a motorway shunt.'

'Don't be rude. It's just very old and altered,' Slider said defensively. 'The left-hand bit shows the real age. The Georgian face is only skin deep, and the Victorian wing's been added, by the look of the roof.'

'I'm glad I brought you along,' Atherton said. 'And now they've got a body. Careless of them. Gin a body meet a body lying down a hole . . .'

'That's "doon", surely?'

'If you insist. But don't call me Shirley. Shall we knock or go round the side?'

'Side,' said Slider. To the right of the house — between it and the next house, from which it was divided by a fifteen-foot hedge of that omnipresent British Leyland spruce that someone was soon going to regret not keeping cut down to a manageable height — was a gravelled parking area on which stood a very dirty, light blue Ford pickup with various items of builder's equipment in the back. Parked at the roadside and blocking it in were a patrol car and the Department wheels — a maroon Orion, which had brought DC McLaren, who had been on duty when the shout came in. At the back of the gravel area was a low wall that gave straight onto the terrace behind the house.

Slider and Atherton crunched over the gravel, stepped through a gap in the wall, and then stopped.

'Now that's what I call a patio,' Atherton said, with a soundless whistle.

'And I thought I was the Philistine,'

11

Slider replied. 'That's not a patio, that's a terrace.'

It ran the whole length of the house, a broad and glorious terrace paved with York stone in slabs so wide and worn and ancient they might have been nicked from a monastery, and who knew but they were? Beyond it there was a steep drop to the lawn, which sloped down to a belt of trees, behind which, but hidden at this leafy time of year, was the railway. It should have been a river, Slider thought, for perfection. Still he coveted, country boy though he was at heart. Sitting on this terrace and gazing at the trees, you could almost believe . . .

Presumably the forces of nature were exacting a toll on the structure, for there was all the evidence of building work going on: a heap of earth and rubble, another of sharp sand, a pile of bricks, three bags of cement, a bright orange cement mixer, a wheelbarrow with two spades and a pick resting across it, and a blue plastic tarpaulin the colour of the inside of a lottery-winner's swimming-pool, with frayed nylon rope through the eyelet holes at the corners.

The tarpaulin was folded back on itself, half covering a long trench dug in the terrace, parallel with its front edge, about three feet wide and two feet deep. The paving stones which had been levered up were neatly stacked away to one side, and an opportunist black cat was sitting on top of them in the sun, its paws tucked fatly under itself and its eyes half closed.

The builder himself was sitting on the low wall with his hands and his lips wrapped around a mug of tea: a stocky, powerfully built man in his thirties, with untidy thick blond hair, bloodshot blue eyes, weather-roughened cheeks and an unshaven chin. He was wearing mud-streaked work trousers and boots, and a ragged blue sweater over a check shirt. His strong hands, grained white with cement, were shaking so that the mug chattered against his teeth; he stared at nothing over the rim, past the blue-black legs of PC Willans, who was standing guard over him with an air of gentle sternness. It was a demeanour, Slider noted, often adopted by coppers towards remorseful domestic murderers.

McLaren came across to report. He was eating a cold Cornish pastie straight from the Cellophane wrapper and his lips were flecked with pastry and whatever the pallid glop was that passed for filling. 'Breakfast, guv,' he justified himself, seeing the direction of Slider's gaze. 'The body's down the hole.' With his free thumb he indicated the builder. 'That's Edward Andrews — Eddie Andrews. It's his wife.'

'And presumably his hole,' Atherton suggested.

'That's right,' McLaren said, with a world of significance. 'He got here very early this morning — earlier than usual — but, bad luck for him, the lady of the house was up even earlier and found the body before he could concrete her in. The plastic sheet was apparently pulled right over, bar a corner that'd blown back, when she found it. It was like it is now when I got here.'

'Householder's name?'

'Mrs Hammond. Lives here with her old dad. Norma's inside with 'em — I picked her up on my way here.' He gestured towards the uniformed constable, Defreitas, guarding the body. 'Daffy's got all the gen about Andrews. He lives round here.'

'On a PC's salary?' Atherton said disbelievingly.

'Well, not on the estate *as such*,' McLaren admitted, 'but only just round the corner. Woodbridge Road. Anyway, he knows this geezer Andrews.'

14

'All right, let's have a look,' Slider said. He went over to the hole and hunkered down. The victim was lying on her back. She had not been tumbled in, but laid out carefully as though in a coffin, decently composed, her clothes straight, feet together, hands folded one on the other. She was a slim woman in her thirties with well-cut blonde hair (helped, to judge from the roots, but not by all that much), wearing a short-sleeved, fitted dress of navy cotton with a red leather belt, bare legs and strappy leather sandals. She had full make-up on, rather on the heavy side, Slider would have thought, for a woman as attractive as she must have been; and her finger- and toe-nails were painted red to match the belt. Her eyes were closed, and there were no obvious marks of violence on her. She might have been fresh from the mortician's parlour.

'Expensive scent,' he said. Even after however long it was lying out in a trench, it had lasted well enough for Slider's sensitive nose to catch it. He felt her hand: it was cold and stiff.

'Expensive jewellery,' Atherton said, looking over his shoulder. She was wearing a wedding-ring and an engagement hoop with five large diamonds, a sapphire and diamond dress ring of more expense than taste, a rather nice gold watch and three gold chains of varying thickness around her neck. 'I wonder why he didn't take them off? The rings and the watch at least. Shame to bury them in concrete.'

'He says he didn't do it,' Defreitas offered.

'Well, he would say that, wouldn't he?' Atherton said.

Slider stood up. 'Things must be on the up in the building trade.'

'It's a good area for it,' Defreitas said. 'Lots of work — quality stuff, and no trouble about payment.' Something about his voice made Slider look up, and he noted that Defreitas seemed upset. He was pale, and there was a rigidity about his expression that suggested he was holding himself firmly in check. His cheek muscles trembled with the effort of control, but he went on steadily, 'Eddie's been doing all right for himself. Just built himself a big new house, down the end of Woodbridge Road. Corner of the main road. Four-ways, it's called.'

'Yes, I know it,' Slider said. He had passed it often over the months while it was being built in what had been the back garden of a big Edwardian house: the

Curse of Infill. He had noticed it because it had irritated him that it was called Fourways when it was on a T-junction, not a crossroads.

'Supposed to be really smashing inside,' Defreitas said. 'Built it for her.' He moved his head slightly towards the body, but without looking at it. 'Her name's Jennifer.' He stopped and swallowed a couple of times. Some men couldn't bear a corpse, even such a seemly and undamaged one as this.

'Take it easy, lad,' Slider said. 'You'll see worse in a long life.'

Defreitas swivelled his eyes towards Slider and then away again. He was a good-looking youngster, with brown eyes and a lean face and the sort of vigorous, slightly fuzzy tight brown curls that look like pubic hair. 'I know, sir. But it's different when it's someone you know, isn't it?'

'What do you know about Jennifer Andrews?' Slider asked.

'She works — worked — part time for David Meacher — you know, the estate agent? — and she did part time at the pub, too. The Goat In Boots, I mean,' he added conscientiously, 'not the Mimpriss Arms.' That was the estate's own pub, built at the

17

same time as the houses: draughty and uncomfortable, an overblown, over-quaint thing of pitch-pine and vaulted ceilings, like the fruit of an illicit union between a village hall and a tithe barn. 'The Mimpriss is a bit rough sometimes. The Goat's where the nobby people go. It's got a restaurant and everything. You know, a posh one — *nouveau cuisine* and all that.'

'How well do you know Andrews?' Slider asked.

'Just to say hello to,' Defreitas said. 'I've seen him in the Goat sometimes. He seems a nice bloke. I've heard people say he's a good builder.'

'You drink in the Goat?'

He seemed embarrassed by the implication. 'Well, I used to mostly go to the First And Last in Woodbridge Road, but they've got music there now and a lot of young kids come in. The Goat's nice and quiet, more like a village pub. Local people like it quiet. They don't like the Mimpriss — lets the tone of the estate down, they say.'

'They're not going to like having a murder here, then,' Atherton observed.

'Oh, I don't know,' Defreitas said. 'A murder like this —' He swallowed again. 'It's quite a toney crime, really. They'll all want to be in on it.'

'No trouble getting them to talk, then?' Slider said.

'Getting 'em to stop, more like,' Defreitas said succinctly.

'Doc's here, guv,' McLaren called.

Out in the road Slider could see reinforcements arriving and the photographer's van drawing up too. A group of onlookers was gathering on the pavement. 'Get some crowd control going,' he told McLaren. 'And we'd better get Andrews back to the shop before the press arrives.'

'When murder comes, can the *Gazette* be far behind?' Atherton enquired rhetorically. 'D'you want me to take him? I can have a crack at him while he's still warm. He's obviously number one suspect.'

Slider turned to look at him.

The morning sun shone on Atherton's face, illuminating the fine, deep lines, that looked as though they'd been grooved with an etching tool, and the indefinable bruised look that Slider associated with people who have been gravely ill. Atherton had not long been back at work, after an extended leave during which there had been doubt as to whether he would come back at all. His knife wound had been slow to heal; and there was the psychological wound as well. But Atherton was not the only one affected by the incident. For some weeks Slider had been obliged to consider the prospect of carrying on in the Job without Atherton, and to face the unwelcome realisation that he didn't want to.

That touched more than vanity. It was dangerous to be dependent on someone else in that way, and Slider had always thought of himself as self-sufflcient. In a long career as a policeman he had made many working alliances and had had some very good partnerships, but he had never allowed himself to become attached to any colleague as he had to Atherton in the past few years. Atherton's wounding and long sick-leave had forced him to realise how strong that attachment had become, and it scared him a little. He had coped with losing his wife and children to Ernie Newman, a man who could have bored for England; had coped — just — with losing his new love, Joanna, before he got her back again. But those traumas were in the social side of his life, and early in his career he had learned to keep the two sides separate. The Job was much the larger part of his existence.

It was not just that Atherton was a good bagman — anyone competent could learn his ways and fill those shoes; it was that he helped him to keep a sense of proportion about it all, something that got harder as time went on. Oh, he could do the job without Atherton, of course he could; it was just that, when he thought about it, really got down to it and looked it in the face, he felt an enormous disinclination to bother. Perhaps he was war-weary; or perhaps it was just the fleeting years. They were none of them, the Boy Wonder included, what they had been. But he had felt that if Atherton didn't come back, it would be time to empty his Post Office savings book and go for that chicken-farm in Norfolk.

Well, the boy was back; but looking fragile. Only yesterday Porson, the new detective superintendent who had taken over from Little Eric Honeyman, had stopped him on the stairs and asked him how Atherton was 'shaking out'. It was one of those maddening Porsonisms: it was obvious what he meant, but how did he get there? Did he think he was saying shaping up, shaking down, or working out? Or had he in mind even some more obscure metaphor for settling down, like Atherton shaking dusters out of the window, or shaking a pebble out of his shoe? Porson used language with the neatness and efficiency of a one-armed blind man eating spaghetti.

Slider had answered him optimistically; things were quiet and there was nothing even a fragile Atherton, given his gargantuan intellect, couldn't cope with. But now here they were with a murder shout, and who knew where that might lead? If there was any likelihood of rough stuff, Slider had already determined, he would make sure Atherton was kept well away from it. But the trouble was, these days, you couldn't necessarily predict the direction the rough stuff would come from. You might knock on any ordinary door and meet Mr G. Reaper in the shape of some crazed crack-head with half a Sabatier set clutched in his germans. And that was the worry, of course, that would wear you down. It was one thing to go into a known dangerous situation, with your body-armour, back-up and adrenaline all in place. But the creeping anxiety that any closed door and street corner, any routine roust, sus or enquiry, could suddenly turn bad and go for your throat, was unmanning. Slider wished he knew how Atherton was feeling about that; but Atherton had not brought up the subject, and Slider would not touch on it uninvited.

Atherton had noted his hesitation, and now said, with dangerous patience, 'I don't think he'll turn nasty, but if he does, I'm sure Willans will protect me.'

Now the pressure was on Slider not to seem to be coddling Atherton, so he agreed. And then, of course, because Atherton had put the thought in his head, he started wondering whether Andrews would turn violent after all. This friendship business was a minefield, he thought resentfully, and went to meet the doc.

It was not, however, the duty police surgeon, but Freddie Cameron, the forensic pathologist, in all his splendour.

'What's this — short of work?' Slider asked.

'I'm actually nearer than Dr Prawalha,' Cameron explained. 'I don't mind, anyway: if I'm going to be doing the doings, I'd just as soon see everything for myself while it's untouched.'

'You don't need to apologise to me,' Slider said, 'except for looking so disgustingly brown.'

'It was only Dorset,' Cameron protested. 'The Madam's got a sister in Cerne Abbas. Lovely place, as long as you don't suffer from an inferiority complex.

What have you got for me?'

Slider took him to the trench. In accordance with procedure Cameron pronounced life extinct, but offered no suggestion as to the cause of death. 'There's nothing at all to see. Could be drugs of some sort, or even natural causes — heart, or a stroke. Can't tell until I get her on the table. Presumably she died elsewhere and was transported here?'

'Unless it was suicide and she took the precaution of lying down neatly in her grave first. And then covered herself with the tarpaulin.'

'Those questions I leave to you, old dear,' Freddie said, and shook his head. 'Don't like this sort of case. Too much room for error.'

'Dead men don't sue,' Slider comforted him. 'Can you give me an approximate time to be working on?'

'Well, she's cold to the touch and stiff, but there's still some warmth in the axilla. It was a warm night, wasn't it? And she's been sheltered down this hole. Could be six to eight hours. Could be more. Probably not less than six.'

'Late last night, early this morning, then?' Slider said.

'Is that enough to be going on with? I'll

have a better idea from the temperature, but I don't want to do a stick here when I've no idea of the cause of death. You never know what evidence you might be destroying. Do you know who she is?'

'She's Jennifer Andrews, wife of local builder Edward Andrews.'

'He the one who dug the hole?' Freddie asked. 'Ah, well, there you are, then.'

'Here I am then where?' Slider asked, resisting the obvious.

'Whoever put her in here took the trouble to lay her out nicely,' Freddie said. 'So presumably it was someone who cared about her.'

'Could be remorse,' Slider pointed out.

'Comes out the same.' Freddie shrugged.

'Get on with your own job, Sawbones, and leave the brainy stuff to me.'

Cameron chuckled. 'You're welcome to it.'

A small door from the terrace let Slider into a coats lobby sporting an array of wax jackets, waterproofs, overcoats, shapeless hats, walking sticks, a gardening trug, a fishing basket, rods in a canvas carrying sheath, green wellies, muddy shoes and an extra long canvas-webbing dog-lead. A narrow door with opaque glazed panels gave onto a loo, an old-fashioned one with a high seat and a stout pipe going up the wall behind it to the overhead cistern. That would give you a healthy flush, he thought. A third door passed him into the house. Here was proof that the Georgian elevation was only skin deep: he was in the beamed hall of a fifteenth-century house, going right up into the roof-space. Some Victorian, during the Gothic revival, had added a massive oak staircase going round three sides of it, and an open gallery on the fourth providing access to the rooms on the upper floor, giving it a sort of baronial-hall look; but the wood of the beams was silvery and lovely, and it worked all right.

He could hear a dog barking somewhere. On his left, the Victorian extension to the house, there were two doors. The first he tried revealed a large, high-ceilinged room, empty of life and smelling pungently of damp. It was furnished with massive, heavy pieces, partly as a dining room and partly as a study or office: a vast mahogany desk with a typewriter and books and papers stacked untidily on it, and a rank of ugly steel filing cabinets occupied the far end. There were two tall windows overlooking the terrace, and one to the side of the house, looking onto the gravel parking space.

The second door opened on the room at the front of the house, a drawing-room, equally huge, with a Turkish carpet over the fitted oatmeal Berber, one whole wall covered floor to ceiling with books, and the sort of heavy, dark furniture usually associated with gentlemen's clubs. Here and there about the room were framed black-and-white photographs. Slider noted amongst them one of a man in climbing gear against a background of mountain peaks, a group of men ditto, the front row crouching like footballers, and another of a climber with his arm across the shoulder of a well muffled-up sherpa, both grinning snow-smiles at the camera.

The room also contained WDC Swilley, an old man in a wheelchair, and a large woman struggling with a dog. The dog was one of those big, heavy-coated, dark Alsatians, and it was barking with a deep resonance that was making the chandelier vibrate.

'Oh, for God's sake, woman, let her go!' the old man said irritably. 'Why must you always make such a fuss? Stand quite still,' he commanded Slider, 'and she won't hurt you.'

The dog, released, sprang unnervingly forward, but stopped short of Slider, sniffed his shoes and his trousers, then looked up into his face and barked again, just once, its eyes wary and suspicious.

'Good girl, Sheba,' the woman said nervously. 'Good girl, then. She won't hurt you.'

Slider had known a good many dogs in his time, and wouldn't have wagered the hole in his trousers' pocket on the temper of this one. He offered his hand to be sniffed, but the dog flinched away from it, and then he saw that its ears were bald and red and scabbed with some skin complaint, which made him both wince and itch in instant sympathy.

'Poor girl,' he said quietly, 'poor old girl,' and the dog waved her tail uncertainly.

But the old man snapped, 'Sheba, come *here!*' and the bitch turned away, padded over to the wheelchair, and flopped down, near but just out of reach.

'I'm so sorry,' the woman fluffed, blushing awkwardly. 'She's a bit upset, you see. She wouldn't hurt a soul, really.'

'Oh, for God's sake, Frances, shut up!' the old man snapped. 'You don't need to apologise to him. And what's the point of having a guard dog if you tell everyone she's harmless?' He looked at Slider with a kind of weary disgust. 'I despair of women's intellect. They have no capacity for logical thought. The Germans had the right idea: confine them to *kinder, küche,* and *kirche.* Trouble is, *this* one's no bloody use for the first two, and the last is no bloody use to me. Who are you, anyway? Another of these damned policemen, I suppose.'

Slider passed from Swilley's rigid expression — was she suppressing fury or laughter? — to look at the old man. He had a tartan rug over his legs, and his upper half was clad in a black roll-neck sweater and a crimson velvet smoking jacket: very sprauncy, but that jacket, with the scarlet of the Royal Stuart plaid, was an act of sartorial vandalism. He sat very upright, and Slider thought he would have been tall once; now he was thin, cadaverously so, with that greyish sheen to his skin and the bluish tint to his lips that spoke of extreme illness. He had a full head of white hair, though that, too, had thinned until the pink of the scalp showed through, like the canvas on a threadbare carpet. His hands, all knuckles and veins, were clenched in his lap, and he stared at Slider with eyes that were surprisingly, almost shockingly dark in that corpse-white face, eyes that burned with some desperate rage, though the thin, petunia lips were turned down in mere, sheer contempt. Some poem or other, about a caged eagle, nagged at the back of Slider's mind. There was nothing really aquiline about this old man's appearance. A caged something, though. If he was the climber in the photographs, it must be a bitter thing to be confined to a wheelchair now.

'I'm Detective Inspector Slider, Shepherd's Bush CID,' he said, showing his brief. 'May I know your name, sir?'

The old man straightened a fraction more. 'I am Cyril Dacre,' he said superbly.

The woman shot a swift, nervous look first at the old man and then at Slider. That, combined with the annunciatory tone of voice gave Slider the hint, and he was saying in suitably impressed tones, '*The* Cyril Dacre?' even while his brain was still searching the old mental card index to see why the name sounded familiar.

'You've heard of me?' the old man said suspiciously.

The woman crackled with apprehension, and Swilley, trying to help, swivelled her eyes semaphore-style towards the bookcase and back, and, concealed from Dacre by her body, made the unfolding gesture with her hands that in charades signifies 'book'. But — and fortunately — Slider really had heard of him and remembered just in time why, so he was able to say with obvious sincerity, 'Not the Cyril Dacre who wrote all those history books I learned from in school?' How many times had he opened one of those fat green tomes and seen that name on the title page? *A Cambridge History of England* by Cyril Dacre. *Volume VII, The Early Tudors, 1485–1558.* A name so well known it had become generic, like Fowler or Roget: 'All right, settle down now, and open your Dacres at chapter seven . . .'

'I am indeed Cyril Dacre the historian,' Dacre said, and there was no mistaking the pleasure in his voice. 'Why does it surprise you?'

'Your name was such a part of my schooldays, it's like meeting — oh, I don't know — a legend,' Slider said. For some reason, when he was at school he had always assumed that the authors of all textbooks were long dead, so it was even more unexpected to come across a live one all these years later. But Dacre didn't look as if he had too tight a grip on life, so Slider didn't think that it would be tactful to put it that way.

Dacre waved a skeletal hand towards the bookcase. 'Of course, my Cambridge History series is only a small part of my oeuvre.' In his head, Slider heard a ghostly Atherton voice saying, *'An oeuvre's enough,'* and resisted it. 'Though perhaps when the account is totted up, it may prove to have been the most influential part.'

'It's an honour to meet you, sir,' Slider said, and looked pointedly at the woman, so that Dacre was obliged to introduce her.

'My daughter Frances. Frances Hammond.' The woman made a little woolly movement, as though unsure whether to step forward and shake hands or not, caught her toe in the carpet and stumbled. Dacre glared at her and made a sound of exasperation. 'Clumsy!' he said, not quite under his breath.

Slider stepped in to rescue her. 'And there are just the two of you living here?'

'Yes, that's all — now,' she said, in a failing voice. 'Now the boys are gone. Left. Grown up, I mean. My two sons, who used to live here.'

Slider sensed another *for God's sake, woman* just under the horizon and turned to the glowering historian to say, 'I should like to talk to you later, sir, but I'd like to take your daughter's statement first, if you'll excuse me.'

Dacre's eyebrows snapped down. 'Excuse you? Where are you going?'

'I'd like to speak to Mrs Hammond alone.'

'Oh? And what do you think she'll have to say that I mayn't hear?'

'We have rules of procedure which we have to follow, sir,' Slider said smoothly, 'and one of them is that witnesses must make their statements alone and unprompted.'

He snorted. 'Statement? The woman can't string two words together without prompting. You'd better talk to her here where I can help her.'

'I'm sorry, Mr Dacre, but I must stick to the rules,' Slider said firmly. 'Mrs Hammond, if you'd be so kind?'

She fluttered again and started towards the door, hesitated, and glanced uncertainly back towards her father. Dacre looked irritated. 'Yes, go, go! I don't need you. Take the dog with you — and for God's sake try to look as though you remember how to walk. Why I wasted all that money on ballet and deportment lessons when you were a child I don't know —'

While he carped, Mrs Hammond called the dog, but it didn't move, only looked up at Dacre, which seemed to please the old man, but made Mrs Hammond blush again. She had to go back and take hold of the dog's collar. Slider held the door open for her, but Mrs Hammond, bent over to tow the dog — for she was a tall woman — misjudged the opening and hit her head on the edge of the door.

Dacre roared, 'You are the clumsiest moron of a female it has ever been my misfortune to —'

She passed Slider in an agony of confusion, and he shut the door on the dragon, feeling desperately sorry for her. She had a red mark on her forehead, and her eyes were bright and moist. 'I'm sorry,' she muttered disjointedly. 'My father — all this is so upsetting. He's in a lot of pain, you see. He has pain-killers, but they don't stop it completely, of course. It makes him rather — cross.'

The childish, inadequate word was somehow the more effective for that. 'Is he ill?' Slider asked.

'Cancer,' she said. She met his eyes starkly. 'He's dying.'

'I'm sorry,' Slider said. She looked away. She had let go of Sheba's collar: the dog

34

was trotting rapidly round the enormous hall, tracking the smell of police feet back and forth across the carpet. 'Is there somewhere we can go to talk?' Slider asked.

She gestured limply across the hall. 'The kitchen — we could — if that's all right?' she said. 'It's where I usually . . .' Slider had to stand aside and make a courtly gesture to get her to lead the way. He could see how her constant ineffectual wobbling would get on Dacre's nerves; on the other hand, maybe Dacre's roaring and snapping was what had made her that way. If tyrants proverbially make liars, surely bullies make faffers?

Chapter Two

It Takes Two To Hombre

The kitchen was on the far side of the hall, in the third section of the house. Mrs Hammond opened the door onto a room as different as could be from the drawing-room — about twenty feet square, low-ceilinged and stone-floored. Its long case-ment window facing onto the road was set deep into a wall two feet thick, and there were beams overhead and a stunning arched stone fireplace with a delicately carved sur-round, which now housed a rather beat-up looking cream Rayburn. Judging by the quality of its stonework, this must have been one of the main rooms of the original house, Slider thought, reduced to the status of kitchen when the house was enlarged.

Slider turned to his hostess. Frances Hammond, *née* Dacre, was a big woman — not fat, but tall, and with that unindented solidness that comes with a certain age. Slider put her in her middle fifties, but it

36

was not altogether easy to tell, for her clothes and hair and general style made her look older, while her face, if one could take it in isolation, looked younger. It was a soft, creaseless face, pink and somehow blurred, with uncertain eyes and a vulnerable mouth. She made Slider think of a child of about ten finding itself trapped by sorcery in someone else's body. Perhaps that accounted for her lack of co-ordination: she moved like someone coping with an alien planet's gravity. But she might have been pretty once, and could have been handsome even now had anyone taken the trouble to encourage her. Her hair, in the dull, too-old-for-her style, was light brown and softly curling, and her eyes were large and brown and rather fawn-like.

'What a splendid room,' he said to her, to prime the conversation.

She looked pleased, but nervous. 'Oh, yes,' she said, moving her hands vaguely. 'I like it. I tend to sit here mostly.' There was a saggy old sofa, stuffed with a variety of cushions, standing endways on to one side of the Rayburn, and an old-fashioned high-backed oak settle facing it on the other side. 'It's warm and quiet, and Father — well, he finds — he likes to be

alone for reading and working and . . .'
She seemed to run out of steam at that
point. Her voice had a faded, failing sound
to it, so that she started her sentences
feebly and lost impetus as she went along.

'You don't worry about his being alone,
in his condition?'

'He rings if he wants me. The servants'
bells are still . . .' She glanced towards the
indicator above the door, one of those
boards with little handbells on brass
springs. 'And he has Sheba with him most
of the time, though sometimes she gets on
his nerves. And then he . . .'

'What's wrong with her ears?' he asked,
turning to look at the dog; it seemed restless, tracking round the kitchen with its
nose to the floor, ears flicking with irritation.

'Oh, it's nothing catching,' Mrs
Hammond said at once, as though she had
been accused of it many times. 'It's a nervous complaint, the vet says. Or maybe
hormonal. It makes it difficult to . . .'
Fade-out again. It was like listening to
Classic FM in a poor reception area. 'She's
a bit upset, poor thing, with all this . . . I'll
just shut her out.'

Mrs Hammond opened a door on the far
side of the kitchen, giving Slider a glimpse

of a stone passageway with doors on either side — storerooms, he supposed — and called the dog. It did not obey, and she was obliged to catch it by the collar and drag it out, nails protesting on the stone floor, and shut the door quickly. Coming back, Mrs Hammond said, 'Would you like a cup of tea? Or coffee. Or anything.'

It would probably soothe her to have something to do with her hands, Slider calculated. 'Yes, please, if it's no trouble. Tea, please.' He waited until she had drawn the water and set the kettle on the hob, and then said, 'It must have been a terrible shock to you this morning to find Mrs Andrews like that.'

Instantly her eyes filled with tears and her mouth trembled; it was as though she had forgotten the dreadful events in the business of taking care of Slider. He was almost sorry to remind her. 'Oh! It was awful. Poor Jennifer!' She put her hands to her mouth. 'Who would do a terrible thing like that?'

'A terrible thing like what?'

Her cervine eyes lifted, puzzled. 'Well — you know — murder her.'

'We don't know that she was murdered,' he said, leaving an opening for her; but she only looked at him in utter dumbfoundedness.

'But —' she said at last. 'But she couldn't have — I mean — how did she get into the hole? With the tarpaulin pulled over her. Someone must have put her there — mustn't they?' She added the last in a kind of horrified meekness, as though expecting him to produce some ghastly official knowledge of bodies and holes beyond the range of the ordinary citizen.

'Someone must have put her there,' he agreed, 'but it doesn't follow they killed her. She might have died naturally, and this person for some reason didn't want to get involved.'

Mrs Hammond stared a moment longer, working it through, and then looked hugely relieved. 'Oh! Yes, I see. That must be it! Oh, I'm so glad it wasn't . . . I didn't want anyone to . . .' She sat down awkwardly on the edge of the sofa. 'Of course, he might think no-one would believe him. They were always quarrelling.'

'They?'

'Eddie and Jennifer.' She looked up at him anxiously, as if she had done something wrong. 'Oh, but I don't mean to suggest . . . It doesn't follow that . . .'

'Most married couples quarrel,' he said.

She looked relieved again. 'Yes, of course. I didn't want you to think . . .'

'That's all right,' he said, in general reassurance. 'What work is it that Eddie's doing on your terrace?'

'Subsidence,' she said. 'All these dry summers. We're clay here, you see, and it shrinks. There was a section of the terrace where the paving stones were sinking, and cracks appeared in the terrace wall.' She paused, thinking.

'So you called him in?' Slider prompted.

'I mentioned it to him, just in passing, and he said he'd come and have a look. And then he said it was subsidence and it was very serious. We'd have to have it done or the whole terrace might collapse.'

'So it was he who suggested you have the work done?'

'Oh! Yes. I suppose so, if you put it like that. But he would know: he's a very good builder. Everyone says so. And he's done lots of little things for us over the years. He's very reliable.'

Slider nodded. 'When did he start work on the terrace?'

'On Monday.'

'And what time did he finish work last night?'

'I'm not really sure. I think it was — perhaps some time after six.'

41

'Didn't he usually come and tell you he was leaving?'

'Oh! No, you see, he could come and go as he liked, round the side. He didn't need to be let in, so he . . .' He waited sturdily and she went on, 'I didn't go out there much while he was working. I didn't want to get in the way.'

'You can't see the terrace from here,' he observed. The only window looked onto the road. 'You say you usually sit in here?'

'My father likes to be alone. He has his end of the house, the two big rooms for his study and sitting room, and his bedroom and bathroom above. I stay at this end. My bedroom's above here, and my sewing-room, and I generally sit here in the kitchen — unless he asks for me, to read to him. Or play chess.' She blushed. 'I'm not very good, so he doesn't often ask me.'

'So it's almost like being in two separate houses?'

'It was the arrangement we had when the boys were little, so that they wouldn't disturb him. Mummy was alive then, of course. She and Father had their end, and the boys and I had ours. Their bedrooms and our bathroom are next to my bedroom, and my sewing-room used to be their playroom. Of course, they're gone now, the boys. Left home. They've got their own lives,' she added with unconscious pathos. 'But Father — we just kept the arrangement the same.'

Slider felt almost shivery, thinking of these two people alone at opposite ends of the house, isolated by the great no man's land of the baronial hall. He thought he had never come across a woman so sad — in all senses — as Mrs Hammond.

He resumed questioning. 'So how do you know that Andrews left after six yesterday?'

'I took Sheba out at about half past six, and he wasn't there then.'

'But he could have left earlier than six?'

'Oh, he wouldn't do that,' she said earnestly. 'Whenever he's worked here for us, he's always started at half past eight and worked till six or later — at least, in the summer. He liked to get the job done, you see.'

Slider accepted this for now. 'How did he leave things? Was the tarpaulin covering the hole completely last night?'

She fluffed. 'Oh! I think so. I didn't really notice. I'm so sorry! I mean, I didn't have any reason to look. I think it was, though.'

Slider made a calming gesture. 'Would

you like to tell me what happened this morning?'

'I — I went to take Sheba out. I was earlier than usual. I didn't sleep well last night. I don't sleep much as a rule; Father sometimes needs me in the night, and it's made me something of an insomniac.'

'Were you disturbed in the night — last night, I mean?'

She looked confused. 'Oh! No — nothing like that. It was very quiet, actually. But I didn't sleep well all the same, so I got up early. I took Sheba out, and — and the corner of the tarpaulin was turned back. I suppose it must have blown like that in the night. As I went past I just glanced at it and — and saw — saw the legs.' Her lips began to tremble. 'It was so terrible.'

'Yes, it must have been a dreadful shock for you,' Slider said encouragingly. 'What did you do next?'

'I couldn't think. I didn't know what to do. I thought I'd better make sure. So I pulled the tarpaulin right back. Then I saw it was Jennifer. Then I — I suppose I was frozen to the spot for a while. And then Eddie arrived.'

'In his pickup?'

'Yes. He pulled onto the gravel and

jumped out and came towards me and — and I — I screamed, I'm afraid. I was frightened. And he said something like, "What are you doing here?" and I said, "It's Jennifer," and he said, "You've found her!" or something like that. And then he looked at her, and he seemed very shocked and sat down on the wall and handed me his telephone and said, "You'd better call the police." So I did.'

'Why were you frightened when he arrived?'

She paused at the question, as though surprised, and then said nervously, 'Well — because I thought he'd killed her. So I was afraid he might — attack me.'

'What made you think that?'

'I don't know. I suppose it was silly. It just seemed obvious at the time.'

'You were quite sure she was dead?'

'She looked dead,' she said faintly. 'You don't mean — ?'

He had no desire to add to her mental burdens. 'No, I'm sure she was. I just wondered why you were so sure. And Andrews seems to have been sure, too. He told you to call the police, not an ambulance?'

She nodded. 'But she looked dead,' she said again. The kettle boiled and she got up and lifted it off with hands that were trembling badly again. Prudently, he waited until she had poured the boiling water and put the kettle down before asking the next question.

'So after you had telephoned the police, what did you do?'

'I went indoors to get Father up.'

Slider raised his eyebrows. 'You just left Andrews there on his own?'

She coloured. 'Was that wrong? But I had to see to Father. He gets so cross if his routine is interrupted.' Her hands moved about feebly as if trying to escape. 'Eddie — he wasn't doing anything, just sitting on the wall. But Father —'

She was obviously much afraid, or in awe, of her father; the thought that Andrews might destroy evidence probably never occurred to her. And if she really did think he had killed his wife, she might not want to remain alone with him. Slider could hardly carp about that, but it was inconvenient: Andrews must have been alone out there for a quarter of an hour or so. 'I believe you told one of the other policemen that Eddie Andrews arrived earlier than usual this morning?'

She handed him a mug of tea. 'Yes. He always started at half past eight, but it was before seven o'clock this morning.'

'Did you usually see him arrive?'

'Well, I see his truck go past the window if I'm in here. Half past eight was his usual time. I didn't expect . . .'

'No, I'm sure you didn't,' Slider said.

There was a scratching, rattling noise at the far kitchen door, and it swung open to admit the Alsatian, which glanced sidelong at Mrs Hammond and then resumed its restless padding around the kitchen, nose to the floor. Mrs Hammond looked guiltily at Slider. 'She can get the door open now, the bad girl. She pushes the latch up. She doesn't like being shut out.' She turned to the dog. 'Basket! Go to your basket.' For a wonder, the dog obeyed. The basket was in the corner, a big wicker one, lined with blanket. The dog turned round three times and flopped down, and then nosed out what looked like a bit of red rag from under the blanket and began chewing it in an obsessive kind of way.

'Good girl,' said Mrs Hammond, with a hint of relief. It must be nice for her, Slider thought, to get her own way in something for once.

Andrews looked up as Atherton came in with the tea. He was more haggard than ever, though his hands had stopped shaking; and despite his burliness of shoulder he looked small sitting at the table with the great solid bulk of PC Willans standing in the corner behind him.

'I didn't do it,' he said, without preamble.

'He denies it: write that down,' Atherton said to the wall.

'I want to go home. You can't keep me here.'

'No-one's keeping you here, sir,' Atherton said blandly. 'You're helping us with our enquiries, that's all. It's purely voluntary.' He pushed a cup across the table to Andrews, and raised the other to his lips in a relaxed, social manner. 'You do want to help us, don't you?'

Andrews' defiance deflated. 'I don't know anything,' he said pathetically. 'I don't know what happened. I would never have hurt her. Aren't I supposed to have a solicitor?'

Atherton, absorbing the sequence of words, said in tones of pleasant interest, 'You can have one if you want, of course. Do you think you need one, then?'

Andrews shook his head slightly, which Atherton took as an answer, though it might just as easily not have been. Andrews was drinking the tea now, staring blankly through the steam. He looked as if he hadn't slept for a week, and he certainly hadn't shaved for twenty-four hours. The shock was genuine enough, Atherton decided. He had seen before how a murderer didn't really take in the enormity of his actions until he was found out, and saw them, so to speak, through someone else's eyes. Only then did he let all the normal human feelings out of the locked room where they'd been kept out of the way while the deed was done.

Start with the easy stuff, Atherton thought, from chapter one of the *Bill Slider Book of Getting People To Blurt It All Out*. 'So, tell me about this work you're doing for Mrs Hammond.'

Andrews blinked, having expected a worse question, and took a moment to recalibrate. 'She was worried about subsidence. Well, some of the pavings had sunk a bit, and there were some cracks in the retaining wall, but I told her it was nothing to worry about. They move about a bit, those old buildings, but they'll stand up for ever. But she insisted I do something about it, so I did.' He looked at Atherton and shrugged slightly. 'I've got a living to make.'

'Cheating her out of her savings, eh?'

He looked nettled. 'I *told* her it was all right. Anyway, the money's all Mr Dacre's. She hasn't got a penny of her own. It was for Mr Dacre to say if he wanted the job done, so he must've agreed.'

Atherton smiled smoothly. 'I see. Of course, you didn't mind taking the money from an old man in a wheelchair?'

Andrews flared up. 'What're you trying to say? I'm an honest builder, anyone will tell you that.'

'Just trying to get an insight into your character.'

'Mr Dacre's a bad-tempered old bastard, and he treats her like dirt, so you needn't take up for him! What's all this got to do with it anyway?'

'Well, you see,' Atherton said, 'here was this handy hole in the terrace and, lo and behold, your wife's body turns up in it. Naturally I wondered whose idea it was to dig the hole in the first place.'

Surprisingly, Andrews crumpled and a couple of convulsive sobs broke out before he covered his face with his hands and sat making choking noises into them, his shoulders shaking. 'I didn't kill her!' he cried, muffled. 'I wouldn't! I loved her! You've got to believe me!'

Atherton waited implacably until the

noises stopped. Then he said, 'All right, tell me about you and Jennifer. How long have you been married?'

'Ten years,' Andrews said pallidly. 'We have our ups and downs like any couple — you know how it is — but . . .' It was one of those sentences not designed to be finished.

'How did you meet her?'

'I was doing a job in St Albans. That's where she comes from. I went to the pub after work one evening and there she was.'

'Working behind the bar?'

Andrews didn't like that. A little point of colour came to his cheeks. 'She was a customer, same as me. She was there with some friends. It's only recently she's started working at the Goat — and anyway, she's a waitress in the restaurant there, not a barmaid.'

'You've got something against barmaids?'

'Not as such. It's just — not something you want your wife doing, is it? She helps out sometimes in the restaurant at the Goat, that's all, because Linda asked her to, as a friend.'

'Linda?'

'Jack's wife. Jack Potter, the landlord. Linda runs the restaurant. It was her idea

51

to start it — she reckoned there was lots of money round here for a posh restaurant. Sharp as a packet of needles is Linda.'

'And your wife also worked for an estate agent, I understand?'

'That's her proper job,' Andrews said. He seemed eager, Atherton thought, to distance the Andrews name from the taint of licensed victualling. 'That's what she was doing in St Albans when I first met her. She does four mornings in the office for David and the occasional Saturday and Sunday, if there's a lot of people wanting to see over houses.'

'And David is?'

'David Meacher. It's his own business. He's got two offices, one in Chiswick High Road, and the other out where he lives, out Denham way. But that's not open all the time. The Chiswick one's the main branch.'

'And that's where your wife worked?'

He hesitated, and Atherton saw his hands, resting on the table, clench slightly. 'Mostly. Sometimes David would ask her to man the other office, when he couldn't get anyone else. But not often.'

'She was working at the Chiswick office yesterday?'

'In the morning.'

'You saw her off to work, did you?'

'We left at the same time. Half past eight — just before. I was only going round the corner, to St Michael Square. She had to get to the office for nine. Nine to one, she did.'

Atherton nodded encouragingly. 'And you got to work at the Old Rectory at about half past eight? And stayed there all day?'

'Yes.'

'Where did you go for lunch?'

'I —' He stopped himself, looking at Atherton suspiciously. 'I didn't go anywhere. I don't stop for lunch. I just worked through.'

'All alone all day? Did Mrs Hammond come out and chat to you?'

'No, why should she? Anyway, I like to get on when I'm working.'

'And what time did you finish?'

'Six. I started packing up when the church clock struck six.'

'And then you went — ?'

Andrews paused, his eyes still but his mind apparently busy. 'I went for a drink.'

'At the Goat?'

'Not in working clothes. They don't like it. I went for one at the Mimpriss. Then I went home.'

'What time did you get home?'

'It would be — about half past seven, I suppose.'

'Your wife was there?'

'No. It was her night on at the Goat.'

'Ah, I see. So what did you do?'

'Got some supper. Watched telly. Went to bed.'

'And what time did your wife come home?'

Andrews looked away. 'She didn't come home,' he said sullenly.

Atherton laid his hands slowly on the table in front of him. They were large, open, relaxed, handsome hands; strong contrast to Andrews battered and whited fists, bunched and wary opposite them. 'Now that's interesting. She didn't come home at all, and yet you weren't worried about her?'

'Course I was worried!' Andrews flashed. 'Who says I wasn't?'

'But you didn't call the police and report her missing.'

'You don't report someone missing when they've not come home just one night.'

'She'd done it before, had she, stayed out all night?'

'No! But — well, a person might go and see a friend and get talking and so forth, and, you know, forget the time. You know what women are like, yackety-yack all day and all night when they get together.' He appealed weakly to Atherton, *hombre à hombre*.

Atherton remained stony, *hombre*-proof. 'But she didn't telephone to say where she was, and you didn't phone around to check? I find that very remarkable.'

'How do you know I didn't?'

'Because you'd have said so. No, you just said you watched television and went to bed.'

'Well, I did phone round,' Andrews said defiantly.

'Who?'

'Lots of people. I don't remember,' Andrews muttered.

'Give me some names.' Atherton cocked his pen at dictation angle.

'I can't remember them all.'

'Give me just one name, then, that I can check.' No answer. 'Well, it doesn't matter, we can get the numbers from BT,' Atherton said cheerfully. 'They're all recorded by computer now, did you know that? Every phone call you make, it's all logged.'

Andrews looked at him resentfully. 'Oh, leave me alone!' he cried. 'Why are you going on at me? I didn't do anything!'

'That was rather the point,' Atherton said, with a sinuous smile. 'Your wife, whom you loved, didn't come home as expected and you didn't do anything. It just struck me as strange.' Andrews said nothing. 'Well, let's move on, shall we? You got up the next morning and went to work again — rather early, I understand. Why was that?'

'Why was what?' Andrews seemed confused by the question.

'Why did you go to work so early?'

'I — I hadn't slept well. Worried about Jen, you see,' he added, on a happy thought.

'Do you usually wash and shave when you get up in the morning?'

'Course I do. What d'you mean?' He caught the purport of the question. 'Well, I usually do, but I was upset this morning. Worried.'

'Of course you were. You tossed and turned all night, woke up early, and thought as you were up you might as well go and make a start at Mrs Hammond's?'

'That's right,' Andrews said. 'Get on with the job, get it finished.'

'Get on with the job of mixing up the concrete to pour into the nice hole you'd dug, perhaps? Filling it in before anyone could discover what was lying in the bottom?'

'No!'

'Only bad luck for you, Mrs Hammond got there first, eh? Pity you didn't start a bit earlier. But I suppose the sound of a concrete mixer at dawn would have been a bit much, wouldn't it? A bit suspicious. Wake up the neighbours, bring them round to complain. And then they'd see what you were up to —'

'No! I tell you, no!' Andrews was on his feet, his face congested with emotion — fear, anger, what? 'It wasn't like that! I didn't kill her! It wasn't me!'

'*Sit down,*' Atherton said icily, and Andrews subsided, trembling. Atherton stared at him impassively for long enough to get him really nervous, and then said, 'It wasn't you that murdered her, eh? Well, you see, when I came in here, I didn't even know she'd been murdered. I thought it might possibly have been death from natural causes, or even an accident. But you seem to know more than me, Mr Andrews. So suppose you tell me how you did it? What did you use? And where did it happen? You know, if you get it off your chest, you'll feel a lot better.'

But Andrews laid his head down on his arms, moaning, and seeing it was not going to stop soon, Atherton decided to leave him to stew for a bit.

Emerging again into the great hall of the Old Rectory, Slider bumped into a bit of a frackarse. PC Renker, newly arrived, was standing at the open door of the drawing-room, from within which Cyril Dacre was concluding a long and fluent tirade.

'— outrageous overreaction! Coming in here mob-handed — bursting into a private residence like a gang of storm troopers! And don't think I can't see you smirk,' he added furiously, as Renker made a face at Swilley. 'Opening doors without knocking — are we living in a fascist state? Yes, you look like a Hun! Pure Nordic type. Love the uniform, too, don't you? What did you say your name was — Reinke? I knew a Reinke in Berlin before the war, ended up as a top-echelon SS man. Complete fanatic. Well, you can get out of here! I insist on my privacy. Yes, and you can take this nursemaid away, too,' he added furiously, gesturing towards Swilley. 'I don't need watching in case I fall out of my chair. I may be old but I'm not senile!'

Slider jerked Swilley out with his head,

apologised tersely, and shoved Renker gently out of Dacre's line of vision. Renker, tall, broad-shouldered, fair-haired and blue-eyed, looked at Slider with a hurt quirk of the mouth. 'I just opened the door looking for you, sir,' he murmured. 'Didn't get a chance to say more than my name, and he was off.'

'He's had a trying morning,' Slider said. 'Go outside and help McLaren. Swilley, wait here in case I need you.' He inserted himself politely into the doorway and faced the smouldering historian. 'I'm sorry to have to disturb you, sir, but I would like to talk to you about what's happened here,' he said firmly.

Dacre looked out from under his eyebrows. 'Well, if you must, you must. I shall have to do my civic duty, I suppose. You're not quite such a fool as some of the others, at any rate.' Slider accepted the compliment gracefully and came in. 'Shut the door,' Dacre commanded. 'I see you've left the Rhinemaiden on guard. I called her a nursemaid, but I rather guessed she was meant as a gaoler.'

'WDC Swilley was just making sure you weren't disturbed,' Slider said smoothly.

'Didn't work, did it? That bloody Hun still came bursting in.'

'There are quite a few reporters outside, sir,' Slider mentioned.

'Ha! The vultures gather. Where there's a corpse . . .'

'We'll try to keep them away from you.'

Dacre shrugged. 'I've nothing to tell them — or you. I slept rather soundly last night, for a change, so I knew nothing about it until Frances came in this morning with her incoherent babble about Andrews having murdered his wife. My daughter,' he added severely, 'falls into a flap at the sight of a spider, so you can imagine the state of what serves her for a mind when she came across a real human corpse on the premises. It is rather hard, by the way,' he pursued, 'to be cooped up in here with your Amazon looming over me — to make sure I don't destroy any evidence, no doubt — when I wanted to see the body.'

Slider, seeing a gleam in the dark eyes, began to suspect he was being teased, and relaxed cautiously. 'It's gone now,' he said.

'Yes, I saw the undertaker's vehicle go past. "Meat wagon" — isn't that what you fellows call it? But if one is to be embroiled in a sordid case of murder, it's hard not to be allowed any of the fun.'

'Why do you think it's a case of murder?'

Slider asked mildly.

'I hardly think Jennifer Andrews lay down in the hole of her own accord, quietly died, and then covered herself up with a tarpaulin. Please, Inspector, don't patronise my intelligence.'

'Someone put the body there, of course,' Slider said, 'but she may have died by accident.'

'No, no, my money's on murder. She was a vulgar, unpleasant woman, ripe for the plucking,' he said largely.

'Someone is dead, sir,' Slider reminded him.

Dacre threw a sharp glance under his eyebrows. 'At my age, and in my situation, death loses its semi-religious glamour. You can't expect me to feign a pious reverence for a mere biological process, and one, moreover, that I am already in the early stages of.'

Slider made no comment on that. Instead he said, 'Tell me what you know about Jennifer Andrews. You said she was unpleasant. In what way?'

'Loud-mouthed, brash and vulgar. The sort of woman who always has to be the centre of attention and doesn't mind how she achieves it. She liked to organise everything that happened around here so that she could manipulate people and situations to her own advantage. She hadn't a scintilla of proper feeling or sensitivity. She flirted with every man over the age of sixteen and even treated *me* with an appalling kind of coy roguishness.' His wrath mounted to a peak as the final, horrible revelation burst from his lips. 'She called me a "dear old boy" and referred to me as her "sweetheart"! If ever a woman deserved to die it was her!'

'Yes, I see.'

'Oh, well . . .' Dacre looked a little shaken by his own vehemence. 'I don't suffer fools gladly.'

Or at all, Slider thought. 'How well did she know your daughter? Did she call here often?'

'She called here from time to time in the course of organising things. And she and Frances were both involved in activities at the church. She's a neighbour: not quite of us, but with aspirations. There is a species of, if I may call it so, village life on the Mimpriss Estate, of which Mrs Andrews longed to be part. Whatever activity there was, she wormed her way into it. Socially ambitious, you see — the worst type. I think she viewed this house as the local manor, and myself as lord of it, so she was always eager to ingratiate herself. She couldn't get anywhere with me, so she attached herself to Frances.'

'Would you say she and your daughter were friends?'

His lip curled. 'Frances hasn't the knack of making *friends*. Never had. She and Jennifer Andrews had acquaintances in common and sat on the same committees. And, of course, the husband did quite a few jobs for us. You took him away, I see.' He nodded towards the windows that looked out on the street. 'Poor devil. Driven to it by that frightful woman. The man should be decorated for performing a public service, not hanged.'

'We're not allowed to hang anyone nowadays,' Slider reminded him.

'More's the pity.'

'You seem to be very sure it was Andrews who killed her.'

'Oh, please, Inspector, play your parlour games with someone else! The body turns up in a hole in my terrace, which by complete chance was dug by the victim's husband — with whom she was on famously bad terms! It's hardly a challenge to the intellect!'

'Why were they on bad terms?'

Dacre seemed to lose interest quite

abruptly. 'I have no idea,' he said, and turned his face away with a stony expression. 'I don't interest myself in other people's domestic affairs.'

'Do you remember when you last saw Mrs Andrews?'

He seemed to consider not answering, and then said, 'On Sunday morning. She called on Frances briefly. Something about arranging the flowers for the church, I believe. I didn't see her — Frances went out to her, in the hall. She didn't stay long.'

'Did she come to see her husband here, while he was working?'

'I sincerely doubt it. But how would I know? I can't see the terrace from here.'

'Do you always sit in this room, then? I noticed there is a desk and typewriter in the other room, which looks out on the terrace and garden. Is that where you write?'

'I don't write any more,' he said irritably. 'In case it has escaped your notice, I am a dying man.'

'I'm sorry, sir. I do have to ask questions —'

'About the protagonists in this sordid affair, perhaps. You do not have the right to interrogate me about my own activities!' He put a hand rather theatrically to his forehead. 'I must ask you to leave me now. I tire easily these days.'

Slider stood up patiently. 'I shall probably want to ask you some more questions later.'

Dacre snorted. 'If you insist on wasting my time in this way, you must take the consequences. However, since Jennifer Andrews was obviously *not* killed on these premises, you would be better advised to find out where she died and how she was brought here. Why don't you try to find out who put her body into the hole?'

Slider felt his hackles rising. 'Thank you for the valuable advice. I would never have thought of that for myself.'

Dacre's face darkened. 'How dare you display your insolence to me! You are a public servant! I pay your wages!'

'And my parents paid yours!' Slider went cold all over as he heard himself say it. In the brief silence that followed Dacre's eyes opened very wide; and then, surprisingly, his face cleared and he began to chuckle.

'Yes, I dare say they did! I am justly rebuked. You must forgive me my occasional self-indulgence, Inspector. At my time of life, being rude to people is the only kind of bad behaviour one is still capable of.'

Chapter Three

Char Grilled

To the right of the Old Rectory, beyond the gravel parking space and hard by the overweening hedge, was St Michael House, which had presumably been named by someone who had never shopped at Marks and Spencer. It was one of those 1920s joke Tudor houses, stucco above and herringbone brick below, with so many pitch-covered beams, horizontal and vertical, it looked as though it had been scribbled out by a child in a temper. It had an oak front door studded and bedecked with extraneous pieces of iron, hysterically quaint diamond-pane casements, and cylindrical chimneys so tall and elaborate they looked like confectionery. If you could have snapped them off, they would undoubtedly have been lettered *Merrie Englande* all through.

Not that WDC Kathleen 'Norma' Swilley, owner of the most fantasised-about legs in the Met, thought in those terms. Walking up the brick front path to start the house-to-house, her verdict was, 'What a junky old dump!' She lived in a brand new flat in a brand new block in West Kensington, and had no use for things antique, false or genuine. The newer the better, was her motto; and if whatever it was could function on its own by means of electricity, so much the better. She'd have had electric food that ate itself if she could.

When she reached the front door, there were so many bits of old iron attached to it that it took her a while to work out that the bell was operated by a pull-down handle on a shaft. The instant it rang, however, the door was opened by the householders, who must have been crouched behind it waiting, and she was glad-handed and whisked into the lounge with the avidity of an Amway induction. Defreitas had been right about that, it seemed: the Mimpriss residents were aching to be in on the act.

The inside of the house was at one with its exterior. The lounge had cast-iron wall lights in the shape of flaming torches, a wheel-shaped iron chandelier supporting electric candles, and a vast herringbone-brick inglenook containing a very small gas log fire. Perhaps to foster illusion, a log basket sat on the brick hearth, filled with real logs and pinecones: Norma bet the old dame dusted them daily, probably with the Hoover attachment. The furniture was all turned oak and chintz-covered; there were display cabinets full of the sort of limited-edition figurines that are advertised in the *Sunday Times* magazine, Vernon Ward framed prints on the walls, dried flower arrangements everywhere, and a row of royal-commemorative plates around the picture rail.

Mr and Mrs Vanhurst Bright — Desmond and Mavis, they assured Swilley eagerly and watched until she wrote it down — were in their sixties and gave the same impression of careful prosperity as the house. His face had the over-soft look of a man who has been thin all his life and only put on fat in retirement, and he wore the willing but slightly tense expression of a very intelligent dog trying to understand human speech. She was thin, brittle and ramrod straight, and looked as though her whole life had been a battle against importunate door-to-door salesmen. She had evidently gone to the same hairdresser as Mrs Hammond, though her arrangement was tinted a fetching shade of mauve; with her chalky-pink face powder and rather bluish shade of lipstick it made her look as though she were slightly dead. She was dressed in a pink cashmere twinset and heather tweed kilt complete with grouse-claw kilt-pin, pearl earrings, two rows of pearls round her neck, more diamond hoop rings than perhaps the strictest of good taste would think necessary, lisle stockings, and well-polished brogues as brown and shiny as a racehorse's bum. He was wearing a lovat tweed jacket over a cad's yellow waistcoat, khaki shirt and green knitted tie, grey flannel trousers, and a beautiful pair of expensive brown Oxfords, which were so unexpectedly large compared with the rest of him that he looked as though he had been inserted into them as a preliminary to being tied up and dropped into the harbour.

Swilley wondered at their immaculate appearance so early in the day. Did they always dress like this, or had they made a special effort in anticipation of a police visit? The house was immaculate too: perhaps they were the sort that would still change for dinner on a desert island. She bet they had twin beds with satin quilts and his 'n' hers library books on the bedside cabinets. Well, good luck to them.

'I'm sorry to have to disturb you —' Norma began routinely, but they jumped in eagerly.

'Oh, no, not at all. Our pleasure,' said Mr Bright, with a social smile.

'Naturally we were expecting to be called upon,' said Mrs Bright, 'and of course we are eager to do anything we can to help in these dreadful circumstances.'

'It's our duty,' Mr Bright added.

'We've never held back when it was a question of duty,' said Mrs Bright, 'however inconvenient.'

'Well, I hope I shan't have to inconvenience you for long,' Norma said.

'Oh, please, not at all, it's no trouble,' Mr Bright waffled happily. 'Won't you sit down, Miss — er?'

Norma sat on a slippery chintz sofa. Mr Bright looked at her legs with a slightly stunned air and sat down opposite her. Mrs Bright arranged herself carefully in an armchair between them and looked to see what Mr Bright was looking at. A spot of colour appeared in her cheeks. 'Would you like a cup of coffee, Miss — er?' she asked, rather sharply. 'Desmond, shall we have coffee?'

He snapped out of it and began elaborately rising and enquiring about the nature of preferred beverage and Norma saw herself reaching retirement in this mock-Tudor embrace and said quickly, 'No, thank you very much, no coffee. I'd just like to ask you a few questions and then I can take myself out of your hair.'

He sat again, trying to keep his eyes from her legs and not succeeding very well. 'Ask away, then,' he said heartily. 'It's no trouble. We're glad to help.'

'Not that we have much we can tell you,' Mrs Bright put in, in a bid for attention. 'We didn't know Mrs Andrews well.'

'She seemed a nice sort of gel,' Mr Bright rumbled gallantly, and Mrs Bright gave him a sharp look.

'I wouldn't say that. I'm afraid my husband is rather susceptible to a pretty face. Mrs Andrews wasn't really One of Us. She worked at the pub, you know, the Goat In Boots.' She gave Norma a significant nod, as though this explained everything. 'She was rather a *forward* young woman. One might almost say *pushy*. She's quite taken over the church social committee, *and* the flower arrangements, and I have to say that some of her ideas of what's fitting for a religious building are —'

'My dear,' Mr Bright interrupted anxiously, 'she is dead.'

'That doesn't change the facts,' Mrs Bright went on relentlessly. 'She didn't understand our ways, and she never seemed to realise where her interference wasn't welcome.'

'Oh, come, I wouldn't say "interference".' Mr Bright seemed anxious for his wife not to expose herself. 'Someone has to organise things and she had so much energy —'

'Well, I have to say I didn't like her,' Mrs Bright said, giving him a nasty look, 'energy or no energy. She attached herself to poor Frances Hammond, who hasn't the sense of a day-old chick, poor creature, and *forced* her way into our circle, and then tried to impose her vulgar ideas on us. There's a time and a place for everything, and *our* church fête is not the time and place for a bouncing castle, or whatever they like to call it.'

Mr Bright appealed to Norma. 'I always found her very polite. Quite a nicely spoken girl. She was always cheerful and pleasant to me.'

'Yes, well she would be, wouldn't she?' Mrs Bright said sharply.

Mr Bright went a little pink. 'I don't know what you mean, Mavis.'

'Work it out for yourself,' Mrs Bright

snapped, with an appalling lapse from British Empire standards, and clamped her thin lips shut.

Norma, fascinated by this glimpse under the carpet, reflected how odd it was that the more determinedly a couple kept up their shop front, the more eager they were to trot out old grievances before a 'safe' audience like a policeman, priest or doctor. She looked at Mr Bright. 'Tell me what you know about Mr Andrews.'

He got as far as 'Well,' when his wife interrupted.

'We didn't know him. I've heard he's a good builder, but we have our own people that we've used for twenty years.'

'Kept himself to himself,' Mr Bright said approvingly.

'He's done one or two jobs next door. I can't say whether he did them well or not,' Mrs Bright went on, finding another grievance, 'but I wouldn't use anyone who wasn't more careful about leaving things clean and tidy. Only a few months ago I had to speak to him quite sharply about parking his lorry outside our house. Quite apart from spoiling the view, it leaked oil all over the road. There's still a stain there.'

Swilley tried another pass over the subject. 'So you have no idea how things stood between Mr Andrews and his wife?'

'I don't interest myself in other people's private business,' Mrs Bright said loftily. 'It's poor Cyril Dacre I'm sorry for. It's a dreadful thing to have happen on one's own premises.'

'All those people tramping about,' Mr Bright joined in, now the topic was safe again. 'Journalists everywhere. And in his state of health —'

'He's very ill, you know. *Cancer.*' She lowered her voice and almost mouthed the word, as if it were indelicate. 'It's dreadful that he should be upset at a time like this.'

'You know him well?'

'Oh, of course. Margery Dacre was one of my *dearest* friends,' Mrs Bright said eagerly. 'She's been dead — oh, ten years now?'

'Ten, it must be,' he confirmed.

'Of course, Cyril Dacre is a *very distinguished* man. We're proud to have him as a neighbour. His mother was a Spennimore before she married — very old Hampshire family.'

'Wonderful brainy chap,' Mr Bright said admiringly, and added with faint puzzlement, 'Odd sense of humour sometimes, but I suppose that comes with being so clever. He writes books, you know.'

'The parties they used to give, before Margery died! She was fond of music. They had a grand piano in the hall, and they had wonderful musical soirées. Quite famous musicians came to play, friends of Cyril's. He had friends in every circle — artists, actors, scholars —'

'That athletic chap, the one who broke the Olympic record, what's his name? Became an MP —' Mr Bright shorted out, frowning with the effort of remembering.

'Dinner parties, garden parties,' she went on, ignoring him, 'intellectual conversation.'

'It was like *The Brains Trust* in there some evenings.'

'Of course, one had to make allowances for Cyril. He could be quite devastatingly rude, but he is a genius after all. And there was that terrible tragedy — his son dying so young. I think that made him a little strange.' She nodded to Swilley as if she ought to know. 'After Margery died Frances took over as hostess; and I must say,' she added, with a hint of surprise at discovering it for herself, 'that one never noticed the difference. Of course, Margery never did say much.'

'Nice woman, but quiet,' Mr Bright agreed. 'Left all the talking to Cyril.'

'And Frances hasn't two words to say for herself,' Mrs Bright concluded. 'But, of course, since Cyril's become so ill all that's stopped. They haven't entertained in — oh, two years. He keeps himself completely to himself now. I suppose,' she added with a sigh, 'that when he goes it will be the end of an era. One can't see Frances keeping up the old traditions. She hasn't many friends. That's why she fell a prey to Mrs Andrews.'

'There's that chap who visits,' Mr Bright said. 'What's his name? Married to the horsy woman — what's her name?'

So far Norma had nothing down in her little book. 'Mrs Bright, if I could just —'

'*Vanhurst* Bright,' she corrected with sharp affront. 'No hyphen.'

'Mrs Vanhurst Bright,' Norma said obediently, 'if I could just come to the events of last night: did you notice what time Mr Andrews left work?'

'Just after six,' she said promptly. 'We were watching the six o'clock news when the lorry started up. The engine makes a dreadful noise — and the tyres crunching over that gravel. We could hardly hear what was being said.'

'I suppose it went past your window?'

'No, he went the other way.'

'And did you hear him arrive this morning?'

'We certainly did!' Mrs Bright said, with tight annoyance.

'Well, people have to work,' Mr Bright said, making all possible allowances.

'But not at that time of the morning. It's inconsiderate to be making noise at half past six in the morning —'

'It was a quarter to seven, dear,' said Mr Bright. 'I looked at the clock,' he added to Swilley.

'It's still much too early,' his wife said, annoyed at being corrected. 'Half past eight is quite early enough; a quarter to seven is beyond reason. I said to Desmond, "I suppose we'll have the cement mixer starting up next, and have to close the windows." People shouldn't have noisy jobs done in the summer when people have their windows open.'

'So you heard the truck arrive and pull onto the gravel? What else?'

Mrs Bright considered. 'Well, I thought I heard someone shout, and then some voices talking — I suppose that was Frances and Mr Andrews — and then nothing until the police arrived and all the fuss started.'

'You didn't look out of the window when

you heard the shout?'

'No. It wasn't loud. More a sort of — exclamation.'

'I didn't hear it,' Mr Bright said.

'In any case, you can't see the terrace from any of our windows because of the hedge.'

'That's why it's there,' he pointed out.

'And what about during the night?' Swilley asked. 'Were you woken by any disturbance?'

'No, not that I remember,' Mrs Bright said. 'Why? Did something happen?'

Mr Bright, surprisingly, proved more on the ball than his wife. 'Well, dear, poor Mrs Andrews must have been put into the hole during the night, or someone would have seen.'

'Oh,' she said, evidently not following.

'Under cover of darkness,' he elaborated. 'If Frances found her there before Mr Andrews arrived —'

'Oh. I suppose so.'

'But you didn't hear anything during the night?' Norma pressed.

'No,' she said, with a world of regret. 'Did you, Desmond?'

'Nothing,' he said, shaking his head.

'Do you sleep with the windows open?'

'Always,' he said.

'That was why we heard the lorry arrive in the morning,' she said. 'I'm sure if he'd driven up in the night and stopped outside we'd have heard. It's very quiet round here at night.'

Swilley extracted herself with difficulty, and went to try the neighbour on the other side of the Old Rectory, but knocking and ringing elicited no reply, and the place had a shut-up, empty look. Out at work or away? she wondered. They would have to try again later. She saw Mackay emerge from three doors down and called out to him. 'Hoi, Andy!' He turned. 'Have you done this one?'

'No-one in,' he called back. 'I've done the next two. I'll do the rest of this row if you like.'

'Okay, I'll start at the corner, then,' she said, and trudged off. Breakfast seemed a distant dream. If the next house was decent, she decided, she'd accept a cup of coffee. With a bit of luck they might break out the biccies, too.

Atherton came back with the keen-eyed look of a police dog entering a vagrants' hostel. 'Open and shut case,' he said.

'Oh, really?' said Slider, leaning on the

car roof and addressing him across it. It was going to be another hot day. The earth smelt warm and the sunshine on the pale stones of the churchyard wall made them hard to look at.

Atherton leaned too. 'Andrews says he went home from work last night, watched telly and went to bed. His wife was out at work so he was all alone. His wife didn't come home all night, but he didn't do anything about it, just got up and went to work this morning as usual — having forgotten to wash and shave — and blow me, there she was, down the hole! Well, you can't help being convinced by a story like that, can you?'

Slider assumed a judicious frown. 'I don't know. Cyril Dacre, the owner of the house and thus the hole, was extremely anxious to lay the crime in Andrews' lap, despite accidentally giving away the fact that he — Dacre — loathed deceased with a deep and deadly loathing, and rejoices that she's dead.'

Atherton slapped a hand to his cheek, wide-eyed. 'Of course, I see it all now! It must have been Dacre. He pursued her up and down the terrace in his wheelchair until she fell into the hole and died of exhaustion. And, come to think of it,

Andrews did say that the work on the terrace was Dacre's idea. He says he told Mrs H there was no need to do anything, but she — i.e. her father, since his was the final authority — insisted.'

Slider shook his head. 'Pity he said that, because Mrs Hammond says it was Andrews who told her that the work needed to be done, or the whole terrace would collapse.'

'So he was trying to distance himself from authorship of the hole?'

'It was a silly lie to tell — too easy to expose,' Slider said.

'Perhaps he hasn't had much practice. This could be the first time he's murdered his wife.'

'We don't know she was murdered,' Slider said, for the third time that day. 'She might have dropped dead of a heart-attack, during a quarrel, for instance, and Andrews — or whoever — panicked and tried to get rid of the body.'

' "Might" is right,' Atherton said.

'Well, we'd better try to expose a few more of Andrews' lies, hadn't we?' Slider said. 'If it was a domestic murder, the most likely place for him to do it was at home: private, convenient, and a thorough knowledge of the tools to hand to boot. The

81

forensic team's going over there when they've finished here, but we might as well have a look first.'

Woodbridge Road was the long road that led from the other side of St Michael Square to the main road. Fourways was at the far end, on the corner with the main thoroughfare. There was a red sports car parked on the hard standing, with the registration number JEN 111.

'Hers, I bet you,' Atherton said.

'Give that man a coconut. Well, if she was working at the Goat In Boots last night, she must have come back here afterwards.'

'Or she might have walked to work.'

'So she might.'

'Or he could have driven it back himself from wherever he killed her.'

'So he could. Not much help, is it? Shall we go in?'

Fourways was a large, modern, well-appointed house, smelling strongly of new plaster, and full of large, modern, well-appointed furnishings of the sort that were obviously expensive without being in any way luxurious or even particularly pleasing. It was the sort of house to which you might invite people you didn't know very well so that they could marvel at how well you were doing for yourself.

It had Atherton gaping. 'Gloriosky, what a gin palace!'

'Every mod con,' Slider agreed. 'Sunken whirlpool bath, electrically operated curtains —'

'The expense of spirit in a waste of shame,' Atherton said.

There was no sign of any struggle anywhere — no sign of life at all. Everything was clean and tidy, the beds made, the bathrooms spotless. There was no dirty crockery in the kitchen: if Andrews had eaten supper on Tuesday night and breakfast on Wednesday morning, he had not only washed up after himself but dried up and put away too.

'As if!' Atherton snorted. 'No man on this planet puts away after he's washed up. It's against nature.'

The kitchen waste-bin contained a fresh bin-liner and nothing else; the toothbrushes in the *en suite* bathroom were both dry, as was the wash-basin, the bath and the floor of the shower. The towels were clean and folded and looked as if they had just been put out.

'It doesn't look as if he's been home at all,' Atherton said.

'He said he was watching television all

evening, but the TV listings are folded open at Monday,' Slider observed. 'Not that that proves anything. He could have known what was on, or just put it on at random when he got home.'

'There was football on last night,' Atherton blinked, feigning astonishment. 'Blimey, even I know that! An international — England versus Italy. If he'd been in, he'd've been bound to look and see what time it started.'

'Maybe he doesn't like football.'

'And the Pope's a Jew.'

'Just trying not to jump to conclusions, that's all. One of us doing it is quite enough. Well, I think we've seen all we'll see here. How was Andrews when you left him?' Slider asked, as they headed for the front door.

'He's gone sulky,' Atherton said. 'Decided his best policy is to say nothing — but he hasn't asked to go home.'

'Oh?' Slider asked significantly.

'I dunno,' Atherton answered elliptically. 'I don't think I'd read anything into it necessarily. He seems to be in a state of lethargy.'

They opened the front door, and found a woman outside arguing with the guardian policeman. She was a small, fair woman in her fifties, with a neat face and figure, wearing a raincoat which hung open over a pink nylon overall, and she was carrying a raffia shopping-bag. She turned to them, her expression a mixture of belligerence and fear, and her sharp eyes effortlessly singled out Slider as the present peak of authority.

'What's going on?' she demanded. 'What's happened? Only I was going past and I see all this kerfuffle. There's not been a burglary?'

'No, I'm afraid it's more serious than that,' Slider said. 'Would you tell me who you are, please?'

'I'm Pat, their cleaner. Pat Attlebury — Mrs.' she added, as though they might already know several Pat Attleburys from whom she wished to be distinguished. 'Tuesday and Friday mornings I do for them, two hours, though there's not a lot to do, really, between you and I. Except for the dust. You always get a lot of dust in a new house,' she explained, still scanning their faces. 'What's going on, then, if it's not a burglary?'

'How about a cup of tea?' Slider invited, recognising a bunny champion when he saw one. 'I expect you know your way around the kitchen?'

Over the requisite cuppa, Mrs Attlebury was perfectly willing to chat. She expressed a properly hushed shock at the news, but she seemed less than grief-stricken about Mrs Andrews' fate.

'It's *him* I'm sorry for. He'll take it hard. Besotted about her. Such a nice man, too — though I'm always having to speak to him about his boots. I mean, all right, the building trade's a good business, and *he's* done all right out of it — look at this place! But building sites mean dirt, you can't get away from that. I think that's what *she* didn't like — always down on him, sneering, you know — as though she thought she was too good for him. Didn't mind spending the money, oh, no! But it was beneath her to be married to a builder, even though he had got his own business. I mean, that's where it is, isn't it? He's like the company chairman if you want to look at it that way. But he wasn't good enough for Mrs Lady Docker Andrews! She didn't like him coming home mucky, if you ask me. Though she had a point. It was bad enough when I used to do for them where they used to live before, but a new place like this shows up every mark, and she would have these pale carpets — madness, I call it. It made it hard for me, and he wasn't careful where he put his feet. Well, men never are, are they? Take off your boots at the door, I said to him over and over, that's all I ask. Well, even this dry weather there's still earth and cement and everything, isn't there? But I couldn't get it through his head. But apart from that, I've no complaints. There's hardly anything to do, really. To tell you the truth, I don't think they're ever in much. He's down the pub often as not, and she's gallivanting God knows where. Which, when you think of it, is a waste, this lovely new house built specially for her and everything. But she wasn't a bit grateful.' She sipped her tea. 'How did she die, then?'

'We don't know yet,' Slider said. 'Did she have heart trouble, do you know, or any chronic condition like that?'

'Heart? Strong as an ox, her,' Mrs Attlebury said. 'Far as I know, anyway. But you'd want to ask him, really.'

'Oh, we will. But it's nice to get these things confirmed. Was she on any medication, that you knew about? Did she ever take sleeping pills?'

'I never heard that she did. There was never any on the bedside table, anyway — or in the medicine cabinet. Her doctor'd be the one to know, I expect. Dr Lands, same as me, she went to, in Dalling Road.'

Slider noted down the name, and she watched him, her mind working. 'So it wasn't a road accident, then, or anything like a shooting or a stabbing? I mean, you wouldn't be asking about pills if it was,' she said ruminatively, and then seemed to feel this comment lacked proper feeling, for she looked at them defiantly and said, 'I hadn't any time for her, if you want to know. She wasn't a nice person, in my view.'

'In what way, not nice?' Slider prompted.

'Fast,' said Mrs Attlebury decisively, and made a face. 'I don't know how he stood her, to tell you the truth. He had a hell of a life with her, poor soul. All right, she kept herself nice, and I don't say she wasn't a smart-looking woman, but it was his money she spent dolling herself up, and she should have been doing it for him, not showing herself off to every Tom, Dick and Harry. I mean, he's out working every hour God sends to make money for her to spend, and she's off gallivanting around and flirting with anything in trousers. Oh,' she said, with a significant look, 'it wasn't a secret. I mean, she didn't bother to hide it. Flirted openly — if it wasn't worse than flirting. I wouldn't put it past her.'

'How did Mr Andrews take that?'

'Well, he didn't like it, of course,' she said. 'What man would?'

'Did they quarrel about it?' Slider asked.

'What do you think?'

'Were the quarrels violent?'

'Shocking! I've heard them going at it hammer and tongs in another room when I've been cleaning. Heard them over the Hoover more than once — well, she was a loud-mouthed woman, you know, voice like a foghorn. And bossy? Always telling you how to do your job. Had to organise everything — you know the sort. She'd organise a pig into having puppies, that one. Well, it's not nice for a man, being taken down by his wife like that, in front of other people, like she did. It's no wonder he got mad.'

'Did he hit her?'

She seemed to realise at last where this was going. 'We-ell,' she said cautiously. 'I can't say I've ever seen him lift his hand to her. He's not that type, to my mind. And, like I say, he worshipped the ground she walked on. Except when she got him riled and he lost his temper. But he's the quiet sort, really.'

'Those are sometimes the worst,' Atherton said wisely. 'Quiet till you push 'em too far, and then — bang.'

'He could be shocking when he was provoked,' she acknowledged, 'but that's the same as any man. But he's never hit her that I know of. He's a nice man. It's her I couldn't stand.'

'Did they have any children?'

'No, and it's a pity if you ask me, because he'd have made a lovely dad, and it might have kept her at home a bit more, clipped her wings. But they didn't, and why I couldn't tell you, though I expect it was her that said no. Selfish, she was. Spiteful, too,' she added, looking towards Slider with an old grievance plainly bursting to get out. 'She changed the flower rota at the church so that I lost my turn, because the week she changed me to I was on holiday. She *knew* that. She just wanted another turn herself; thinks she's God's gift — her with her dead sticks and dandelions and runner beans! Load of rubbish! I mean, who wants to look at that ugly stuff instead of proper flowers? I do a nice arrangement, roses and pinks and pretty things like that. But she says, Oh, Pat, she says, that's so old-fashioned! Nobody does that sort of thing any more! Never mind if they don't, I said, it's what people want to look at that matters, and they don't want to look at your rubbish, modern or not. It's like that modern art, dead cows in fish tanks and all that stuff. It's just plain ugly, I said to her. But you might as well talk to the cat. And, of course, Mr Tennyson backs her up. That's why he gave her the rota — thinks the sun shines out of her eyes, and no wonder, the way she makes up to him. Making up to a reverent! It's disgusting to my mind. But she'd flirt with anything in trousers, that one.'

She stopped abruptly, remembering the occasion, and what was required of it. She sipped her tea again, and then said, 'Oh, well, they say you shouldn't speak ill of the dead, but I speak as I find, and it has to be said, she was a right cow.'

Outside in the sunshine, having seen her off, Slider turned to Atherton. *De mortuis?*

'At least.'

'I've heard things can get pretty fierce at those flower-arranging classes.'

Atherton snorted. 'And this from the man who thinks oasis is a band!'

'At least we've got a motive now,' Slider said.

'The old green-eyed monster: an oldie,

but a goodie. And we've bust Andrews' story wide open. Mrs Prattlebury left the house clean yesterday morning, and there's not so much as a builder's footmark to be seen, so he couldn't have gone home after work last night.'

'Unless he cleaned up after himself.'

'Hoover ye lightly while ye may? But he wouldn't, would he? If that's his alibi, he'd want it to look as if he'd been there. He wouldn't cover his tracks. It's not as if there were oceans of gore to clean up.'

'No, you're right, of course. I have to admit that it looks as if he didn't go home.'

'Crikey, if Mr D. Thomas is convinced, it must be so! Where next, guv?'

'I think we should pay a little visit to the Goat In Boots.'

'Ah, *nunc est bibendum*.'

'Come again?

'I said, it's a fruity notion. Lay on, McDuff. I'm right behind you.'

Chapter Four

Shorts And Whine

The pub was not open yet, and Slider and Atherton walked in on an argument about whether it should be. Jack Potter, the landlord, was in favour of staying closed for the day, out of respect for the dead.

'It's not as if we've got the brewery to please,' he said. He was a wiry, flexible-looking man with a slight and incongruous paunch. He looked in his late forties, with thick black hair brushed back and slightly too long, bulging eyes, and a loose mouth. They came upon him bottling up behind the bar, shifting plastic crates of light ale about with the absent, practiced strength of a circus juggler. He was wearing denim shorts, because of the heat, and a dark red polo shirt, which left his stringy, muscled arms bare. They were obviously strangers to the sun, for they were gleamingly white, and so generously veined and tattooed they looked like Stilton.

'It doesn't seem right to me to open up when Jen's — you know,' Potter went on, with syrupy tact.

'She's not "you-know",' his wife Linda said irritably. 'She's dead. It's not an indecent word.'

He glanced at her, hurt, and then appealed to Slider. 'Well, it doesn't seem respectful, anyway. What do you think?'

'I can't advise you on that,' Slider said.

'It's not as if she died in here,' Linda objected. She was fortyish, professionally smart, so well turned-out that you would never remember after meeting her whether she was attractive or not. Her appearance was designed, like waterproofing, to repel. She was in full fig even this early in the morning, right down to her earrings, with her hair lacquered to immobility in one of those ageless styles only suburban hairdressers can achieve. She had eyes hard enough to have etched glass, and a chain-smoker's voice rough enough to have sandblasted it afterwards; but a determined inspection revealed that under her makeup she looked pale and shaken, and her eyes were ringed. She clutched a packet of Rothmans and a throw-away lighter in one hand, and a man-sized Kleenex crumpled up in the other. 'I mean, no-one could be

94

more sorry than me that she's dead, but when it comes right down to it, she wasn't family. Family you shut for,' she decreed. 'Not friends.'

'But she worked here, Lin,' Jack protested. His eyes were red and watery, and moistened further even as he spoke. 'I think people would expect it. I mean,' he appealed to Slider again, 'they're classy people round here. It's all lounge trade — you know, shorts and wine. You don't want to go offending them. And there won't be a soul on the estate doesn't know about it by lunchtime.'

Linda's voice hardened. 'I've got a full restaurant tonight, and five tables booked for lunch already, and I'm not giving all that away. Besides, they'll all want to talk about it,' she added, with an acidulous knowledge of human nature, 'and where are they going to go and do that, if not here? We'll have sales like you never saw for a Wednesday. Call it a public service, if you like, if it makes you feel better, but the long and the short is I'm not closing up for the sake of an empty gesture. It won't bring Jen back.'

Jack looked cowed. 'All right, love, if you think so. I just want to do what's right, that's all. I mean, Jen was —' His lips trembled and his eyes seemed in danger of overflowing. He took out a handkerchief and honked briskly into it, and then emerged, looking almost shyly at Slider and Atherton, to say, 'Can I offer you gents a drink, atawl?'

Linda shot him a hard look, and Slider said, 'It's a bit early for me, thanks all the same.'

'Cuppa coffee, then?'

'Jack, they want to ask questions,' Linda said impatiently. 'You get on with your bottling up, or you'll have the twirlies in before you're ready. If you'd like to come through to the snug where it's quiet . . .' she said to Slider and Atherton.

Slider fielded her smoothly, 'I know how busy you must both be, so to save time I'll talk to you while my colleague has a word with your husband, if that's all right.'

Linda Potter looked as though no-one had ever conned her in her life, but she nodded briskly, and walked away before him into the private bar.

The pub had obviously been a number of separate rooms, before most of the walls had been knocked out to make one large irregularly shaped one, low-ceilinged, beamed, the upright timbers showing where the walls had once been. The bar was three sides of a rectangle, and the snug was behind the wall on the fourth side, with a wooden serving-hatch through to the bar, and a little brass bell hung on a bracket beside it for service. The snug had one casement window of diamond panes too small and old to see through, though the sunshine streamed in strongly and illuminated the eternally falling dust. The air was heavy with the smell of furniture polish. The cherry-red carpet was tuftily new. There were three small round imitation antique oak tables, and banquettes and Windsor chairs upholstered in a chintz-patterned material. A beam running the length of the wall opposite the bar supported a range of the kind of junk pubs display to make them look homey: leather-bound books, pewter mugs and plates, a copper kettle, a crow-scarer, a set of donkey-boots, wooden butter-pats, wicker baskets. Since the real-ale, real-pub revolution there was a whole new vocabulary of clutter, and presumably merchants who combed the antique shops of the realm and supplied it by the yard.

Mrs Potter slapped the hatch shut, sat down on a banquette, crossed her legs, and extracted a cigarette one-handed from the packet. It was such a dextrous, professional action that it reminded Slider of a prostitute he had once seen up an alley near King's Cross extracting a condom from its wrapper without looking, using only her left hand. He shook the thought away.

'Smoke?' said Mrs Potter.

'I don't, thanks,' said Slider, pulling out a chair and sitting opposite her, sideways on to the table.

'I don't usually in here. Get a lot of non-smokers in our class of trade, and I like to keep the snug smoke-free. But this morning — sod it! I'm not going to get through today without my fags. You watch 'em come in later, all the ghouls, to pick over the body.'

She put the cigarette into the dead centre of her crimson lips, and Slider reached across to take up her lighter and strike the flame for her. She looked at him over the cigarette with her eyebrows raised, and then leaned forward, sucking the flame onto the tobacco with little popping puffs. Then she leaned back again, dragged deep, blew long and ceilingwards, and said, 'Ta,' with just enough surprise in her voice to convey the words, 'It's nice to meet a gentleman with manners. You don't get too many of them these days.' She folded her free arm, the one holding the Kleenex, across her chest, and propped the other elbow on it so that the cigarette was in the operative position just in front of her face 'Well,' she said. 'So how did it happen? Everyone's talking about it, but nobody seems to know anything. Not that that stops them talking,' she added viciously. 'But they say — well, if she was found where they say she was — it looks like she must've been done in.'

Her eyes behind the mascara were frightened, and she looked at him with flinching courage, waiting to hear the worst; dreading it, but facing up to it all the same. The spirit of the Blitz. He liked her a little better. He put the lighter down neatly on top of the cigarette pack and said, 'We don't know yet what the cause of death was.' And because of the fear in her eyes, he added, 'There were no obvious signs of violence on her.'

'Oh.' Linda relaxed slightly. 'Well, I suppose that's something. But you do think it was murder?'

'We're keeping an open mind about it. But however she died, someone must have put her body where it was found.'

Her mouth hardened. 'Well, you don't have to look far for him, do you? Eddie

Bloody Andrews. Is that right you've arrested him?'

'He's helping us with our enquiries.'

'Same thing.' She dismissed the distinction. 'He's the one all right, take my word for it. Bastard! I don't know how Jen put up with him.'

'Womaniser, was he?' Slider suggested.

'It wouldn't surprise me. But that's not what I meant. No, he was a jealous swine, always following her around and spying on her. But men are all the same.' She brought the Kleenex into play, dabbing her eyes and blowing her nose carefully so as not to smear her makeup.

'You don't have much of an opinion of men,' Slider observed.

'I've seen too many freeloaders. I've been in the trade all my life, you see. My dad had a pub. My grandad, too. I grew up in a pub — served behind the bar as soon as I was old enough. Then I married Jack. He's not from the trade — he was a merchant seaman till he married me, then he gave it up and we started off managing a tied house in Watford. Then we got a tenancy in Chiswick, and then we bought this place.'

'How did you meet Jennifer?'

'I met her at the birth-control clinic

when we moved to Chiswick. We sort of hit it off. She didn't have much good to say about men either, and no wonder. Worst thing she ever did was marry that Eddie.'

'You don't like him? Why is that?'

'Oh, what, apart from the fact that he's murdered her, you mean?' she said sarcastically, and then took a puff at her cigarette to compose herself. 'No, I'll tell you. He's one of those men who has to own a woman. Thinks if you put a ring on a woman's finger she's your property, at your beck and call every minute of the day. Jen couldn't have any life of her own. And jealous? He's mad. I mean literally — unbalanced, if you ask me. Always following her about and spying on her, accusing her of this, that and the other.' Mostly the other, Slider gathered. 'Terrible rows they had, because of course she wouldn't take it lying down. You can't, can you? Let 'em start walking all over you and you might as well be dead. But it didn't matter what she said. He wouldn't have been happy unless he had her under lock and key twenty-four hours a day.'

'Did they have money problems?'

She looked surprised. 'Why? Did someone say they did?'

'I was wondering why she took the job with you.'

'Oh, it wasn't for the money, it was just to get away from him for a bit. He's got plenty of money — doing very well for himself.'

'Generous with it?'

She seemed unwilling to grant Eddie Andrews any mitigating features. 'She never wanted for anything. But then she never asked him to keep her. She had her own career.'

'Working for the estate agent?'

'That's right.' She nodded. 'She was earning her own living before she met him, and if you ask me she made a big mistake ever giving it up, because it just gave him ideas. She couldn't stand being stuck at home doing nothing all day, so she took it up again part time.'

'Why part time?'

'Because *he* made such a fuss about her going out to work! That's why he built her that house — thought it would keep her home. It was a cage, that's what that was. But Jen was wise to it. She came to me and asked me for a job, to give her a reason to get out.'

'Why didn't she do the other thing full time?'

'Meacher's didn't want her full time. Anyway, it was evenings she wanted to get away from him. Of course, he was furious. He couldn't stand any wife of his working in a pub.'

'I thought she worked in the restaurant?'

She looked at him shrewdly. 'Is that what *he* said? God, he's a snob! He makes my blood boil! He's not the bloody Duke of Westminster, he's only a bloody builder, but he thinks himself so-o superior! Can't have his wife being a barmaid, oh no! Can't have her consorting with people like Jack and me! Publicans? The way he talked to me, you'd think I was a common prostitute! I said to him, you want to change your attitude, mate, I said, 'cause if you're not careful they'll stuff you and stick you in a museum, and good bloody riddance!'

'They didn't have any children, I understand.'

'Jen didn't want any, and who can blame her? *He* wanted 'em, but then it wouldn't be him had to go through it all, would it? Jack's the same way — all sentimental about "kiddies". Never mind morning sickness and backache, losing your figure, to say nothing of childbirth, and then being stuck in a house for the best years of your life changing nappies and wiping noses. No, she wasn't having any of that, thank you very much. Of course, it was another thing he held against me — as if I made her mind up for her!'

'You say he accused her of having affairs,' Slider said. 'Was there any truth in the accusations?'

She coloured angrily. 'Of course there wasn't! What are you trying to say?'

He made a small open gesture with his hand. 'Mrs Potter, I don't *know* the people involved. I'm not saying anything — I'm asking.'

She calmed a little. 'Well, there wasn't, that's all. It's just his morbid imagination. He wanted her locked up like some Arab woman, you know, and he couldn't stand it that she wanted a life of her own. I mean, Jen's smart, pretty, full of life, always into everything; all he ever wants to do is sit slumped in a chair watching football on the telly. Never wants to go out anywhere or do anything, just wants to go home and lock the door with Jen inside. Well, she doesn't want to spend her life doing house-work, which is all he'd've let her do if he had his way. And then he accuses her of things she hasn't done, the nasty-minded, jealous little snob.'

'Did he hit her?'

'Oh, yes, he's done that too. When they've rowed. I don't know why she stayed with him. I mean, he was earning the money, and Jen always liked the good life, but I would never have to do with a man that'd hit a woman.'

She stubbed out her cigarette with shaking fingers and immediately racked the packet for another. Slider, with a reputation now to maintain, lit it for her. Then he said, 'I understand Jennifer was working here last night. Was that her regular evening?'

She looked sidelong at him. 'She didn't have regular times here. I just asked her, or Jack asked her, when we were busy. But yesterday — well, it was a bit different.' She sighed out a mouthful of smoke. 'I can't believe it was only yesterday. My God, I still can't believe she's dead.' She took a few more serious drags to steady herself. Slider waited in sympathetic silence, and at last she went on, 'I'll tell you how it was. Jen was at work at Meacher's in the morning — till one o'clock, she did — and about, oh, quarter, twenty past one she came here, came round the back to the kitchen to talk to me. Well, we were standing chatting when suddenly Eddie turns up —'

'Eddie Andrews came to the pub yesterday lunchtime? From his work at Mrs Hammond's house?'

She glanced an enquiry at him. 'That's right.'

'He said you didn't allow working clothes in the pub.'

'That's right, we don't. Well, it's all lounge trade here. But we don't mind in the garden. Not that you really get working clothes coming in very often — people like that go to the Mimpriss, where they've got a public bar. But, of course, working at the Rectory, this is closer, so I suppose he just popped across for a drink. Anyway, the first I know about it is he comes into the garden with a pint in his hand, and sees Jen standing at the kitchen door talking to me. So he comes over and says, "What are you doing here?" and Jen says, "Talking to my friend, do you mind?" And he says, "Yes, I do mind, I don't want my wife hanging around pubs."'

She looked at Slider to see if he appreciated the insult, and he nodded encouragingly.

'So I can see Jen's really fed up with him, and she says, "I don't care what you want. As it happens, Linda's asked me to work tonight and I've said yes," which I hadn't, but of course I had to back her up, so I said that was right, and he gets mad and says he won't have it and there's a bit of a barney, and at the end of it Jen says she'll do as she likes and if he don't like it he can do the other thing, and she walks off. So then Eddie starts mouthing off at me, how I'm a bad influence on Jen and all that old toffee, but I'm not taking it so I tell him to clear off. I said I've had enough of you, I said, and you're barred from now on. So he says I wouldn't drink here if you paid me, and he tips his beer out all over my clean kitchen step and walks off.'

'Weren't you afraid?'

'What, of him? If he'd tried to hit me, I'd've decked him first — and he knew it. He's all mouth and trousers, that one. A bully, like most men: if you stand up to them they cave in. You get to know who's dangerous in my trade and who isn't. But then I wasn't married to him.'

'Go on,' Slider said. 'Did Mrs Andrews come in to work that evening?'

'Well, she phones me up in the afternoon, about ha'pass three. She sounded upset, and I said what's up, and she just says, oh, men, I hate 'em all. So I told her I'd barred Eddie, and she said thank God for that, at least there was one place she could go to get away from him, and I said do you really want to come in tonight, because of course Tuesday isn't a busy night in the bar, and she said, yes, is that a problem, so I said did she fancy helping out in the restaurant instead because I had an office birthday party, twelve covers, coming in, and you know what those parties are like, it takes for ever to get the order down with 'em all talking and changing their minds. But she said no, she'd do the bar, and Karen — that's our bar girl — could do the restaurant. So that's how we left it, and she was to come in at seven.'

'And did she in fact come in at seven?'

'Oh, yes. Well, I didn't see her, but Karen came through and said Jen had just arrived. As it turned out the restaurant was really busy — we had a lot of casuals in as well as the bookings — so I never got a chance to go through to the bar, and by the time I'd finished Jen was gone.' Her eyes moistened abruptly. 'So I never got to say goodbye. I mean, not that I'd have known it was the last time — but — you know.'

'Yes, of course, I understand,' Slider said, and she nodded and retired into the handkerchief again, and then emerged for a therapeutic puff. 'And you didn't see her or speak to her again?' She shook her head. 'And what about Eddie? Did you see him at all last night?'

'Oh, he came in that evening, all right, but I didn't see him. Jack'll tell you all about that. Of course, if we'd known what was going to happen, we'd have got the police on to him, but we didn't know,' she said harshly. 'No-one could have known, that's what I say. I mean, he led that poor woman a hell of a life, but I'd never have thought he had it in him to do what he did, the evil bastard.'

Atherton sat on one of the bar stools as Slider was led away by the female of the species, and said to her mate, 'You carry on with what you're doing. What are twirlies, by the way?'

'Eh?' Jack seemed distracted. He was watching his wife's departure with what looked like perplexity, and came back to attention with difficulty. 'Oh — they're the ones who turn up every day on the dot of opening, if not before — pensioners, usually, with nowhere else to go. They dodder into the bar the minute you unlock and say, "Am I too early?" Too early — twirly. See?'

'You perform a social service, really, don't you?' Atherton said. 'Like the public library.'

Jack Potter took him seriously. 'Well, yes, we do. The public house has a unique place in the social fabric of this country. There's nothing like it anywhere else in the world, did you know that? And this was a village pub once — back in history.'

'Really?' Atherton marvelled.

'Oh, yes. It's any age, this place. All these beams are genuine, you know.' He slapped the nearest in a horsemanlike way. 'There was a village here goes back to Doomsday, before they built all this lot on top of it.'

'It's an unusual place to find in this part of London,' Atherton said.

'Oh, there's a lot of old stuff about, if you know where to look,' Potter said. 'Trouble is, most of it got messed up before anyone started caring about that sort of thing. The First And Last — in Woodbridge Road, you know it? — that was an old coaching inn, stage coaches and all that, though you'd never know to look at it now. But this one, being out of the way, it got missed out when all the modernising was going on. And now it's listed, so the outside's protected at any rate. But it's a nice place, and we get a very nice sort

110

of clienteel round here. Shorts and wine trade, like I said —'

'And the occasional murderer,' Atherton remarked.

Jack looked upset. He leaned on his hands on the bar, pulling the bar-towel taut between them. 'Don't say that! I can't bear to think of it. That poor woman! It *was* murder, then? Nobody seemed to know, but people were saying . . .'

'What do you think?'

'I don't know. I don't like to. I mean, Eddie and her were always having rows, but I never would have thought he'd go so far as to . . .' He filled in with a shake of the head. 'How did he do it, anyway?'

Atherton said, 'I don't want to go into that. Tell me about yesterday.'

'Well, he was here yesterday lunchtime, and they had a bit of a barney out in the garden, but I didn't actually see that. Linda will tell you all about it. She ended up barring Eddie, and I wasn't sorry. He had it coming. I mean, he was a nice enough bloke most of the time, but it made it awkward, with Jen and Lin being friendly, and her working here. I mean, you never want to get in between a husband and wife rowing, see what I mean? I'd've stayed out of it, kept neutral, if I could've.

But with the situation what it was — and I didn't like the way he behaved to my wife. Very rude to her he was. So I'd've ended up barring him myself sooner or later.' He looked at Atherton to see if he believed him. Atherton already had a fair idea who was the Lord Warden of the Trousers in this family.

'And Jennifer Andrews was working here last night, was she?'

'That's right,' he said, though his eyes moved about a bit.

'She was here all evening?'

'That's right,' he said again.

'In the restaurant or in the bar?'

'Well, she came on to help me in here, so that Karen — that's our girl — could help the wife out in the restaurant. Had a big party in, Lin did. Jen came on about seven, or a bit after, and then Karen went through to help Lin.'

'And what time did she leave?'

'What, Karen?'

Atherton curbed his impatience. 'No, Jennifer.'

Jack Potter stared at him, and his face congealed with guilt. 'Look,' he said. Atherton looked, but he seemed not to be able to go on. His eyes shifted sideways and back. 'Look,' he said again, pleadingly now, 'I want to tell you the truth, but you've got to keep it from the wife. I mean, it's nothing bad,' he added hastily, 'but I don't want Lin coming down on me for it. She's got a sharp tongue, my wife, and — well, married life's hard enough, d'you know what I mean?'

Atherton smiled, inviting confidence, persuasive as the Serpent on commission. 'Every marriage has its little secrets,' he said.

'You're not wrong!' Jack said gladly. 'Women? I tell you, it's a juggling act, keeping 'em sweet. Well, look, strictly between you and me — the thing was, Jen wasn't really working here last night. She'd arranged it with the wife lunchtime, and all I knew was what they'd arranged between them, about Karen going in the restaurant and everything. So Jen comes in at about seven, like I said, or a bit after, and Karen goes through, and Jen and me chats a bit, because there's no-one in the bar yet; and then she says, Jen says, "Look, you don't really need me here tonight, do you?" Well, Tuesdays are quiet — in the bar at any rate. So she says, "You can manage without me," and I says yes, and she says, "Good, because I've got to go somewhere, to see someone." And she gives me a wink,

113

just like that, you know.'

'Did she say where she was going?'

'No,' he said, and seemed to find it a naive question. 'Well, the thing was, she wanted me to cover for her. Now Eddie was barred, it meant he couldn't come in and check up on her, so he'd think she was in here, and —' He shrugged.

'What time did she leave?'

'About half seven, it must have been. She went out through the back, down the passage past the ladies' and out through the garden, and that was the last I saw of her. She said she'd be back later but she never. Luckily Lin never came through until after ten, so I just told her Jen had finished and gone home.'

'Why didn't she want Linda to know where she was?'

'Well, Lin's a bit — careful with the money. It's not that she's not generous, I don't say that, but she's the one that keeps the books and everything and she's — careful. She wouldn't've liked if it I'd paid Jen for the evening and she wasn't here.'

'But then why did you have to pay her, if all you were doing was providing cover for her?'

'Well, if I hadn't paid her, Lin would've known she wasn't here.'

'Why shouldn't your wife know Jennifer wasn't here?' Atherton asked, patiently trotting another circle.

'Well, Lin's a bit, you know, strait-laced,' Jack said, with what seemed like sudden inspiration. 'She would never tell a lie, my wife, which is why Jen never asked her to cover for her.'

'Did you think Jennifer was going to meet another man?'

Jack looked defensive. 'I don't know, I don't know where she was going. It was probably all innocent, but Eddie wouldn't've thought so, which is why she needed me to cover for her. I'm sure it was all innocent. She just wanted to get away from Eddie.'

As yarn went, Atherton thought, this was multi-coloured lurex thread. He went on unravelling. 'So what would you have done if your wife had come through during the evening and found Jennifer not there?' Atherton asked.

'Well, she wasn't likely to, with a big party in, but Jen said if she did I was just to say she'd felt a bit iffy and gone home; but as it was, Lin was really pushed and never come through till closing, so she never found out, and I never said.'

'And what about Karen? Didn't she come through at any point?'

'Oh, yes, she was fetching the drinks for the restaurant. But I just told her to keep schtumm. She's a good girl, she does what I tell her.'

'I see. But surely the customers would know Jennifer wasn't there, and let it out some time?'

'Well, they wouldn't expect her to be there anyway, so why should they mention it to Lin that she wasn't?' Atherton offered no reason. 'You won't tell her — Linda — will you?' Jack pleaded, and laughed unconvincingly. 'There's no harm in it. I just want a quiet life, that's all.'

Atherton let it go. 'What about Eddie Andrews? Did he come to check up on his wife at all?'

'Twice,' Jack said, seeming relieved to reach something more stable underfoot. 'First time he came it was around eight, eight thirty. He'd had a few by then, I could tell. He comes bursting in through the door over there, but I nipped out smartish and stopped him, and told him to get out. "You're barred," I said, "and besides which we don't allow work clothes in here." '

'He was in his work clothes?'

'Oh, yes, mucky boots and all. So I grabbed him by the shoulder and hustled him out, and he was, like, trying to look behind me and saying, "Where's my wife?" so I said she was in the storeroom and he wasn't going to annoy her, not on my premises, and I shoved him out. And he stood there a bit, arguing with me, but I just said I wasn't moving until he'd gone, so after a bit he got into his pickup and drove off.'

'And the second time?'

'That must have been near eleven o'clock. Not long before closing, anyway. He came in just like before, only I was serving someone and I wasn't quick enough to catch him before he got up to the bar. Anyway, he asks where Jen is and I told him she'd left and gone home, and he said I was lying, she'd gone off somewhere and I knew where. Well, in the end I told him if he didn't clear out I'd call the police — which he didn't want, because he was well over the limit and still driving about in that truck of his. So after a bit he goes, and that was the last I saw of him.'

'Where was your wife at the time?'

'She was in the kitchen clearing up and getting ready for the morning. She didn't see any of it, fortunately, but I told her afterwards, of course. I mean, I told her Eddie'd been in drunk looking for Jen after Jen'd gone home. She said, Lin said, I ought to phone Jen and warn her, but I said Jen could take care of herself and we shouldn't get involved, and she saw the sense of that.' He stopped and gazed at Atherton with fawning eyes. 'I didn't know how it would turn out. I mean, covering up for Jen, I was just doing a favour for a friend, that's all. I didn't do wrong, did I?'

'That's entirely your business, sir,' Atherton said, 'but as far as these timings go, we shall have to have a statement from you about it.'

'Yes, I do see that.' He bit his lip, frowning anxiously. 'But it wasn't my fault he killed her, was it? I mean, who'd have thought he'd do a thing like that? All right, he got drunk and mouthed off a bit, and he had hit her once or twice, according to what Lin says, but I'd never have thought he had the balls to really do it.'

Atherton thought of Eddie Andrews, drunk and looking for his wife, being fobbed off so easily by Jack Potter, and was inclined to agree with him.

Chapter Five

Eyes That Last I Saw In Tears

In the CID room, the sandwiches were out in force. 'I don't suppose anyone got me anything,' Slider said plaintively.

General mastication was arrested for a micro-second of guilty silence; then McLaren said, 'I got an egg and cress here you could have.'

'I don't want to deprive you.'

'No, it's all right, guv, I got plenty.'

That was true. He was already eating a sandwich, and Slider saw on his desk, besides, two jumbo sausage rolls (made with real jumbos, to judge from the grey colour of the filling), a Cellophane-wrapped Scotch egg, a Twix, a big bag of salt 'n' vinegar crisps, an apple turnover and, betrayed by its slippery stench, a Pot Noodle sweating it out from the microwave in the coffee-room next door. Slider accepted the sandwich. It was the depressing sort of low-grade egg and cress on white sliced, with margarine instead of butter, and the thin slices of hard-boiled egg which, given nothing to weld them together, fall out of the side of the sandwich when you lift it. But beggars, Slider reckoned, couldn't be critics, and he was famished.

'You can have my Kit Kat as well, boss,' Norma said, slinging it over, belatedly troubled by conscience.

'Thanks,' said Slider.

'Don't mensh.'

Hollis had already got the name and details up on the whiteboard, along with the photographs of the body and its position. 'My second murder since I've been here,' he said with satisfaction. 'And I thought it was going to be quiet.'

'We don't know that it's a murder,' Slider said patiently, but he still had no takers. Over the groans he said, 'She might have died of natural causes: pegged out in the middle of a naughty, for instance, leaving someone in an embarrassing position, or a blind panic, with a body on their hands. Don't let's get carried away. Remember Timothy Evans.'

'What, the Christie murders geezer?' Mackay asked thickly, through a cheese-and-pickle gag. 'What's he got to do with it?'

'He went to the police station to say he'd put his wife's body down a drain, but the officers assumed he was confessing to murder, and he never smiled again.'

'Careless talk costs lives,' Atherton remarked.

'And careless listening, too,' Slider warned. 'So let's wait for the post-mortem report before we go assuming anything.'

'My money's on murder anyway,' Mackay said, swallowing. 'And it doesn't take a genius to guess who.'

'Disappointed?' Hollis said,

'Oh, I like a challenge, me. But it's got to be the husband, hasn't it?'

'I met Murder on the way: he had a face like Eddie A.' Atherton said. He intercepted Slider's look and said defensively, 'You can *et tu* me all you like, but our Eddie's story's got more holes in it than the Labour Party manifesto.'

'All right,' Slider said, settling on the edge of a desk, 'I can see you're not going to heed my warnings, so let's have it out in the open.'

Atherton, stretching his elegant legs across a good part of the room, extended his thumb. 'Point one — to begin at the beginning: Andrews says that the work on the terrace was at Mrs Hammond's instigation, that she practically begged him to do it, though he told her it wasn't needed. But she says he told her it had to be done, the terrace would fall down otherwise. Why would he lie about that, except to cover up that the existence of the hole was all his idea? And what was the hole for, if not to conceal his wife's body?'

'He may just have wanted the work,' Norma said.

'Everyone says he's doing very well,' said Atherton. 'She was dripping jewellery, and he has just a stately pleasure dome decreed —'

'Eh?'

'Built himself a big new house, which, vile though it is in every detail, is someone's idea of luxury.'

'He might have put himself into debt satisfying her and building it,' Norma pointed out reasonably. 'We don't *know* he didn't have money troubles.'

'Good point.' Slider nodded. 'That's something to check up on.'

Norma went on, 'All the same, I can't see why he lied about whose idea the work was. It's nothing to us if he persuaded Mrs H. to part with unnecessary cash. It does look as if he's trying to dissociate himself from it, which looks guilty. So I'll give you half a point, Jim.'

'Ta very much,' he said, and extended his forefinger. 'Point two: he says he went home from work and stayed there all evening, had supper, watched telly and went to bed. But the house is as immaculate as if the cleaner had just left it — which I propose is the case. Mrs Chatterbury did for them on Tuesday morning after both Andrewses had gone to work, and she was the last person to set foot in the house before we arrived.'

'But hang on,' McLaren objected, 'surely Mrs Andrews would've gone home at some point? I mean, minimum, a smart-looking bint like her wouldn't've stayed in the same clobber all day, would she?'

'You'd expect her to've gone home to change before going to the pub for the evening,' Hollis seconded.

'According to Jack the Lad, she wasn't going to the pub for the evening,' Atherton pointed out. 'She was going on a date.'

'All the more reason, then,' said Norma.

'Check on that,' Slider said. 'What was she wearing at lunchtime? But I suppose she might have changed without leaving any trace in the house, though God knows why she should.'

Atherton sighed and extended his

middle finger. 'Point three: Andrews says he worked through his lunchtime and stayed home all evening, whereas we already know he made three visits to the Goat In Boots. Why is he lying?'

'Because he's dead stupid,' McLaren said pityingly.

'Harsh words from a man who has to write L and R on the bottom of his shoes,' Swilley said.

'And point — whatever this finger is,' Atherton pursued patiently, 'we have from several sources that the Andrewses were on bad terms and given to quarrelling, and that he was a jealous beast and had been known to hit her. We know he was looking for her, and probably the worse for drink. *Ergo*, dear friends, we may postulate that he found her — somewhere — and had a row with her; killed her — somehow — and put the body in his nice handy hole, meaning to fill her in with concrete in the morning. Unfortunately for him, the early-rising Mrs H. got there first. Simple.'

'You are,' Swilley agreed. 'What's all this somewhere and somehow stuff? You sound like a chorus from *West Side Story*.'

'Well, obviously,' Atherton said kindly, 'there are a few minor details left to be filled in. That's just routine legwork, and since you are *numero uno* in the legs department, Norm, I feel I can safely leave that to you.'

Slider retrieved crumbs of hard-boiled egg-yolk from his chest and said, 'There's a great deal we still have to find out. Where the death took place and how the body was transported to the terrace of the Rectory are two that spring to mind, whether it was murder or not.' There was a general groan, and he raised his voice slightly. 'Whether it was murder or not, we are still dealing with a crime: not reporting a death is an offence,not to mention attempting to conceal a dead body, and our old friend obstruction. But to ease your turbulent minds, I will say that I am now much more inclined to think that it was Eddie —'

'Hallelujah! A conversion!' said Atherton.

'And the best way we can overcome his natural reserve is to apply some facts to his story.'

'Or electrodes to his *cojones?*' Atherton suggested hopefully.

'I thought that was Spanish for rabbits,' Norma objected.

'Comes out the same,' said Atherton.

Slider went on patiently over the top of them, 'We must find out exactly where he was all through the evening and last night and present him with it. When he knows we know nearly everything, I think he'll cough up the rest. If he did love her, he'll want to tell us — it's just a matter of helping him to get there. We also need to find out where Mrs Andrews was for the whole of the day —'

'And what she was wearing,' Norma added.

'Nothing like some nice, knobbly facts to trip up a liar,' Slider concluded. 'So how about garnering me some?'

Atherton stood up, sighing. 'Here we go. Another *crime passionelle.*'

'Sounds like an exotic fruit-flavoured blancmange,' said Norma.

'Blancmange?' McLaren pricked up his ears, like a dog hearing its name.

'Never fails,' Norma said witheringly. 'Mention food . . .'

'You what?'

'Confection is good for the soul,' Atherton explained kindly.

'Yeah, I read that,' McLaren said, starting on his apple turnover.

'An alimentary deduction,' Atherton concluded.

Slider was in his own room doing the

preliminary paperwork when Hollis shoved his head round the door.

'Guv? Some good news.'

'I'm up for that.'

'They've found a handbag in the back of Eddie Andrews's pickup.'

'A handbag?'

Hollis followed his head in. 'Funny, everyone says that when I tell 'em. It's like being stuck in a lift with Edith Evans.'

'What do you mean, everyone? You mean I'm the last to know as usual?

'Oh, not the last, guv. I thought *you'd* like to tell the Super.'

'Always grateful for crumbs. What sort of handbag?'

'It's Jennifer Andrews's all right. Got her driving licence and all sorts inside. I suppose he chucked it in there meaning to get rid of it later, and forgot. Or didn't have time.'

'We must have it tested for prints.'

'They're doing that,' Hollis nodded.

'Not that it will help to find Andrews' dabs all over it. There's no reason why they shouldn't be there.'

'No, guv. But there's every reason why the bag shouldn't be in the back of his pickup. I can't see someone like her riding on the sacks, can you?'

'Quite. If it had been in the cab, now —'

'Well, no-one can think of everything.'

'But where a woman is, there shall ye find her handbag also. Meaning —'

'Get Forensic to check the back of the motor for any traces of *madarm*,' Hollis said smartly, 'dead or alive.'

'You're quick. You'll go far.'

Hollis looked hopeful. 'Is it enough to arrest him on?'

'If he can't provide a decent explanation, I think it probably will be.'

Half an hour later Slider was back in the CID room with the good news.

'Andrews burst into tears at the sight of his wife's handbag, and offered no explanation as to how it got into the back of his pickup, so I'm here to tell you, ladies and germs, that with Mr Porson's blessing, Andrews is now officially nicked.'

'For murder?' Anderson asked.

'Hold your horses. We still don't know what she died of. Suspicion of interfering with the body is all we've got so far, but it means we can get stuck in.' There were murmurs of satisfaction around the room. 'Right, the house-to-house continues. Norma, you're going to look into Andrews' finances. Let's have the BT record for his home number — that will give us some corroboration as to whether he was home or not, and may help us with the whereabouts of Mrs. Find out if either or both had a mobile and get the call records on them — McLaren, you can do those. And someone had better call her GP and find out if she had a heart disease or was taking anything.'

'Guv, what's the SP on the post?' Anderson asked.

'Doc Cameron's doing it this afternoon, if we're lucky.'

'Blimey, that's quick,' said Hollis.

'Close personal of the guv'nor,' McLaren said. 'It pays to be popular in this game.'

'How would you know?' Norma asked cruelly.

Freddie Cameron telephoned very late. 'What are you doing still there?'

'What are you?' Slider countered.

'Struggling with this corpse of yours.'

'Metaphorically, I hope.'

'Thanks to you I'm now thoroughly behind with the rest of my work. It was an absolute stinker — *absit omen* — but I think I've cracked it at last. Would you like to guess?'

'Can't be anything obvious, if it took you so long.'

'Thanks for the vote of confidence. Mine in you to solve the crime, let me say, is as solid.'

'Crime? It is murder, then? I'm glad to hear it, because we've got the husband binned up.'

'You arrested him? That was bold of you.'

'We found her handbag in his truck, and Porson agreed that was enough to start with. But we'd sooner know what crime we're dealing with. So far all we've got is interfering with the body.'

'Ah, yes, now, we knew she must have been moved, but the hypostasis confirms it. The distribution suggests she was left at first in a sitting position for several hours. Sitting as if on a chair, with the legs bent at the knee. And she was tied to whatever it was to keep her in position.'

'Tied up?'

'With something broad and flat, like a luggage strap, for instance, passed around the upper body, but with the arms inside. Definitely post-mortem. No ante-mortem ligature marks. Tied quite loosely: her weight had fallen forward against the strap.'

Slider digested that. The being tied in position suggested it had been for purposes of hiding the body, presumably until it was late enough and quiet enough to take it to the trench. In the back of Eddie's truck, sitting on a sack under a tarpaulin? Something like that. 'So what did you decide in the end was the cause of death?'

Freddie hesitated. 'If it came to court, it's one of those cases where defence would probably bring in their own expert opinion to contest my findings, so you'd better try your utmost for a confession. But I'd say it was suffocation.'

'I've never known you so cautious,' Slider said. 'Suffocation? Surely that leaves definite signs? Petechiae, for instance? And cyanosis?'

Cameron chuckled. 'There's my educated copper!'

'It's a misspent youth hanging around morgues. Well, am I right?'

'You are,' Cameron agreed. 'But, you see, petechiae aren't caused by the lack of oxygen itself; it's the raised venous pressure that does it — due to, for instance, constriction of the throat or thorax. Cyanosis — and oedema, for that matter — are congestive signs. Where asphyxia is not accompanied by any violence or struggle, the classic signs can be completely absent. Plastic-bag suicides, for instance, are often quite pale.'

'So what's the actual cause of death in those cases?' Slider asked.

'Probably a neurochemical reaction of the heart. The heart just stops; which, of course, leaves an appearance of natural death. Which is what makes it fun.'

'So you're saying she could have died naturally?'

'My personal belief is not, though it was a close decision, I have to tell you, even on my part; and my assistant — who likes to err on the safe side of not sticking his neck out — doesn't agree with me. But I would say she was smothered.'

'Smothered? You mean with a pillow, or something?'

'Little Princes in the Tower job,' Freddie agreed.

Slider laid this against the image of the drunken marital row and found it wanting. 'But how could you smother somebody without a violent struggle?'

'It happens — probably more often than we like to think — with the frail and bed-ridden. It's the front runner for easing your terminally ill relly out of life without having the State come down on you for the price.'

'Mrs Andrews was hardly frail and bed-ridden.'

'Quite,' Cameron said. 'But a healthy and active adult could be smothered without violent struggle if she was first rendered helpless or comatose.'

'Made drunk, you mean?'

'Possibly, or drugs. I'd put my money on sleepers — I've sent blood and stomach samples off to the lab, by the way, so we shall see what we shall see. But if she was slipped the appropriate mickey, and fell into a nice deep one à la Sleeping Beauty, the rest would be easy.'

The dirty little coward, Slider thought indignantly. His native caution asked, 'If there are no signs, what makes you think that's what happened?'

'This is where I triumphantly produce the pedigree angora from the depths of the old silk topper,' Cameron said, 'and announce that purely owing to my analytical genius and thoroughness of method, I have found some slight bruising on the inside of the mouth, consistent with the lips having been pressed against the teeth by the pressure of the killer's hands on the pillow — or whatever he used.'

'But you say your assistant doesn't agree with you?'

'It is *very* slight bruising,' Freddie admitted. 'It wouldn't be necessary to press very hard, you see, if she was comatose. If I hadn't been sure it wasn't natural death . . . No signs of violence, but Freddie "The Bloodhound" Cameron wasn't satisfied. Don't you want to know why?' he prompted when Slider didn't speak.

'I was afraid to ask. I'm beginning to think you're after my job.'

'No, no, my dear old thing, I leave all that messy dealing-with-the-public to you. I prefer my Smiths and Joneses as mute and docile as possible. But look here,' he became serious suddenly, 'this woman was rather tarted up, wasn't she?'

'Yes, that's what I thought,' Slider agreed.

'And if you place a pillow over the face even of a sleeping victim, the other result, apart from death, is that the old maquillage gets smudged.'

'You mean — ?'

'I think it was touched up after death.'

'Good God!'

'Yes,' said Freddie, 'it struck me as a bit macabre, too. I found smears of the coloured foundation cream *inside* the nostrils, where a woman would have to be very clumsy to get it when making up her own face; and even more telling, traces of mascara on the right eyeball and contact lens. No-one alive would leave that where it was. You'd have spots before the eyes — and that stuff smarts, too.'

Slider thought a moment. 'Of course, touching up the makeup doesn't in itself mean it was murder. But it must have been meant to conceal something. Why else would it have been done?'

'That I leave to you, dear boy,' Freddie said, 'and, frankly, you're welcome to it. I'd stand up in court and swear to the bruises, but the defence could easily put up someone else to say they didn't exist.'

'So we've got to hope for the lab to show something up?'

'You can hope,' Freddie said grimly, 'but if it was a sleeper, and if it shows up, and if it was a normal dose, what's to say she didn't take it herself, voluntarily? Then you're back to my expert opinion on the bruises versus the defence expert opinion.' Slider was silent. 'Oh, and by the way, talking of the lab, there was a quantity of semen in the vagina. I sent a sample off to be typed. No sign of forcible penetration, though.'

'From what we hear she didn't need to be forced.'

'But if you get a suspect, it might be a help to prove she was with him.'

'If it's the husband's, it won't prove anything. Oh, well,' Slider sighed, 'it's early days yet.'

'And you have miles to go before you sleep,' Freddie said. 'Talking of which, I should be long gone. I'm supposed to be taking the Madam to the golf-club dinner tonight. Must go home and get into the old soup-and-fish. And scrub off some of the smell of offal — Martha says it's like a slaughtermen's convention being in the car with me.'

'You? Never! You're a mountain breeze, Freddie.'

'Thanks, but best friends notoriously don't tell. Better to rely on one's wife for brutal frankness. I'll be in touch when the lab report comes back. Goodnight.'

'Goodnight.'

'Oh — and, Bill?'

'Hello?'

'Go home, there's a good chap. It's after seven.'

The flat was empty when he got back: Joanna was away overnight, doing a concert in Swansea, from which it was not practicable to drive home to sleep. Or, at least, Joanna didn't think it was. Some musicians, he knew, drove back and pocketed the 'overnight' allowance, but Joanna said, 'I'd sooner relax, wind down and go for a drink after a concert than hammer down the M4. And I should have thought as a policeman you wouldn't want me to drive all that way when I'm exhausted,' so after that there was nothing more he could say. And she was right, of course. He'd got to the ridiculous stage of worrying about her whenever she was out of his sight, particularly when she had a long drive to do, which was often. She was an excellent driver, he knew, but it wasn't the excellent drivers who caused the accidents.

She was right to stay away; but still he felt rather pathetic and hard-done-by, coming home to an empty house after a hard day at work. Where was the warm greeting, the nicely adjusted bath-water, the 'supper in half an hour, darling' that a man ought to have the right to expect? Joanna wouldn't be alone this evening. After the concert she would go for a drink — or more likely several — at the hotel where they were all staying. He expected it would turn into quite a late session, since she was more inclined to hang around with the brass players than anyone in the string section, and everyone knew brass players were boozers. Joanna didn't much like other violinists — tea-drinkers, she called them — and he put it down to her having been corrupted early in her career by that trumpet player she used to go out with, Geoffrey whatever-his-name-was. Geoffrey! What kind of name was that for a grown man? he asked, with savage illogic. Then there was Martin Cutts, the man they called Measles, because every girl had to have him at some point. And that big trombone player with the beard who always put his arm round Joanna's waist when he was talking to her . . . Slider would not allow himself to think about what else brass players had the reputation for being besides boozers. As Joanna had said, in her limpid way, 'You either trust me or you don't'; and, of course, it wasn't that he didn't trust her. He did, completely. Absolutely. But you couldn't expect hormones to be logical, and his hormones had a vivid imagination and no sense of proportion whatsoever.

He stumped off to get himself a large malt — Aberfeldy, he decided, since he needed soothing — and went with it in his hand to look in the fridge. There was salady stuff, he saw with deep indifference:

salad was not what he wanted, when he'd had nothing all day but McLaren's spare sandwich. Salad! Rabbit fodder! Well, what did he expect? Hot food didn't spring into existence, like Athene out of Zeus's head, just because he thought about it. For a moment he contemplated cooking himself something, but the silent emptiness of the flat was striking lethargy deep into his bones, and after a moment he took out the cheese box instead. Too far gone even to make himself a sandwich, he cut some thick wedges of Cheddar and put them on a plate with some oatcakes; hesitated, and added a chilly tomato (Dutch! In the middle of summer!) that he knew even then he would leave.

He was half-way to the sofa when he remembered he hadn't turned off the answering-machine and, dumping his plate and glass, went back into the hall. The little red light was blinking away like a contact-lens wearer in a sandstorm. He pressed Replay. There were several messages about work for Joanna, one irritatingly casual, 'Hi Jojo, it's Ted Bundy, give me a ring, okay? Chiz!' (Jojo? Who the hell was Ted Bundy? And why did he assume she knew his number? He hated people who said cheers instead of goodbye.) And then a click and one for him.

'Hello, Mr Slider, it's Yvonne here from Ralph Easterman.'

That was the estate agent to whom he'd transferred the ex-marital home in Ruislip, after the original two had failed to shift it. She went on, sounding annoyed, 'You seem to have made some new arrangements. Um, it would have been helpful if you could have let me know, because actually I did take someone round there this afternoon, and it was a bit embarrassing. So, um, could you give me a ring, please, and confirm whether you are taking the house off the market or not? Thanks very much. 'Bye.'

That was all. Slider stood a moment, frowning, while his magnificent analytical brain went to work on it. Then he picked up the receiver and, with a peculiar sensation of unfamiliar familiarity, tapped in what for so many years had been his home number.

Irene answered. She had always been one of those annoying people who answer the phone properly, with the full number, as specified in the *GPO-Debrett Book of Telephone Etiquette*, 1965 edition; but this time she just said, 'Hello?' in the uncertain tone of someone who has arrived by appointment at night at a lonely house on the moors and found the windows dark and the front door standing open.

'It's me,' he said. 'What are you doing there?'

She didn't speak at once, and he heard in the background the sound of the television on loudly in the sitting room, with the peevishly upraised voices of some soap-opera characters being unpleasant to each other. Suddenly and painfully he was back there in the cramped little hall with its smell of incipient food, glimpsing through the open door the children sitting on the floor gaping at one of the early-evening banalities, in which there was always someone with their hands on their hips saying aggressively, 'What's that supposed to mean?' His children, his home, his wife: the encrusted habit of so many years which, however little pleasurable it had been at the time, was so very hard ever afterwards to scrape off the old hull.

Then Irene said tautly, 'Wait while I shut the door.' Clatter of the receiver being put down; click of the sitting room door being shut, and the soap stars were cut off in mid plaint. Then Irene was back, with an air of speaking without moving her lips. 'I didn't want the children to hear.'

Why? he wondered. Had he become an indecent secret? But he had a more urgent question. 'The estate agent left me a message on the answer-machine —'

'Yes, she was round here today. She wanted to show someone round. I told her the house wasn't for sale any more.'

'You did what? *Why?* What are you doing there, anyway?'

'Why shouldn't I be here if I want to?'

'Irene!' he said, exasperated. 'Are you saying you've moved back in?'

'Brain of Britain,' she said disparagingly.

It was a bit of a blow. 'You might at least have told me.'

'Why should I? It's my home, isn't it?'

'Is this permanent?'

'I don't know. Maybe. Any objections?'

'Well, yes, as it happens! It may be your home, but it's not his. I'm damned if I'm going to subsidise Ernie Newman. What's happened, anyway? Has he lost all his money on the horses or something?'

'Don't be ridiculous,' Irene said icily. 'Ernie isn't here. Do you really think I'd — ?'

'What, d'you mean you've left him? You've split up?'

She paused, selecting her words. 'Ernie and I aren't living together any more.'

My God! What did he feel about that? Vindication — he'd always known it wouldn't work. Triumph — the smug, boring prick that his wife had preferred to him had lost after all. Dismay — Irene without Ernie became his responsibility again. Fear — what was she going to demand of him in these new circumstances, and how was he going to cope? And also — and not least — horrible, embarrassed sympathy for Irene herself, because whosever choice this was, it must be humiliating for her.

'So it didn't work out, then?' he heard himself say, and his voice sounded definitely peculiar.

'I didn't say that.' She sounded strange too. 'It's just that, for the time being, at least, we're going to have separate homes.'

'There's something going on here,' he said suspiciously. 'I know you. You've got that tone of voice when you've done something you know you shouldn't — like when you bought the conservatory furniture without asking me. Marilyn Cripps was behind that, as I remember. I bet you've been talking to her.'

'Oh, you love to play the great detective, don't you? You think you're so clever!' She was trying to sound scornful, but there was a quiver of defiance in it.

'What's that bossy bitch up to now? Why has she turned you against Ernie?'

'Don't you call my friend a bitch! She hasn't done anything of the sort. And what do you care about Ernie all of a sudden? You've never done anything but sneer at him, when he's never done anything to you —'

'Apart from waltz off with my wife, you mean?' He knew as he said it that it was a mistake but he couldn't stop himself in time. The trouble with these marital rows was that the script was all engraved on the brain from years of television, and lumps of it tended to come out of their own volition.

Irene was furious. '*Your* wife? Pity you didn't think a bit more about *your* wife when you started messing around with that dirty little cow you're shacked up with! I told you I'd make you damn well pay, and I will!'

'Marilyn is behind this,' he concluded.

'She gave me some good advice, simply because she has my welfare at heart — unlike some people!'

'She told you to move back in?'

'Yes. So that I can take you for every penny you've got!'

He tried to assemble the words so that she would hear them. 'Irene, it doesn't work like that any more. Divorce is all no-fault, these days — didn't your solicitor explain that to you?' A suspicion took hold of him. 'You have spoken to a solicitor, haven't you?'

There was a tell-tale pause. 'I don't need to. Marilyn knows all about it. She's got a friend who's a solicitor who deals with divorce all the time. She practically does nothing else but divorce, this friend. So Marilyn's quite well able to advise me, thank you.'

A huge tired sadness overwhelmed him, so that he couldn't even be angry. Irene was such a plonker when it came to people with big houses and Range Rovers. '*Please* listen to me,' he said. 'They don't take fault into account any more. Unless there are special circumstances, they always end up dividing everything fifty-fifty. Including the house — which means selling it, so that the proceeds can be split. The courts won't automatically give you the house, like in the old days, just because you're living in it. And they won't automatically expect me to go on paying the mortgage.'

'I don't believe you,' she said stonily. 'Why should I believe you?'

'You don't have to take my word for it,' he said. 'Any solicitor will tell you. But it would be so much better if you and I came to an amicable arrangement first. Look,' he said gently, 'do you really not want to live with Ernie?'

'I don't know,' she said. 'I don't know what I want.' Her voice broke, and she was obviously close to tears. Behind her he heard the television grow suddenly loud, and she said sharply, away from the receiver, 'Go back in and shut the door.'

'Is it Daddy?' he heard Matthew's voice ask wistfully, and his heart lurched painfully. 'Can I talk to him?'

'Go back in, Matthew, I want to be private. Go on! It isn't Daddy, it's — a friend.'

There was a pause, during which he could imagine Matthew accepting what he knew was a lie, and turning away, obedient but hurt. Then the sitting room door shut again.

Irene said, 'I must go. I can't talk about this now.'

'We must talk about it some time,' Slider said.

'Oh, that's big, coming from you, isn't it?' she said resentfully.

'Please, Irene, don't let's quarrel.'

'I can't talk now,' she said again. He could tell she was trying not to cry. 'Don't call me — not here. I don't want the children upset. I'll call you.' And she snapped the phone down.

Slider put his end down too, and stared at it unhappily for a moment, reflecting that it did things to a man to know that whenever he spoke to a woman he was going to leave her in tears. He went off in search of his whisky. What a time for Joanna not to be here! He needed more comfort than alcohol, even a glass of the good stuff, could give him.

Chapter Six

Up To A Point

Nobody loves an estate agent, but David Meacher was a handsome, well-groomed man in his late forties. His suit was beautiful, his shirt and shoes exquisite, his silk tie daring without being vulgar, his hair thick and glossy, his face firm and alert and lightly tanned. He was on his way out of the Chiswick office door and held a poser-phone in one well-manicured hand, and in the other a car key whose leather fob bore the Aston Martin badge. Slider hated him instantly and effortlessly.

'Hello,' Meacher said, in a cultured, well-modulated voice, and smiled a professional smile. 'Do come in.' He stepped back into the shop again and held the door open for Slider, but with the poised look of a bird about to take to the air. 'Can I leave you in Caroline's capable hands?' he asked rhetorically, gesturing towards the very young, very fair, very nervous-looking girl behind one of the desks.

'I don't think so,' Slider said. 'Are you David Meacher? I'm Detective Inspector Slider of Shepherd's Bush CID. I'd like a word with you, if I may.'

Meacher's expression became grave and helpful, the look of a serious, responsible and well-intentioned citizen. 'Oh! Of course. About Jennifer Andrews, I suppose? I read the paragraph in the paper this morning. It's a terrible business. Well, do come in and sit down.' He retreated to the largest and handsomest of the desks and waved Slider to a deep-buttoned leather swivel chair on the supplicant side of it. 'Er — Caroline? Could you go and put the kettle on, there's a good girl.'

The fair girl departed through to the back of the shop, and Meacher took his place at the desk and rested his hands on it, leaning forward just a little, like the headmaster of a fee-paying school interviewing applicants. 'I suppose,' he enquired delicately, 'that it was murder?'

'Why should you suppose that?' Slider delicated back.

Meacher withdrew a fraction. 'It said very little in the paper, but when a body is found in those circumstances . . . You're not saying it was an accident?'

'My mind is completely open at the moment,' Slider said blandly. 'I'm still trying to establish exactly what happened.'

'Of course,' Meacher said, with just a touch of impatience. 'I supposed that was why you were here.'

'You were one of the last people to see her,' Slider suggested casually.

'I doubt that,' he jumped in sharply. 'She finished work here at one o'clock on Tuesday. There must have been lots of other people who saw her after me, in the afternoon and evening.'

Slider looked mildly puzzled. 'Why do you think she was still alive in the afternoon and evening? I didn't say what the time of death was.'

'Oh, but —' He frowned. 'I'm sure it was in the paper.'

'It wasn't.'

Meacher's frown cleared. 'Well, murders usually take place during the night, don't they? I just assumed. Are you telling me she was killed just after she left here, then?'

'No, I'm not telling you that,' Slider said. Unfortunately, there was truth in what Meacher said: it was natural to assume that murder took place at night. He had to give him that one. 'Would you tell me, please, about her last morning here?'

Meacher gave a faint shrug of his elegantly clad shoulders. 'There's nothing to tell. It was a normal day. She arrived at the usual time — nine o'clock — did the usual things, and left at one.'

'She was in this office the whole time?' He assented. 'And were there any unusual incidents? Did anyone come in to see her? Did she take any personal telephone calls?'

'Absolutely nothing happened that I know about, except what you'd expect from a normal working day.'

'And when she left, did she say where she was going?'

'I assume she was going home. I don't know whether she actually said she was.'

Slider was silent a moment. He felt there was something here, something to be found out. But this was a very cautious witness: unless he could ask the right question he wasn't going to get at it. You didn't get to be a wealthy estate agent by giving things away. 'What was she wearing?' he asked abruptly.

'What?' It took Meacher by surprise.

'What was Mrs Andrews wearing at work on Tuesday? What clothes was she wearing?'

Meacher hesitated, his eyes watchful. 'I

don't think I remember.'

'Try.'

'She was always smart. I really don't remember in detail.'

'Perhaps your assistant would remember.'

'Caroline wasn't here. She and Jennifer do different days.' Slider raised an eyebrow, and he said impatiently, 'That's the point of it. She and Jennifer and Liz, my other assistant, each do part time, covering the week between them. They're never on together.'

Slider nodded. Because of the employment laws, three part-timers cost less than one full-timer. All females, Slider noted. It was funny how ripely handsome businessmen like Meacher always had to assemble a harem about them. He continued to regard Meacher in silence, and finally the estate agent felt obliged to break it, and said, 'I think it was a navy dress. Yes, with a red belt. I remember now.'

Why had he pretended not to know? What was he afraid of? 'How well did you know Mrs Andrews?' Slider asked.

'She's worked for me for a couple of years. I wouldn't say I know her well,' he said indifferently.

At random Slider said, 'What sort of car

do you drive, sir? An Aston Martin, is it?'

Meacher paused a fraction before answering. 'No, I sold the Aston last year. It cost too much to run. I have a black BMW now.'

'Registration number?'

'The same as my Aston — DM 1. I transfer it from car to car. Why do you ask?'

'Just routine,' Slider said. He was poking sticks down holes, that was all; but lo, he'd unearthed another saddo with a personalised number-plate. Any connection? 'What did you do on Tuesday afternoon? Were you here in the office?'

Another faint pause. 'No, I went over to my other office, in Denham. I wasn't there all the time either, though. I was out looking at properties some of the time — empty properties.'

'And in the evening?'

'I had a meal with a friend and went home. Why? What have my movements to do with anything?'

'As I said, sir, it's just routine. We like to know where everyone was who was connected with the subject.' He was framing another question when Meacher changed the subject abruptly.

'It's poor Frances I feel most sorry for. It

must have been a terribly upsetting thing for her, finding the body like that. I'm an old friend of the family, you know.'

'No, I didn't know that.'

'Oh, yes. I've known her for a very long time. I was a friend of Gerald's — her husband. He and I were at school together. Between you and me, he treated her rather badly over the divorce. She ended up without a roof over her head and the two boys to look after, while Gerry took off to South Africa with the girl and the loot.' He gave a half-roguish, half-apologetic smile. 'I have no brief for him. He behaved like a complete swine. Frances would have been out on the street if her father hadn't invited them to go and live with him. Not that that's been a bed of roses. I have the greatest admiration for Cyril, but he can't have been an easy man to live with. Though, of course, Frances's mother was still alive then, which helped.'

Slider listened with interest to this considerable slice of volunteering from what should have been a donation-free zone. It was a smokescreen, he thought, but meant to distract him from what? It offered, however, a fertile new field for consideration.

'You'll have telephoned Mrs Hammond, then, when you heard about it?' Slider suggested. 'Perhaps that's where you got the idea that it happened in the night.'

It was extraordinary to watch the thoughts flitting across Meacher's face as he wondered what to lay claim to, and what traps were being set for him. There's such a thing, Slider thought, as being too clever.

'No,' Meacher said at last, 'no, I haven't phoned her yet. Well, I only heard about it this morning — read it in the paper — haven't really had time. I didn't want to intrude. People don't want endless enquiries after their well-being at a time like that, do they?'

Slider stood up to go. 'Well, thank you for your time, Mr Meacher. Oh, by the way, could you let me know where you went after you left here on Tuesday?'

He looked uncomfortable. 'I told you, I went to the Denham office, and then to look at some properties.'

'Yes, sir, but I need some addresses. Perhaps you'd be so kind as to make me out a list of the places you went, and the approximate times?'

Meacher reddened. 'I say, what is all this? Are you trying to accuse me of something? Why should I have to tell you where I was every minute?'

'No-one's accusing you of anything, sir,' Slider said soothingly. 'It's a matter of eliminating people from the picture. We get hundreds of reports in from witnesses, and it's just as important to eliminate the people we don't suspect, so that we can be left with the ones we do.'

Meacher seemed to accept this explanation without probing its structure, promised but without grace to see what he could do, and saw Slider off the premises with an air of wanting to be sure he'd really gone. Slider went back to his car with his mind whirring like a sewing-machine. Something was going on, but *what? Had* he telephoned Frances Hammond and got details of the finding of the body from her? If so, why had he denied it? Why had he mentioned her at all? And why the hesitation over what Jennifer Andrews had been wearing? And what *had* he been up to on Tuesday afternoon?

He telephoned the station and Mackay answered. 'Oh, guv, we got the word from Jennifer Andrews' doctor. She wasn't on sleepers or tranks or anything. And no heart disease. He says she was perfectly healthy as far as he knew. He hadn't seen her for eighteen months, and then it was only a holiday jab.'

'All right,' Slider said. 'Nothing from Forensic?'

'Not yet. But the Potters described what she was wearing, and it was the same at lunchtime and in the evening as what we found her in. So it looks as though she might not have gone home at all.'

Except that her car was there, Slider thought. Did she just leave it there without going into the house? It seemed unlikely she would have gone in and left no mark — no cup or glass used, no cushion dented, no towel crumpled. Unless, inexplicably, Andrews tidied up afterwards. Or perhaps her car was with her elsewhere when she was killed, and the murderer drove it back.

'Okay. Get on to this, will you? David Meacher, her employer, has a mobile phone — get a list of all the calls he made from it on Tuesday.'

'Okay,' McLaren said. 'But what's up, guv? What's he suspected of?'

'I don't know. All I know is he's keeping some little secrets from me, and I want to know what they are.'

The Crown and Sceptre was a Fuller's pub, so it was worth the extra distance from the station. Atherton came in singing a cheery little policeman's ditty. 'If I had to do it all over again, I'd do it all over you . . .'

Slider, waiting in their favoured corner, looked up. 'What are you so cheerful about?'

'Why not? I've been on a pub crawl,' Atherton reminded him. 'Is that for me?'

'Do I usually buy my pints in pairs?'

'I'll take that as a yes.' He sat down and took the top off the pint. 'Ah, that's better. First today.'

'I thought you'd been on a pub crawl.'

'I can't drink at a pub with no ambulance.'

'Did you say ambience or ambulance?'

'Yes. And I'm here to tell you that the First And Last is about as like unto a coaching inn as my dimpled arse is like a Moor Park apricot.'

'Who said it was a coaching inn?'

'Jack Potter of the Goat In Boots, that's who. The F and L, however, is a brewery's delight. The lounge is all plastic rusticity and elastic Muzak —'

'That's easy for you to say!'

'— and the public is stuffed with every electronic money-snatching device from bar pool to a Trivial Pursuit machine.'

'I gather you didn't like it.'

'The Mimpriss at least was ghastly in an honest, unenterprising way. A bit like the Dog and Scrotum — oversized and under-privileged. How was your estate agent?'

'Smooth, plausible and shifty.'

'So what's new?'

'He sold his Aston Martin and bought a BMW.'

'The man has no taste. No wonder you didn't like him.'

'Who says I didn't like him?'

'Shifty is generally deemed to be a pejorative term.'

'He had a personalized number-plate, too — DM 1.'

Atherton raised his brows. 'Now there's a coincidence. Is bad taste catching, I wonder?'

'I don't know, but there was something about him that didn't ring true. I don't know what, but I wonder whether he didn't know more about Jennifer Andrews than he was admitting to.'

'Ah, well, it wouldn't surprise me, after what I've heard this morning,' Atherton said, putting his hands on the table in preparation for a speech.

But Slider wasn't listening. He had seen a shadow outside the window, and now the door opened and Joanna appeared, brown, bare-shouldered, ruffle-haired, with her fiddle case in her hand and her sunglasses pushed up on the top of her head. His heart sat up and begged. 'Here she is,' he said.

Atherton looked, and then glanced sideways at his boss. 'I knew I didn't have your full attention.'

Joanna came over to them, wreathed in smiles. 'Ah, my two favourite policemen!'

Atherton made a wrong-answer buzz. 'That should have been "My favourite policeman and my second favourite policeman." Thank you for playing.'

Slider stood up and kissed her across the table. 'Pint?'

'You know the way to a girl's heart. God, the motorway was awful this morning! The queue for the Heathrow spur was backed up ten miles down the M4.' She chatted, as newly arrived drivers do, about the journey. Atherton listened, while Slider fetched her drink.

Putting the glass on the table in front of her, Slider said, 'Who's Ted Bundy?'

She looked up. 'How do you know Ted Bundy?'

'Why do you always answer a question with a question?' Atherton said to her.

'Why do you?' she countered.

Slider sat down. 'There was a message on the machine last night for "Jojo" to call Ted Bundy. He seemed to think you knew his number well enough for him not to have to leave it.'

'What it is to have a detective in the family,' Joanna said, licking the foam off her top lip in an unstudiedly sensuous way that made Slider's trousers quicken. 'He's a trumpet player.'

'Ha! I knew it! And why does he call you Jojo?'

'Because he's a nerk,' she said. 'Ted's all right, but you wouldn't want to get cornered by him at a party. And everyone knows his number, dear heart,' she assured her fidgety mate. 'He's a part-time fixer — organises small ensembles for private parties and catering gigs and the like. All right if you haven't got any other work: not much money, but usually plenty to drink. I once subbed in on a gig he fixed for a wedding reception at the Heathrow Hilton. I still can't remember much about it, but the bride flew off on the honeymoon alone while the groom was having his stomach pumped at Hillingdon Hospital.'

'Innocence itself. I hope you feel suitably chastened,' Atherton said to Slider.

'Oh, shut up,' Slider scowled, and to

Joanna, 'I missed you.'

'I missed you too,' she said.

'Well, that's all right, then.'

'What have you been up to while I was away?' Joanna asked generally.

'A murder on the Mimpriss Estate,' Slider answered.

'Sounds like that Agatha Christie novel where everybody dunnit,' Joanna said. 'Anyway, you can't have a murder on the Mimpriss Estate. It's far too posh.'

'Well, up to a point, Lord Copper,' Atherton said, amused.

'To be fair,' said Slider, 'we can't be absolutely sure it was murder.' He outlined the case so far for her.

'If Freddie Cameron says it's murder, don't you have to take his word? He's never wrong, is he?'

'Hardly ever.'

'You've got the old man saying the victim was a bossy cow, the cleaner saying she was a multiple adulteress, and the friend saying she was an angel and the husband a jealous monster,' Joanna summarised. 'But whether she did rude things, or the husband only thought she did, it comes out the same, doesn't it? Obviously he's the best candidate.'

'Especially when I tell you my latest

news,' Atherton said. 'Andrews was in and out of various local pubs all Tuesday evening, in his work clothes, drinking steadily, and at intervals telling anyone who would listen that he was looking for his wife, and when he found her he was going to kill her. And at ten forty-five or thereabouts he got chucked out of the Mimpriss for trying to get into a fight with the landlord. Don't you want to know what about?'

'Do tell,' Joanna invited daintily.

He told. Brian Folger, the landlord of the Mimpriss, was one of those leering, slippery customers whose every word and gesture is loaded with sexual innuendo. 'The way he thrust a cloth-shrouded hand inside a glass to dry it was positively gynaecological,' said Atherton. Folger was a thin, bald man with little, suggestive eyes, and a wet, carnivorous mouth like one of those meat-eating plants. All the time he spoke his fingers were straying as if of their own accord into various cavities, slipping into his mouth and up his nose and into his ears like an involuntary overspill of lubricity. Atherton had caught himself thinking that Folger's nose even looked like a penis — long, fleshy and flexible with a bulbous end. It gave a whole new significance to sneezing.

Folger made no bones about the quarrel with Eddie Andrews. 'Oh, he comes in here a lot. On his way home from work usually. Well, some pubs don't allow working clothes. I say the money's the same, and a working man's got a right to his pleasure, hasn't he? We've got nothing in here to get dirty. I don't mind what stains a man's got on his trousers, as long as he gets the right thing out of 'em. His money, I mean! Ha ha!' All his conversation was like that.

'I bet his customers love him,' Joanna remarked.

On the evening in question, Andrews had come in at about half past six and had a couple of pints, making them last an hour. 'He said there was nothing to go home for, because his wife was out working that evening,' Folger had said. 'I made a little joke about his wife being a working girl, see, but he never picked up on it. Anyway, he went about half past seven. Then he comes back middle of the evening.'

'What time?' Atherton had asked.

'It must have been about an hour later. Half eight, say. He has a pint. He's looking depressed, like, so I ask him, how's the lovely wife, still showing off her assets

164

down the Goat? He says no, she's not there. He thought she was, but he's gone over there and just seen her drive off somewhere. He's driven past his house, but her car's not there either. So I say something about what she's up to, and he gets a bit shirty. I say, you want to learn to take a joke, mate, and he says how would I like it if everyone was after my wife. I says, my wife? I'd sell bloody tickets, I says, only who'd buy one? So he says if he knew where she'd gone he go after her and wring her neck. And he drinks up and he's off again. About ten to nine, by then.'

'Did he say where he was going?'

'Nah, he just storms out in a temper. Anyway, he's back again about ah pass ten. Getting to be a right little bar-fly, I says to him. He has a couple o' shorts in quick order, and I ask him if he's found his wife yet. He says no and mutters something about he's not gonna let her work at the Goat any more, so I says, little joke, like, if Jack Potter's finished with her, I wouldn't mind having her behind my counter. He says he doesn't want her to be a barmaid, I says, who said anything about being a barmaid?' Folger winked horribly. 'Then he starts getting nasty. I'm not having that. I tell him to get off his high horse, everybody knows why Jack Potter give her a job. If that's all he's giving her — because between you and I and the bedpost, Jack Potter never says no to it if it's free, and all the nice girls love a sailor, know what I mean? Anyway, I says to Eddie, when she gets sick of the notes at the Goat, she can come over here and give me a turn — and I'll even pretend she's the barmaid if it makes everybody happy. So then he tries to start a fight with me, and I chuck him out. Must a' been about quart' to eleven then.'

At this point in the narrative, Joanna said, 'What a sweetheart. Do you think there's any truth in any of it?'

'Maybe,' Atherton said thoughtfully. 'Jack Potter was very nervous and very evasive when I spoke to him, and his story sounded like a load of Tottenham. He said Jennifer went off somewhere, which fits what Folger says Andrews told him, but he didn't seem to have a convincing reason for covering for her.'

'That'd stand a follow-up,' Slider said.

Atherton nodded, and went on, 'Andrews was also in the First And Last during the evening — after his first visit to the Goat, to go by the timings — and he was there again at around eleven, trying to get a drink, being refused, and telling the barman his wife was cheating on him and if he found her he'd kill her.'

'People say that sort of thing all the time,' Joanna said. 'Doesn't mean they'd really do it.'

'But in this case,' Slider said, 'the person he said it about is dead. I'm sorry, because I didn't want to think Andrews was guilty of murder — and such a cowardly murder, if Freddie's right — but it's certainly looking bad for him.'

Atherton lowered his pint to half mast with some satisfaction. 'I think I'd better have another little *parlare* with the guv'nor of the Goat, see if I can't make him come clean about the real nature of his relationship with Jennifer A.'

'All right, and when you've done that, I'll interview Andrews again. Now we can table his movements up till eleven o'clock, it may be enough to make him tell us the rest.'

'Especially when you apply the delicate sympathy over how badly you think he was provoked,' Atherton said.

'That's not cricket,' Joanna said sternly.

'I wonder where she did go, though,' Slider mused. 'And was it innocent or guilty?'

'If she was guilty with Jack, she was probably guilty elsewhere,' Atherton said. 'One thing, though — we now know she drove away from the Goat, so that means either she or the murderer brought the car back later in the evening or night. If anyone saw it arrive back, we might have something.'

'Talking of having something, are we going to nosh?' Joanna said. 'I'm starving.'

'I'll go,' Atherton said. 'What does anybody want?'

While he was up at the counter ordering their food, Joanna asked Slider, 'Were there any other messages for me?'

'A couple about work. I haven't cleared them off the tape.' He hesitated. 'I've had some news, though.'

'Oh?'

'Irene's moved back into the house.'

She stared, reading his face. 'With the children? Has she split with what's-his-name, then?'

'It's hard to tell. She was very evasive about it — all she'd say was that they've decided not to live together for the time being.'

'Oh, Bill, what now? It's not going to be more trouble for us, is it?'

'It needn't be for you.'

'If it is for you, then it is for me. What's going on? Is she trying to get you to go back to her?'

'I don't think so. It sounds,' he said slowly, 'as if her friend Marilyn has told her that if she moves back into the marital home she'll get a better settlement in the divorce.'

Joanna thought about that for a moment, sipping her pint. Slider watched her, knowing that she was choosing her words — perhaps her thoughts, too — carefully. She didn't want to say unkind or disparaging things about Irene, to seem petty, spiteful, grasping or demanding, to belittle anyone's pain or inflate her own. She wanted to come out of it all with her character intact — not to make herself look good, he knew, but because her own self-esteem rested on it. 'And will she?' was what she eventually said.

'Yes and no.'

She grinned at him. 'I used to be indecisive, but now I'm not so sure.'

'What I mean is that the courts decide these things on relative need. They don't take fault into account any more, which is what I can't get her to understand. Okay, while she was living with Ernie, her needs would have been assumed to be taken care of, though not the children's.'

'You mean you wouldn't have had to pay maintenance for her, only for them?'

'Right. But even without Ernie, the courts will expect her to get herself a job. They won't expect me to keep her for ever.'

She raised her eyebrows. 'I didn't know that.'

'Nor does she. The good old days of skinning the erring husband down to his socks are over — though it's all going to change again, apparently, when the new legislation goes through in 1999.'

'And what about the house?'

Atherton came back. 'Grub's on its way. What house?'

'Mine,' Slider said.

'Oh, sorry, private conversation?'

'I don't know what there is about my life that you don't already know.' Slider shrugged.

'Oddly enough, neither do I,' Atherton said. 'Shall I go away again, or hum loudly?'

'Don't be silly.' He turned to Joanna again. 'The house is pretty academic, really. It's not in negative equity, thank God, but what's left after the mortgage won't be enough to buy a greenhouse. But if she goes to court they could order it sold so that the proceeds can be split. And then where would she be?'

Joanna looked grave. 'Homeless?'

Slider rubbed his hair up the wrong way in anxiety. 'I can't let that happen.'

'Wouldn't she go back to Ernie?'

'But if she didn't? Or couldn't? I've told her if we agree to a settlement between us, the courts will uphold it. But with Marilyn needling her, she doesn't trust me.'

Joanna laid a hand briefly on his. 'She must be mad.' Atherton looked at her and away again. He didn't think she'd grasped the implications yet. Then she asked, 'What sort of settlement?'

'I couldn't let them be homeless,' Slider said again.

Now she saw. She removed her hand and put it back round her pint. 'You'd go on paying the mortgage.'

'Until the children leave school,' he said.

'Or university, or home, whichever is the latest,' she qualified. Her voice was as neutral as Bird's Instant Custard. 'You'd go on paying the mortgage, and the house insurance.'

He nodded minimally. 'And the bills — gas and electricity and so on.'

'Yes.'

'And maintenance for the children, of course. And for Irene?'

He looked at her helplessly. 'She's never been out to work since we were married. She couldn't get a job now. What could she do?'

'Bill, that's your whole income accounted for. What are you supposed to live on? Something has to give.' She knew what. Living with her he didn't have rent to pay, but he had been contributing to household expenses. That's where the only slack was. Joanna would have to keep him, effectively, so that he could keep his family. She tried not to let her mouth harden, but she could never hide from him. 'Let her go to court,' she said at last.

'They're my responsibility,' he said.

She looked at him with enormous sadness. 'And I'm not.' It wasn't a question. They were back to where they had begun: Irene and the children were real life to him, and she was fun and magic and fantasy, but essentially separate, independent, outside him, the thing that, however little he would ever want to, he could jettison, because she could manage without him. He could put down his pleasures, but not his burdens.

Atherton felt the pain of both of them

acutely, and wished to be anywhere but here. Any moment now she would nobly offer to leave him, and Bill would accept sadly and go back to prison with Irene because it made financial sense. Atherton didn't want to be here to witness it. He had been against Joanna and Bill getting together in the beginning, but he knew now it was the best thing for Bill, and it was too late by an extremely long chalk for him to go back. Atherton didn't want to see the two people he was fondest of in the world commit suicide.

Fortunately, at that poised moment, a figure loomed up to the table and said, 'One sausage, egg and chips and one chilliburger and chips, was it?' They all looked up, and after a blank instant Joanna said, 'That's right.'

The woman smiled and set the plates down. 'And there's a lasagne to come, and I'll bring your knives and forks. Any sauces, atawl? Salt and pepper? Vinegar for your chips?'

When the interruptions were over and they were alone again with their food, Joanna said, 'Isn't it strange how of all the spices in the world, the only one that's routinely offered is pepper? A weird sort of hangover from the Middle Ages.'

'There's spices in my chilli,' Slider said, with an effort.

'In it, not offered separately. Imagine her asking, "Salt and cinnamon?" or "Mace and nutmeg?"'

'But they're sweet spices.'

'All spices are sweet. Pepper's sweet.'

Atherton joined in helpfully, 'Have you tried black pepper on strawberries?'

They talked about anything but the cloud that hung over them. Atherton could see how a man more stupid, more selfish, more violent in his passions than Bill — like Eddie Andrews, perhaps — might end up murdering the cloud because he could neither face up to it nor see any way out from under it. But facing up to things was Bill's forte, poor devil, and Joanna was not enough of a selfish bitch to force the issue. Too good for her own good, really.

Chapter Seven

Publican's Tail

Slider got back to the factory with a headache. He tried to sneak it up to his room to seduce it with aspirin, but as he tiptoed past the door to the shop, Paxman, who was duty sergeant, spotted him and called after him. 'Sir! Bill!'

Slider turned back resignedly. 'Thanks for the knighthood.'

'Eh?' Paxman's stationary eyes were troubled. He was a big man, solid as a bull, and he had never quite got to grips with Slider's humour.

Slider waived the flags. 'Did you want something?'

'There's someone waiting to see you.'

'I was born with someone waiting to see me,' Slider said sadly.

'Name of Potter. Mean anything? Looks like a cat on hot bricks. I put him in interview room two, but I can get rid of him for you if he's trouble.'

175

'No, I'll see him. Thanks.' Atherton had just gone off to the Goat to re-interview him. Slider rubbed his forehead. 'You haven't got any aspirin, have you, Ted?' he asked. Paxman had. Slider washed them down with a gulp from the water-cooler in the charge room. They lay sulkily on top of his chilliburger and chips, with which they were obviously not going to play nicely.

Jack Potter was pacing about the interview room, looking worse than Slider felt. He turned eagerly as Slider came in. 'I was just thinking of leaving,' he said.

'I'm sorry, I've only just got in,' Slider said. 'Have you been waiting long?'

He gave a short laugh. 'Cold feet,' he said. 'I don't want to say what I've come to say, but it's on my conscience. And if I don't and you find out anyway, it'll look worse than it is. Besides, I don't want anyone coming round the Goat asking questions in front of the wife.' There was a question mark at the end of the last sentence, and a fawn in the eyes.

'If it's about you and Jennifer Andrews —' Slider began.

Potter's scalp shifted visibly backwards as his eyes widened. 'How the hell did you know?'

'Detective Sergeant Atherton's on his

way round to interview you at this very minute,' Slider said.

'Oh, blimey! He won't go and — ? I mean, Linda's there, my wife, that's why I came here. If Lin finds out she'll skin me alive. Your bloke won't blurt it out?'

'I'm sure he'll be discreet,' Slider said. 'He's a man of the world. Why don't you sit down and tell me about it?'

Potter sat automatically, his eyes flat with apprehension. 'I wanted to tell you when you came round that first time, but with Lin in the house — suppose she'd walked in and heard? You do see? I did feel bad, with Jen — with Jen —' His eyes filled abruptly with tears. 'I can't believe she's — you know. Did he do it? Did he kill her? Eddie?'

Slider avoided the question. 'Tell me about you and her,' he said, sitting down opposite him.

Potter took out a handkerchief and blew his nose. 'I never meant it to happen. I mean, with Jen being Linda's friend, it was a bit too close to home. You don't shit on your own doorstep, know what I mean? But she was always around, Jen was — *you* know,' he went on pleadingly. Nothing propinks like propinquity, Slider thought. 'I mean, she was a bit of all right. You never met her, but she was a real smasher. And when she started coming on to me — well —'

'What man could resist?' Slider said.

Potter looked relieved at his understanding. 'It's not that I was looking for it. I'm not the running-around sort. Oh, I've had my moments,' he added modestly. 'I mean, before I married Lin I was in the merchant. Well, it goes with the job, know what I mean? I've had women all over the world. Some of them eastern tarts, you wouldn't believe the things they can do! Oh, don't get me wrong, I love my wife. All right, since I been married there's been one or two occasions, but all very discreet. But, well, when it comes down to it, a man's a man, if you get my drift, and when it's offered him on a plate —'

'Jennifer Andrews offered herself on a plate?'

He shrugged. 'Let's face it, Jen was a sparky girl. I wasn't the first and I won't be the last.' He didn't seem to see the incongruity of those words. 'But Linda thought Jen was a snow-white lamb and Eddie was the coal-black villain, and no shades in between, get me? Though if you ask me that man had the patience of a Jonah, with what she put him through.'

'He knew about her — infidelities?'

'Yes and no.' Potter frowned a little. 'Funny thing, that. I mean he was jealous, and I don't say he didn't have cause, but I don't think he knew anything definitely. That was the ironic bit, really,' he said, with a mirthless laugh. 'I don't think he believed half of what he said he thought she'd got up to. I reckon he probably thought a lot of the time that he was probably being jealous about nothing, when all the time he was probably right.'

Slider felt disinclined to untangle that sentence. He got the general idea. 'So let's get this straight, you and Jennifer Andrews were having an affair? How long had it been going on?'

'Oh, best part of a year, but it was only occasional. I mean, it was tricky for both of us, both being married. We done it once or twice upstairs at the Goat, when Lin was out, but I didn't like leaving Karen on her own down the bar, and you never knew if she might come up for some reason. And it's always hard for the likes of me to get time off. You wouldn't believe the hours involved in running a pub! But, well, Linda likes to have a day's shopping up west every now and then, and I cover for her, so in return she sometimes tells me to have a day off. I'm a bit of a motor-racing fan, I like going down Silverstone or Brands Hatch once in a while. At least,' he dropped a ghostly wink, 'that's what I tell the wife.'

'But instead you met Mrs Andrews — where?'

He grinned. 'Well, that was the beauty of it, Jen being in the estate-agent business: she'd always have keys to houses they were selling, and we'd use one of them. It was a bit exciting sometimes, wondering if the owners were going to come back early and catch us.' He caught himself up abruptly, and appealed to Slider, 'It was just a bit of fun, and no-one ever knew about it, so where was the harm?'

Slider refused the wig and gown. 'So has this got something to do with Tuesday evening?' he asked.

'Well, yes, it has. You see, lately she hasn't been much interested — Jen. Got other fish to fry. She used to hint stuff, to get me going. She wasn't a nice person, you know. She was a bit of a prick-teaser, if you want the truth. She liked to brush past me when Lin was in the room, and say things that meant one thing to me and something else to Linda. For a couple of weeks she'd been winding me up, and then when I tried to do something about it, pushing me away and saying she had someone else and she didn't need me. Only when I got mad at her she'd threaten to tell Lin.'

'But two could play at that game, surely?'

He looked uncomfortable. 'Well, yes, and I said that to her, but she always said I'd never do it, because if I split on her to Eddie, he'd come straight round to me and then Linda would find out, and that would hurt me worse than it hurt her — Jen — because when it came down to it she didn't care if Eddie did find out, but I did care about Lin. Well, I love my wife, you see.' He slithered his eyes sidelong. 'And in any case, the pub's in her name. I couldn't get a licence 'cause of a little bit of trouble I had a long time ago. So everything belongs to Lin, officially. If she chucked me out, I'd get nothing. Jennifer knew that, of course. So she used to say to me, "You just be a good boy and do what I say and don't get any funny ideas. Because I shall be gone soon anyway," she said.'

'Gone? Where?'

'She never said. I s'pose she was just hinting she'd take off one day. She was always saying she was bored with Eddie. I mean, he's a nice enough bloke, but he's dull, and she's a bit of a bright spark, know what I mean? I never thought she'd stop with him for ever. Ambitious girl, was Jen.'

'So that's why you agreed to cover for her on Tuesday night?' Slider asked. 'She blackmailed you into it?'

'Well, yes, I suppose you could say that. And of course, once I'd covered for her, I couldn't let Lin find out. That's why I couldn't say anything when you came round the pub. But you won't let on, will you? I mean, I didn't do anything wrong, just told a little porkie or two, and what man doesn't do that to the misses?'

'Do you know where Jennifer went?'

Potter's look was eager now, willing to help. 'No, I don't, and that's straight up. She just said she had to see someone. Well, naturally I thought it was another man. She was — excited, see? All worked up and — sort of electric, like it was a bit dangerous. She liked a bit of danger, did our Jen. That's why she liked using clients' houses — give her a charge to think someone might walk in. I said to her, You'll go too far one day, I said. I s'pose,' he added dully, 'that's what happened in the end.'

'So she left at about seven thirty, and you've nothing more you can tell me?'

'That's right. Old Eddie only just missed her. When he came in the first time and I went to chuck him out, he said he'd just seen Jen drive away and he wanted to know where she was going. I said she'd gone home with a headache, and he said I was lying, because she'd gone in the other direction, so I said in that case I didn't know where she was because she'd told me she was going home. Well, I *didn't* know where she'd gone, did I? I s'pose he realised I was telling the truth — anyway he seemed to believe me and away he went. But the second time he come in he was pretty drunk, and he said, I know you know where she's gone, he said, and if you don't tell me I'll smash your face in. I said to him if there was any smashing of faces in, it'd be me that done it to him, and I told him to go home and sober up, because I didn't know where Jen was and that was all about it. Well, after a bit I managed to get rid of him, and that was that.'

'You don't think he knew about you and Jennifer?'

'No,' Potter said, with clear certainty. 'He'd have said if he did.' Interesting, Slider thought: evidently Eddie hadn't believed the guv'nor of the Mimpriss. It just went to prove that jealousy is all in the mind. 'No,' Jack said, 'he just thought I knew who she was with and wouldn't tell him, but I think he believed me in the end that I *didn't* know. Because I didn't, did I?' This accidental cleaving unto veracity seemed to give him some perilous comfort.

'Do you know who else Jennifer Andrews was — seeing?'

Potter shook his head. 'Well, no. I don't know for certain that she *was* seeing anyone else. I just wouldn't be surprised if she was. I mean, no-one found out about her and me, did they?'

It was possible, of course, that the landlord of the Mimpriss was merely making mischief and guessing right by accident; but the picture Slider was forming of Jennifer Andrews suggested that she liked to wield her power over people and enjoy the credit for her bad behaviour. If he read her right there would be at least one other person who knew about Jack Potter, but it would be someone who couldn't make use of the information, as Potter couldn't about the last mystery appointment.

He no longer wondered that someone had wanted to murder her. He only wondered there had not been a queue; he'd have taken a low number himself. But it was still obvious who was clutching ticket number one. It was time, Slider thought, to have another chat with Eddie. He must remember, if sympathy for this long-suffering man threatened to overcome him, that if Freddie Cameron were right, it had not been a murder of impulse, of the man driven to a hasty lashing out he instantly regretted. If she had been smothered while comatose, then a degree of premeditation had been present. He must have waited for her to fall asleep: plenty of time for temper to cool and better instincts to take over.

When he returned to his room, he found Hollis looking for him. Hollis, a scrawny man with failing hair, bulbous pale green eyes and a truly terrible moustache, was also cursed with a Mancunian accent and a sort of strangulated counter-tenor voice. He covered his aspects by cultivating an air of gentle self-mockery, as though he were weird by choice. 'Sitrep, guv,' he said, as Slider came along the corridor.

'You what?' Slider said absently.

'We've got the list of calls for the Andrews house from BT,' Hollis explained. 'None at all made on the Tuesday.'

'None?'

'Not a tinkle. So either they weren't fond of talking —'

'Or they weren't home,' Slider concluded. 'Well, it all helps.'

'We've got the list from Meacher's mobile, and we're putting names to numbers now. Andrews didn't have a mobile, but Mrs A. had a car phone, and we're waiting for that list. Oh, and Norma says the Andrews' finances check out. He had a loan to finance building the house, but the repayments have been met all right, and there's money coming in as well as going out.'

'Okay. Anything come yet from Forensic?'

'Not yet.'

'Oh, well, I don't suppose it'll be much help when it does. That's the trouble with domestics.'

'Send you clean round the bend,' Hollis agreed solemnly.

'I'm going to have another chat with our prime suspect,' Slider decided. 'You'd better come with me.'

Nicholls was custody sergeant, a lean, handsome Scot from the far north-west, with blue eyes and a voice like silk emulsion. 'Come to get a confession?' he asked, walking Slider and Hollis along to Andrews' cell.

'It'd be nice to get him to talk at all. Mostly he just stares at the wall. Interviews with him are as exciting as a Thomas Hardy novel,' Slider sighed.

'Well, I hope you bring it home before I go on my holidays,' Nicholls said. 'It'd be like missing the last episode of *Murder One*.'

'That gives me two weeks, doesn't it? Where are you off to, by the way?'

'Norway.'

'I've never seen the point of Norway. It's just Scotland on steroids.'

'Och, Mary fancied it for the kids. They love canoeing.'

'A sort of fjord fiesta, then?'

Nicholls grinned. 'Lots of healthy outdoor activities to wear the wee anes out, so that we get quiet evenings alone for once.'

'For once? That's how you got six kids in the first place.'

'Oh, aye, I forgot.'

'You'd better not forget again,' Hollis warned. 'You can't afford any more on a sergeant's pay.'

'Nae worries, old chum. Don't you remember, I've had the Snip?'

'How could anyone forget?' Slider winced. Nicholls adored his wife, and had wanted to curb his rampant fertility without having Mary risk the Pill. Now with the enthusiasm of the convert — or, as Slider thought of it, of the tail-less fox — he was a crusader for the operation. Pale, doubled-up young constables hurrying out of the canteen were a sure sign that Nutty was in there on his break, campaigning.

'You should try it, Bill,' he said seriously. 'No more worries, no more condoms. It makes a vas deferens to your sex-life, I can tell you.'

'The condommed man ate a hearty breakfast,' Slider murmured, as they reached the cell door. Nicholls brought the key up to the lock. 'Can I have a look at him first?' Slider asked. He slid back the wicket and applied his eye to the spy-hole. Eddie Andrews gave the impression of having settled into his cell, as if he neither expected nor hoped to be released. He was sitting on the edge of the bunk with his hands clasped loosely between his knees, and didn't move or look up at the sounds at the door. Slider stepped back.

'Is he like that all the time?'

Nicholls had a look too, and nodded his handsome head. 'Just sits quiet like a good wee boy. No trouble at all.'

'Eating all right?'

'Eats and drinks, says thank you —'

'Thank you?'

'I told ye it was bad. He asks no questions. Doesn't want a solicitor. Doesn't want anyone told he's here.' He met Slider's eyes gravely. 'I don't like it, Bill. The quiet, obliging ones are often the ones you lose. It can mean they've made up their minds to go. We've got his belt and shoelaces, but they'll always find a way if they're determined.'

'You think he's one of those?'

Nicholls hesitated. 'I'm not just sure. It could be he did it and wants to be punished. Or it could be shock, and he's just not connecting up. But he's not in a normal state of mind, and that's a fact.'

'All right, Nutty, thanks for the tip. Can I have him out?'

Slider signed for Andrews and they took him along to the tape room. Andrews was docile, almost dreamy, as Slider went through the preliminary procedures. He needed shaking out of it.

'Now then, Eddie, you told us that on Tuesday night you had one drink in the Mimpriss and then went home, and stayed home all evening watching television. Is that right?' Andrews nodded. 'For the tape, please.'

189

'Yes,' Andrews said, in a lacklustre voice. 'We've been through all this. Why can't you leave me alone? I've got nothing to say.'

'What programmes did you watch on the television?'

'I've told you before. I don't remember'

'Just tell me one.' No answer. 'Did you watch the football?'

'Yes,' he said, after a hesitation.

'Who was playing?'

'I don't remember.'

Hollis intervened, in a voice of utter amazement, 'You don't remember the Man United-Aston Villa match? That wicked goal in extra time by Sheringham?' He mimed a header into the net.

'Oh — yes — I remember now,' Andrews said, blinking at him. 'That was it. The football.'

Hollis shook his head sadly. 'Man United didn't play that night. It was an international.'

'Come on, Eddie, don't waste my time!' Slider took the ball neatly on his toe. 'We know you weren't home watching television. You were out on a drunken pub crawl. You were in the Mimpriss three times. The guv'nor there's told us about the argument you had with him, over what your wife was up to.'

That got a reaction. His hands on the table tightened. 'My wife wasn't up to anything.'

'That's not what Mr Folger says,' Hollis said, with a knowing grin. 'He knew all about your wife and Jack Potter. Fruity stuff!'

'It's not true,' Andrews cried. 'Don't you talk like that about her! Brian Folger's a foul-mouthed liar!'

'And then later you were in the First And Last,' Slider picked up the pass, 'telling the barman there your wife was cheating on you —'

'She wasn't! It's not true.'

'— and that when you found her you'd wring her neck.'

'It's not true!'

Slider leaned forward a little. 'Eddie, you were there and you said those things. We know that. We've got witnesses to everything you did that evening, the pubs you went to and the times you were there and what you said. There's no point in going on lying when we've got witnesses. Why not give up and tell us the truth? You must have had reasons for what you did. I want to know what they are. I want to hear your side of the story.'

Andrews looked across the table at him, and the little spurt of energy that had been generated died away. He sighed. 'I've got nothing to say to you, except what I've already said.'

'You've got to tell me, Eddie,' Slider said gently but insistently. 'Because, you see, it's looking really bad for you. You left the First And Last at ten past eleven, vowing to murder your wife. And some time between then and one o'clock, she was murdered.' Andrews kept silent, looking down at his hands again.

'You said she didn't come home all night, but her car was there on the hard standing in the morning. How did it get there, if she didn't come home? Did you drive it back from the place where you murdered her?'

No answer.

'Her handbag with her car keys in it was found in your pickup. How did it get there if you didn't put it there?'

No answer.

'Eddie, we'll find out, just as we found out what you were doing the rest of the evening. We always find out. So why don't you tell me about it now, get it all out in the open? I promise you you'll feel better.' Andrews sighed. 'I want to hear your side,'

Slider urged. 'You must have been under terrible pressure, to do what you did, because I know you loved her. You were driven mad by her behaviour. I understand that. I know what she was like.'

Now he looked up. 'You don't!' he said, and his red-rimmed eyes blazed briefly. 'You don't know anything about her — none of you!'

'All right, you tell me, then,' Slider said, settling back as if the story was just beginning.

'It was all my fault!' Andrews cried. 'She didn't do anything. It was all down to me.'

'Yes,' Slider nodded encouragingly, while Hollis almost held his breath, trying to turn himself into paint on the wall. 'Go on.'

'I was jealous. But I had no right to think those things. I loved her, and I thought bad things about her, and now she's dead!'

'I'm so sorry, Eddie,' Slider said tenderly. 'Tell me all about it. After you left the First And Last. Where did you meet her?' Andrews stared, haggard, bristly, flame-eyed, goaded. 'Tell me what you did to her.'

'I didn't kill her!' he cried.

'All right, but tell me what you did. Where did you go after the First And Last?'

'I don't know. I don't remember. I just wandered about all night. Every time I went past the house her car wasn't there, and it made me mad wondering where she was. So I just wandered. I fell asleep for a bit, sitting in the van. And then in the morning I went to work, straight to Mrs Hammond's. I didn't go home because I didn't want to find out she'd been out all night. I thought she was with another man. But I had no right, you see! I thought bad things about her, and they weren't true! If I'd only trusted her! And now she's dead, and it's my fault, all my fault.' He put his head down into his hands again, and made moaning noises.

Slider felt Hollis looking at him, waiting for him to pull the rabbit out of the hat, perform the *coup de grâce* — or what Atherton called the lawnmower. Oh, the responsibility of greatness! 'Tell me, then, Eddie. Get it off your conscience. Tell me how you killed her.'

Outside the tape room, Hollis shoved his hands deep in his pockets, hunching his spindly-looking shoulders like a depressed heron, and said, 'Oh, bollocks. He was *that* close, guv.'

'Tell me,' Slider sighed.

Nicholls came back. 'Any joy?' He read their faces. 'You couldn't crack him, even after I gave you a full psychiatric profile?'

Slider smiled unwillingly. 'Come off it, Nutty. You haven't got the figure to play Cracker.'

'Robbie Coltrane hasn't got my voice,' Nicholls countered modestly.

'There is that,' Slider agreed.

'Is that right you're playing the female lead in Mr Wetherspoon's opera?' Hollis asked.

'Operetta,' Nicholls corrected. He had famously once sung the Queen of the Night aria from *Zauberflöte* in a police charity concert, but Commander Wetherspoon's next production was to scale lesser heights. '*HMS Pinafore*. I'm the captain's daughter.'

'Well, everyone likes Gilbert and Sullivan,' Hollis said reasonably.

'That's his reasoning,' Nicholls said neutrally. 'He's sinking to the occasion.'

It was a new age, Wetherspoon had told the assembled troops during one of his recent descents on the Shepherd's Bush nick from the Valhalla of Area Headquarters. 'Caring is the watchword. Relating to the People. We are the People's police service.' There had been a distinct sound of retching at that point, but Wetherspoon was one of those elevated beings who didn't care whether he was popular or not, and he had carried on unmoved. 'It's not enough to Relate, we have to be Seen to Relate. It's all about Trust, boys and girls. Above all, we mustn't appear elitist.' So it was goodbye, Wolfgang Amadeus, hello, Ruler of the Queen's Nayvee.

'Never mind, you'll look lovely in a bonnet,' Slider said comfortingly. There was nothing in the least effeminate about Nicholls: it was just that his features were so classical, he looked equally good in a dress or trousers.

'It could be worse,' he said philosophically. 'At least it's still music. There was a moment when he was toying with *Aspects of Love*.'

'So what now?' Hollis asked, as he and Slider headed back upstairs.

'We'll have to do it the hard way.'

'Oh, that'll be a nice change.'

'Someone must have seen him,' Slider said. 'Someone always does. And we haven't had the forensic reports yet. If necessary we'll go over the whole of west

London on our hands and knees.'

Hollis smiled behind his ghastly moustache. 'When you say "we", sir, I assume your own hands and knees will be otherwise engaged.'

'Naturally. I've got to go and see the Super.'

Detective Superintendent Fred 'the Syrup' Porson was in his room, pacing about dictating to a hand-held recorder. He was hardly ever seen sitting down — a man of constant, restless energy. When Slider appeared in the open doorway he raised his eyebrows in greeting as he finished his sentence, clicked the machine off and barked, 'Come in. Enter. I was just going to send for you.'

Slider came in and entered, almost simultaneously. Porson was a tall, bony man with a surprisingly generous nose, a chin like a worn nub of pumice-stone, and deep, cavernous eyes below craggy, jutting eyebrows that could have supported a small seagull colony. It was hard, however, to notice any of these things when looking at him: the eye was ineluctably drawn to the amazing rug which had given him his sobriquet. It wasn't just that it was ill-fitting, it was an entirely different colour from his remaining natural hair, which prompted the constant nagging question: *why?*

The thing that drove the language-sensitive Atherton mad, however, was that Porson talked like Peter Sellers playing a trade-union representative doing his first ever television interview. He chucked words about like a man with no arms, apparently on the principle that a near miss was as good as a milestone.

'Now then,' he said, as Slider closed the door behind him, 'the Andrews case: as regards the suspect, what is his current status at this present moment, *vis-à-vis* confession?'

'Hollis and I have just had another crack at him, sir,' Slider reported, concentrating on the portrait of the Queen on the wall behind the Syrup's left shoulder. 'But he still won't cough.'

Porson frowned. 'We are in an advanced state of the clock with regard to this one, if I'm not mistaken?'

'We've got six hours to go, before it has to go before the Muppets.' After thirty-six hours, a magistrate's authorisation was needed to detain an arrestee any longer.

'All we've got against him is the handbag?'

'And his refusal to tell us where he was and what he was doing. And the fact that he was heard threatening to kill her.'

Porson walked about a bit, deep in thought. 'I think we'll let him go,' he said at last.

Slider was surprised. 'Sir, I think the Muppets'd let us keep him. He's the obvious suspect, and his statement has been shown to be —'

'Oh, yes, yes, I'm quite well aware that his whole story has been a tinsel of lies. Nevertheless, if he's decided to dig his teeth in, then there's no point in banging our heads against a glass ceiling.'

'But if I carry on working on him —'

Porson shook his head. 'We can't afford to be giving free bread and board to every Tom, Dick and sundry. There's such a thing as budget restraints, you know. I've seen 'em like this one before, and believe you me, he's not going to come across until we present him with irreputable evidence. That's my judgement. Your job, Slider, is to get the evidence, and you'll concentrate on it all the better if you're not running up and down stairs waiting on him like a housemaid's knee!'

'Yes, sir,' Slider said blankly. The knee threw him somewhat.

'Besides, I'd just as sooner let him go while we've got some time left on the clock, in case we want to bring him back in again at some future eventuality.'

'Well, it's for you to decide, sir.'

'It is, laddie, it is, and I've decided.' Porson looked at him sharply. 'You think he'll make a skip for it, is that it?'

'No, sir, probably not, but —'

'Well, if he does, that's all grist to our mill, isn't it? No, my mind's made up: send him home, keep an eye on him, and meanwhile, let's see your team come up with some new evidence. Time to look in some fresh directions; get a new prospective on the case.'

'It's a long road that gathers no moss,' Slider concluded.

He didn't realise he'd said it aloud until Porson, terrifyingly, clapped him on the shoulder. 'That's the idea,' he said approvingly. 'Neil Desperado. Well, carry on. Keep me informed. And if you want any help, my door is always here. Knock, and ye shall find, as they say.'

Tufnell Arceneaux, the doyen of the forensic laboratory services, was a big man with a big voice. Slider always had to hold the receiver away from his ear when Tufty came on.

'Bill! How's she hanging, my old mackerel?'

'Limp as a three-legged dog.'

'That's terrible! Trouble at t'mill?'

'Trouble everywhere. I hope you've got good news for me.'

'Depends on how you feel about no news. I can't find anything in your victim's blood or stomach contents — nothing of significance, anyway.'

'Damn.'

'Hold fast, chum! That doesn't mean there isn't anything there to be found,' Tufty bellowed. 'I suppose you can't give me an idea of what I'm looking for?'

'I wish I could. Her doctor says she wasn't written up for any sleepers or tranks, and there was nothing in the house or in her handbag. But Freddie Cameron says —'

'Ah, the ineffable Freddie! Yes, I've read his report. Well, old hamster, I've been through all the normal prescription drugs from soup to nuts, and scored a big fat zero. Nix. *Nada*.'

'What about alcohol?'

'Oh, she'd been drinking, all right, but there's not enough alcohol there to account for coma or collapse.'

'There must be something,' Slider said in frustration.

'Very likely, old love, but I can't test for "something". Tell me what to look for, and I'll look for it.'

'I wish I could,' Slider said. 'It's one of the vast army of things I don't know yet. Anything interesting on the victim's clothes?'

'I'm just your bodily fluids man. I passed the clothing to a minion who is e'en now working on it for you.'

'What about the semen, then? Though with my luck it'll probably turn out to be the husband's.'

'I'm hoping to get round to the basic tests tomorrow. You know the problem: too much work and not enough assistants. They're always promising us more man-power tomorrow, but somehow tomorrow never comes. I've sent the semen off for DNA profiling, too, but as you know, dear, it's easier to lift a live eel with chopsticks than to get a quick result from the DNA lab.'

'Well, never mind, I dare say I shall still be in the same position when the results come back.'

'Dear boy,' Tufty boomed, 'you sound infinitely pathetic!'

'I'm up to my gills in pathos —'

'Not to mention bathos and Abednego. How are things on the domestic front? Got your love life sorted out at last? Getting it together with your lovely Euterpe?'

'My turkey?'

'Your lady musician,' Tufty translated kindly.

'Oh! She's a joy, but the other side is not so harmonious.' He told Tufty, who knew Irene of old, about the latest development.

'You do have all the luck,' Tufty acknowledged, in what were for him muted tones. 'My sympathy, old horse. And just when you thought you'd got her nicely bedded in with El Alternative! But you know what the old Jewish proverb says: life is like a cucumber — just when you think it's firmly in your grip, you find it's up your arse.'

'That's the most helpful thing anyone's said to me all day.'

'Go and see Irene face to face, that's my advice. You know you're at your most persuasive in the flesh. One look into your sad, doggy eyes, and she'll be putty.'

'You might have something,' Slider acknowledged.

'And meanwhile, go out and have yourself a good meal and bottle of decent wine.

You've got to rejuvenate the manly juices.'

'That's already in the plans,' Slider said. 'Joanna and I have been invited to dinner tonight with what Fred Porson would call a Gordon Roux chef.'

Tatty chucked. 'Ah, the dear old Syrup! What a character!'

'It takes one to know one,' said Slider, amused.

Chapter Eight

Apart From That,
Mrs Lincoln . . .

Oedipus was sitting in one of his outrageous positions — this time balanced on the top of the chairback of the fireside Queen Anne.

'He can't be comfortable,' Joanna observed.

'He just does it to prove he can,' Atherton said. 'It's a form of intellectual intimidation. The less he appears to want to be noticed, the more he expresses his mental dominance over me.'

Oedipus had his paws tucked under and his eyes shut, but his ears moved like radar saucers, following every movement of Atherton in the kitchen, freezing with special alertness at the sound of the fridge door opening. Joanna leaned against the frame of the door between the sitting-room and the tiny kitchen, watching: she knew better than to offer to help. Slider had taken non-participation one step further and, nursing a G and T, was sitting in the other fireside chair reading the paper, something he hardly ever had time to do.

'You know who's missing from this gathering,' Joanna remarked, watching Atherton frying something.

'Who?' he said absently.

'I love the way you shoogle those things in the pan! Wonderfully professional wrist action.'

He glanced her way. 'White woman speak with forked tongue. Who?'

'Sue, of course. She loves your cooking.'

'Don't start that again,' he warned. 'If she wants to see me she's only got to ring.'

'She gave you all the encouragement a nicely brought-up girl can give. It's for *you* to ring *her.*'

'Why?' he said brutally, slinging the fry-ees onto plates.

'Because she's not going to make all the running. She's a womanly woman.'

'And why should you think I want a womanly woman? Move, please, you're in the way.'

Joanna rolled herself round the supporting jamb as he passed her in the doorway. 'What would be the point in any other sort?'

'Sit down,' he told her, and raised his voice slightly, 'Bill, are you joining us?'

Joanna regarded her starter of two miniature fishcakes in a puddle of pink sauce, decorated with a twig of watercress. The whole thing was like a bonsai garden: tiny tree, two pebbles and a sunset pool. 'The trouble with your food is that it looks so professional, it's discouraging for people like me. I cook things best eaten with the eyes shut.'

'It's no more difficult,' Atherton said, pouring wine.

'It is,' she said indignantly.

'I like your food,' Slider said stoutly. 'It's filling.'

'Oh, thank you! What's this sauce?'

'It's a sauce. Dill, mostly.'

'Why is it pink?'

'Why does Superman wear his knickers over his tights?' Atherton countered. 'Do you think I'm going to reveal all my secrets to you?'

Slider sampled cautiously; he wasn't fond of fishcakes. 'Delicious,' he discovered, with relief.

Atherton looked at him cannily. 'I expect you'd prefer a nice half-a-grapefruit with a dazed cherry in the middle, but, dear heart, you are not going to get it in this house.'

Slider smiled at him with perfect concord. 'This stuff,' he said, lifting the watercress with his fork, 'is just the Islington equivalent of a cherry tomato and two slices of cucumber.'

'Eat it, it's full of iron. You need iron at your age,' Atherton said.

They ate companionable, but the empty fourth side of the square table now seemed a rebuke. Atherton cursed Joanna for bringing the subject up again. He had 'dumped' Sue, according to his own script, because she was getting 'too heavy'. Any minute, he had complained, she was going to use the dreaded C-word. He liked his carefree bachelor life, and there were thousands of women in the world that he hadn't had yet. But Joanna had said to him — only once, and casually, but it was enough — that she believed he had dropped Sue out of fear that Sue would drop him first.

The idea nagged at him; and alone and immobile in the hospital there'd been plenty of time to be nagged. Of his numerous previous girlfriends, only Sue had sent a card, only Sue had visited him. He had been half touched, half angry at her attentions. Getting her claws into him while he was vulnerable, he had told himself cynically; but even his angry half didn't really believe that. He had enjoyed her visits. She didn't seem to feel the need to be bright and cheery; hadn't even minded when he was too down to talk to her. On those occasions she had just sat and read the paper for half an hour, and it had been nice simply having her there. He had found himself looking forward to her visits, and had had to force himself not to ask as she left when she would be coming again.

Only as he grew stronger, and his ambivalence about going back to the Job had troubled him more, he had rejected what he saw as a despicable dependency. The idea of him, the randy young copper's role model, settling down to banal domesticity — Darby and Joan facing each other like Toby jugs across the fireplace — appalled him. Since he left the hospital he had not contacted her. A bit of him had been hurt that she had not contacted him, but mostly he told himself that he was relieved that he didn't have to go on being grateful to her for rallying round in his time of need.

But if he was honest — which he tried not to be too often — he had to admit that the house had seemed horribly cold and empty when he first returned to it; even since Oedipus had come back from his temporary stay with Bill and Joanna, he had felt lonely in it. Him, lonely! Logic told him that it was just the aftermath of shock. He hadn't felt up to going out on the pull yet: didn't want to have to show a stranger his scar. Besides, his nerve had taken a bashing: he had come face to face with his mortality. All those things, he told himself, only made him *feel* that he was lonely. He was still the same Jim Atherton underneath, the old tom-catting free spirit who depended on no-one.

All of which was both true and untrue in about equal proportions. He looked across the table at his boss, who wore an almost visible aura of sappy contentment whenever he was with Joanna, despite all his other troubles; and he wished he had Bill's courage simply to admit he needed to love and be loved. Bill could acknowledge not just to the world but to *himself* that he was not complete without Joanna; the idea terrified Atherton. If the integrity of his shell were once breached, what chaos might not come flooding in?

He cleared the plates and went out to the kitchen for the main course — chicken breasts with lime and bay on a bed of polenta, with mangetouts and baby carrots

— and as he laid it all out he suffered a brief spasm of revulsion for the whole performance. Was not this dilettantism a denial of life? Who was he doing it all for? What was the point? But he took himself firmly in hand and dismissed such barbarous thoughts, marched the plates in by the scruff of their necks. When cast away on a desert island, *always* dress for dinner.

The other two — thank heaven — had changed the subject. 'So what's this committee meeting you've got to go to tomorrow?' Slider was asking Joanna.

'Just the usual shinola, I expect. In the old days it used to be all about not letting enough women into the orchestra. Now women are accepted, it's all about what they ought to wear. Long black or long coloured? Patterned or plain? The LSO is anti-sleeveless; the LPO won't allow tails.'

'Eh?' said Atherton.

'For women,' she explained. 'The arguments are endless.'

'So that's what concerns you all in the nineties? Do you want to finish up the Macon, Bill, or go on to the red?'

'Oh, red, thanks.'

'Joanna?'

'I'll have another splash of white, thanks. No, clothes are just on the surface. The deep concern is one none of us wants to look in the face.' She sipped and replaced her glass. 'I think there's a move afoot to get rid of some of the older players.'

'Because they're no good?' Slider asked.

'Good God, no! Because the marketing men think concert-goers only want to look at dewy youth. They think grey hair and glasses put the punters off. And for all I know they might be right,' she shrugged.

'Surely music-lovers can't be that shallow,' Slider protested.

Atherton looked at him with amusement. '*You* say that, with all your experience of human nature?'

'I've heard comments about Brian Harrop, our second trumpet,' Joanna went on. 'I think they're trying to get him out. He plays like an angel, but, hey, he's bald on top and white round the sides and wears half-moon glasses on the platform. Who wants an old giff like him?'

'Eat your nice din-dins,' Atherton said sympathetically.

She picked up her knife and fork, but passion drove her on. 'I know what it's really about. They want to bring in Dane Jackson, who was Young Musician of the Year last year, because he looks like Nigel Kennedy, and he can do all that fast-fingering, pyrotechnic stuff they teach in College now. Never mind that he can't actually make a nice *sound* on the thing. They don't teach that any more.'

'Careful, dear, you're sounding bitter,' Atherton said.

'Why shouldn't I? All these kids coming out of College have got technique to die for, they can play things most of us couldn't get near, but they're not orchestral players. They don't know how to fit in and, what's more, they don't want to. Brian knows every piece in the repertoire and a thousand that aren't, he knows how to get the right sound at the right moment, and he can adapt to any first trumpet's playing so that they sound like one. Dane Jackson loves himself first, the music a poor second, and the ensemble way down the list. If he plays in a Mozart symphony, he's going to make sure what you hear above all else is Dane Jackson.'

'But if it's what the audience wants,' Slider said doubtfully, 'I suppose it has to be. They're the ones buying the tickets.'

'I can't argue with that,' she said abruptly, and addressed herself to her chicken.

'You agree?' Slider said, surprised.

She grinned over a forkful. 'I didn't say I

agreed, I said I couldn't argue with it.'

'Let's pick up the phone, here, and dial for Ronnie Real,' Atherton said expansively. 'We're talking what's Now. And Now is about Image. Youth is Cool, and Cool is where it's at. Okay?'

'You think you're joking,' Joanna snorted. 'You should hear them at the meetings!' She sighed. 'They're all so bloody earnest and humourless, that's the worst thing. When I think of some of the old characters who were around when I first started playing —'

'Here it comes,' Atherton said to Slider. 'Anecdote Alert!'

'Another Bob Preston story,' Slider agreed.

'Well, why not? I feel like a treat,' she said defiantly. 'We were doing a recording of the Capriccio Italienne, and of course there's that really fiendish cornet bit in it: fast, A-transposition and full of accidentals.' She da-da'd the phrase, and Atherton, at least, nodded. 'Anyway, every time we got to it, Bob fluffed it, and finally after about five takes the conductor looked across and said sarkily, "First cornet, would you like me to take it slower for you?" Bob says, "No, actually, could we do it a bit faster, please?" The conductor looks amazed. "But could you play it faster?" he says, and Bob says, "No, but it'd be a shorter fuck-up." ' She sighed. 'I loved that man!'

Atherton fetched the pudding, and they got on to discussing the case.

'I think Porson's right to let him go,' Slider said. 'The old man may be a bit strange, but he knows his onions. Being held by us was probably just enough punishment to keep Andrews comfortable. Being all alone in the house — the house he built for her — may work on his guilt and bring him to the point of remorse where he has to confess.'

'But he didn't kill her at home, did he?' Joanna said.

'We didn't find anything to show that he did,' Slider said. 'The trouble is, if he didn't kill her in the privacy and comfort of his own home, where did he do it?'

'In the cab of his pickup is the next best bet,' Atherton said. 'But it could equally well have been in the long grass or round the back of the bike sheds. We just don't know.'

'Not on a hard surface,' Slider said, 'or the back of her head would have been bruised or abraded. Of course, since she was found lying in the earth, the presence of earth or grass on the back of her clothes and hair wouldn't tell us anything.'

'But wherever he killed her,' Joanna said, 'how did he transport the body? I suppose if the handbag was in the pickup, it suggests the body was too.'

'It could be. But that's another problem: why didn't the neighbours on that side of the house hear the pickup driving up?'

'Oh, come on,' Atherton objected. 'Who pays any attention to the sound of traffic? Your brain edits it out.'

'But the sound of crunching gravel —'

'Well, he'd be nuts to drive it over the gravel,' Atherton said impatiently. 'He'd park it on the road.'

'*He*'d still have to walk over the gravel — and with a body over his shoulder,' Slider said. 'Surely they'd hear that? It's the point of gravel — it's an alarm system.'

'Couldn't he have got to the terrace any other way?' Joanna asked.

'Up through the garden,' Slider said.

'But that would mean crossing someone else's garden first,' Atherton said. 'There's a footpath at the end of the row, but there's three houses between it and the Rectory. That's four fences to get the body over. Of course it's possible, but would anyone?'

'Where does the footpath go to?' Joanna asked.

Slider raised his eyebrows. 'To the railway footbridge. But of course, good point! From there he could have got onto the railway embankment, which runs parallel with the gardens: only two fences, and cover in between. Maybe we oughtn't to get too hung up on the pickup.'

Atherton cocked his head. 'Time for a general appeal for witnesses, do you think?'

'We haven't enough manpower to extend to house-to-house much further,' Slider said, 'and Porson's already burbling about budget restraints. Yes, maybe it's time to ask him to go public. But on a limited scale — local television, perhaps. We don't want sightings from Aberdeen and Abergavenny clogging up the system.'

'Why don't *you* ever do the TV appeals?' Joanna said, slipping a hand on his thigh under the table. 'It'd be a feather in my cap having a celeb for a lover. Your handsome face all over the silver screen —'

'Not in these trousers,' Slider said firmly. 'I'm a private man and I intend to stay private. Det sups get the big money — they can have the exposure as well.'

'Mr Modesty!'

Atherton was still musing. 'What I can't understand is why he retouched the makeup. It seems to me that, if Freddie's right about that, it's a point against its being Eddie. If he was going to bury her in concrete, it wouldn't matter what she looked like.'

'It is odd,' Slider acknowledged. 'Maybe the oddest thing about the whole business.'

'But, to my mind, it's only her husband who *would* do a thing like that,' Joanna said. 'Why would anybody else care what she looked like? It's a strange, obsessive kind of thing to do. I can imagine him plotting the murder, carrying it out, and then brooding over the body — you know, like those chimps that won't be separated from their dead babies and keep on licking and grooming them.'

'I see your reasoning,' Slider said. 'But is he obsessive in that way?'

'Don't ask me, I've never met the bloke,' Joanna said. 'But if he says he loved her, and she was a bad hat, maybe that was enough to make him obsessive.'

'How much of a bad hat we've still to discover,' Slider said, and looked towards Atherton. 'You know, I'm wondering if there wasn't something between her and Meacher. Given the way she was with

Potter, her other boss — and the availability of empty houses to do it in.'

'Eddie says Meacher sometimes asked her to work at weekends, and he obviously didn't like it,' Atherton agreed cautiously.

'Maybe that was just an excuse. I got the feeling Meacher was keeping something back from me, and he's never come in with the list of where he was that afternoon. There's something about that man I don't like.'

'I thought it was everything about him you didn't like,' Atherton said. 'The ordinary bloke's hatred of the man of style and taste —'

'None of your sauce,' Slider countered. 'You forget I have it in my power to retaliate. There are jobs and jobs, and I'm the one who gives 'em out. For instance, Andrews' pickup had an oil leak — left stains on the ground where it was parked. Now that might give us a clue as to where it was on Tuesday night.'

Atherton rolled his eyes. 'No! Mercy! You want me to go and investigate every oil patch in west London? I don't have the stomach for it! I don't have the trousers for it!'

'Well, just watch your lip, then,' Slider warned. 'And go and get my coffee. Can't you see I've finished?'

Atherton jumped up, cowering, grabbed the plates and shuffled out, one shoulder hunched and his left leg dragging.

Joanna replaced her hand on Slider's thigh. 'I love it when you're masterful,' she said, batting her eyelids. 'Would you like to sleep with me tonight?'

'I'll think about it,' he said lordly-wise, but his smirk gave him away.

Morning streamed into Slider's office to fidget with his hangover and remind him that nothing worthwhile was ever had without payment. They had been drinking brandy late into the night, and he was beginning to think brandy didn't agree with him. Certainly morning had come too soon and was being far too loud about it. Still, at least the windows were decently grey again, now that the awful cleanliness of the Barrington era had worn off. Det Sup Porson had a proper respect for crud. Dirty windows saved on net curtains.

He was talking to Atherton when Mackay came in with the long-promised cup of tea.

'You took your time,' Slider grumped.

'Sorry, sir. I got sidetracked,' he said, putting the cup down without taking his eyes from the typesheet in his hand. Slider sighed and patiently poured the slops back into the cup and found a paper hanky to wipe the cup's bottom. 'I left yours on your desk, Jim,' Mackay said.

'Safest place,' Atherton said.

'The thing is, guv,' Mackay went on, 'it's these phone numbers. Mrs Andrews' car phone. On the Tuesday she made two calls to a number that turns out to be David Meacher's mobile. The first was a short one at one fifty-five — lasted only thirty-five seconds. The second was a long one — nineteen minutes. Cost her a small fortune — or would've,' he corrected succinctly. 'That was at eighteen thirty-one.'

'Half past six in people-time,' Atherton translated.

Slider reflected. 'Well, there's no reason she shouldn't phone her boss, I suppose. I wonder where she was, though, and why it couldn't wait until she got home? Any others?'

'Well, I dunno if it means anything, but about half past five she phoned a number that turns out to be the vicarage of the vicar that does the church in St Michael Square.'

'The Rev. Alan Tennyson,' Atherton said.

'That's right. Well, we know she was very inty at the church, so there's nothing funny about that, but I did wonder —'

'Whether she asked for spiritual advice?'

'It wasn't a long enough call for that — four minutes. But seeing as it was the day she died, she might have said something to him that would give us a hint.'

'Quite right,' Slider said. 'We'll look into it. Anything else?'

'She phoned the First And Last just before eleven o'clock. Ten fifty-five, to be exact, one minute fifty seconds. I wondered if she spoke to Eddie. Maybe that was when he arranged to meet her somewhere, wherever it was he killed her.'

'The barman said it was after eleven that Eddie came in,' Atherton reminded him. 'After closing-time, which was why he refused him a drink. But I suppose he could have got the time wrong.'

'Or the pub clock could be fast,' Slider said. 'It's a thought, anyway. What about Meacher's mobile?'

'Nothing that strikes the eye, guv,' Mackay said, 'except —' He hesitated. 'Well, I dunno if it's anything to do with anything, but he did make a call to the Target Motel that morning. At half past eleven.'

'Half past eleven? He was still in the office at that time, wasn't he?'

'Well, that's what I wondered. If he used his mobile instead of the office phone, maybe he didn't want anyone to hear what he was saying. And it being a motel, naturally I thought —'

'That his call had naughty purposes,' Atherton concluded. 'It's shocking the effect the word "motel" has on people.'

'Well, why don't you pop round there and find out?' Slider told Mackay. 'No, no, don't thank me. I like to reward virtue. Meanwhile,' he said to Atherton, 'I think you may pay a visit to the parish priest, and see if you can get any more information about Mrs Andrews and her little proclivities.'

'Pretty large ones, from what I've heard,' Atherton said, unfolding his long body from the window-sill like an hydraulic arm. 'What about a Meacher follow-up?'

'I'll do that,' Slider said. 'I need the fresh air.'

Meacher's office was womanned by a very smart, well-preserved female in her forties who was very nearly pretty. Her hair was dyed blonde, but very nicely, and her makeup was perfect, except that she had eaten off her lipstick leaving only the out-liner, which gave her rather a clownlike look. A lipstick-stained coffee cup on her desk completed the story, and the stale-laundry smell of instant coffee on the air suggested to the trained mind that she had only just finished it and hadn't yet had time to renew the lippy. It was easy when you knew how, Slider told himself, and asked her for the boss.

She replied, with a clipped smile and an authoritative voice, 'I'm sorry, he's at the other office today. Can I help you?'

'You must be —' Slider sought memory for the name. 'Liz — I'm sorry, I don't know your other name.'

'Liz Berryman,' she admitted, looking a query.

'Detective Inspector Slider, Shepherd's Bush CID.'

'Oh! Yes,' she said, and her face became grave. 'About Jennifer, I suppose. That was a terrible thing. I suppose it was murder?'

'We're treating the death as suspicious,' Slider said cautiously. The eyes behind the mascara were watchful and intelligent. 'I suppose you didn't know her very well?'

'Oh, I knew her all right,' she said bit-terly. She looked down, and then up again as though coming to a decision. 'I suppose you know about her and David?'

Slider sat down in the chair on the other side of her desk with an air of settling in for the spill. 'Funnily enough, that's what I was going to ask him about when I came here.'

'If he'd tell you. It's supposed to be a big secret. But *I*'ll tell you if he won't.' She translated his waiting expression as an enquiry into her motives. 'I don't owe him any loyalty on that score. What loyalty did he ever show me, or anyone? And they were both married people. Besides, it's everyone's duty to help the police, isn't it?'

'I wish everyone thought so,' Slider said. 'So Jennifer and David Meacher were having an affair, were they?'

'If that's what you want to call it,' she said sourly. '*He* tried to keep it a secret at the office, but *she* was always brushing up against him, and saying things no-one else was supposed to understand. She was always calling him, too, when it wasn't her day on. She'd disguise her voice sometimes and pretend to be a client if it was me answered the phone, but I knew it was her, all right. I expect she did the same thing at his home. Her sort always do. I pity his poor wife.'

'But Mr Meacher said that you and she

were never here at the same time,' Slider queried.

'That was the basic principle, but our times overlapped, so as to make sure the office was always covered. And she did extra hours when we were busy. And, of course,' she added harshly, 'she liked to hang around after I arrived talking to David and looking sideways at me to see if I'd noticed.'

'Why would she do that?' Slider asked mildly.

She glowered at him. 'Why don't you just come right out and ask me? I've got nothing to hide, though David seems to think I have. But I wasn't the one who was married. I was perfectly entitled to do whatever I wanted, especially given —' She stopped, biting her lips angrily.

Slider was there at last. 'It used to be you,' he said. 'He dropped you for Jennifer?'

She coloured. 'There was no dropping about it! He wanted to go on seeing me as well, but when I found out about Jennifer I told him there was no way I was going to share, let alone with that vulgar, brassy — well, tart's too good a word for her. He wanted to have both of us. That's when I got out — and I was right to.'

'But you were already sharing with his wife,' Slider said, though he had guessed what came next. Oh, Lord, what fools we mortals be!

'He promised to marry me. I would never have started it otherwise. He said he was going to leave her, that he was only waiting for the right time to tell her. But when he took up with Jennifer, I realised what a fool I'd been. He never meant it. It was just what he said to get me into bed.'

'Well, at least you've realised it now,' Slider said encouragingly. 'Some people never see the truth, even when it's under their noses.'

She didn't answer that, only stared broodingly at the computer screen, alone with her thoughts. And Slider thought, Yes, she's discovered the truth, but she's still here, working for him. Why is that? Just to be near him? Still in love with him, in spite of everything? What *was* it about some men?

'So when did it start between him and Jennifer?' he asked.

Miss Berryman's attention snapped back into place. 'Oh, right from the time she first came to work here. In fact, I wouldn't be surprised if that wasn't *why* he gave her the job — so as to have more opportunities for it.' She looked into Slider's eyes as one coming to the worst and barely credible thing. 'They used to do it in the clients' houses, you know. The ones we had keys for. On their beds. God knows what would have happened if they'd got caught.'

Slider wondered for a moment whether the two-timing Meacher had known he was being two-timed by Jennifer. What a pair they were! 'And yet,' he said aloud, 'you wouldn't have thought she was his type. I wonder what he saw in her.'

'Oh, I understand she was fabulous in the sack,' Miss Berryman said, in a hard voice. 'As for her, she thought David was worth a mint, and she couldn't wait to get her claws into him. She'd have found out!'

'Found out what?'

She looked at him with narrowed eyes. 'I do the invoices, and I know how to get into his accounts on the computer. The business is on the rocks. If his wife doesn't bail him out again, he'll go bust. Well, serve him right, I say. I know I'll lose my job if he folds, but it'd be worth it just to see that smug look wiped off his face.'

'His wife has money, has she?'

'Oh, she's rich as Croesus. That's why he'll never leave her. I learned *that* the hard way.'

Instructive, Slider thought, out in the street, though it didn't get him much further forward. So Jennifer was making the beast with two backs with Meacher, who had previously been bonking Liz Berryman. And what price now the little fluffy one he'd seen the other day — what was her name? — Caroline? Meanwhile, Jennifer was Doctor Dolittling with Jack Potter on the side, and who else? Oh, brave new world, that had such people in it. He should have known Meacher was a villain. Any man who'd sell an Aston to buy a BMW couldn't be all good.

In his car, he dialled the number of Meacher's Denham office, but all he got was an answering-machine in Meacher's voice.

'I'm sorry we can't come to the phone right now, but if you'll leave your telephone number and any short message, we'll get back to you.'

Slider put down the receiver with irritation. Why 'right now'? Was there some other, less immediate sort of now during which the telephone might possibly be answered? And why 'get back to you'? The phrase had such overtones of hardship dauntlessly overcome, conjuring images of the faithful family dog, accidentally left behind, struggling mile after mile over unfamiliar terrain to find its way home to the masters it adored. Get back to you, indeed! Slider knew perfectly well that his dislike of David Meacher was in essence irrational; but the mark of maturity, he always felt, was the ability to sustain irrational prejudices with grace and dignity. He made a few more telephone calls, and then rang Joanna.

'Fancy a trip out into the countryside?'

'You mean now? As opposed to finishing the pile of ironing I've just started, Hoovering the sitting room, cleaning the bath and putting in a solid hour's practice? That's a hard one to call.'

'I've got to go out to Denham to interview a bloke, and there's a really nice pub in Denham village — the Kestrel — where they do toasted bacon and tomato sandwiches. I thought we could meet there for lunch.'

'What beer do they do?'

'Marston's and Brakspear's, if memory serves.'

'You're on.'

'You're not working today, are you?'

'Just that committee meeting at six.'

'Hedonist!' he said.

★ ★ ★

The Denham office of David Meacher Estate Agents turned out to be a wooden hut standing all alone beside the bypass between a garden centre and a timber yard. Traffic thundered past, bypassing for all it was worth, and four lanes and a central reservation divided the hut from the pavement on the other side where there was a row of shops, a pillar-box, houses, and pedestrians. However cheap the hut was in terms of rent and rates, it was unlikely to pay its way in walk-in trade, Slider thought, as he parked in the lay-by. The hut had two shop windows and a door in between. The windows were filled with cards advertising houses for sale, but half of them had 'sold' stickers across them, and they all looked very yellow. A hecatomb of dead flies lay inside on the window-sill, and the door had its blind pulled down and a 'closed' notice hanging from a suction hook. There was a hand-written notice stuck to the inside of the glass of the door, instructing interested parties to contact the Chiswick office; but this, too, Slider noticed, was yellowed with age and exposure to sunlight. Without any hope, he banged on the door, but there was, as he expected, no answer.

He returned to his car. The lay-by was tenanted by a flower-seller, a young man in cut-offs and teeshirt perched on a camp stool reading a paperback, guarding a greenpainted barrow displaying the indestructible flowers of the roadside: long-stemmed rosebuds that would never open, multi-headed chrysanthemums whose petals would fall off in one shattering lump ten minutes after you bought them, and the sort of scentless carnations that looked exactly the same whether they were alive or dead. The lad looked up as Slider approached, but not with any expectation of making a sale. Slider wondered how he — or whoever employed him — could possibly make a living. Who bought these joyless objects, which could not merit so exuberant a title as 'blooms'? Someone going to the funeral of an office colleague, perhaps, cramming it into a working day between meetings? A businessman with sweat rings under the arms of his striped shirt and fear of discovery in his heart, hurrying to a clandestine lunch with his mistress in one of those tomb-like exurban Italian restaurants, where the food is frozen in individual dishes for ease of microwaving, and the coffee is reheated from day to day?

'Know anything about the estate agents there?' Slider asked. The young man shook his head. 'Has anyone been in there this morning?'

'Never seen anyone go in there,' he said.

'You here every day?'

'Mostly.'

'What time is it usually open?'

He shook his head again. 'Never seen it open.' He eyed Slider keenly. 'Police?'

Am I that obvious? Slider thought. 'I'm looking for the owner,' he said.

'I think they've closed down,' the young man said. 'It's been shut up like that since I been coming here. Never seen anyone go near it. You only got to look at the weeds.'

Slider looked back, and noticed, sure enough, the ragwort and dandelions growing up between the cracks in the pavement and between the pavement and the hut's wall. This was a pavement that never knew the touch of human foot. People drove into the garden centre and the woodyard, or parked briefly in the lay-by for the flower-seller's wares and then drove off again.

'Thanks,' Slider said. It was all Hatton Garden to a hatful of mice that this man had no trader's licence, but Slider had no wish to appear ungrateful, and besides, he reckoned the lad had already devised his own punishment. He got into his car, thought for a moment, looked at his watch, and then in his notebook for Meacher's home address. If he wasn't there, at least there might be someone who knew where he was.

Chapter Nine

Babes and Suckers

Meacher's house was as irritating as the man: a large and lovely 1930s mansion, built in the Lutyens-Jekyll vernacular, with cottage casements, elaborate tile-hanging, mossy paths, and a garden of full-blown, tangled beauty whose natural, untended look was the ultimate in artifice and must have taken endless work to achieve. It was down a quiet lane on the outskirts of Denham, and when Slider climbed out of his car, only the distant waterfall-roar of the M40 spoiled the rural idyll.

Slider had more than half expected to find no-one home, but after a long delay, the door was flung open to reveal a woman holding a black Labrador by the collar. 'Can you just come inside,' she said, without waiting for him to speak, 'so I can shut the door? Bessie's on heat and I don't want her to get out.'

Slider obeyed and stepped into a large

vestibule full of beautiful old furniture covered in clutter, terracotta walls covered in watercolours and prints, the woodblock floor covered in an old Turkish carpet and muddy paw-marks. A tall Chinese vase of obvious antiquity was filled with blue and white delphiniums spitting their petals everywhere. Coats hung over the newel post of the stairs, a heap of books and papers sat on the third step waiting to go up, a George III side table was littered with opened and unopened mail, dog-leads and a tin of saddle-soap, and the air smelt of furniture polish, dogs, earth and damp. Slider soaked it all in. He was in the presence, he knew, of genuine Old Money. None of your Chiswick-and-Islington, upper-middle-class, fresh-painted spotlessness here: this was how the real nobs lived, the sort of country gentry his father had worked for and whose houses Slider as a child had occasionally entered. There had always seemed to him an effortlessness about everything they did, which he as a struggling mediocrity to whom nothing came easily had deeply admired; but with later wisdom he supposed that, like the garden, it looked effortless because someone behind the scenes had put in a great deal of hard work — in the case of his childhood icons, probably a grim-faced, uniformed nanny.

The present example released the dog, which instantly danced smiling up to Slider to bash his legs with its black rudder of a tail and invite him to play. He stroked the big, domed head and the dog instantly reared up and placed huge paws on his stomach to make the stroking easier. Over its head, he looked at the woman.

She was tall and thin, probably in her late fifties, tanned, with a mane of streaked grey hair, which seemed to grow naturally back from her face like Tenniel's illustrations of Alice. She was dressed in black leggings and a body-hugging sleeveless pink top, something like a leotard, over which she wore a loose, baggy white shirt, hanging open and with the sleeves rolled up. Her feet were bare and her toe-nails were painted. Her large-featured face must once have been staggeringly beautiful, and even now, though her skin was tired, her neck crepy, and the veins on her hands like jungle creepers, she was still stunning.

'Mrs Meacher?' he asked.

'Lady Diana Meacher,' she corrected, though not as if it mattered very much.

'I beg your pardon, ma'am. Detective Inspector Slider of Shepherd's Bush CID.'

He removed one hand from the dog's head to reach for his ID, but she waved the formality away.

'I suppose you've come about this wretched Andrews woman? You'd better come through. Do you mind the kitchen? I was potting some fuchsia cuttings. You won't mind if I carry on?'

He followed her down the passage beside the stairs, glimpsing through open doors rooms that were larger performances of what the hall had rehearsed. The dog trotted after them, nails clicking on the parquet, but when they reached the kitchen it turned and went away again, back the way they had come. The kitchen had an Aga under the mantelpiece instead of a range, and fitted cabinets round two walls, but otherwise was pretty much unchanged from the 1930s, with the original tiles, quarry floor, wooden dresser and shelves. A huge deal table stood in the middle of the room covered in newspaper on which stood a potting tray full of earth, ranks of small plastic flower-pots and jamjars full of rooted cuttings. An ancient yellow Labrador with filmy eyes and a nose the colour of milk chocolate lay in a basket by the Aga and did not get up, and there were three vast dozing cats, two sitting on the top of the Aga and the other on the window-sill by the open window onto the garden. Out on the lawn another three Labradors, two black and a yellow, were racing about, ears flapping, having a glorious game with a stick. Slider felt sorry for poor Bessie, gynaecologically excluded from the fun. Wasn't that just a woman's lot?

Lady Diana followed the direction of his eyes. 'Rusty, Leo and Bob. The chap in the basket's Billie, who's too old to bother with miscegenation. Bessie's the only girl, poor bitch. I'll take her out later for a run round the garden, but she has to stay on the lead when she's in purdah, and I just haven't time now.'

'I don't want to disturb you,' Slider said. 'I was really looking for your husband.'

She looked at him with large, intelligent, beautiful eyes, whose tired orbits had been delicately shaded with grey eyeshadow, the lashes darkened with violet mascara: even when not expecting to be seen, he noted, she tended her garden. 'He's not here,' she said abruptly. 'I don't know where he is. Probably looking at some property. Or he may be at his health club, or propping up a bar somewhere, who knows? Look here, I suspect this is going to turn into a long session. Why don't you make us some coffee, while I carry on with these cuttings? I've promised two hundred for the church bazaar tomorrow, and they're still in water. I don't know why I do these things. The coffee machine's over there, and the coffee's in the blue tin on the shelf above it. Can you manage that?'

'I can manage that,' he said. While he was managing, the black Labrador reappeared with a small, much-chewed rag doll in her mouth, which she laid at his feet, smiling and waving her tail. He thanked her gravely, and she trotted off again.

'That's Lucy, her baby,' Lady Diana explained. 'Bessie's frightfully maternal and won't be parted from the thing, except when she's on heat, and then she gives it away to all and sundry. So, you were looking for David?'

'I tried his Chiswick office, and they said he was at the Denham office, but when I went there —'

She snorted. 'Oh, that! David's alibi. Some men have a potting shed, some men have the club. David has a hut on the A40. They all serve the same purpose. What do *you* do when you don't want anyone to be able to contact you?'

'I'm a police officer. We don't need any

other excuse,' Slider said, smiling. 'So the Denham office doesn't actually do any business?'

'It did once, back in the eighties when estate agency was flourishing. David opened branches — the hut and another office in Chalfont St Peter — took on extra staff, planned to conquer the world. But the recession and the property crash ended all that. He closed the branches and sold the building at Chalfont, but he kept the hut.'

Bessie reappeared with a dog-lead in her mouth. She ran up to Slider but when he put his hand out she jumped away and carried the lead to her mistress. Lady Diana took it absently and put it on the table. The bitch gazed at her hopefully for a while, and then pattered away again.

'Why did he keep the hut?' Slider asked.

She filled a pot with compost and shook a cutting free of its companions. 'Male pride, partly. He couldn't bear to think that his days as a business mogul were over. He loved having three branches and six employees, driving from one to the other and being paged in between. He doesn't really like business, you see, just the trappings of it. For instance, I thought it would break his heart to part with the

Aston, but I think he actually likes the BMW better because it's got more gadgets.'

Slider nodded, watching her long fingers dive into the soil like fish getting back into the water. 'What was the other reason?'

'For keeping the hut? Oh, for his affairs, of course,' she said brutally. 'He has a sofa in there that turns into a bed. There's nothing else in there now, except for the answering-machine — equally useful for genuine enquiries or messages from his tarts. He changes the call-in code all the time so that I can't collect them before he does. As if,' she gave him a burning look, 'I care any longer what he does.'

Slider nodded. The machine was making a noise now like an advert for instant coffee. 'You cared once, then?'

'I married him for love, strange though that seems now,' she said. 'My family were against it. They saw him for what he was — a hollow man. But to me he seemed so sophisticated, charming, urbane. And he told me he loved me. Women are fools where words are concerned. A man can behave as badly as he likes, as long as he tells you he loves you.'

'Perhaps he did love you,' Slider said. 'Why wouldn't he?'

'I was beautiful when I was a girl,' she said, reaching for another cutting.

'You're beautiful now.'

She paused, and then looked up, and gave a puzzled laugh. 'You're a strange sort of policeman.'

'Are policemen all the same, then? Like women are all the same?'

She shook her head wonderingly. 'You can't go round saying that sort of thing, you know. Talking to people as if they were human beings. As if you knew them.'

Bessie came trotting in at that delicate moment with another gift for Slider. When he disengaged it from her jaws it proved to be a pair of white cotton knickers. Slider held them up to Lady Diana with a look of innocent enquiry, and she blushed.

'That wretched dog! She's been in my chest of drawers again. She's worked out how to open a drawer by gripping the knob in her teeth, but she can only open the small ones, so it's always something embarrassing she brings out.'

'Perfectly decent, respectable knickers,' Slider said blandly. 'Nothing to be ashamed of. Marks and Sparks finest.'

'Oh, throw the wretched things away!' she protested, laughing. 'Bessie, you bad bitch, I shall have to lock you out of the bedrooms next. Go and lie down. Lie down! Is the coffee ready? You're very handy about the kitchen, I must say.'

By the time Slider had poured two mugs, and drawn up a high stool to perch on at the other side of the table, his hostess seemed to have accepted him completely. Bessie was lying down with the old dog, rolling about and play-biting its ears and paws; the cats were fast in sleep, a clock ticked peacefully somewhere deep in the house, and the coffee aroma mingled with the smell of warm compost. Everything was set for confidences.

'Would you like to hear the whole story?' Lady Diana asked. 'I suppose you only came to enquire about David and the Andrews woman, but it might help to place it in context.'

Slider exuded comfort and being settled here for the morning. 'I want to hear everything you want to tell me,' he said, with perfect truth.

She sighed just discernibly. 'You have a wonderful — what's the police equivalent of a bedside manner? Do people always end up by telling you absolutely everything?'

'I wish I knew,' said Slider.

She was born Lady Diana Seldon, youngest daughter of an old family with a new earldom. 'Grandpa was created by Edward VII, but we'd been at Old Warden for five hundred years. I think that's what attracted David in the first place. Property — real estate — is his passion.'

'I'm interested in architecture myself,' Slider mentioned.

'Architecture!' She gave him a humorous look. 'Oh, David hasn't any artistic sense. What he loves about houses is their size, age, extent and value. Their saleability. It's a purely commercial passion. He may have the body of a demi-god, but he has the heart and mind of a grocer.'

'Cruel,' Slider said.

'Not at all. Praise where praise is due. David has the uncanny ability to put a price on any property after the briefest inspection. He can balance location, bedrooms, condition and come up with exactly the figure the market will bear. And he has an incredible memory for what's on his books: he can match a client to a house without even looking in his filing system. He just loves selling houses. He was born to be an estate agent.'

It sounded like the ultimate insult. 'They also serve?' Slider suggested.

'Oh, don't worry, he doesn't need

defending. He loves his calling. His other ambition was to be an MP, so you see popularity doesn't figure in his calculations.'

Slider smiled at the jest, but not too much. There was a great deal of pain here somewhere and he had no wish to press on a bruise. 'How did you meet him in the first place?'

She took another seedling and slipped it into the ready earth like a Norland nanny slipping a baby into its cot. 'Daddy was selling some property — a couple of Victorian houses in the village. He contacted Jackson Stops, and they sent round David.'

Her fingers stopped firming the earth for a moment and she stared at nothing. 'He was very handsome, and so fresh and eager. Nothing like the men I'd been used to seeing who were bored with everything, or pretended to be. He was rapturous about the house — it was rather touching. I thought he was loving it, the way I'd always loved it, almost as a person —' She glanced at him to see if he understood, and he nodded. 'Of course, I didn't realise until a long time later that all he wanted to do was to sell it.' She gave a little snorting sigh. 'That's what turned Daddy against him in the end — David kept urging him to sell up and move somewhere more convenient. Daddy had never liked him, but he put up with him for my sake, and he thought it was rather touching that David should worry so much about his health and welfare, even if he did show it in an inappropriate way. But he finally understood that David wasn't concerned for him at all: he just wanted to handle the sale.'

There, in the peaceful kitchen, Slider heard the whole story. Lady Diana had fallen in love with David Meacher more or less at first sight. As the youngest of the family and everyone's pet, she had remained at home long after the others had married and/or moved away. Even her eldest brother, the heir, was living in a flat in Chelsea and running an interior-design shop jointly with a schoolfriend from Eton.

'I suppose I'd never really grown up,' she mused. 'I was happy just going on doing what I'd always done at home — dogs, horses, parties, the family. I had lots of friends, and I'd always had plenty of boyfriends, but I'd never been serious about any of them. I suppose I thought I might marry one day, but I wasn't in any hurry. When you're pretty and popular,' she said frankly, 'you don't feel the same pressure as other girls. I was approaching my thirtieth birthday, but I was still the baby of the family and Daddy's pet.'

Bessie, who had fallen asleep with her head pillowed on the old dog, groaned in her sleep, rolled over and stretched out, exposing her swollen nipples to the cooler air from the window.

'But David was so different. I suppose I fell in love with him because he was different. And he seemed determined from the beginning that he was going to have me. He was always single-minded like that about anything he really wanted.'

He courted her hard, and she was flattered and fascinated. She had started seeing him regularly, but it was not until she announced that she meant to marry him that her family had become alarmed. 'They simply never imagined I could be doing more than amusing myself with him, because — as Bob, my brother, said — he just wasn't one of us. I was furious. I was desperately anti-snobbery in those days and, in any case, as I was always pointing out, David had been to a decent school and everything. It wasn't as if he ate peas with a knife or wiped his nose on his sleeve. The more the family argued, the more I was determined to have him. And in the end Daddy said I was old enough to make my own mistakes, and made everyone else shut up.' She shrugged. 'Of course I found out they were right about David and I was wrong, but it was too late by then. I was married to him and that was that.'

'You never thought about divorce?'

She shook her head. 'Pride, at first. I couldn't have admitted my wonderful love affair was a fish story. And, of course, I did love him. Later I suppose it was just stubbornness. I wouldn't be beaten by him. And fear, too.' She looked at him sidelong. 'I'm not used to being on my own. I don't think I'd like to have to go out there again as a single person.'

'I don't suppose you'd stay single for long,' Slider said.

'Very gallant of you.'

'No, just the truth.'

She moved away from the compliment. 'But to have to start again, go out and meet people, all that dreadful who-are-you and what-do-you-do business — ghastly enough at sixteen, but at fifty-eight? No, I don't think I could go through that again. So we go on as we are. A *modus vivendi* has been reached. I ignore his infidelities and pay his bills. He plays the dutiful husband on public occasions for the sake of my cheque book.'

'But doesn't he make a living? Didn't you say he was a good estate agent?'

'He is, but he's a lousy businessman. He'd have done better to stay with a firm like Jackson, but of course he was ambitious and wanted his own company. What man doesn't? And I was ambitious for him. I set him up, and I bailed him out whenever he made a bad decision, which was often. I suppose that was part of the trouble.'

'How's that?'

'All the money in the marriage is mine. Daddy made a large settlement on me when I married — fortunately, very well invested. David knew that. He married me at least partly for my money — no, please, don't protest.' She stopped Slider with a lift of a muddy hand. 'The trouble is that he's an old-fashioned creature underneath and thinks a man ought to wear the trousers and bring home the bacon. He has affairs to put me in my place, and the worse his business does, the more women he flaunts in front of me. It's his way of asserting his masculinity.'

'It must have been very hard for you,' Slider said gently.

She looked at him nakedly. 'I'm crazy to put up with it. That's what my family says.

But I married him. You can't just shrug off responsibility because it's inconvenient, can you?'

'No,' said Slider uncomfortably.

'And they don't really mean it, anyway,' she went on. 'Bob's wife drinks, for instance, and sometimes she steals things, but he'll never leave her. Not just *noblesse oblige*. Either you're that sort of person, or you aren't — don't you think?'

'I used to,' Slider said. 'Lately I've wondered whether everything isn't changing.'

'I know what you mean.' She nodded rather glumly, and then said, 'Is there any more coffee?'

He took her mug and went to refill it, and her voice followed him across the room in a puzzled way. 'I was right, you are a strange sort of policeman. Dangerous, too.'

'Dangerous?' he said, amused.

'Look how much I'm telling you. Why should I do that?'

'Because I'm interested.'

'Exactly.' She tried for a lighter tone. 'I imagine all the young policewomen are nuts about you.'

He came back with the coffee. 'They don't even notice me. They think I'm dull and safe.'

'I bet they don't.'

'Tell me what Jennifer Andrews was like,' he said firmly.

'Haven't you seen her?' She seemed surprised.

'I never met her alive,' he pointed out. 'What was she like as a person?'

'Pretty, smart, lively. Rather obvious. Vulgar, of course. And she was man mad.'

'What did your husband see in her?'

'She was a conquest,' she said. 'I don't know if you know women like her, but she was very mannish in some ways — brassy, confident, at home in pubs, handled her drinks and cigarettes like a man, liked to drive fast, took the lead in conversation. Women like that are a challenge to some men.'

He nodded. 'And what did she see in him?'

She shrugged. 'Another scalp on her belt.'

'Is that all?'

She hesitated. 'I have a theory that women like that are really not interested in men at all. What they are trying to do is get their own back on women. She wasn't taking David *for* her, she was taking him *from* me.' He stirred a little restlessly at this advance into the psycho-Saharan dunes without a water-bottle, and she noticed it. 'They always go after married men, you notice,' she justified her argument. 'What they're really trying to do is to take their father away from their mother. They're scoring off Mummy.'

'You knew her quite well?' he suggested noncommittally.

'Not well, but better than I wanted to.'

'How did David meet her?'

'Oh, that was through Frances Hammond. I suppose you know David was friendly with her husband?'

'I understand they were at school together.'

'Yes, though not in the same year. Gerald was three years older than David, but I suppose he saw a kindred spirit in him. They became great chums after they left school, at any rate. The four of us spent quite a lot of time together — David, Gerald, Frances and I — though really it was more for David's sake than mine, because they weren't really my sort of people. Then after Gerald left, David set himself up in a sort of avuncular role to Frances, listening to her problems and offering advice. One of the things he advised her to do was to get herself involved in local affairs, as a way of taking her out of herself. Be more like Diana, he told her: I don't suppose she liked that any more than I did. But she joined the parish council, anyway, and met Jennifer Andrews, and at some point introduced David to her. I expect he bumped into her at the Rectory. Then Jennifer said she wanted a part-time job, and David took her on.'

'Was it a genuine job?'

'Oh, yes, I think so. At first, anyway. She'd done that sort of work before. I expect she wangled the meeting so that she could ask him for a job; and David, of course, always liked taking on more staff. That was why his business failed. But at least Jennifer knew what to do, unlike some of them.'

'But then at some point they began to . . . ?'

'What a delicate pause. Yes, they "began to". I don't know exactly when — he did *try* to be discreet, though not very hard — but I don't suppose they lost much time about it, when there was so much goodwill on both sides.'

'I'm sorry, this must be very painful for you.'

'I don't care any more.' She eyed him with a hard, defiant look. 'No, really. I used to, but there comes a point when it all just stops. He can do as he pleases, as long as I don't have to know about it.'

'But you did know about Jennifer Andrews.'

'Yes, and now that she's dead, I suppose it will all be dragged out into the open for people to paw over.' She sighed. 'I must say you were a pleasant surprise compared with what I'd expected.'

'A uniformed constable with big boots who licked his pencil?'

'Come, I'm not as out of touch as all that! I thought it would be a callow youth with a moustache and an attitude, who'd look around this house with a serves-you-right expression.

'What would he think served you right?'

She looked at him slightly askance for a moment, and then said, 'No, don't play games with me. It doesn't suit you. You know she came here that evening, so why not ask me about it straight out?'

Long experience kept Slider's face impassive. 'Fair enough,' he said. 'What time did Jennifer Andrews arrive here on Tuesday night?'

'It must have been about nine o'clock. I heard the car drive up and the dogs started barking. I thought it was David coming back. I was upstairs, in my bedroom — I'd just gone up to look for my reading glasses. I went and looked out of the window and saw her getting out of the car. She has a red sports car with a personalised number-plate.'

He noted the incipient scorn in her voice on the last words, and said diffidently, 'Your husband has one, too, hasn't he?'

'I imagine that's where she got the idea. I suppose they were alike in some things — a taste for the meretricious and showy. Perhaps that's what they saw in each other.'

'What was she wearing?'

'Wearing?' The question seemed to surprise her. She thought a moment. 'A navy dress, sleeveless, with a red belt. And a red silk scarf over her hair. She pulled it off as she got out of the car and it hung round her neck.' She looked to see if that was enough and then went on with the story. 'I went downstairs and opened the door to her. She was in a temper and she'd been drinking — I could smell it on her breath. She demanded to know where David was. I said I had no idea, and she screamed, "Liar!" at me. I saw no reason to put up with that sort of thing so I started to close the door. She shoved her foot in the way of it. The dogs were barking their heads off and I told her she'd better move it before it got bitten, and she laughed in a sneering sort of way and said she knew all about the dogs and how they wouldn't hurt a fly.' Her eyes filled suddenly, shockingly with tears. 'That was the moment when it really came home to me. This dreadful woman knew all about my dogs. She probably knew everything about me and my home and family. He'd *told* her. She and David had discussed me and my private affairs together. It made me feel — quite *sick* for a moment.'

Slider nodded with painful sympathy. 'It must have been a dreadful shock. What did you do?'

'I told her David wasn't there, and that if she was so desperate to see the inside of my house she could come in and search for him if she liked. She said she'd already seen the inside of my house. She said that she and David had — had made love here once when I was out.' Her hands were trembling slightly, he noticed. She saw him looking at them, and put down the cutting she was holding and folded them together to keep them still. 'I said she was an unprincipled slut and told her to go away. She said she'd go all right when I'd told her where David was, because he'd stood

257

her up. She'd been waiting for him for nearly an hour in Romano's — the Italian restaurant at Baker's Wood, just up the road from here, do you know it?'

'I know the one.'

'It's a dreadful place.' She met his eyes. 'It was the first glimmer of light for me, thinking of her sitting in there alone all that time waiting for him. David and I went there once in desperation when there was a power cut at home. There was mould on the salad and the lasagne felt like rubber and smelt like sweat.'

'God, yes, I know what you mean.' Slider remembered his earlier thoughts about the flowers and the businessman's assignation. Out of the mouths of babes and sucklings? 'And where was David, in fact?'

'I said I didn't know, and I didn't. Do you think I would stoop to lie to a woman like that?' He looked at her steadily. 'He went out to the office that morning and I hadn't seen him or heard from him since; but that was quite usual. We lead our own separate lives for most of the time.'

'Had you been in all day?'

'No, I was out several times, shopping in the morning, to the bank early in the after-noon and to take the dogs out later. He could have been home while I was out, if that's what you mean.'

He nodded. 'What happened next with Mrs Andrews?'

'Nothing happened. She talked for a bit, told me more than I wanted to know about her relationship with David. She asked me several more times where he was, and then left.'

'At what time?'

'She couldn't have been here more than ten minutes or so.'

'Did she say where she was going?'

'No, and I certainly didn't ask. I was simply glad to be left in peace — though it wasn't for long, of course, because at about half past nine her wretched husband arrived.'

Now Slider did jump. 'Eddie Andrews came here?'

She raised an eyebrow. 'Didn't you know that?'

'No. You've filled in a gap for me.' Allowing for the drive here and back, it probably accounted for the missing time between his leaving the Mimpriss at ten to nine and returning there at ten thirty.

'He came looking for his wife, of course. He, at least, had the grace to apologise for disturbing me.'

'Was he drunk?'

'He'd been drinking. I think he was more upset than drunk. I felt rather sorry for him, really. He couldn't manage to come straight out with the question at first. He was beating around the bush, and I supposed he didn't know whether I knew about David and Jennifer, so I put him out of his misery and said I knew all about it, and that she had been here looking for David. Then his face —' she paused, thinking '— it *collapsed* with misery. He hadn't been sure, and now he was. I felt as though I'd kicked a puppy. He was such a pathetic little man.'

'How long was he here?'

'About a quarter of an hour. He was rather shaken and I felt sorry for him so I took him into the kitchen and gave him a cup of coffee — I had some already brewed. He asked where David was and I said I didn't know but that he obviously wasn't with Jennifer, since she was looking for him, and that I was pretty sure that he had finished with her.' Slider looked the question and she shrugged. 'I thought it would be better for him to think so — and it rather looked that way, to judge by Jennifer's desperation.'

'And what did he say to that?'

'He said, "But has she finished with him?" ' she said glumly.

'Ah,' said Slider.

'Yes, it was rather horribly perceptive. Anyway, he drank the coffee, thanked me very courteously, and left — that would be about a quarter to ten.'

'Did he say where he was going?'

'He said he was going to look for her, and when he found her, he'd wring her neck.' She met his eyes with a clear look. 'People say that sort of thing.'

'I know,' Slider said.

'Yes, I suppose you do. Well, he drove away and that was that.'

'And what time did your husband come home?'

The clear eyes moved away. 'I don't know. Not exactly. I went to bed at about eleven, and read for a bit before putting out the light. I was probably asleep by about half past. I didn't hear him come in. I was up early the next day and took the dogs out for a long run. By the time I got back he'd left for work.'

'He didn't wake you when he came in?'

'We have separate rooms,' she said, her voice as neutral as wall-to-wall beige Wilton.

'And you didn't see him when you got

up? Did you see his car?'

'He keeps it in the garage. I didn't go and check whether it was there or not.'

'So you don't actually know whether he came home at all that night?'

'I just assume that he did. But, no, if you put it that way, I couldn't say for certain.'

'Do you take sleeping pills?' Slider slipped the question in, and it was sequitur enough not to bother her.

'I didn't that night, though I do have diazepam for when I need it.'

Slider noted it mentally, though Tufty would surely have tested for that. He went on, 'What did your husband say when you told him about your visitors the evening before?'

'I didn't see him to speak to until Wednesday evening. And by the time he came home, I'd heard about Jennifer being dead, so I didn't mention it. I wasn't sure how he felt about her death, and I didn't want to know. The whole subject was too fraught to open up.'

'So you've never spoken to him at all about both the Andrewses coming here on Tuesday evening?'

She eyed him defensively. 'You seem to find that remarkable, but I don't go seeking out unpleasantness. It's a subject I would far rather not raise with anyone, and especially not with my husband. Why should I? It's not my business.'

'If Andrews killed his wife, and it was because she was having an affair with your husband —'

'If?'

'It's all supposition at the moment. We don't know that Andrews did it.'

She looked at him for a moment, but her eyes were focused through and beyond him. 'I suppose as a loyal wife I ought to be providing David with an alibi, but I'm a hopeless liar, and it's always safer to stick to the truth, isn't it? And the truth is that I don't know what time he came in on Tuesday night. But it doesn't matter, does it? Wherever he was, he wasn't with her.'

Chapter Ten

Fresh Words And Bastards New

'She thinks he did it,' Slider said to Joanna as they sat thigh to thigh in a quiet corner of the Kestrel. 'Or at least, not to put it too strongly, she's afraid he might have.'

Joanna lowered the level of her pint of Marston's by a quarter and put the glass down in the beam of sunshine that came in through the crooked, ancient casement window for the express purpose of turning it to liquid gold. 'But if she did, wouldn't she be sure to give him an alibi? Or do you think she's so fiendishly cunning she's trying a double bluff on you?'

'Good God, no! That sort of thing only happens in books. But there are people who just tell the truth, you know, because it's the right thing to do. Not many of them, granted.'

'She really impressed you, didn't she?'

Joanna looked at him curiously. 'The way you've described her to me, stunningly beautiful, intelligent, noble, good — it's enough to make a person chuck.'

'Don't be silly,' he said comfortably, nudging her knee. 'But if Meacher was out all night —'

'If. She didn't say he was.'

'Quite. But he didn't tell me he had an assignation with the Andrews woman that evening. He didn't tell me he'd been having an affair with her —'

'Would you, in his position? It doesn't mean he bumped her off.'

'Why are you so keen on him?' he asked resentfully.

'My darling dingbat, you've just had a thorough job done on you by a master — or should one say mistress? — of the art. You loathed Meacher on sight and you adored Mrs ditto, so it hasn't occurred to you that if he was out all night, *she* hasn't got an alibi either. Why shouldn't she have killed this ghastly woman?'

'Ridiculous!'

'Is it? Maybe she didn't know before that the affair was going on. Bleach-bag comes to her door and spills the beans, demands where Meacher is as if she's got a right to know, *and* brags that she's done it on the marital premises. Who has a better motive now?'

'I hate it when you're reasonable.'

'Maybe Jennifer never left the house again. Maybe Mrs M. did her right there and then on the doorstep in a fit of righteous, wifely rage.'

'Lady Diana, not Mrs M. And anyway, Jennifer wasn't killed violently, remember. Freddie thinks she was drugged to helplessness.'

'Even better. Lady Diana got her inside, gave her a drink, and drugged her.'

'With?'

'*I* don't know. I can't do everything for you.'

'She says she does have sleeping pills,' he said reluctantly.

'There you are then! She did her, bunged her in the pantry, then late at night drove her to the Rectory and shoved her down the hole, knowing that everyone would suspect Eddie Andrews, and that there was nothing to connect the deed with her.'

'It holds together —'

'Of course it does. I'm brilliant!'

'— so far, I was going to say. But why didn't Eddie see Jennifer's car when he arrived? And how did it get back to Fourways?'

'Lady D. hid the car temporarily, and took Jennifer home in it so as not to leave any traces in her own, of course.'

'And got back home — ?'

'Somehow. Bus, train, taxi, shanks's pony. Aeroplane.'

'I see. And if she did it, why did she tell me about the visits of the Andrewses at all?'

'She didn't know how much you knew. The fact that you were there was a worry. She had to think fast.'

'She did?'

'Notice,' Joanna pursued, 'how she cunningly deflected suspicion away from Eddie Andrews, by telling you she felt sorry for him and gave him a cup of coffee. That was so that she could plant the seed about her husband in your mind.'

'Why should she do that?'

'Because hubby is a much better smoke-screen. If *he's* guilty, she's innocent. You have to be innocent to be someone's alibi.'

'But she *wasn't* his alibi.'

'Which makes her even more innocent — too good even to lie for her own husband.'

'I love it when you're unreasonable,' he grinned, glad to discover she wasn't serious. They stopped talking while their toasted sandwiches were put in front of them. When they were alone again, he said, 'Joking apart, what we've got now is a much better motive for Eddie. If Jack Potter was right, Eddie didn't really believe, deep down, that Jennifer was straying; after his visit to Lady Di, he knew for certain that his worst fears were founded. I'm afraid he's still the front runner. We'll have to check up on Meacher, though.'

Joanna said, 'Poor thing, you so wanted it to be him instead of Eddie, didn't you?'

'It still might be. The thing that puzzles me about him is, why didn't he call Mrs Hammond when he heard about the body being found on her premises? If he was such an old friend, and was sorry for her . . . It's as if he's trying to distance himself from the whole thing.'

'Could be any number of reasons,' Joanna shrugged. 'People don't phone each other like anything, every day of the week. Especially when they ought to.'

'True,' he sighed. 'Well, it looks as though we know where Jennifer was going, anyway, when she left the Goat and told Jack Potter she was going to meet someone. But why didn't he keep the appointment?'

'Probably he was finished with her and that was his noble way of letting her know.'

'Unnecessarily cruel. I know restaurants like that. Lady Di said she went there once and had rubber lasagne that smelt like sweat.'

'Very graphic. I can see why you liked her.' Joanna grinned suddenly. 'It reminds me of the story of the man who went to a very bad Chinese restaurant. When he'd eaten his main dish the waiter came and asked him if everything was all right. He said, "Well, the duck was rubbery," and the waiter said, "Thank you, sir. We have bery nice rychees, too."'

When they emerged into the sunlight and walked towards their cars, he said, 'What time do you think your meeting will be finished?'

'I expect it'll last a couple of hours. Why?'

'I thought if I could get away early enough I ought to go and see Irene and try and sort things out.'

'I thought she said don't ring us, we'll ring you?'

'Yes, well she can't expect to make all the rules,' he said irritably. 'Besides, it's my house as much as it's hers, and if I can't stop her going there, she can't stop me.'

'It's rather more yours than hers, I would have thought, since you pay the mortgage and everything.'

'What do you mean by that?'

Joanna blinked. 'Sorry, which bit of the sentence are you having difficulty with?'

'I thought the subject would come up sooner or later. It all comes down to money, doesn't it?' he said angrily. 'These things always do.'

'What things?'

'Divorce, first wives versus second wives, the whole palaver! Mortgages and maintenance and who gets the pension! The next thing you'll be complaining that we live in penury while she swans about in a big house, and that I never spend any money on you.'

She whipped round on him like a cobra striking. 'Hold it right there! In the first place I'm not your wife, second or any other sort. In the second place I haven't the slightest interest in your money or what you do with it. All I want is for this business to be sorted out so that people can stop hurting each other, and you and I can have a little life together, and I can stop having to watch you turn grey and wrinkled as you wonder what the next ghastly cock-up will be. And in the third place,' she went on, forestalling his attempt to break in, 'if you ever speak to me like that again I shall smack you round the ear with a wet fish.'

'You'd assault a police officer?' he said feebly.

'In a second.'

They looked at each other for a moment. 'I'm sorry,' he said. 'Abject grovel. I get so strung up about it all.'

'I know. Just don't take it out on me.'

'I'm really sorry.' He kissed her contritely and she kissed him back. 'I don't deserve you.'

'I know,' she said.

'I miss my children.' It burst out of him without his meaning it to.

'I know,' she said again, in a different voice.

'Matthew sounded so sad on the phone the other night. And if I can't get her to agree to a settlement and the lawyers come between us, there'll be a contentious divorce and she'll get custody, and I'll be just another weekend father. I'll have to spend every Saturday of my life in McDonald's.'

She stepped close. 'Don't cry outside a pub, it looks bad.' He put his arms round her. 'It will come out all right,' she said.

'Go and see her, talk to her. Who could resist you? You'll work it out.'

'I love you,' he said.

'I know,' she said for the third time, and he felt her smile against his chest.

Atherton suspected Slider had sent him off to interview the priest on the assumption that it would keep him safe, and resented it. Of course, he mused, many priests through the ages had been seriously bonkers, so it didn't mean a thing — which Slider must know as well as he did, so it rather spoilt his argument, but he went on feeling resentful for as long as it suited him anyway.

The priest's house was across the road from the church with which St Michael and All Angels shared him. Atherton needed Slider to tell him the vintage of the church — St Melitus — though he put it down tentatively as (?) late Victorian, or at least not very old (?); but his own eye was enough to tell him that St Melitus Church House and Community Hall had been built, if that was the right word, within the last twenty years. To judge from its neighbours, a large Edwardian house had been knocked down to accommodate it, and it stuck out like a baboon's bottom: a flatfaced, ugly building of pale yellow brick with a roof too shallow and metal-framed windows too large for it. It had a porch, which was just a square slab of concrete meanly supported on two metal poles, and some unnecessary panels of barge-boarding by way of ornament, from which the paint was peeling like an unmentionable skin disease. The Community Hall was a single-storey extension to the side, with a flat roof and wire-cast windows. Bountiful Nature was represented by a plant-pot in the shape of giant boot made of something grey, which looked almost entirely but not quite unlike stone, which stood beside the Church House porch and contained the leggy ghosts of some dead pansies and a flourishing crop of chick-weed. The whole complex was surrounded by a liberally stained concrete apron for parking, and had all the warm invitation and spiritually uplifting charm of one of the less popular stalags.

Atherton thought of the aspiring beauty of St Michael's and the solid harmony of the Old Rectory, and wondered when it was that the church had completely lost its marbles; and what God thought of an organization that so passionately promoted ugliness. He rang the Church House doorbell, and it was answered by a tall man in khaki chinos, and a black teeshirt inscribed in white letters *If Jesus is your Saviour CLAP YOUR HANDS!*.

'Mr Tennyson?' Atherton enquired politely.

'Yes — are you from the police?'

'Detective Sergeant Atherton. I spoke to you earlier.'

'Yes, that's right. Come in.'

Inside, the house smelt like a school, Atherton discovered: dusty, with a faint combined odour of socks and disinfectant. 'Come through,' Tennyson said, leading the way to the back of the house. Here there was an open door labelled 'Waiting Room', a narrow room facing onto what would have been the garden if it hadn't been concreted over. It had french doors and two large picture windows — metal framed with wired glass — and since it was on the sunny side of the house it was as hot and dry as the cactus house at Kew. The low window-sills were of chipped quarry tile — as if the room had once been meant to be a conservatory — and along them lay a weary row of dead flies and wasps, desiccated corpses that Atherton could almost hear crackle in the sunshine beating in. The room contained a beat-up

274

sofa and two 'office' armchairs, a coffee-table bearing a sordid array of ancient, coverless magazines and a tin ashtray, the whole underpinned by a cherry-red cut-pile carpet pocked with cigarette burns, and spillings of something that had turned into that strange black toffee you find on carpeted pub floors.

'Nice place,' Atherton said. 'It must cut down on time-wasters.' Five minutes alone with your troubles in this room, he thought, and you'd slit your wrists — except, of course, that the window glass was unbreakable. On the whole, he'd sooner spend a night in the pokey.

Fortunately, Tennyson didn't understand his comment. 'It's a bit warm, but I'm afraid the windows don't open. They've warped, I think. Probably just as well,' he added, with unexpected bluntness. 'Nobody thinks twice these days about stealing from the Church.'

Tennyson was an interestingly gaunt man in his forties, with thick, bushy grey hair and deep-set brown eyes, handsome except that his skin had the dull pallor of the lifelong costive. He had a good, resonant voice, with a faint trace of an accent Atherton couldn't pin down — somewhere north of Watford Gap, anyway. Tennyson sat in one of the chairs and Atherton, after one dilating glance at the sofa, perched gingerly on the other. Somewhere in the room was a smell of babies, and he was rather fond of the trousers he had on.

He couldn't resist asking, 'Don't you sometimes long to exchange this for the Old Rectory?'

Tennyson shook his head. 'Couldn't afford it. I dread to think what their heating bills are like with those high ceilings. And the rooms here are better suited for our purposes. Besides,' he added, 'it just wouldn't be secure. Anyone could break in with those old windows, leave alone the fact that the garage doors don't lock.'

'How do you know that?' Atherton asked with interest.

'Frances Hammond's one of our stalwarts. I know the house very well. The oil man delivers through the end doors, and our sexton uses the tap in there, to get water for the flowers on the graves. Mrs Hammond doesn't mind. She's only too eager to help. Our best helpers are usually lonely women,' he added, not entirely as if he were glad about it.

'And talking of lonely women,' Atherton suggested.

'You want to know about Jennifer Andrews,' Tennyson picked him up. 'I wouldn't have said "lonely" was the best adjective in her case.'

'No? What would you have said, then?'

'Predatory.' Tennyson clasped his hands between his knees and stared broodingly at the carpet. Don't do that, Atherton wanted to warn him, you'll go blind. 'She was one of my flock, a member of the PC, she was on the flower rota, the bazaar committee, the coffee rota, the Happy Club, the Refugees Aid — she was into everything that was going. A valuable helper — but I didn't like her.'

'Are you allowed to say that?'

He glanced up with a bitter look. 'I'm a clergyman, not a saint. I'd sooner have Mrs Hammond's wool-gathering than Jennifer Andrews' help, for all her energy. Frances Hammond has the same urges, but at least she knows how to behave herself.'

'Urges?'

He paused, as if selecting the appropriate words, but when he spoke, it came out with the fluency of an old and oft-rehearsed complaint. 'There is a certain type of woman who is just attracted to priests. Altar babes, we call them. Something about the dog-collar turns them on

277

— it doesn't matter who's wearing it. Young, old, married or single. Sometimes they just gaze at you from afar and sublimate it by helping; but sometimes they make a nuisance of themselves. The worst sort throw themselves at you, always hanging around, trying to touch you, wangling ways of being alone with you.'

'Jennifer Andrews was one of those?'

'The worst. The sort that, when they finally get the message that you don't want them, make trouble out of spite. You're damned if you do and damned if you don't with women like that. Have you ever wondered why there are so many stories about priests messing around with parishioners? Sometimes the only way to avoid being falsely accused is to go ahead and do it.'

'It happens to coppers too,' Atherton said. 'The glamour of the uniform. Are you married?'

'No,' said Tennyson, 'but don't think that would stop them. My married colleagues get pestered to death just the same.'

'Did Jennifer Andrews falsely accuse you?'

Tennyson gave him a horrible look. 'What are you implying?'

Atherton spread his hands. 'I wasn't

implying anything. It was a straight question.'

'What you're really asking,' Tennyson contradicted, 'is whether I slept with her. And the answer's no.'

'But she wanted you to?'

'What do you think?' Tennyson said morosely, staring at the floor again.

Atherton summoned reserves of patience. This interview was not without peril after all. If the hideous surroundings didn't drive him to suicide, he could be bored to death, or choke on the smog of the vicar's gloom. He decided to try a direct question of fact.

'When did you last see Jennifer?'

'Tuesday afternoon,' he said promptly. 'I thought you knew that. Isn't that why you're here?'

Atherton adjusted smoothly. 'I want to hear it in your own words. Where did you see her?'

'She came here, of course. It was about six o'clock, or just before. She rang up earlier to ask if she could come and see me and I said no, it wasn't convenient, but she came anyway. She knew I'd be here, preparing for the mid-week service at seven. The woman knows my schedule better than I do. If there was any justice in law, clergy could get these women taken up as stalkers. Anyway,' he said, responding to Atherton's prompting expression, 'she turned up here, smelling of drink, and said she needed to talk to me. I brought her in here.'

Atherton glanced around him eloquently. 'That ought to have cooled her ardour a bit.'

'That's why I did it. She made a fuss about it, said why couldn't we go to my sitting room or the kitchen. Said why didn't I offer her a drink and why was I being so unfriendly. I told her I hadn't much time before service and if she had anything serious to say she'd better get on with it. So she dropped the smarm and took the hint, and it all came out. Her — lover, boyfriend, what you will — had dumped her.'

'Did she say who it was?'

'Oh, she made no secret about it. It was her boss. She'd been telling me all about it for weeks, trying to make me jealous — though she'd pretend it was a religious or a moral problem she had, so that she could tell me all the details. Thought it would get me excited. That's the trouble with these altar babes, they're cunning. And you've got to listen to them, or they're straight off telling everyone you don't care.'

Atherton tried a curve ball. 'So this was her boss at the pub, was it?'

The bushy eyebrows rose. 'Good Lord, no. The estate agent, David Meacher.'

'Have you ever met him?'

'Once or twice, at St Michael's events. Just to recognise him. He's chummy with Mrs Hammond. What he saw in Jennifer, I don't know.'

'I should have thought it was pretty obvious,' Atherton said mildly.

'I suppose you're right,' Tennyson said glumly. 'Anyway, she said she'd met him that day at a motel somewhere — one of their usual places. They'd spent the afternoon in bed, and then he'd calmly told her it was to be the last time.'

'Should you be telling me all this?' Atherton asked in wonder.

He scowled. 'You asked. I'm co-operating. Isn't that what you want?'

'I'm delighted,' Atherton said hastily. 'I just wondered whether —'

'It wasn't a secret. And she's dead now anyway, so what does it matter? I've told you, she just liked telling me these things as part of her game of seduction. I had to pretend to give her advice, tell her to give up her activities and be faithful to her husband, but that was part of it too, for her.

Gave her a thrill.'

This bloke was definitely in the wrong profession, Atherton thought. With his misogyny he should have been a fashion designer. 'When she told you this about being dumped, how was she? What was her mood like?'

'She was furious. She thought he had some other woman lined up, and she wasn't going to be dumped for anyone else. She said, "He's got some game going, and I'm going to scotch it." She even asked me if I knew what he was up to — as if I would! I said, "I hardly know the man," and she said, "All you men like to stick together." Then she said she was going to get him back, whatever it cost. I told her she ought to be satisfied with her husband, and stop running around with all these men.'

'There was more than one, then?'

'You ought to know,' Tennyson said, shortly and obscurely. 'But she seemed particularly keen on David Meacher — or that's what I'd thought. But when I said that about not running around, she said, "I'd drop them all in a moment if you made it worth my while." '

'What did she mean by that?'

'Use your imagination! She meant if I'd

go to bed with her. Not that she would have given up the others even if I did. She collected men like badges. It was quantity she liked, not quality.' He stopped abruptly, as if he thought that was a bit too uncharitable even for him. 'Well, anyway,' he went on, in a milder voice, 'I told her that was out of the question, and got rid of her. I said she knew what she ought to do, and that I had to go and get ready for service.'

'And what did she say to that?' Atherton was fascinated by this glimpse behind the scenes of an English vicarage.

'She said she knew what to do all right, that she was going to make Meacher see her again that night, and when she got him alone, he'd come back to her. And then she went.'

'What time was that?'

'About half past six, I suppose. I went to the window to make sure she'd gone, and she was sitting in her car outside. I thought she was lying in wait for me, but then I saw she was talking on the phone. And after a bit she drove off, still talking.'

Ringing David Meacher, Atherton thought, to make an assignation. That accounted for two of her mystery phone calls. Almost twenty minutes, that had been: he must have been hard to persuade. 'How well did you know her husband?' he asked next.

'Not at all. He wasn't a church-goer, and she didn't tend to have him with her at social things. I only knew what she told me about him, which wasn't much. It was mostly the things he'd bought her. Like her car — a Mazda RX5. Red.'

Atherton nodded. 'Dashing. And expensive.'

'He bought her a personal number-plate, too. Cost him thousands.'

Poor sucker, thought Atherton. It didn't sound as if he got much of a return on his investment. But it was all beginning to shape up nicely now. Motive was not everything, but it was a lot, and Eddie Andrews was coming out more of a martyr every minute.

The department was seething like a hedge full of sparrows when Slider got back. The extra help which had been drafted in crowded the confined space, no-one was at his own desk, phones were ringing, and there was a cluster round the whiteboard like dealers expecting a stock-market crash. Files and papers migrated across the room majestically as continents, and McLaren sneezed sloppily whenever anyone got within spraying distance.

'I'm not feeling well,' he said plaintively, as Hollis went past.

'Maybe it's everything you ate,' Hollis said heartlessly.

Atherton was perched on a desk, looking as elegant and pleased with himself as a particularly fashion-conscious gazelle with a Harvey Nichols card. 'Talking of eating,' he said, 'what *was* that meat in the canteen today?'

'What d'you think I am? A pathologist?' Hollis retorted.

'And the lemon sponge,' Atherton's voice descended to a tomb of horror, 'was made with synthetic flavouring.'

'Dear God!' Hollis responded like a poor man's Christopher Lee. 'I can't believe it!'

'Contrary to what you may think,' Norma said witheringly, 'your stomach is not the focal point of the universe. Some of us manage to raise our minds a fraction higher.'

'I shall treat your contempt with the remark it deserves,' Atherton retorted.

Slider felt the moment had come. 'If I can interrupt your lemon harangue for a moment,' he said. Sadly, no-one noticed. Ain't it always the way? he thought. He tried something else. *'Ten-hut!'*

That got them. All eyes turned his way. 'Ten hut?' Norma said wonderingly.

'He never forgets a phrase,' Atherton said kindly.

'Gather round, children, and let's see where we are,' Slider said. 'Atherton, how was your priest?'

'Turbulent,' Atherton replied, and gave his report. Then Slider recounted his morning's discoveries.

'So where does that leave us?' Norma asked, at the end of it. 'Are we still after Eddie, guv, or are you putting Meacher in the frame?'

'Eddie's still got to be favourite,' Hollis said. 'Closest to the victim, won't say where he was, and everything we find out about the woman gives him a better and better motive. Trying to knock off a priest —' He shook his head in wonder at the depravity of humankind, and blew reproachfully through his moustache. 'And if Andrews didn't know until Lady Di told him that Jennifer was knocking off Meacher, that could have been the last straw. A night of ghastly revelation, all his fears confirmed, then — bang.'

'I agree,' Atherton said. 'Meacher's got no motive. If he'd already chucked her, why should he want to kill her?'

'Because she wouldn't be chucked,' Norma suggested. 'And maybe she was planning to make trouble.'

'Who with?' Slider said. 'Meacher's wife already knew about her.'

McLaren made a nasal contribution. 'With the new bint, whoever she was, that he was chucking her for, that probably didn't know about her, but she might chuck him if she did, the new one might, if she told her about her — about herself, I mean, Jennifer.'

'What did Horace say, Winnie?' Slider asked the air.

'You don't know for sure that there *was* another woman,' Atherton said. 'It might be just what Meacher told her to get rid of her.'

'All right, but Meacher hasn't got an alibi,' Norma continued doggedly.

'We don't know that he hasn't,' Slider said. 'We'll have to check — when we can find him.'

'Why don't you ring him on his mobile, sir?' Swilley urged. 'Ask him where he is?'

'Thank you, Wonderbread, I did think of that. It's switched off.'

'That's suspicious for a start,' Atherton said. 'For a man like him, turning off your

287

mobile is like voluntary castration.'

'We know his reg number. Shouldn't we put out an "all cars", guv?' Anderson asked, with the eagerness of a former Scalextric owner.

'He's not a suspect yet,' Slider said. 'I can't gear up an expensive pursuit just because he's turned his mobile off. He'll answer eventually, or turn up somewhere. Meanwhile, let's hear what else we've got.'

'Forensic report on the house is negative,' Hollis said. 'No sign of a struggle anywhere, nothing that looks as if it'd been used for smothering.'

'What about the handbag?'

'We might have something there, guv. There's a set of marks on the handbag that don't belong to Andrews or the victim. A good, clear set.'

'Interesting,' Slider said. 'But, of course, she could have said to anyone at any point, "Chuck my bag over, will you?"'

'We've put 'em through the system, and they come up negative. Whoever it was, they had no previous.'

'That's what you'd expect in this case,' Slider said. 'It might be an idea to eliminate the staff at the pub, anyway.'

'What about at the estate agent's?' Anderson said.

'Yes, if nothing else, it'll be a way to get hold of Meacher's for the record,' Slider said.

'If the prints proved to be Meacher's, it wouldn't help either way,' Norma said. 'He could have handled her bag quite legitimately at work.'

'Yes, I know. I don't think the prints are going to be useful, except maybe as supporting evidence,' Slider said. 'What else?'

'We've had the report back from Mr Arceneaux about the semen sample,' Hollis said, 'and it seems there are two different types present.'

There was a crash as someone at the back of the room knocked something off a desk. 'All right, don't get excited,' Slider said. 'So she had sex with two men that day? Assuming for the moment that Meacher was one —'

'The priest could have been the other,' Atherton said. 'He could have been lying about not succumbing to her charms.'

'Or it could have been Eddie in the morning before going to work,' Anderson said.

'Or Potter in the storeroom before she left on her date,' Mackay said.

'Or person or persons unknown,' Atherton concluded impatiently. 'Are we going to start looking for an entirely new and unconnected suspect?'

'Why not?' Norma said, at least partly to annoy Atherton. Slider had noticed a slight friction between them of late. For some reason, Swilley had disapproved of Atherton's dating WDC Hart, the loaner who had come as his temporary replacement and stayed on for a few weeks after his return. Hart had gone back to her home station, and as far as Slider knew the affair was off; but something about the situation had annoyed Norma, and the banter that she and Atherton had always exchanged now sometimes had an edge to it. 'If she was stock-taking, she could have met another lover that night that we don't know about yet, who turned nasty — which would put Eddie telling the truth all along.'

Atherton looked lofty. 'What makes it Eddie for me is the car. If anyone else had killed her, I can't see they would have risked taking her car back. Only Eddie knew that Eddie wasn't home: anyone else risked having him come out to look as they parked it. And there again, the car keys were in her handbag, which was in his pickup. I can't see how you can get round that one.'

'She must have had a spare set,' Anderson said.

'Yes, but who would have had access to them, except Eddie? People keep their spare keys at home,' Atherton pointed out.

There was a silence of general consent to that. Slider moved on. 'All right, how's the welly brigade getting on?'

'The back garden's a blank, guv,' Hollis reported. 'Trouble is, it's been so dry there's nothing to take footmarks. They've done an inch by inch search of the Rectory garden from the bottom up and found nothing. Nothing on the wall at the bottom, either, to show anyone going over with a heavy object. Plenty of evidence of people walking along the railway embankment, but there's a broken fence-panel at the bottom of the footbridge, and apparently kids get through onto the embankment there, so it needn't have been Eddie. And there is an oil patch on the road not far from the footpath entrance, which could be where Eddie's van was parked. But lots of people have leaky cars.'

'Get a sample and have it tested,' Slider said. 'It should be possible to match it to the pickup.'

'Or otherwise,' Hollis concluded. 'And, of course, he could have parked there any time.'

'Well, that's a fine upstanding body of

negatives,' Slider said. 'Unless we get some eye witnesses —'

'When's the public appeal going out, guv?' someone called from the back.

'Tonight on the regional news at six thirty. So you'll all be drawing overtime tomorrow. I hope you're pleased.' A general response of mixed yesses and noes. 'And we shall need a team for tonight. Any volunteers?'

'I don't mind, sir,' said Defreitas, who was amongst the uniformed men drafted in.

'By golly, I hate a volunteer,' Hollis said. 'What's up with you, Daffy? Ain't you got no home to go to?'

Defreitas looked embarrassed. 'As a matter of fact, no. The wife and me are not getting on. I'd just as soon stop out, and earn a bit extra while I'm at it.'

'As the actress said to the bishop,' Atherton concluded for him.

'What about you, Jim?' Hollis said. 'With your lifestyle, the extra wad must come in useful.'

'Count me out,' Atherton said. 'I've got a date tonight.'

Norma glanced at him sharply, and he gave her a defiant look in retum.

'I'll leave you to sort out the rota,' Slider said to Hollis. 'Meanwhile, let's get back on the street, boy and girls, and ask those questions. I want you to ask about vehicles: Eddie's, Jennifer's, and let's include Meacher's this time. I'd like to end up with a complete log of where they were every minute. Re-interview the householders in St Michael Square. Any luck with the neighbour on the other side, by the way?' he asked Norma.

'No, boss, still no answer. I think they must be away.'

'Well, it's probably not important. They wouldn't be likely to have heard anything from that end, anyway. But keep trying. And let's extend the house-to-house to the surrounding streets. Any nocturnal comings and goings. Any sightings of our three vehicles. What time did Jennifer's car get back home? Talk to the householders on the other side of the railway, whose windows look onto the embankment: did they see Eddie, or anyone else, humping a suspicious-looking bundle along there late at night? And let's have a team at the footbridge to find who are the regular users, and whether they saw anything. The back garden's still the best way to the terrace. Swilley, keep chasing Forensic for the report on her clothes. She was somewhere before she was down that hole.'

Chapter Eleven

Do You Remember An Inn, Miranda?

When patient telephoning eventually located Meacher, he was back at his office in Chiswick. Having clapped a metaphorical hand over the jam-jar, Slider and Atherton hurried round while he was still buzzing with irritation.

'I've been looking at properties, if you must know. I wasn't aware I had to account for my whereabouts to you, or anyone.'

'You've been out on business with your mobile turned off?' Atherton said.

'I turned it off to save the battery. I forgot to recharge it last night — if it's any of your business. Really, this is too much!'

'Do you think we might talk to you privately for a moment?' Slider asked emolliently. Meacher's assistant — a different one, Jennifer's replacement, he assumed, a flatfaced young woman of obviously high breeding and presumably correspondingly low pay — averted her gaze abruptly at his words and concentrated on her computer screen, cheeks aglow.

Meacher also looked, and then, with a theatrical sigh, said, 'Oh, very well, if it will get you to go away and leave me in peace. Come through to the back. Victoria, I shall be five minutes. No calls until I come back.'

'Right-oh,' Victoria said, with false cheerfulness; her eyes followed them anxiously as Atherton and Slider trooped after Meacher into the small back office and shut the door. The room contained a sink with a hot-water geyser and a table with tea- and coffee-making equipment on it, four filing cabinets, and boxes of stationery stacked against the unoccupied wall. Another door, ajar, revealed a lavatory and washbasin. There was nowhere to sit and barely room to stand, and this seemed to please Meacher, who almost smiled as he leaned against the sink and folded his arms across his enviably suited chest with an exaggerated air of relaxation. He looked guilty as hell to Atherton, who was almost ready to give up the Eddie theory in favour of nailing this sartorial rival.

'Right, make it quick,' Meacher said. 'I have a business to run.'

'It can be as quick as you care to make it,' Slider said evenly. 'Just tell me where you were on Tuesday night, and we'll be off.'

'It's none of your damn' business where I was. I don't have to answer to you,' Meacher said impatiently.

Slider sighed. 'This is just time-wasting. I thought you were in a hurry?'

'I'm not in a hurry to tell you my private business.'

'Not as private as all that,' Atherton said, in a tone calculated to annoy. 'The Target Motel hardly counts as private property within the meaning of the act. Rather a hackneyed choice for a man of your sophistication, I thought, by the way. Or did you think that was all she merited?' Meacher stared. Atherton added kindly, 'The "she" I'm referring to is Jennifer Andrews, just in case you were going to waste more time by asking.'

'I don't know what you're talking about,' Meacher said, while his mind worked frantically behind his fixed eyes.

'Yes, you do,' Slider said. 'You and Jennifer Andrews spent Tuesday afternoon together at the Target Motel.' Meacher's confidence had been such that he hadn't even bothered to use a false name. 'The registration clerk has identified Jennifer from her photograph, and he says you've been there several times before and he's quite willing to pick you out from a line-up if necessary. And,' he added a body blow to the reeling Meacher, 'the post-mortem found semen in Mrs Andrews' vagina. Fortunately the sample is good enough to get a DNA fingerprint from.'

Slider was punting on this last, since until they had a sample from Meacher to compare with, they couldn't know the semen was his; but it was a fair guess that they hadn't gone to the motel to play bridge. Meacher seemed to sag as the confidence trickled out of him into a little heap of sawdust at his feet.

'What intrigues us most, you see,' Atherton followed up with a smart left hook, 'is that you didn't tell us this before. You spent the afternoon engaging in social intercourse with Mrs Andrews — the last afternoon of her life — and didn't think to mention it. Does that seem like the behaviour of an innocent man to you?'

Meacher rallied enough to get his gloves up. 'Why should I mention it? I didn't want my private life pawed over by a pack of prurient policemen.' That wasn't easy to say, and Atherton gave him grudging admiration. Meacher even looked surprised at himself, but followed up his advantage quickly. 'Anyone could guess that as soon as you knew about *that* you'd start imagining all sorts of other things — just as you are doing, it seems. Yes, I saw her in the afternoon, but that's the last time I saw her, and I know nothing about her death. *Now* are you satisfied?'

Slider pulled his chin judiciously. 'Well,' he said slowly, 'there is just one other little matter. You agreed to meet her in Romano's restaurant at eight fifteen that evening, but you didn't show up. After waiting for three-quarters of an hour she went round to your house in a state of agitation, looking for you. She spoke to your wife, and told her all about it.'

Meacher started at that. So, Slider thought, Lady Diana still hasn't told him. Now, was that odd of her, or not?

'After leaving your house, Mrs Andrews disappears from view — and so do you,' Slider went on. 'So when I discover you've concealed information from me about your relationship with her, I can't help wondering if she didn't find you after all, when she went looking for you. If perhaps you and she were together for those vital hours. You do see my problem, don't you?'

Meacher made a few silent passes before he managed to strike speech. 'It's preposterous. You can't march in here accusing me of murder —'

'I didn't hear you say murder,' Atherton said quickly, looking at Slider. 'Did you say murder, sir?'

'No, it was Mr Meacher who said murder.'

'Don't play your infantile games with me!' Meacher spluttered. 'I know a great many influential people. If you think you can come in here making these ridiculous accusations —'

'Not so ridiculous from where I'm standing,' Slider said. 'If you were innocently engaged all night, the night she died, tell me all about it, and then I can cross you off the list. You won't get rid of me otherwise.'

Silence fell in the little room. Beyond the door to the shop, the gentle murmur of Victoria's voice could be heard answering a telephone enquiry, interspersed with the flat clacking of the keyboard as she typed in information. The tap behind Meacher dripped softly into the stainless-steel sink, heartbeat slow, clock steady. Beside him, Slider felt Atherton almost quivering with eagerness restrained, like a sheepdog at the beginning of the trials who has just seen the ewes released at the far end of the field.

'Very well,' Meacher said at last, trying to sound stern and condescending and not quite managing it. 'I'll tell you about it, but only so that I don't have you hanging around here ruining my business day after day. I had been seeing Jennifer, but it was all over. She'd been seeing someone else — she didn't tell me who — and she was obviously more interested in him than me. I told her when we met at the Target that I didn't care to share her favours. She said very well, in that case we had better call it a day.'

'Did this genial conversation take place before or after sex?' Atherton asked.

Meacher's face darkened. 'How dare you? It's none of your damned business whether —'

'We've been over this already,' Slider said patiently. 'The only way out of this situation is to tell me the truth. If Jennifer was happy to split up with you, why did she arrange another meeting with you later that night? And why didn't you turn up?'

'Oh, all *right!*' Meacher cried petulantly, and then remembered Victoria and lowered his voice. 'All right, if you must know I was getting tired of her. She was getting more and more demanding, wanting to see me every day, being ridiculously possessive. It was becoming unpleasant — and dangerous: she was starting to get careless, and I was afraid any minute her husband was going to find out about it. I didn't fancy having him after me. He didn't strike me as the understanding sort. So I told her when we met at the Target that it had to end. She didn't like it. In fact, she got quite hysterical. I had to take her to bed to calm her down.' He intercepted an expression of distaste on Atherton's face and said angrily, 'Do you want the facts or don't you? Because if you're going to stand in judgement over me like some —'

'Go on,' Slider said. 'What time did she leave the motel?'

'About half past three, I suppose. I didn't notice exactly.'

'And where was she going?'

He shrugged. 'She didn't say. Home, I imagine.'

'How was she when she left? What was her mood?'

'She was all right — quite calm. She

seemed to have accepted the situation: I was surprised when she rang me again.'

'This was at half past six?' Atherton put in.

'That's right.' He didn't question how they knew. 'She said she must talk to me. I said couldn't it wait? She said no, there were important things we had to sort out. Then she started crying and begging. The last thing I wanted was to see her again, but I had to promise to, to stop her crying. So I said Romano's at eight fifteen.'

'But you weren't intending to keep the appointment?'

He hesitated. 'I hadn't decided. I thought I would. But as the time approached I couldn't bear the thought of sitting in a restaurant with her making a scene. So I didn't go.' He looked from Slider to Atherton and back. 'You say she went to my house?' he asked thoughtfully.

'Your wife told her she didn't know where you were. Quite an elusive character, aren't you?' Meacher said nothing. 'Would you like to tell us where you were between nine p.m. Tuesday night and nine a.m. Wednesday morning?'

'I was with someone.' They both waited, looking at him. 'I was with a woman,' he said impatiently.

'All night?' Slider asked.

'All evening and all night. I went to her flat at around eight thirty, and I stayed with her until I left to come to the office in the morning.'

'Name and address?'

'I'm certainly not going to tell you that,' Meacher said, loftily as a gentleman whose honour has been impugned. 'What do you take me for?'

At the moment, I wouldn't take you on a bet, Slider thought, but he said patiently, 'Mr Meacher, unless we can speak to this person and ask her to verify your whereabouts, you remain unaccounted for. I can't cross you off the list.' He stopped there, and maintained an insistent silence, while Meacher stared at the floor, apparently weighing things up.

'All right,' he said eventually, and with a show of reluctance. 'I was with Caroline Barnes — my assistant, whom you saw last time you came harassing me here. But I don't want her upset. Her relationship with me is our private business. If you have to ask her questions, for God's sake be tactful. She's very young and very sensitive.'

Slider took down her name, address and telephone number, with weariness at his heart. This was going to be nothing but an added complication. Neither Meacher's reluctance nor his capitulation rang true.

'Oh, there is just one other thing, sir,' he said, as they were turning to go. 'We have a set of fingermarks on Mrs Andrews' handbag which don't belong to her or her husband, and we would like to eliminate anyone who might have touched it during the last day. Would you be so kind as to come along to the station and give us your fingerprints for comparison purposes?'

Meacher stared long and hard, trying to work out if it was a trap, but Slider looked steadily and blandly back, and eventually he agreed. 'I can't come right away — I have some things to clear up here first.'

'Very well, sir, but as soon as you can, if you wouldn't mind.'

'Things to clear up!' Atherton said, when they were out on the street again. 'You can bet your last banana he's ringing up his alibi. He'll write the script and she'll read it out when we come asking.'

Slider didn't disagree. 'We'll have to go through the motions, but it'll be one of those alibis you can't prove or disprove. It just leaves us with the same questions. Why should he want to kill Jennifer? If it was him, how did he do it, and where, and how did he transport the body? And if he didn't kill her, where was he, and why all the subterfuge?'

'You really did hope to cross him off,' Atherton discovered.

'Of course. One suspect at a time is enough for me.'

'But you quite like Eddie and don't like Meacher,' Atherton pointed out.

'Right. I hoped if he wasn't cross-offable, he'd be definitely suspect. One or the other. Look, why don't you get over to this Caroline sort right away, and get her story? Even if you can't get to her before he does, you might unsettle her by turning up so soon. Or wear her down with your charm and finesse.'

'Or warn her she's next in line, after Jennifer, when he's tired of her,' Atherton suggested.

'You're devious!'

'Maybe I am, and maybe I'm not,' Atherton said mysteriously. 'Where are you off to?'

Slider looked at his watch. Just after half past four: at that moment, someone some-where in the country was saying, 'I think she's really clever, that Carol Vorderman.'

'I think I'll go and have another look at

the Old Rectory,' he said. 'I'd like to see if what Mr Tennyson told you about the garage doors is right.'

As Slider had remarked before, there were two sets of wooden double doors in the left-hand third of the Old Rectory's façade. The far left pair were older, of tongue-and-groove with a simple brown Bakelite doorknob, the wood uneven, shrunk with age and split at the bottom, the black paint generations thick, so that it was cracking down the grooves where it was unsupported. There was an old-fashioned keyhole, heavily bunged up with paint. The other pair of doors had a Yale lock and a newish brass mortice-type key-hole below, so it was easy to tell which pair the vicar had meant. Slider tried the Bakelite handle, and it turned, the door opening towards him effortlessly: Tennyson was right. But the moment he opened the door a fusillade of barking smote his ear and made him jump, and he closed it hastily and stepped back. A moment later the open kitchen window was pushed wider and Mrs Hammond looked out, her soft face creased with anxious enquiry. From the simultaneous boost in volume, Slider guessed that Sheba was in the kitchen with her.

'It's all right, it was only me,' Slider said. 'Detective Inspector Slider,' he added, in case she had forgotten him.

'Oh! I see,' she said, like a willing-to-please child asked an incomprehensibly difficult question.

'I wonder if I could have a look at your garage and storerooms? Would that be all right? May I?'

Mrs Hammond bit her lip, thinking it through. 'You'd better come in,' she said. Yes, Slider thought, that would be a good start. She withdrew her head, and he walked down to the front door. She had some difficulty in opening it, and when eventually she confronted him, she said, 'It's a bit stiff,' and gave a placatory laugh, not with amusement but as a threatened cat purrs. 'Warped, I'm afraid. Mostly people go round the back — those who know.'

She looked at him anxiously, neat in her middle-aged print frock with matching fabric belt. Marks and Sparks: he recognised the one-size-fits-all style of it. Apart from the anxious expression, her face was a smooth indeterminacy framed by her amorphous, middle-aged waved hair. There were thousands of women like her, millions, he thought, up and down the country, going about their dull, useful routines: women who defined themselves by their men, as daughters, wives, mothers; whose time had been used up with cooking, washing-up, fetching, listening, agreeing. Their lives had been lived always at one remove, on the dry shore above the high-tide mark of passions, in a sheltered place out of the stinging wind, out of the swing of the sea. Great events did not happen to women like her. They did not rub shoulders with murder. How bewildering it must all be to her.

'I'm sorry to disturb you,' he began politely, and she jumped in with, 'Oh, it's all right, Father's having his physiotherapy at the moment.' Her being disturbed was not in question with her, it was her father who mattered. 'That's why Sheba's in with me, to keep her out of the way. She's been rather upset since all this . . .' She led the way back to the kitchen. The dog barked once behind the door at their approach, and as Mrs Hammond opened it, backed away, looking at Slider and growling, but with the tail swinging hesitantly, just in case. 'It's all right, Sheba. Be quiet, there's a good girl,' Mrs Hammond said, catching hold of the collar. 'Just let her sniff your hand, and she'll be all right.' The dog sniffed his offered hand briefly, and then, released, smelt his shoes extensively, with embarrassing canine frankness. Then, apparently satisfied, she went back to her basket in the corner and curled down. Slider noted she was chewing the piece of rag again. Obsessive behaviour. That dog must be an animal psychiatrist's dream.

Mrs Hammond asked. 'Can I get you a cup of tea?'

'No, no tea, thank you. I'd just like to see what's beyond the kitchen door, here, if I may. You have storerooms, I believe?'

'Yes, and the boiler-room, and the garage. Is there something wrong?'

'No, not at all. Nothing to worry about,' he said, with his most reassuring smile. 'I'd just like to get the geography straight in my head, if you wouldn't mind.'

She looked unreassured, but opened the further door and stepped back to let him through. He found himself in a stone-floored passage about four feet wide, the whitewashed walls of rough stone, like the outside of the house. There were two doors on either side, of solid tongue-and-groove, painted dark green, and the only light came through the glass panel of the door at the far end.

'This is the oldest part of the house,' Mrs Hammond said. 'This and the kitchen. It probably goes back to the fourteenth century, or even earlier. A friend of ours who knows about houses told us.'

'Is that Mr Meacher?' Slider hazarded.

She flushed. 'Oh! Yes — yes, it is. Do you know him?'

'Yes, I've met him,' Slider said. 'What's in these rooms?'

'Nothing in particular,' she said. 'They're just storerooms.'

'May I have a look?'

'Oh. Well, if you want. They're not locked.'

He could see that. They had only country latches, and no keyholes, though the doors to the left — the street side of the house — had bolts on the outside. When Slider opened the first left-hand door he found that the room was quite empty except for a bundle of torn hessian sacks in the corner. It was about eight feet long by six wide, and windowless. The walls were whitewashed, and the door was rather battered and splintery at the bottom, with grooves down to the pale wood under the paint as if it had been gouged with a garden fork.

'We used to keep the gardener's tools in

here,' Mrs Hammond said, 'but there's a shed outside now, which is more convenient. So we don't use it for anything, really.'

Slider thought of his house at Ruislip, which assumed no-one had more belongings than could dance on the head of a pin, and wondered at having so much storage space you could leave a whole room empty. Glorious waste!

The first room on the right was the same size, but had a small, high window, and smelt strongly of apples. There were boxes of them stacked around the walls, a sack of carrots, strings of onions on hooks on the walls, and jars of jams and fruit on a long shelf along one wall. There were other boxes too, of tins of dog food and tomatoes and so on, and various bits of junk lying around — a jumble of empty flower-pots, a child's cot mattress, a set of pram wheels with the handle still attached, an ancient vacuum cleaner, a stack of books. 'The dry store,' she said, waving a nervous hand round it. 'Nothing here, you see. Nothing important, anyway.'

The second door on the left gave onto another windowless room, which was furnished with self-assembly wine racks, about a quarter full with bottles of wine, some looking authentically dusty. The second room on the right housed nothing but the smell of oil and a massive boiler, its tin chimney bending precariously before disappearing through the wall, with the fine carelessness of earlier, uninspected days.

The door at the end of the corridor was locked, but the key was in it. It gave onto a garage in which the Range Rover now stood. On the far side again was another half-glass door, unlocked, beyond which was the empty garage whose doors he had tried earlier. There was a cold-water tap in the middle of the far wall, and in the wall at the back of the garage was another door. Slider opened it, and found a tiny yard, walled in all round, containing what was obviously the filling-cock to an underground oil tank.

Slider closed the door again and turned to Mrs Hammond, who was waiting at his elbow nervously, as if expecting to be ticked off about something.

'When I tried those doors just now,' Slider said, nodding to the pair, whose cracks and chips and missing chunks were cruelly revealed by the bright sunshine outside, 'they weren't locked.'

She moved her hands anxiously. 'Oh,

well, no, they don't lock, you see. At least, I think there was a key once, but I don't know where it is now.'

'So those doors are always unlocked?'

'Well, yes.' She searched his face for clues as to where the rebuke would come from. 'You see, the oil man brings his pipe in through here and out to the back yard.' She gestured towards the rear door. 'For the central heating. It means I don't have to be in for him. He can just come when he likes.'

'Aren't you worried about people breaking in?' Slider asked.

She looked mildly surprised. 'But why should they? There's nothing here they could steal.'

'The Range Rover?'

'Oh, but they couldn't get it out, could they? I *never* leave the keys in it. And the doors to that garage *are* locked.'

'Someone might go through into the passage — there's all your father's wine, for instance. That must be valuable. And they could get through the kitchen to the rest of the house.'

She shook her head. 'I lock the door at night — I mean the door from the garage into the passage. And Sheba's in the kitchen at night. She'd bark if anyone broke in.'

'And on the night in question, the Tuesday night, she didn't bark?'

'Oh, no. I'd have heard her. I always wake if she barks.' She seemed to falter. 'Is there something wrong? Did you — were you — ?'

'It occurred to me to wonder,' he said, 'whether Mrs Andrews was left in your garage during that night, the Tuesday night. Or perhaps in one of your storerooms. I don't like to upset you by the thought, but —'

She still seemed puzzled. 'Oh, no, she couldn't have been,' she said. 'I'm sure she was never in any of the storerooms, or the garage, except when I was there. Why should you think so?'

He tried to find a gentle way of making her understand. 'You see, we know that she was moved at some point — that she wasn't laid straight in the hole where you found her. She was put somewhere else first, for some hours and then moved later.' Mrs Hammond seemed to pale, and put her fingers to her mouth as she understood him at last. 'And it occurred to me that perhaps whoever killed her used your garage at first —'

'That's horrible!' she said, through her fingers. 'No, I don't believe it. I'm sure she

never was — not there! Oh dear, I can't —'
She turned away, and with her back to
him, fumbled a handkerchief out of her
pocket and blew her nose. 'No, it's not
possible,' she said, muffled but for once
definite. 'Sheba would have barked.'

They returned to the kitchen. The dog
looked up briefly at them and then down
again, resting her nose on her paws, her
sore red ears twitching.

'Your bedroom is above here?' Slider
asked.

Mrs Hammond turned to him. Her eyes
looked a little pink and frightened. He had
upset her by talk of the body, he saw, but
how could it be helped?

'My bedroom and the boys' rooms and
our bathroom. Do you want to see?'

'No, thank you, not now. Your father's
bedroom is at the other end of the house?'

'Over the dining-room; and Mother's was
over the drawing-room, with their bathroom in between.' She searched his face
again. 'But he has a bell by his bedside to
call me, if he wants me. I'm a light sleeper.'

It was sad how anxious she was to avoid
blame, he thought. 'And in fact your father
didn't call you on Tuesday night?'

'No, he had a good night. He slept
through.'

'Yes, so he told me. Does he take sleeping pills?'

'No, but he does have pain-killers. He was offered sleeping pills, but he wouldn't have them. He doesn't like the idea.'

Slider left no further on than when he had arrived. All the same questions remained to be answered. It had to be Eddie, didn't it? But if he did it, *where* did he do it? And where did Meacher come in? There was a hole in the story somewhere, and he was running out of leads. He had to hope that Porson's appeal to the Great British Public would turn something up.

He was on his way back to his car when something that Lady Diana had said came back to him, and he diverted to the Goat In Boots. Mrs Potter was 'upstairs, resting', according to her husband. 'This business with Jennifer has knocked her bandy,' he confided. 'Well, it's got to all of us, really. One minute someone's with you, and the next —' He shook his head dolefully. 'I could go and wake her for you,' he offered doubtfully.

'No, it's all right, I've just got one question, and you can answer it just as well. You've told me that when Jennifer left for her meeting on Tuesday night, she was wearing a navy dress with a red belt?'

'That's right.'

'Can you remember whether she had a red scarf as well?'

'What, on her head, you mean?'

'On her head, round her neck — anywhere.'

Jack pondered weightily. 'I dunno,' he said at last. 'I can't say I remember really. She could have had, but —'

Karen, the barmaid, who was polishing glasses nearby with her ears on stalks, interrupted these musings impatiently. 'But she did, don't you remember? A red silk scarf. It was tied to the strap of her handbag.'

Oh, very seventies, Slider thought. 'You're sure about that?' he asked Karen.

'Yes, course I am,' she said. '*You* remember, Jack?'

'Can't say I do. But she could have. I wouldn't swear one way or the other.'

'That's all right,' Slider said. 'Thank you,' to Karen. 'It's just a small point, but I wanted to clear it up.' So the scarf was real, he thought as he walked across the square; and sometime during the evening she had lost it. Somewhere between the Meacher house and the grave. It was something to file away at the back of the mind. Probably it wasn't important — not important unless it turned up in an interesting place, that is.

The CID room was crowded again: the troops, together with various hangers-on who had nothing better to do, were waiting around the television for the appeal to come on. It would be Porson's first television appearance since he came to Shepherd's Bush, and the excitement was as palpable, and probably of the same kind, as among spectators at a Grand Prix hoping for an accident.

Anderson and Mackay were playing the Porson game. 'What's the Syrup's favourite part of north London?' Mackay asked.

'Barnet, of course. Too easy.'

'What's his favourite place in Leicestershire?'

Anderson looked blank. '*I* don't know. I've never been to Leicestershire.'

'Wigston,' Mackay said triumphantly.

'Never heard of it. You can't have that one.'

'All right, how does he like to travel, then?'

'Dunno,' Anderson said, after some thought.

'By hairyplane,' Mackay said triumphantly.

'*Hairyplane?*'

'For God's sake, shut up, you two imbeciles,' Swilley said impatiently. 'Here's the boss.'

Slider squeezed through to the front. 'Where's McLaren?'

'Gone home, guv. Sick as a parrot,' Mackay said.

'About time, after he's infected all of us,' Anderson put in.

'Atherton back yet?'

'He's just coming in,' Swilley said, gesturing towards the door.

Atherton slithered through to them, looking glum but resigned. 'Caroline Barnes confirms the alibi,' he told Slider, without preamble. 'I tried to shake her, but she stuck to it, though she looks nervous as hell. She says he came round, they had supper and went to bed.'

'A simple story.'

'And none the less incredible for that. So there we are.'

'Yes, there we are,' Slider said. He pondered. 'It could be true.'

'But then again . . .' Atherton sighed.

'Maybe someone will have seen Meacher's car parked outside,' Slider suggested.

'Yes, that would be handy. But of course if no-one remembers seeing it, that doesn't prove it wasn't there. And knowing our luck —'

'Shh, here it comes,' Swilley said. There was a chorus of hoots and wolf-whistles, which Slider silenced in the interests of discipline. However odd Porson was in his mannerisms, he was still the boss, and Slider could not let them mock him in front of him. But in fact, Porson was surprisingly good on the screen. The portentous, trade-unionist delivery did very well on television, and under the unnatural lighting everyone looked as if he could be wearing a wig; the regional news presenter, indeed, looked as if he was breaking in a face for a friend. And the Super only slipped in one Porsonism, when he affirmed that anyone calling with information would have their unanimity respected — and even then you had to be alert to catch it.

When it was over there was a storm of applause, not entirely ironic. Then the hangers-on drifted away, and the night team went to their desks to wait for the first telephone calls. Atherton stood up and stretched, brushed down his trousers, and said, 'Well, I'm off.'

'Oh, yes, you've got a date, haven't you?' Slider said absently.

'Yup. How do I look?'

Slider examined him. 'Too excited.'

'Somewhere at this moment a woman is preparing for an evening of bliss with me,' Atherton said, 'and there isn't a thing she can do to me that I don't deserve. If she plays her cards right, she could be staring at my bedroom ceiling till dawn.'

'Who is this thrice-blessed female?'

But Atherton only smiled enigmatically and sloped out like a cat on the prowl. And the first phone rang.

Chapter Twelve

Lettuce, With A Gladsome Mind

He half thought that Irene would be out on a Friday night, but when he had called her to suggest the meeting she had grudgingly agreed.

'Matthew won't be here, you know,' she said. 'Friday's Scouts night.'

Slider tried not to sound disappointed. 'It's you I want to see.'

Perhaps his choice of words touched her, for she became defensive. 'What time d'you expect to get here? Though knowing you that's a silly question.'

'I'll try and get away by seven, so I should be with you before half past.'

'Half past seven? You don't expect me to cook for you?'

'I can pick up a sandwich or something and eat it in the car,' he said, already resigned.

But she said, 'Oh, I can make you a sandwich. I can do *that*,' as if some other and outrageous personal attention had been in question.

So when the Syrup's broadcast was over he detached himself from the tentacles of the department and hurried down to the car before anyone could think up any more urgent questions for him.

It was a fine summer evening; the air was heavy with the baleful stench of barbecue. Everywhere flesh was being scorched by flames, and a pall of oily smoke hung over London. It was like living in the sixteenth century, he thought. Funny how willing people were to eat burnt sausages and limp lettuce, provided you put them on a paper plate and made them do it in discomfort out of doors. At least he could be sure Irene wouldn't do that to him. Barbecuing was men's work: she was a very traditional woman.

When he reached the house he thought for a minute there was someone else there: he'd forgotten she'd changed her car since she'd been with Ernie. She had a Toyota Celica — what Porson would call a Cecilia, of course. A bit posh for Irene. He assumed Ernie had put some money towards it, if he hadn't bought it entirely, and wasn't sure how he felt about that; then told himself it was damn well time he stopped feeling like anything about Irene and Ernie, if he really intended her to be his wife *quondam* but not *futurus*.

He had a key, but tactfully rang the bell, and stood on the doorstep of what he had called home with many painful feelings, which were only sharpened when she opened the door to him and stood looking at him nervously and with an inadequately hidden expectancy.

'Hello,' he said, since she didn't seem to be going to.

'I thought you'd be late.' She didn't move to let him in.

'Shall I go away again?'

'Don't be silly,' she said, and stepped back at last. She was nervous, and she had too much scent on: it hung in the hall like a cloud of insecticide and made his eyes burn. She closed the front door, and he suddenly felt nervous too, trapped in this small space with her, not knowing what she was feeling or what she might say. It was absurd not to know how to behave with his own wife of so many years; and he looked at her back as she shut the door and thought, *She's been to bed with Ernie Newman,* and it completely threw him.

Horrid images flashed up in his mind without his volition: her with Ernie; her with Ernie in the nude; her doing with someone else what she had only ever done with him before. Sex was such an absurd stroke revolting thing when it was someone other than oneself doing it.

'Are you all right?' Her voice brought him back to reality.

'What? Yes — yes, of course.'

'You looked as if you had a pain, or something.'

'No, I'm all right. You look very nice,' he said almost at random, but found that, indeed, she did. She had always been neat and pretty; tonight her smooth short dark hair was curling slightly with the heat, so that it looked like duckling feathers, and the descent from severity suited her. Her makeup was carefully done, and her pale mauve cotton dress left bare her slender arms, which were lightly tanned. 'Is that a new frock?'

'This old thing? I've had it years.' But she seemed pleased, almost fluttered. 'No-one says "frock" any more,' she went on, her eyes scanning his face on a mission of their own.

'Bishops do.'

'Don't be silly,' she said again, automatically; and then grew brisk. 'Well, don't stand about in the hall like a visitor. Come into the lounge.'

Everything was perilously the same: the three-piece suite, the carpet, the television tuned to some appalling sitcom which, to judge from the *Beano* jokes and weirdly 1950s stereotypes, had been written as a school project by a team of bright fifth-formers.

No, one thing was different. There was no little button nose pressed against the screen. 'No Kate?' he asked.

Irene's eyes slid away. 'I arranged for her to go to Flora's for the night.'

'Oh.' Slider wondered why she was embarrassed. Did she feel guilty for depriving him of his daughter? Or was it something else? What? Her guilt made him feel wary. Was there trouble here for him?

'I thought it would be better for us,' she went on with elaborate casualness, 'to be on our own so we could — talk freely.'

'Oh,' said Slider again. A horrid thought was struggling to be born, and he was reluctant to be its mother.

'Well, sit down, then. Would you like a drink?'

'Have you got any beer?' he asked — a *num* question if ever there was one. But she was full of surprises tonight.

'I've got a can of lager in the fridge. I thought you might like one.'

He smiled. 'Just one?'

'Well, it's a four-pack, actually. They don't sell single cans in Sainsbury's. No, stay there, I'll get it.'

She went out, and he got up and turned off the television, having lost his immunity to it since living with Joanna. Into the sudden quiet, sounds jumped from the open french windows: children's voices — next door's, playing in the garden — and a clatter of cutlery from somewhere, a distant lawnmower, a car in the street accelerating past and changing up a gear, a dog barking with the monotonous rhythm of one who knows no-one's coming. He walked to the window to look out. The square of garden was neglected: the grass needed cutting, and the borders between the dull shrubs had gone all Isadora Duncan with gracefully unfettered weeds, where once there would have been a Coldstream Guard of annuals. Neither of them had been here to do anything, of course.

Burnt-sausage smoke rose up from the garden to the left, spiced with a whiff of paraffin; the sky was hazy and quivering with it. As he stood brooding, there was a characteristic thump-and-scrabble sound as a black cat came over the fence from next door and trotted by fast with its ears out sideways and the cunning-gormless look of a cat with prey. It had a barbecued spare rib clenched in its teeth, and only glanced at Slider as it passed, intent on escape. It reached the opposite fence, crouched and sprang up, and disappeared to crunch in peace in the empty garden beyond.

'Oh, there you are.' He turned back at Irene's voice, and seeing her with a tray in her hands hurried to relieve her of it; but she said, 'No, it's all right, just take the *Radio Times* off the table, will you?'

She put the tray down on the coffee table, which was drawn up to the sofa, and sat, evidently expecting him to sit beside her. On the tray was a tumbler of lager with the can beside it — the glass was too small to take the whole fifteen ounces — and another tumbler of what looked like gin and tonic. There was a plate on which stood a pork pie flanked with lettuce, cherry tomatoes, slices of cucumber and a teaspoonful of Branston pickle, a knife and fork, a paper napkin, and a jar of mustard.

'I thought you'd prefer it to a sandwich,' she said.

His heart hurt him. Cans of lager, and now a pork pie. She didn't approve of pork pies, she thought them common, but she knew he liked them, and there was a little tremor in her voice when she said, 'I thought you'd prefer it,' which told him she had deliberately arranged this treat for him and was waiting to feed off his pleasure and surprise. And she'd laid it out so nicely, with traditional pub garnish; and remembered the mustard. He wanted to howl and bite the furniture. 'This all looks very nice. Thank you,' he heard himself say. It sounded falsely avuncular to him, but she seemed satisfied.

'Dig in, then. I know you must be hungry. I had something with Matthew before he went out.'

He cut the pie and loaded his fork with Dead Sea fruit — or was it coals of fire? She waited until his mouth was full and then asked him brightly, 'How is your case going?'

He chewed and swallowed with painful haste. 'I didn't know you knew about my case.'

'I didn't. I don't. But you've always got one on, haven't you?'

'It's a murder, actually — a domestic. Bit of a puzzler,' he said telegraphically.

'Oh, then I'm surprised you've got time to come and see me,' she said. 'When you've had a murder before you've hardly had time to come home to sleep.'

Ah, a hint of acid: this was more like the old days. But he couldn't afford to revel in comforts like that.

'I wanted to talk to you properly,' he said evenly. 'Can we be civilised and talk without recriminations on either side? I think this is too important for quarrelling.'

She looked away from him for a moment at the blank television screen. He was close enough to see the fine lines around her eyes under the makeup, the sad, tired droop of her mouth. He knew her so well, and discovered now that he didn't know her at all, as though she were a character in a new drama played by a very familiar actor. He felt no *attachment* to her. At some point all his belonging feelings had redirected themselves towards Joanna. It made things easier; but harder, too, in a way, because it meant he didn't know what Irene was thinking. His domestic thoughts moved to Joanna's rhythm now; framed themselves in her idiom.

'Yes,' she said. 'You're right. I'm sorry I

blew up at you on the phone the other day. I was a bit tense.'

'I know. Nothing about this is easy, for any of us. But we've got to sort it out, and it's better that we do it between us, just you and I, without any third parties getting in on the act.'

'What does your *mistress* think of that?' she said, with a flash of the old spirit.

'What's decided between you and me has nothing to do with her,' he said steadily.

She said nothing, reaching out for her glass, drinking at it straight, like a poker-player, without looking at him.

'Irene,' he said gently, 'what's happening between you and Ernie? Don't you really want to live with him any more?'

'I don't know,' she said, and put her glass down. She didn't look at him. 'I don't know what I want any more. It all seemed clear once. I was fed up with you never being home, being stuck here alone with the kids all the time, no proper social life. I used to think sometimes, what was the point of being married at all? And then Ernie was so kind to me, and — everything,' she concluded, hopeless of defining her former bridge-partner's charms. Slider thought he knew — some of it, at least.

Irene had always been a sucker for the trappings of middle-class advancement. It was what she had always thought she wanted. And everyone wanted attention. God, he knew that! It was the origin of so much crime.

She seemed to have got stuck, and he tried to help her along. 'So when he asked you to come and live with him . . .'

She made a strange little noise, like a snort of amusement, except that she didn't look very amused. 'Oh, *he* didn't ask *me*. He's much too shy. Well, not shy exactly, but he doesn't value himself highly enough. He'd never have thought he was good enough for me. No, I had to ask him.' She flicked a glance at him. 'I suppose you think that's funny?'

Oh, far, far from it, he thought. 'I never had anything against Ernie,' he said.

'You could have fooled me. You've always been so rude about him.'

'Defence mechanism. I was jealous,' he said thoughtlessly.

'Were you?' she said, turning to him fully as though she had only been waiting for that. The fearful eagerness in her eyes warned him, too late, to look where he was treading. He *had* been jealous of Ernie, but it was mostly on account of his children, and a bit of atavistic resentment of another man taking his possessions. It was not the sexual jealousy that Irene was wanting him to mean. But how could he explain that to her? While he was not explaining, she carried on, stupidly brave, 'Ernie's been good to me, but it hasn't all been roses. The children haven't really taken to him, and it's strange living in his house. You'd laugh, but I miss this house in a way, and now I'm back here — well . . .' She paused, gathering her words. 'I only told him I wanted to think things out for a bit, but what I think is — what it seems to me —' She swallowed. 'I think I'm still a bit in love with you.'

He couldn't say what she wanted him to say. He sat there, stupidly silent. She died, like someone in variety with the wrong act before the wrong house, but could only carry on, stranded there in the middle of his unreceptiveness with her hopelessly inappropriate script.

'What I mean is — it would make so much more sense for us just to go back to where we were. There's the children to think about. The house — you can't afford two places, can you? It makes no sense to be paying rent and housekeeping for this place, and not living here. Oh, Bill,' she rose up like a surfer on a wave of urgency, 'we could be comfortable! I know it wasn't ideal before, but I understand more now. I'd be more patient about your job — and you could try and be home more, so we could have more of a life together.'

'Irene —' he began helplessly.

'I'm your wife!' she cried desperately. 'Doesn't that count for anything?' He was silent. She turned her face away. 'I don't want to live here alone,' she concluded.

He had to speak. 'I can't go back to the way it was. I can't come back here.'

'You don't want to.'

It took courage for her to ask that, and courage for him to answer with the truth. 'I don't want to.'

'Well,' she said after a moment, in a flat voice, 'that's that.' She drank some more of her gin and tonic. 'I suppose you're really in love with her, then — this woman?'

'*Please* don't let's quarrel about it.'

'I'm not going to quarrel. Just give me a straight answer to a straight question.'

It seemed best to, now. 'Yes, I'm in love with her. I love her.'

'Are you going to marry her?'

'We haven't talked about it. One day, maybe.'

She looked at him starkly. 'I spoke to a

solicitor, after you told me all that on the phone the other night. I went to see one yesterday. She confirmed what you said about no fault. And she says I can't stop the divorce, that it's automatic after a time, whether I want it or not.'

He nodded, very gently. 'That's the law now.'

'Do you want a divorce?'

The house seemed to hold its breath. Even the barbecue smoke beyond the window paused, and the distant cutlery ceased to rattle. He'd have given anything not to answer, but this was another case where his anything wouldn't even buy the handles. He had to speak. 'Yes,' he said.

Her shoulders went down in an exhalation, and Ruislip started up again. She finished her drink, pulled out her handkerchief and blew her nose, and then said in a different voice, quite briskly, 'Well, thanks for telling me. I needed to hear it from you straight.'

'I'm sorry,' he said.

'No, it's all right. Things come to an end. I just didn't want to face it, I think, that's all.'

'What do you want to do?' he asked her cautiously.

She hardly paused. 'I suppose I'll go

back to Ernie,' she said.

Her courage was staggering. He had never admired her so much. 'You don't have to, you know. You can stay here. I won't let you want.'

She shook her head. 'I don't like living without a man; and the children need someone.'

'I thought you said they didn't get on with him?'

'It's early days. Everything's strange, still. They'll get used to him. He's a good man.' She looked at him. 'My mother would have liked me to marry someone like him. She was never sure about you being a policeman.'

'Nor was I,' he said, wanting to laugh, God knew why. It was just the thought of Mrs Carter weighing him up and finding him wanting. It was so beautifully Victorian. A policeman is not a *gentleman,* dear, however nice he may be. 'I get less sure all the time.'

'Does she mind it?' she asked curiously. 'The hours and everything?'

'She's a musician, you see,' he said. 'She has hours herself.'

'Oh. Well, that's different, then. She'll understand.'

'Yes,' he said. 'It's different.'

336

He didn't go straight home. He drove around a bit, not really aware of where he was going; just going, with that instinct to escape the emotional scene that throughout history had made men leave home, fleeing their mother's pain, their wife's, their children's, going to the Crusades, to war, to the Colonies, the Antarctic, the Moon, the pub; hopelessly fleeing the eyes that always went with them, followed them for ever and all the way to death's dream kingdom. He wanted to be tired enough to sleep: that other escape. He thought suddenly of Eddie Andrews, and his story that he had driven about all night and didn't remember where. Well, it was plausible. Hard put to it, Slider could probably have dredged up some kind of memory of his own itinerary, but then Slider's emotional turmoil was kindergarten stuff compared with Eddie's.

When he got back to Turnham Green, Joanna was just parking, and waited for him outside the front gate while he eased his car into a space further up the road, the last roadside gap in all west London. The time would soon come when they'd have to build cars with retractable stilts so that you could park above one another.

'You'll never guess what!' she called to him as he approached.

With an effort, he remembered her meeting. 'They're going to allow you to wear trousers?'

'Phooey! I'm talking sensational news here.'

'Sensational good or sensational bad?'

'Good. Well, I think so.' He reached her and she slid her arms round his waist. 'Jim Atherton had a date tonight.'

'I know, he told me.' His brain caught up belatedly. 'How do you know?'

'Because I know who it was with!'

'You don't mean Sue?'

'Yes! Isn't that terrific? Our subtle campaigning the other night must have worked. Aren't you pleased?'

'Oh, yes, I like Sue.'

'I think she'll be good for him.' She realised at last that he was elsewhere, and scanned his face anxiously. 'What is it? Did you see Irene? Did it go badly?'

'Yes and no. She's agreed to a divorce, and she's going back to Ernie.'

'What's the "no", then?'

'She's agreed to a divorce, and she's going back to Ernie. Do we have to discuss this in the street?'

'Yes. I want to know why you're upset.'

He drew a deep, long sigh that came all the way up from his boots. 'It's easier to fight with her than admire her. She was so brave.'

'Oh,' said Joanna, and turned to walk up the path with him. She had her key out ready, and let them in, and once the door was closed put down her bag and put both arms round him again. Some of his muscles took the opportunity to slump into her familiar curves, and he closed his eyes a moment and rested his face against her. It was a thingummy devoutly to be wished, to consummate and then to sleep.

'Is it all settled now?' she asked carefully.

'Yes, all settled. We've agreed maintenance and everything. Provided she doesn't go back on it.'

'Which is always a possibility, if lawyers get involved.'

'Or her friend Marilyn. But for now . . .' For now the arrangement was the best that could be hoped for. She would have a home with Ernie Newman, and Slider could sell the Ruislip house — which, with the market picking up, now looked possible — relieving him of having to pay the mortgage, insurance and other associated bills, which had been a huge chunk out of his wages. So he wouldn't be stony broke and utterly dependent on Joanna after all. He'd be able to pay for his food and petrol, at least. So everything was peachy, wasn't it?

'Did you see the children?' Joanna asked, going instinctively to the heart of it.

'No, they were out,' he said.

She detached herself enough to look up, saw the closed eyes and the tired lines beside the mouth. 'Bill?'

He opened his eyes then, and she saw he was almost spent. 'Can we go to bed?' he asked. 'Right now?'

She squeezed him hard and reached up to kiss him. 'Come on, then.' They walked interlinked towards the bedroom and the haven of her bed where he was king and emperor, all-powerful, always wanted; safe. 'You big, dumb, strong ones are always the first to go,' she said, unbuttoning his shirt. 'You should learn to let it all out.' But he never would do that, couldn't, and she knew it.

The public appeal was getting results. Atherton greeted Slider with the news when he came in.

'It's the best response we've had since Hunt missed a typing error on a flyer, and we invited the whole of F Division on a sponsored wank.'

'I've just been to see Mr Porson and congratulate him on his performance,' Slider said. Porson had been as happy as a randy dog in a Miss Lovely Legs·competition. It was touching, really. 'He said his wife recorded him on video as a momentum of the occasion.'

'He didn't!' Atherton said admiringly.

'He did. Had a good time last night?'

Atherton grew inscrutable. 'Yes, thank you,' he said, with grammar-school politeness. 'I've got some good news and some bad news.'

'Bad news first.'

'McLaren hasn't called in sick. The good news is that the fingermarks on the handbag are not Meacher's — official.'

'That's good news?'

'Well, it wouldn't have helped us if they had been, would it? We know he was with her. At least this way there's a chance they may be useful.'

'True, O king. What about the staff at the Goat?'

'Haven't done them yet. Mackay's seeing to it.' Atherton eyed his guv'nor, wondering how events went with Irene last night and trying to gauge the answer from his expression. But Slider's mild worried frown was practically permanent and told him nothing, and he could hardly ask for intimate confidences if he wasn't prepared to offer them himself, so he went away unsatisfied and got on with his work.

The trouble with public appeals was that they generated so much work, panning the rubbish for the real information, which occurred with about the same frequency as gold nuggets. It was mid-morning before McLaren tapped on Slider's open door and said nasally, 'Guv, I think we got one.' Slider beckoned him in. 'It's a Mr Tarrant, lives in Hamlet Gardens, says he was walking his dog Tuesday night, saw a man and a woman talking at the end of the footpath down to the footbridge. Quarter past eleven, give or take.'

'What does he sound like?'

'Posh-ish voice. Not young. Sounds normal.'

'Right then, send someone round to get his story.'

'Can't I go, guv?' Slider hesitated about inflicting biological warfare on the general public. 'Everyone else is busy. I could get you a sandwich on my way back,' he added guilefully. 'From that new place, where they do the nice bread and everything.'

'Trying to bribe a senior officer?' Slider said sternly.

'No point in bribing a junior,' McLaren pointed out logically. He dragged out a handkerchief and blew into it.

'Yes, go,' Slider said hastily. Anything to get rid of him.

Mr Tarrant turned out to be older than his voice, a well-preserved man in his sixties, a retired chartered accountant. He had the ground floor of an Edwardian terraced house converted into a one-bedroom flat, with no room to swing an environmental health inspector, but at least with the tiny square of garden. 'I wouldn't think of having a dog if I didn't have a garden,' he told McLaren, as he made tea in the galley kitchen, so small that McLaren had to stand in the hall and watch him through the door, 'but even so, I take Tosca out twice a day. Dogs need a lot of exercise. People rarely understand how much they do need. A five-minute stroll to the nearest tree isn't enough, you know. Tosca has a brisk walk for an hour, twice a day. That's what keeps me fit.'

'Yes, sir,' McLaren said encouragingly. 'You do look fit.'

'Man was made to walk. Best exercise in

the world. We do all too little of it these days. Children especially. Taken everywhere by car — driven to school, even! When I was a boy everyone walked to school. Most people walked to work, as well. It's no wonder there's so much obesity. And ill health,' he added as McLaren blew again. 'Now *I* never get colds.'

McLaren was resigned to having hobbyhorses aired in front of him. It was funny how many people saw a policeman as a captive audience. He let Mr Tarrant ramble on until the tea was made, and then, sitting down in the tiny living-room with the big yellow Labrador watching him doubtfully from uncomfortably close quarters, he eased the old boy round to the topic of Tuesday night.

'I often take my walk around St Michael Square because it's quiet and away from the traffic. On that particular evening I had just come round the end of the churchyard and I was intending to go over the railway footbridge and back down Wenhaston Road, but I saw there was a young couple standing on the pavement just where the footpath to the bridge comes out.'

'Yes, I know.' McLaren answered the slight query at the end of the sentence.

'Tosca was investigating the railings so I

just waited for a moment to see if they would move away, but when they didn't, I walked on along the side of the church and made the circuit round it and went home via Woodbridge Road.'

'So why didn't you go over the footbridge, then?'

Mr Tarrant frowned slightly. 'Well, they looked as if they were having an argument. I didn't want to interrupt them.' He eyed McLaren, and gave a self-conscious cough. 'If you want the truth, I'm a little nervous of young people in general; and I've once or twice received abusive language and even threats from couples when I've interrupted them, quite innocently. I'd always sooner avoid trouble of that sort, and it didn't matter to me which way I took my walk.'

'So this couple were having a barney, were they?'

He nodded. 'That's what it looked like. Of course, I couldn't hear what they were saying, being across the road from them. At one point he looked as if he was threatening her. He leaned very close, poking his face at her — you know — like this.' He demonstrated the aggressive tortoise position of the head. 'And another time he grabbed her by the shoulder, and she sort of pulled herself away angrily, like this.'

This bloke should be on telly, McLaren thought. 'Can you describe what they looked like?'

'Well, she was blonde, I could see that. Short hair. She was wearing a dark dress of some sort — with bare arms.'

McLaren got out the photo they were using of Jennifer. 'Is this her?'

Mr Tarrant looked at it carefully, turning it to catch the light from the window. 'It might be. I couldn't say for sure. She had her back to me, you see, so I didn't see her face. But the hair looks all right.'

'What about the bloke?'

'Oh, just ordinary. Tall. Youngish — not teenage, you know, but a young man. In his twenties or thirties, I'd say.'

'Beard? Moustache? Glasses?'

'No, nothing like that.'

'What colour hair?'

'Just ordinary, really. Brown, I suppose. Light brown. Short. Curly, I think.'

McLaren jotted things down in his notebook. 'Do you remember what he was wearing?'

Mr Tarrant looked apologetic. 'Well, you see, most of his body was hidden from me by the woman. They were standing face to face, quite close to each other, so I could only see her back, and his head over the top of hers. I really wouldn't like to say what he was wearing, no.'

'But you saw his face, all right? Do you think you'd recognise him again?'

'I might do,' he said doubtfully.

'Do you wear glasses at all, Mr Tarrant?'

'For reading. I can see distances quite well. I'm long-sighted, you see.'

'All right. Now, you say this man was tall? How tall?'

'As tall as you, or taller, I should think,' Mr Tarrant said. 'He was quite a bit taller than the woman.'

McLaren considered. Jennifer's height in life had been five-six, and Eddie was five-eight, a difference of only two inches. McLaren himself was five-ten — nearly five-eleven in his thick-soled shoes. 'But of course it was dark, wasn't it?' he said aloud. 'And you were across the road.'

'Yes, that's true,' the old man said, not quite sure where McLaren was going.

'And what with the whatjercallit — you know, like when you're drawing pictures?' He waved his hands expressively.

'Perspective?' Mr Tarrant suggested.

'That's it. The perspective could make him look taller than he was.'

'It might,' Mr Tarrant said hesitantly.

'He might only have been an inch or two taller than her?'

'Yes, I suppose it's possible.'

'And can you say what time this was?'

'A quarter past eleven. The church clock struck the quarter just as I was coming round the corner.'

Back at the factory, McLaren sought out Slider with Mr Tarrant's statement in his hand and a song in his heart.

'The time's perfect, guv. A quarter past eleven. Eddie left the First And Last just after eleven, where he'd been swearing to find Jennifer and kill her. It's five minutes from there to the footpath. This Mr Tarrant ID'd Jennifer from her picture, and he reckons he could pick out the bloke from a line-up. The description fits as far as it goes — clean-shaven, a bit taller than her, with short, light-coloured hair. I questioned him about vehicles and he thinks there could have been a pickup parked just along from the footpath, where the oil stain was found.'

'What's your idea, then?' Slider asked, always ready for fresh input.

'He's looking for Jennifer, he finds her. End of story.'

'You call that an idea? That'd be a low

output for a glass of water.'

'Well, guv,' McLaren said, thinking on his feet, 'he's got his motor nearby. Maybe he gets her into that, pretends to've swallowed her story, whatever it was. She thinks they're driving home. Instead he drives to some quiet place, parks the motor, and kills her.'

'With?'

'Oh, something he'd got in the cab. His jacket, or a bit of cloth or something. Afterwards, when he calms down, he realises what he's done. Doesn't know what to do. When everything's quiet he drives back, lays her out nicely in the trench, does her makeup and hair to make her look nice. Remorse and all that. He spends the rest of the night in his cab somewhere, sleeping. Means to come early the next day to fill her in. But Mrs Hammond gets there first.'

'Hmm,' said Slider, a sound McLaren had come to know.

'You don't like it?'

'It's not a theory, it's a sieve,' Slider said. 'For instance, if he's going to kill her, why not take her home and do it there, in real privacy?'

'The way I play it, he's never thought it out. He's just acting off impulse.'

'And how come she was waiting for him by the footpath? What was she doing there?'

'Maybe she was on her way home in her car and he saw her pass and flagged her down.'

'No prizes,' Slider said.

'Well, guv,' McLaren said, 'at least we've got Mr Tarrant's evidence that he saw them quarrelling not long before she died. You can't get over that.'

'I'll try not to,' Slider said. 'All right, d'you want to go and take over a phone, now, give someone a break?'

'Okay, guv,' McLaren said philosophically. He had worked long and hard on that statement, but time would prove its worth. He turned to go.

'Oh — and where's my sandwich?' Slider called after him.

McLaren looked blank. 'Blimey, I forgot all about it.'

Chapter Thirteen

Bridesmaids Revisited

By the time Detective Superintendent
Porson came to see how they were getting
on, a few more pieces had been added. The
most interesting, and one that perhaps
helped McLaren's theory along, was that a
man leaving the First And Last just before
eleven on Tuesday night had seen Jennifer's
car parked on the hard standing in front of
the Andrewses' house as he walked past. He
had noticed it because he had recently been
looking to buy a new car and had fancied
the Mazda RX5 himself, but was going to
have to go for something more practical because of the kids. He had noticed it was red
and that it had a personalized number-
plate, something like a name with an interesting number. He had added that he
thought the engine was still ticking.

'That gets rid of one of our problems,'
Atherton remarked, 'that of the murderer
getting her car back home. It looks as if

either she met him on foot, and was killed close to the Old Rectory, or was taken away and brought back in the killer's motor.'

Other sultanas in the pud were 'a van of some sort' parked down the end of St Michael Square, not far from the footpath, at about half past eleven, according to a woman driving past on her way home; this more or less accorded with the oil stain on the road. Then there was a man on the railway embankment 'between half past eleven and midnight', according to a woman drawing her bedroom curtains in a house on the other side of the tracks. The man had been 'messing about in the bushes', said the woman, and when invited to expand her information thought he had been 'covering something up' with his coat or a blanket or something.

A further piece fell into place when an anonymous caller said he had been crossing the footbridge at about half past eleven on his way home from the station and had seen a man and a woman making their way along the embankment. He had assumed they were heading for the bushes for a bit of how's-your-father. No, she wasn't struggling or anything; they were holding hands. She was just walking along behind him like he was leading her. No, he didn't want to leave his name, thank you, but they could bank on his story. He was quite sure it was Tuesday because that's the only night he'd been out that way.

McLaren had his faults, but you had to grant he wasn't dogmatic. 'All right, he didn't do her in the cab, then. Maybe he invited her for a walk along the embankment, and did her there, hid her in the bushes, and carried her up through the garden later. It's better that way, 'cause of not having to drive up in the middle of the night and have the neighbours hear the engine.'

'But why would she go for a walk with him on the embankment?' Slider asked.

'Why wouldn't she?' McLaren said simply. 'She was his wife.'

'Overcome with passion,' Atherton suggested ironically.

'Five minutes from home and a comfortable bed?' Slider objected.

'You're showing your age,' Atherton grinned. 'Younger people like adventure and thrills, acting on the impulse of the moment.'

Slider frowned. 'There is Jack Potter's evidence that she liked doing it in dangerous places; but hidden in the bushes on the railway embankment is not particularly dangerous, especially with her own husband.'

'Dangerous? It turned out to be fatal,' Atherton pointed out.

The reasoning went down all right with the Syrup. 'I don't think you want to get too bogged up as regards the whys and wheretofores, when dealing with people of this calliper. In my experience they frequently do things that to you and I would seem quite irrationable. Let's just stick to the established facts as we know them, and let the CPS worry about the presentational angle.'

'We haven't got many established facts,' Slider said. 'Only semi-established possibilities.'

'Well, pickers can't be choosers,' the Syrup said comfortably. He swivelled a finger in his ear thoughtfully. 'Let's see, Eddie Andrews — he's had two days to think about it now, hasn't he, since we let him go?'

'Yes, sir.'

'Hmm. Two days. I should think the onermous silence at home ought to be getting on his nerves a bit by now, don't you? Remorse and ecksetera eating away at him, not to mention the investigation hanging

354

over him like the Sword of Damascus. He knows that we know his entire statement was a virago of lies. And he knows we're watching him. With a uniform parked more or less outside his door, he'll have read the handwriting in the wind, all right.'

'You want me to go and talk to him again, sir?' Slider suggested.

'Yes, do that. Have a little chat. Shake the kettle and see if it boils. You might just persuade him to put his hand up like a good boy, and save us all a sackload of trouble.'

'Yes, sir.'

Porson looked at him sharply. 'And take Atherton with you. If anyone can scare Andrews —'

'Atherton?' Slider said, in surprise.

'He's highly articulated — got all the la-di-da chat and the posh grammar. That sort of thing can throw a simple man like Eddie Andrews right off balance.'

'Do you think so, sir?' It was an unexpected insight.

Porson met his eyes with a gleam of humour. 'He scares the shit out of me,' he said frankly.

'Porson called you articulated,' Slider told Atherton, when he passed on the message afterwards.

'Like a lorry,' Atherton said in delight. 'But I've always said I'm in the van when it comes to vocab.'

'I'll have no truck with puns,' Slider told him curtly. 'Let's get going.'

Andrews looked terrible: unshaven, dirty, with matted hair and red-rimmed eyes. He let Slider and Atherton in without question or comment, and wandered before them into the sitting room, where he slumped down in a chair without looking at them. The room was untidy, with glasses and crockery on the floor, an empty baked-beans can with a spoon standing in it perched on the television, newspapers strewn about, a duvet and pillows falling off the sofa.

'I've been sleeping down here,' he said, when Slider asked about them. 'I can't stand it upstairs. I can't stand it anywhere, if you want to know.' He looked round the room as if noticing the untidiness for the first time. 'Pat didn't come Friday. She sent a note. She says she's not coming any more. I don't blame her.' He put his head in his hands and rubbed and rubbed at his eyes. 'This house — I built it for her. Everything she wanted — whirlpool bath, automatic oven. She chose everything —

carpets, furniture, wallpaper, everything. Fitted wardrobes, I put in, with a light that comes on when you open the door. Her dream home. Anything she asked for I gave her. Self-defrosting fridge. Automatic washer-dryer. Digital microwave. But it wasn't enough. I couldn't keep her.'

'Woman is fickle,' Atherton commented.

Eddie lifted his head, his eyes unfocused. 'She cheated on me. I didn't want to believe it. I told myself they were all lying. I don't know. Maybe they were. No, she cheated on me. But she loved me, really. You got to understand. Underneath, it was me she loved.'

'That last night, Eddie,' Slider said gently. 'We know you met her after you left the pub at closing time. Down by the footpath that leads to the railway bridge. Someone saw you there talking to her. Did you have a quarrel?'

He stared as if Slider were talking a foreign language. 'Quarrel? What about?'

'You tell me. You met her by the footpath, didn't you?'

'Later you were seen on the railway embankment,' Atherton added.

'The embankment,' he said. 'Yes, I remember. I did go there. When I was walking about.'

'You were hiding something in the bushes. Covering it with something,' Slider suggested.

'It was Jennifer, wasn't it?' Atherton said. 'Jennifer's body.'

'Jennifer's body,' he repeated. He looked exhausted, run to the end of his strength. The Kindly Ones, Atherton thought, had bayed him at last.

'You were seen walking with her along the embankment to the bushes. But she never came back, did she?' Slider said. 'What did you do, Eddie? Tell me.'

'Her body.' Eddie looked at him in agony, his eyes focused now. 'She's dead.' He quivered all over, as a frightened dog shivers. 'I'll never see her again. Oh, what have I done?'

'Tell me about it,' Slider urged, and to Atherton, his gentleness was a terrible thing, as a sword is terrible; and yet to a man fleeing the Erinnyes perhaps a welcome thing. Andrews looked at him with the hope with which such a man might look at his executioner: the hope only of an end to it all.

'Yes,' he said at last. 'I want to tell you.'

Porson read the statement aloud as he hoofed restlessly about the room.

'I found out she had been cheating on me. I swore I would kill her. I was looking for her all evening. I had been drinking a lot. I met her by the path that leads down to the footbridge over the railway and we quarrelled. I led her onto the embankment and killed her in the bushes and covered her with my jacket. Later when it was quiet I carried her up the garden and put her in the hole I'd dug on Mrs Hammond's terrace. I was going to fill the hole in in the morning, but Mrs Hammond found her first. Now I'm sorry she's dead and want to get it off my chest.'

Porson paused in his peregrination and tapped the paper with his finger-nail. 'Good work,' he said. 'And within the week, too. An expertitious result like this will bring us a lot of kewdos with the Powers That Be, I can tell you, Slider. Especially as it's a nice, clean, straightforward case: confession plus corroboration, obvious suspect, comprehensive motive, creditable witnesses — nothing to tax the imagination of the twelve men and true. I think there's no doubt the CPS will prosecute on this one, and a conviction will do us no end of bon.'

For a rare moment he was still, away in some pleasurable place of plaudit. His big hands twitched as he received a commendation and shook the hand of the Assistant Commissioner, as a dreaming dog's paws twitch at that special rabbit moment.

Slider stirred a little, unhappily. Confession is as confession does, he thought, and there was something unsatisfyingly bloodless about this one. The show without the substance. Someone somewhere wasn't inhaling. But he must try to be specific for Porson: he didn't know him well enough to play the old instinct card, as he could have done with Dickson in the dear dead days of long ago.

'He doesn't say how he killed her,' Slider said. 'Or how he met her there. And what became of the jacket?'

'Eh?' Porson said, dragged unwillingly back to cold reality.

'The jacket, sir. He wasn't wearing one in the morning, and we've been over every inch of the embankment and the garden. There was no jacket in his pickup, either.'

'Well, he could have dumped it anywhere,' Porson said.

'But why would he? It wasn't as if there was any blood.'

Porson looked kindly. 'Well, obviously this statement is only a preliminary starting place. There's plenty more work to be done; d'you think I don't know that? But you don't need to lose any sleep. He's put his hand up, that's the main thing. This is not the moment to go picking hairs and getting bogged down in the fine print. Cut yourself a bit of cake, Slider: you've done a good job.'

'Sir,' Slider said, unconvinced.

'Come on, you don't need me to tell you how the thing works: he feels relief after confessing, and out comes all the rest — if he's handled the right way up. That's down to you — asking the right questions is your providence.'

'Yes, sir.'

'I've every confidence in your interrogatory technique.'

'Thank you, sir.'

Porson was on the move again. 'As he's here voluntarily, we're not on the clock, that's one good thing. We won't arrest him unless he looks like taking a wander — that'll give us a chance to get all the witnesses taped up and labelled. Get the old chap who saw them — Tarrant, is it? — get him in and we'll do a line-up. And get the motor witnesses to come and look at the book and pick out the van they saw in the square. Tomorrow will do for that.'

'Yes, sir.'

'Meanwhile, give Andrews half an hour, spot of grub and a cup of tea, and then have another go at him. Take him through the timetable, and run him gently up to the murder so he doesn't even see it coming, get my drift?'

Slider got it. Excitement was making the Syrup unusually direct. Quite comprehensive, in fact.

Slider was late home, after the failure of the Porson Plan Mark 1: Eddie Andrews cantered gently up to the fence, had not precisely refused, but had jumped carelessly, scattering brushwood. He was willing to co-operate — too willing, in Slider's view: he followed wherever he was led, like a bloodhound on an aniseed trail, and the result was a less than compelling narrative. He didn't deny anything, but he didn't offer any explanations for the things that bothered Slider, either; he seemed to want the answers laid out for him as well as the questions. It left Slider restless. Everything added up to Eddie Andrews, and nothing added up. It was like eating without swallowing, making love with gloves on.

Talking of which, Joanna was home, and miffed that she had had a rare Saturday evening free and he had not been there to share it with her. 'I know it's not your fault. I'm not blaming you. I'm just saying it's a pity, that's all.'

'What did you do?'

'Had something to eat. Watched that film we taped the other day. The Clint Eastwood thing.'

'Oh, I wanted to see that,' he protested.

'Don't worry, by the time you get the leisure to sit down and watch it, it will be far enough in the past for me to watch it again.'

He was mollified. 'I don't suppose there's anything to eat in the house?'

'Didn't you get anything?'

'Not since . . .' He pondered. 'Breakfast, actually.'

'They let you starve all day? You ought to stand up for yourself.'

'Like Narcissus?'

'What an educated quip. You sound like Atherton.'

'Never mind all that. Your mind should be on me. Food, woman, food!'

Obligingly, she looked in the fridge. 'Well, there's salady stuff.'

'I hate salad. I wish it was winter.'

'That was practically a pout. Actually, when I say salad, it's just a sort of honeymoon salad — lettuce alone. There's some cheese and a bit of pâté left, but the bread's a bit old.' She looked at her lover's suffering face and said, 'Tell you what, there's some bacon in the freezer compartment. I could whack that into the microwave to defrost it, and make you a toasted bacon sandwich. How would that do?'

'I love you,' Slider confessed.

'So you say. It's just my cuisine you fancy, really.'

'You have a beautiful and curvaceous cuisine, but I love you for your mind, as well.'

One bacon sandwich thing led to another, so Saturday night was not a total flop after all; but Sunday started badly. He overslept and woke feeling doomed and heavy in the legs, and Joanna rushed in in a panic and said her car wouldn't start.

'I'll have to take yours.'

Slider hated to be without a car. And he hated anyone else driving his. Irene wouldn't have asked; but with a new relationship you have to tread gently. He gave his objection mildly. 'Can't you go by public transport?'

'Not possibly. I've got a rehearsal in Milton Keynes this morning, then that blasted dedication service or whatever it's

364

called at Eton, and then back to Milton Keynes for the concert in the evening. I can only just do it *with* a car. Why do I take on these ghastly economy-class dates?'

'Because you need the money.'

'You've only got to get to Shepherd's Bush, haven't you?'

He couldn't refuse against such reason, little as he liked it, and heaved himself out of bed. 'You ought to get rid of that old wreck and get yourself something reliable,' he grumbled, searching his jacket pocket for his keys.

'Are you talking about my car or my man?' she asked, eyeing his gummy state.

'And how am I supposed to get to work?'

'You could cycle up the avenue, but you haven't got a bike. Or you could call out the AA and take mine when they've fixed it.'

'I haven't got time for that.'

'You'd better have, or I'll have to take your car tomorrow as well,' she said, taking the keys from his nerveless fingers and kissing him hard on the lips in the same movement. "Bye. Love you. Good luck with your murderer.'

'See you tomorrow,' he said glumly, knowing she would not be back before midnight.

Things didn't get better. Eddie Andrews was still in pliant mood, and willing, not to say eager to make a further, expanded statement. But the details he added were vague in the extreme, and when pressed to be specific about times, places and materials he fell back on, 'I can't remember,' and 'It's all confused — just a blur in my mind.' He seemed more cheerful, and was eating well. Now he had confessed, the responsibility had been taken from his shoulders: it was a syndrome Slider had seen before — indeed, it was the basis of the Catholic Church's success — but in this case he didn't find it comforting.

Andrews readily agreed to an identity parade, but Sunday was not a good day for organising a line-up, and Slider had to rummage through the staff to make up the numbers.

'I'll do it,' Swilley said kindly, when Slider asked for volunteers.

'I don't think his heart could stand it. McLaren — no, of course he knows you. Anderson, then. For me, laddie.' Anderson got up, grumbling. Slider surveyed the room. The uniform loaners were in plain clothes today. 'What about you, Defreitas?'

'Not me, sir. I'm allergic to line-ups.'

Defreitas said hastily. 'Take Renker. He wants a break.'

Renker stood up. 'I don't mind, sir.'

There was a chorus from around the room.

'Don't do it, Eric!'

'Never volunteer, son!'

'I wouldn't touch it with a ten-foot pole, mate!'

'Yeah, whatever happened to him?' Renker enquired. ' "Stretch" Polanski, the ten-foot Pole?'

'That's it!' Slider exclaimed. 'Not another word! Anderson, Renker, Willans — front and centre. You've volunteered. And when all this is over, I'm going to run away and join the circus.'

The three men filed out from their desks with a show of reluctance. 'I thought this *was* the circus,' Renker protested. 'Otherwise, how come all the clowns?'

Slider rolled his eyes. 'Everyone's a comedian. Get downstairs, you three. And for God's sake, try not to look like policemen.'

Tosca waited in the front shop, where she and Nicholls fell instantly and deeply in love, while Mr Tarrant did his duty. He did not pick out Eddie Andrews.

'No,' he said regretfully after a long and careful scrutiny of the line, 'it isn't any of those. The one at the end — number eight,' this was Renker, 'he's about the right height. But he's too fair. Number two's hair is more like it.' This was Anderson. 'But he looks too heavy and broad. And I don't think he's quite tall enough. And three, four and five are much too short.' Number four was Andrews.

Slider took Mr Tarrant out. 'I'm sorry,' the old man said. 'I wanted to help. But none of them looked right to me, and I couldn't say they did if they didn't.'

'Of course not,' Slider said. He hovered over a delicate area. 'Regarding the height of the man you saw, sir, in your statement, you did say he was only "a bit taller than the woman"?'

'No,' Tarrant said anxiously, 'I said he was *quite* a bit taller than the lady. I did tell the other officer, the one who came to my house, that I thought he was a very tall man, but your officer talked about perspective and about it being dark, and he pointed out — well, he persuaded me I was mistaken. But *I did* think at the time that he was very tall. Tall and slim.'

'And with fair, wavy hair?'

'Brown,' Mr Tarrant said firmly. 'A

lightish brown, perhaps, but not fair or blond. And definitely curly. Quite tight curls.'

McLaren was unrepentant. 'He wasn't all that sure what he'd seen, guv. I had to help him out a bit. I didn't twist anything, just talked him through it, so as to get it down clearly.'

'Clearly?' Slider was keeping a tight hold on himself, but it wasn't easy. 'He says brown hair and you write fair? He says curly and you write wavy?'

'Well, guv, I mean, how's he going to tell the difference anyway between light brown and fair? I mean, he's across the road, and it's quite wide there. And it's dark, and he's an old bloke, and his eyes are probably not up to much.'

'McLaren, you are a waste of space!' Slider raved. 'You have the intellect of a brick! If he couldn't see across the road, what's the bloody point of having him as a witness?'

McLaren shifted uncomfortably. 'I don't mean to say he can't see, but — you know — I was just, sort of, guiding him a bit.'

Slider put his head in his hands. 'All you had to do was to take down what he said. Just let him tell you, and write it down.'

'But, guv, we've got a confession,' McLaren pointed out. 'You can't get over that.'

'A paraplegic terrapin could get over that! Mr Tarrant says Andrews was nothing like the man he saw. He also picked out a Transit van from the cards, not a pickup, as the motor he saw parked on the square — an identification, incidentally, confirmed by the other motor witness we had. The phone-in who saw a man and a woman on the embankment didn't leave his name. And the woman across the railway lines was too far away to identify the man she saw in the bushes. How long do you think it would take defence counsel to knock that house of cards down, balloon-brain?'

'But Andrews still confessed. We know it was him. He knows it was him. We'll get other evidence — bound to.'

'Andrews is in a highly suggestible state of mind, and his confession is extremely suspect. And now you've contaminated the field. How are we supposed to know now what he really remembers and what's been suggested to him? You were given a simple task to do, basic police work, and you made a complete Horlicks of it. I'm disgusted with you.'

'Sorry, guv,' McLaren said, with a stubborn lack of contrition.

'Oh, go away,' Slider said. He still had to go and tell Mr Porson his prince was a frog.

Porson, annoyingly, was inclined to side with McLaren. 'It's a nuisance, of course, but I don't think the situation is irredeemiable. It's not as if we've got *no* corroboration. We know he was drinking all evening and threatening to kill her, and we know she was having affairs. And her handbag was found in his pickup. We've got enough to be going on with, and other witnesses will come forward in time. Andrews isn't asking to go home, is he?'

'No, sir, but —'

Porson held up his hand calmly. 'There you are, then. Andrews is here completely gratuitously. And if he wants to make a voluntary statement of his guilt, then it's his perjorative to do so.'

Slider stumped up to the canteen for a cup of tea and a quiet fume. He found Atherton there at a table on his own, resting his elbow on the table and his chin in his hand like a Scott Fitzgerald debutante, dunking his teabag delicately with the other hand.

'Your problem is, you always want to know everything,' he said languidly, when Slider had unpocketed his troubles. 'You want all the teas dotted and the eyes crossed. Porson's probably right. And Eddie probably is guilty.'

'Probably? Where's your intellectual curiosity?'

'Oh, I can't be bothered with all that on a Sunday.'

Slider took a few deep breaths and drank some tea. 'And to have to stand there while Mr Porson mangles language at me,' he grumbled, diminuendo.

'You don't really mind that,' Atherton told him. 'That's just psychosemantic.'

Somewhat restored, Slider went downstairs again and found Swilley looking for him. 'I think we may have got something here, boss. A woman's phoned, who says she was Jennifer's best friend. And she says she saw Jennifer on the Tuesday evening.'

Janice Byrt lived, worked and generally had her being in that strange and lost part of Hounslow that lay under the flightpath of Heathrow. Once there had been only little villages, tile-hung farmhouses and rustic churches. Then arterial roads had linked them with ribbons of mock-Tudor semis, traffic lights and neat set-back arcades of shops. But the placid life still went on, in a world where people wore hats, and walked to the shops pushing babies in prams; for few had cars, and their sound was but as the trickle of a stream, and you could hear the birds when you went out of doors.

And then the airport came. Now the great white bellies of arriving and departing jumbos flashed like monstrous fish above them, crushing down the sky and leaving a shimmering wake of hot kerosene like a snail's trail over the frail roofs. Roaring cars and bellowing lorries sucked up whatever air was left, and, to prevent any pocket of peace taking root, satellite dishes on every house probed the sky for new sources of bedlam, while shops and pubs vomited endless loops of strident pop.

In this insanity of noise and stink, a race of people clung to existence, like those bizarre microbes that manage to live inside volcanoes. The thirties semis had been armoured with triple-glazing and wall insulation, and a cheerful, and to all appearances normal, life went on, monument to man's astonishing adaptability. Janice Byrt had a little hairdressing establishment on one of the traffic-lit corners where one arterial road crossed another, and the music of the day was regularly informed with the screaming brakes and tinkling glass of yet another driver's belief that red lights were optional. Her shop front was painted pink, with pink ruched curtains in the windows and the name of the salon hand-painted in curly magenta writing on a pink background over the top: *Hair You Are.* It was an especially good joke, Slider discovered, because Janice came from Lowestoft, where they pronounce 'here' as 'hair'.

She lived in the flat above the shop. Slider parked in the service road in front of the parade, and then found the archway several shops down that led to the granite stairs, which led to the balconies at the back, which gave access to the flats. Inside, the traffic noise was several degrees lower, and when a plane came over it was still possible to carry on talking, though the whole flat trembled like a vibrating bed in a motel, so that Janice's collection of china figurines tinkled together as though they were chatting in tiny china voices.

'You get used to it,' she assured Slider when he asked about the noise. 'I hardly hear it any more. And those new jumbos are ever so much quieter.'

Slider felt as though his brains were being scrambled by a master chef with an extra large whisk, but there certainly could be no more pleasant, normal and relaxed person than Janice Byrt seemed. He supposed it was natural selection. Those who went bonkers were carried off screaming to a suite at the Latex Hilton, and the rest just got on with their lives.

She had been shocked to learn of Jennifer's death. 'I didn't know a thing about it,' she said. 'Well, I don't have time for newspapers, and I never watch the news on telly — too depressing, all that war and MPs and stuff. It wasn't till a friend of mine rung up this morning — she'd seen it on the news last night, and of course the name made her jump. She said she wasn't really watching, but when she heard the name she looked up, and there was Jen's picture all over the screen! That give her such a fright! So she rang me up this morning, and she say to me, "What d'you think about our Jen getting killed like that?" and there, I say to her, "I don't know what you're talking about, girl."' Her accent became stronger as she grew agitated, Slider noticed.

The friend who had rung her lived in St

Albans. 'Val and me were Jen's brides-maids when she married Eddie. Would you like to see the photo?'

Slider accepted with interest, and was handed a framed photograph from its place of honour on one of the crowded shelves of the chimney alcove. It was a typical wedding-photographer's line-up: bride and groom flanked by two bridesmaids and best man, grass under foot and grey stones of the church out of focus behind. There was Jennifer with a glittering smile and meringue hair, scarlet lips and nails, all in white grosgrain, tight bodice and puffed sleeves that Princess Di had made fashionable up and down the land back in another age. She held red roses and white lilies wired into one of those bizarre flat-fronted sheaths designed by florists purely for holding in wedding-photos, and a silver cardboard horseshoe dangled on white ribbon from her wrist. Her other hand rested on the sleeve of a younger, blonder Eddie, bundled into a blue suit patently not his own, and looking, from his expression of bewildered euphoria, as if he'd just had his brains beaten out with a lump of pure pleasure in a silk sock.

To Eddie's other side stood the best man, a scrawny, raw-faced, crop-haired youth who looked as if he'd only just learned to walk upright. To Jennifer's other side stood a plump, dark-haired bridesmaid, and Janice.

'That's me,' she said helpfully, pointing. The bridesmaids were in matching Princess Di jobs in bright pink taffeta with circlets on their heads, and small, flat, round bouquets of Valentine-pink roses that looked like Las Vegas wedding-parlour pizzas. 'They were lovely frocks,' she said wistfully, 'only Val had the figure for it and I didn't. My sleeves kept slipping down.' Slider remembered being told just recently that no-one said 'frocks' any more. Who was that? Yes, poor Janice was small and weedy and flat in every dimension and looked as if her frock was independently rigged like a bell-tent, and she merely standing inside it, looking meekly out of the hole at the top. In a pneumatic-bust competition with Val, she was definitely the twin who didn't have the Toni.

Janice took the picture back from him and caressed it with a thumb. 'It was a lovely wedding. Val's married now, got two children. I'm the only one not married. That's the only time I was ever a bridesmaid, too.' She put the picture back in its special place, probably unaware that she had just told her whole life's philosophy in four sentences.

'You've known Jennifer for a long time?'

'We went to the same school. She was Jennifer Harris then.'

'In St Albans?'

She nodded. 'She was my best friend. I was ever so shy, and then, well, my mum and dad moved from Lowestoft when I was fourteen, so I didn't know anybody, and I felt really awkward and, sort of, out of it. I was never much good at making friends. But Jen just came over to me on the first day and started talking to me, and after that she sort of looked after me, and let me go about with her. She was lovely! I mean, she was pretty and everything, and so lively, too, always into everything, always laughing and teasing the boys. She was never scared of anything. And popular! I never did know what she saw in me.'

Slider nodded encouragingly. Every Dame Edna needs a Madge, he thought; and often the wildest extroverts were the most insecure underneath. They needed one quiet, loyal, reliable lieutenant who loved them blindly and uncritically — and also, who would never be a rival. 'Did you wear glasses at school?' he asked unwarily, out of his thoughts.

'Yes,' she said, surprised. 'I wear contacts now. How ever did you know?'

He waved it away. 'Doesn't matter. Please go on. You kept up with Jennifer when you left school?'

Jennifer went to work in an estate agent's office, and Janice became a hairdressing apprentice, and was still permitted to hang about with Jennifer's gang, and play buffer and straight man in Jennifer's games of seduction with the boys. 'Of course, it wasn't the same after she married Eddie, but we still kept in touch, and after she came to London, I decided to come too, to be nearer.'

Though quiet, plain, and shy with boys, Janice was no duffer. She had worked her way up the hairdressing hierarchy and finally opened her own salon which, though not in a fashionable place — or perhaps because of that — had a large and loyal clientele. It was making her a nice little pot of money. 'I don't really have anything to spend it on,' she said to Slider, but without self-pity. 'I don't go out much, and I bought the flat cheap from the council years ago so there's no mortgage. I like to buy things for my nephews — my brother's boys — and I like nice holidays. But it still builds up. I suppose,' she laughed deprecatingly, 'it's for my retirement, really.'

Over the years, too, Jennifer had come to value the quiet friend more, and had increasingly entrusted her with her confidences. 'People think not being married I must be really sheltered. But that's funny what women will tell you when their hair's wet. I think they feel vulnerable — well, no-one looks their best like that, do they?' She laughed the little laugh again. 'I think it's a bit like being a priest — you know, the confessional? I bet I've heard things that would make your hair stand on end. Well, not yours,' she amended humbly, 'you being a policeman, but most people. And you don't have to do everything to know about it, do you?'

'I should hope not,' Slider said. 'So tell me what happened on Tuesday.'

'Well, Tuesday's my half-day closing. Of course, Jen knew that. She turns up, oh, about ha' past four, it must have been. I could see right away she was upset. She comes right in and says, "Give me a drink, Jan, before I start crying and make a fool of myself." So I made her a gin and tonic, a big one. That was her drink, gin and tonic. I always kept some in for when she dropped in. I like a Cinzano, myself, or a sherry.'

'Had she already been drinking, do you think?'

'She wasn't drunk, if that's what you mean. But I could tell she'd had a couple. But she was too upset and angry to get drunk. She was burning it up, sort of.'

Slider nodded. He knew that mood. 'What was she upset about?'

'She'd been with one of her men that afternoon — David.' She looked at Slider to see if he knew about him, and he nodded again. 'She said, "He's dropped me, Jan, the bastard's dropped me. Now what am I going to do?" You see, it was different with David. She was always having affairs, but they never meant much. But she had high hopes of David.'

'High hopes?'

'Well, he was posh — you know, educated and upper class. Went to a public school and everything. And he was rich, too. Jen had always wanted someone like that. Eddie — he was a mistake, really. She married him too young. If she'd stayed single a bit longer she never would have married him at all, because they weren't suited. He was dull, you know? No ambition. Jen wanted to go up in life. And she thought with David she'd really found the right man.'

'Didn't she know he was married?'

'What, David? Yes, of course, but he didn't love his wife. She was much older than him, and it was never a love match in the beginning. That wasn't a problem. Jen was crazy about David, and what with everything he said she thought he felt the same. She was just waiting for him to say the word, and then she was going to leave Eddie and he was going to leave Diana — that's David's wife's name — and everything would be all right. You see, Eddie's ever so jealous, but he'd never start anything with a person like David. He's very polite with people like that — scared of them, almost.' She sounded faintly puzzled by the idea; Slider thought of the Syrup saying that Atherton would scare Eddie with his grammar. Was this his day for having insights thrust upon him from unlikely sources?

'So what had happened between her and David?'

'Well, apparently they'd met as usual that afternoon — at a motel somewhere, I think.' Slider nodded. 'And they were laying in bed afterwards and he suddenly says that was to be the last time, he didn't want to see her any more. Jen was absolutely flabbergasted.'

'Did he say why?'

'She said he had some other woman on the go, and things were getting serious with her, and he was thinking of marrying this woman, and he couldn't afford to have his affair with Jennifer messing things up, because this other woman was very proper and if she found out she'd have nothing more to do with David, and he didn't want to lose her. Well, Jen said, "I thought you loved me," and he said, "It's got nothing to do with love." Well, you can imagine how Jen felt when he said that! It turns out this woman's going to come into a lot of money, you see. So Jen said to him, "What do you need money for? You're rich enough." And then he sort of laughs and says that he hasn't got a penny, all the money is Diana's, and what's more she's fed up with him, Diana is, and threatening to cut him off. So he's got to make sure of this other woman right away. So he says, "I'm sorry, my dear, but it's curtains for you and me." '

She stopped with a fine dramatic sense, and looked at him, large-eyed, for his response.

'Jennifer must have been very upset.'

'She was. She was crying fit to break her heart at first, because she really thought he

383

was going to marry her, and now it turns out he was just toying with her.' Lovely phrase, Slider thought. 'So I say to her, Jen, I say, if he ha'n't got any money, you don't want to marry him anyway, and she say, I do, Jan, I love him. I don't care if he's rich or poor. And besides, she say, I can't stay with Eddie no more. I don't care what happens, she say, but I'm getting out of that.'

'Did she say why she couldn't stay with Eddie?'

'No. Just the usual, I suppose.'

'What's the usual?'

'Well, he was terribly jealous, was Eddie, and never wanted to let her out of his sight. He'd've locked her up if he could have, literally. They were always having rows. And, then, he used to hit her as well.' She looked at him sidelong to see what he thought about that. 'That's another reason she ought never to've married him, but there, she didn't know at the beginning. It was only when he lost his temper with her, when they had their rows, not, like, all the time. But still, I think it'd been getting worse lately. Anyway, she said she'd got to get out.'

'Yes, I see. What happened next?'

'Well, after a bit, she calms down, and

she says, "I'm not giving up. I'm going to see him again and make him take me back." David, she meant. She reckons if she can just get him to meet her, she can talk him round. She was a great talker, was Jen.' Her eyes filled with tears and her lips trembled at her own use of the past tense.

'Did she say when she would see him?'

'She was going to ring him and make him meet her that evening. She cheered up once she thought of that, and she went to my bathroom and washed her face and did her makeup again, and then she went off. That would be about ha' past five. And that's the last time I saw her.' She blew her nose carefully. 'I can't believe I'll never see her again. She was my best friend in the world. I don't know what I'll do without her,' she said bleakly. She looked towards the net-curtained window as another full-bellied jet, pregnant with tourists, battered the air over her roof. The romance and glamour had gone out of her life. Now there was just Hounslow, and other people's hair, for ever and ever.

Slider suppressed his pity. She wouldn't want it, in any case, who had none for herself. 'When she left here, do you know where she was going?'

'What, you mean right away? Well, I can

guess. It was what she said about, if it didn't work with David, she was getting out anyway. She said to me, "I've got a couple of other irons in the fire," she said, "and I might as well make sure they're still hot, just in case." She couldn't just leave Eddie, you see, unless she had someone to go to, because he'd've come after her and knocked her about and made her go back. I mean, she knew she could always come here, but I couldn't have helped against Eddie. And she wouldn't want to live with me, anyway. She wasn't someone that would want to be without a man.' Janice seemed to accept this practical attitude to the heart's obligations without offence; indeed, with approval.

'So you mean, if David wouldn't marry her, she was going to get one of these other men to?' He was fascinated and appalled by Jennifer's philosophy as it was revealed by her friend. Suppose other women thought like this, seeing men as a commodity, like meat with an income attached?

Janice nodded. 'Though, really, it was just one. I don't think she ever had any chance with Alan, because he was a reverend, you know, a vicar, and she wasn't really cut out to be a vicar's wife.'

Understatement of the decade, Slider thought. He wondered, though, how hot the turbulent priest's iron had been. Had he protested too much to Atherton about his resistance to Jennifer's charms? Had he, in fact, been her lover?

'Yes, we knew she'd been to see the vicar,' Slider said. 'That fits in. But who was the other man, do you know?'

'He was a policeman, as it happens,' she said, with a nod and a shy smile to Slider. 'She was quite excited about him, though he was married too; but she said he was very passionate. I think she half wished he had David's class, because she fancied him a lot more. She didn't tell me his name, though. She had a nickname for him. Duffy, I think it was. No, Daffy. That's right, Daffy.'

Bloody Nora, Slider thought, as a lot of little pieces tumbled into place. And then he remembered Steve Mills, one of his firm who had become a suspect in a murder case he had investigated; and, like the famous petunia, he thought, Oh, no, not again!

Chapter Fourteen

Stalling Between Two Fuels

Defreitas was as white as paper. 'I didn't kill her, sir. You've got to believe me. I didn't. I wouldn't.'

Slider's anger was cold. 'Then why the hell didn't you tell me about your involvement? What am I supposed to think when you conceal important evidence like this?'

'I thought it wouldn't come out,' Defreitas said miserably. 'You see, things are difficult at home. Me and my wife aren't getting on. I hoped —'

Now Slider remembered how Defreitas had got out of the identity parade; and further back, the crash from the back of the CID room when he had mentioned that there were two types of sperm in the victim's vagina. 'My God,' he breathed, 'it was you she met on the footpath! It was you who was seen with her on the embankment!'

Defreitas looked as though he might cry.

'I couldn't tell you, sir. I was afraid if it came out no-one would believe me, they'd think I did it. But I didn't, I swear it!'

Slider's mouth turned down. 'You swear it? What use is your word to me now? My God, I don't think you begin to see what you've done!'

'I'm sorry, sir. But I didn't destroy any evidence, or lie about anything. I just —'

'You just let us bring Eddie Andrews in on the basis that it was him who met his wife by the footpath. Don't you understand? The heaviest evidence against him was that he was seen arguing with her shortly before her death, near where her body was discovered — near a place where he might have killed and concealed her. Now it turns out that person was you! Where do you think that leaves you?'

Defreitas saw now. He shook his head slowly from side to side, not so much in negation but like someone in pain. 'No, sir. No, sir. You don't believe that. She was all right when I left her. I would never have done a thing like that.'

Slider wanted to believe him. He seemed a nice lad. But images were chasing across his brain. The witness who saw Jennifer being led along the embankment towards the bushes. The witness who saw a man covering something with his jacket. In his mind Slider saw it: kisses, panting, a quick, practiced coupling in the bushes — two people who'd done it before and knew how to get it done. Then something wrong was said, sharp words, a quarrel: Jennifer threatening to tell his wife; Defreitas, still kneeling over her, losing control. Then a quick movement and his jacket over her face, smothering her . . .

Thus far it played like panto. But after that, questions arose. Why would Defreitas go back to move her body from a place where it might lie concealed for days to a place where it would certainly be immediately discovered, by the householder or the builder? To implicate Eddie, was the only answer to that — and if it were so, it was a foul and despicable act; but risky, stupidly so. Defreitas had not previously impressed him as stupid; though people in unprecedented situations did do silly things.

But why had she not struggled? If she had, there would have to have been more bruising about the face, at least. Why — and how? — had he restored her makeup? And how had her handbag got into Eddie's pickup? No, it didn't make sense as it stood; but he could see how easily it would make sense to someone less particular —

or someone who had an anti-police agenda, like the tabloids, and their readers, if it got that far. Exposure of that sort would cause great embarrassment to the Department; and even if they eventually charged someone else with the murder, there would always be those who believed Defreitas had 'got off'. His future would be blighted.

But his career was blighted now, anyway — perhaps over. Slider came back from long thoughts to find pleading eyes on him. 'You'd better have a bloody good alibi,' he said. 'And now you'd better tell me what happened.'

Defreitas had been drinking in the Goat on Tuesday evening. 'I only had the one pint. I was making it last. I didn't want to go home. I'd had a row with the wife earlier, you see, so I'd been out since about half past nine, just walking about. I got to the Goat about a quarter past ten and just went in for a pee, but by then I was fed up with walking the streets so I decided to have a pint.'

Just before closing time Jennifer had telephoned there asking to speak to him. 'Karen took the call. Jen didn't give her name, just asked to speak to me, and

Karen passed it over. She was busy — I don't think she really noticed. Jen said she'd been phoning round trying to find me — tried the First And Last and a couple of other places she knew I used. She said she wanted to see me right away. I said, where are you? and she just said, meet me at the footpath to the railway bridge in five minutes. So I went.'

When he met her she had come straight out with it, and said it was time he put his money where his mouth was and married her.

'I was thrown — I mean, we'd never talked about that. As far as I was concerned we were just having a bit of fun, and I thought she felt the same way. But when I said that she got angry and started to create. Said a lot of things, about, you know, leading her on and taking advantage of her and so on. The usual old Tottenham. I said no-one had deceived anyone and she was old enough to know what was what, and if anyone had been doing any leading on it was her. Which was the truth,' he added, seeing Slider's frown. 'I mean, it was her come on to me in the first place.'

'And you were the helpless victim, forced to have sex with her against your will,' Slider said with distaste. Defreitas reddened. 'Go on.'

'Well,' he continued, 'she said it wasn't like that for her, that it was serious — though I swear she'd never even hinted anything like that before. I mean, if she had, I can tell you I'd've never have — well,' he checked himself, 'anyway, she said now she couldn't stand living with Eddie any more and she'd got to get out. Well, I said what went on between her and Eddie was her business, and I couldn't help her. Then she said if I didn't agree to marry her, she'd go straight round and see Becky — my wife — and spill the beans. Well, then I got mad with her and said if she dared go anywhere near my house I'd —'

'You'd kill her?'

Defreitas swallowed. 'I don't think I said that, sir. But I was angry. It's the last thing I wanted then, her going round my house, with things like they are between Becky and me.'

They had argued heatedly for a while, and then suddenly Jennifer had back-pedalled, apologised for the threat, said she didn't mean it, and started sweet-talking him instead.

'It was all lovey-dovey then. She was very persuasive when she wanted. I couldn't

393

resist her,' Defreitas admitted. 'She started sort of rubbing herself against me, and then she suggested us going down on the embankment and — and doing it.'

He hadn't taken much persuading. After the argument his blood was up, and much else besides. They went down the footpath and climbed over the fence onto the embankment. There was no-one around — Defreitas didn't think they'd been seen. They went into the bushes: 'We'd done it there before.' He took off his leather jacket and spread it on the ground and they had sex.

'We weren't there long. I mean, it was a quick job. Truth to tell, I think she had her mind on other things. I think she was just . . .' he hesitated '. . . making sure of me. She'd got me mad, and now she was softening me up again.'

An echo in Slider's mind: stock-taking. Who had said that of Jennifer?

'And as soon as it was over,' Defreitas went on, 'she was up and off.' She had straightened her clothes and her hair, and they had walked back to the footbridge. 'She told me to go the other way — over the footbridge and down Wenhaston Road — in case anyone saw us. She went the other way, back to the square. She said she had someone else to see. I said at that time of night? Because it was about twenty to twelve by then. She just laughed and turned away. And that's the last time I saw her, until —'

Defreitas had gone straight home, arriving at about five to midnight. His wife was already in bed. He had washed, cleaned his teeth, and got in beside her and slept. His wife was not speaking to him the next morning, and he had got into work late for the early shift, which started at six; and so on his arrival had been sent straight round to the Old Rectory to discover the cold body of the woman he had inseminated warm only hours earlier. Slider, furious as he was with the man, could sympathise with Defreitas in that ghastly situation.

In his rage, Porson towered like a demiglot. 'I find it totally incredulous that an officer of your experience could behave in such a way! Do you think you're some kind of special case, that you can just flaunt the rules whenever you feel like it?'

'No, sir.'

'No, sir? Is that all you've got to say? I don't think you realise the trouble you're in, Defreitas. Your lamentacious conduct

395

has put this whole case in jeopardy. As to your career —'

Defreitas tried a few feeble words of defence. 'Sir, as far as my relationship with Jennifer Andrews is concerned —'

Porson, walking fast back and forth across the office, turned at the end of a width with such a jerk his hair visibly swivelled before his face caught up with it. 'Yes, and if this was twenty years ago, I'd have had something to say about that score, as well! It's incomprehensive to me that you could even contemplate an affair of that sort. When I joined the Job, a policeman had to be beyond repute, in his private life as well as on duty. The public demanded impeachable behaviour at all times, and for a married officer to have carnival knowledge of a woman other than his own wife would have been a disciplinary offence of the severest consequence, I can tell you!'

When the mute and miserable Defreitas had eventually been sent on his way, Porson signalled to Slider to shut the door, and, on a last little spurt of anger, walked another width and muttered, 'These young officers don't seem to learn anything! Think they can just carry on any way they please, as if the Job was just a job. That kind of attitude is a milestone round our necks. It's no wonder the public don't trust us!'

'What about disciplinary action, sir?'

'That's for Uniform to decide. Suspended pending investigation certainly. After that, I don't know. Not my providence, thank God. But I shall have to report, and I shall make a strong recommendation that he gets more than his knuckles rapped for concealing information. What's more to the impact, how does this affect the case?'

'It removes quite a bit of the evidence, or rather the suppositions, against Andrews. And of course it blows a hole through his confession — which was already a bit flimsy to my mind.'

'Yes, you never were happy with it, were you?' Porson stood still and looked straight at Slider. 'Do you think Defreitas did it?'

Slider looked straight back. 'No, sir.' He explained the questions which Defreitas as suspect would leave unanswered. 'We ought to be able to substantiate his story. They know him at the Goat, so they ought to be able to say when he arrived and left, and Karen, the barmaid, will probably remember the phone call.'

'That doesn't clear him of the murder.'

'No, sir. But even if Mrs Defreitas doesn't know exactly what time he came in, I think it's unlikely he could have got out of bed again in the middle of the night to go and move the body without her knowing. I think we can clear Defreitas all right. The infuriating thing is that we'll have to waste manpower doing it.'

Porson nodded. 'I'll see he gets his come-uppance, don't worry.'

'To my reasoning, Eddie Andrews is still our best suspect,' Slider went on. 'For one thing, putting the body in the trench — that only made sense for Andrews, who would be the one to fill the hole with concrete the next morning. For anyone else, putting her there wasn't hiding her, it just hastened discovery. And for another, there's this thing about making her face up again. It doesn't make sense. As an action, it's just bonkers. And who but Andrews would have been bonkers in that particular way about killing her?'

'But still, you don't think it was Andrews?' Porson asked cannily.

'It isn't that, sir,' Slider said. 'I don't see who else it could have been; but we just don't have enough evidence against him.'

'Well, there's still plenty of phone calls coming in.' Porson said philosophically.

'We'll have to let him go again, but if he did it, you'll find the evidence all right. And if it wasn't him, something will break sooner or later. Don't worry about it. You'll get there. I've got every confidence in you.'

Just when you think you've heard it all, Slider thought, the old man comes down all sensible and kind and touches your heart.

Back in his own room he found Atherton waiting for him. 'News?' Slider asked, reading his lieutenant's eye.

'Two of them,' Atherton said. 'The owner of the Transit that was parked just down from the footpath has come forward. Renker's checking him out, just to be absolutely sure, but it all looks perfectly innocent.'

'Oh, well, that clears up a point,' Slider said. 'What's the other?'

Atherton eyed him. 'I don't know if you'll like it. We've had a call from a long-distance lorry driver — bloke called Pat McAteer. He was driving an artic on Tuesday night — well, he'd been driving all day Tuesday, tacho notwithstanding, but we'd better not go into that if we want his co-operation. Anyway, he was heading for a ferry crossing on Wednesday morning and he'd got a bit ahead of his schedule so he pulled off the motorway to catch a couple of hours' sleep in his cab in a safe lay-by he knows on the A40. When he pulls into the lay-by he's not pleased to see someone else is there before him.'

'Don't tell me!'

'A light-coloured Ford pickup — light blue, he thinks. He's going to move on when he sees the driver's sleeping in the cab, so he reckons he's safe enough. He sets his alarm to wake himself in good time and gets into his bunk and goes to sleep. When he pulls out in the morning, the pickup's still there, and the bloke's still asleep.'

'Does he remember the number?'

'Enough of it. I suppose we'll have to check the other possible combinations through the PNC, but I'm willing to bet it was Eddie's all right.'

'Well, we knew he must have gone somewhere for the rest of the night,' Slider said. 'Get someone out there to check if there's an oil stain, and try and get a sample. Forensic may be able to match the oil from the pickup, to give us a bit of corroboration.' He read Atherton's face. 'All right, what's the catch? What time did McAteer arrive and what time did he leave?'

'He pulled into the lay-by at one o'clock, and he pulled out again at five. So you see the problem? We've got Eddie missing from just after eleven, when he left the First And Last, to about six forty-five when he turns up at the Rectory. Even driving like the clappers, it's going to take Eddie half an hour to get to the lay-by — three-quarters, really, in a pickup — and the same to get back.'

'So the alibi doesn't cover him for the actual time of the murder — supposed actual time.'

'Yes, but when would he have had time to lay out the body? Suppose he fell upon her the instant she left Defreitas, at eleven forty-five; give him fifteen minutes to do the murdering, he's only got an hour to conceal the body and get back to the lay-by.'

'And we know she wasn't put straight into the trench,' Slider said. 'She was left sitting up somewhere for a couple of hours. Of course, she could have been sitting up in the back of the pickup.'

'So we've got two possibilities,' Atherton said. 'Either Eddie slept in the cab until, say, two a.m., drove back to the Rectory — quarter to three — shifted the body, laid it out, did the makeup — got to allow an hour for that — quarter to four — and then drove back —'

'To the *same* lay-by —'

'Arriving at half past four in order to be seen by the lorry driver at five, and then slept, or pretended to sleep, until six when he left to go back to work in order to fill in the trench — which is physically possible —'

'And which is pure Vaudeville.'

'Or he was there and asleep in his cab between one and five —'

'Which means he wasn't the murderer, and we've got to start all over again from nothing,' Slider said glumly.

'Even William Hill wouldn't give you odds on that,' Atherton said. 'As Mr Porson would say, it's back to the drawing-pin.'

Atherton volunteered to give Slider a lift home.

'Haven't you got a date, or anything?' Slider asked.

'Not even anything. But you shouldn't have to ask that. Don't you know Sue's doing Milton Keynes as well as Joanna?'

'Oh,' said Slider, unsure whether that was a snub or not. He sat quietly for a bit, watching Atherton from the corner of his eye as he drove. Atherton drove well and stylishly, as he did most things — perhaps a little on the generous side when it came to accelerating and braking, but that was the way of youth. As a long-term married man Slider had got used to thinking of Atherton as younger than he actually was. But his age was showing in his face now, after the trauma of his wounding. The portrait had been brought down from the attic: he would probably never get back that fine careless rapture.

Slider wondered what the score was between him and Sue. His last answer might have been a snub, or an irony, or a revelation of the truth; but Slider was naturally delicate of enquiring into a colleague's personal life. Then he thought, What the hell? He can always tell me to mind my own business.

'So is it on again between you and Sue?' he asked, as unprovocatively as he could.

Atherton swivelled an eye briefly. 'What do you care?' It was said flippantly, not with rancour.

'Self-defence. She's Joanna's friend. If you upset her, she'll complain to Jo, and Jo will come down on me for damages.'

'Bollocks. Just admit you're nosy.'

'Don't tell me,' Slider said, looking ostentatiously out of the window. 'I wouldn't listen now if you begged me.'

After a moment, Atherton said, 'We're going out again. How serious it is I don't know yet.' All the flippancy had dropped from his delivery, and the sudden stripping away of defences made Slider nervous. There was a balance and a distance that had to be maintained between working colleagues. Once he and Atherton had kept it effortlessly, but since Joanna, and particularly since the wounding, it had been shifting about like a sand dune on fast forward. Unsure of its present position, Slider didn't say anything; and into the silence, like any victim of interview-technique, Atherton gave more. 'I missed her. Even before I got wounded. God knows why. I mean, she's not glamorous or exciting —' Slider glanced at him, and he interpreted it easily enough. 'That's always been a minimum requirement. After all, I have a reputation to keep up,' he protested.

'You're not that shallow,' said Slider.

'Don't over-estimate me,' Atherton said with a touch of bitterness. 'I have been just that shallow. And don't forget you can drown in an inch of water.'

That sounded so profound they both

had to think about it for a moment.

Then Atherton resumed. 'All those weeks in hospital gave me time to think. I'd always been so terrified of getting involved, but I remembered you saying to me once that there was no alternative, that if you weren't involved you weren't anything.'

'Did I? I'm hardly one to dish out advice.'

'No, you're right. Whatever you get wrong,' and his tone suggested it was legion, 'you're in there, facing the balls.'

'Eh?'

'At the crease. Batting. I thought you'd like a cricketing analogy.'

'This conversation is getting weird,' Slider said. 'Just tell me how come you got in touch with Sue again.'

'I wanted to see her,' Atherton said simply, and then added with deeper honesty, 'I was peeved. I thought she ought to have been more attentive, considering my plight. And I thought, considering what a fabulous catch I was, she ought to chase me a bit. That's what I'm used to. When Joanna said that with Sue I had to make the running, I thought, Dream on, Phyllis! But when I managed to disengage the ego for a bit, I decided I might just give it a try.' He grimaced. 'Anything for a new experience.'

'She's a nice person,' Slider said, ignoring the self-mockery. This was serious, he could see.

'She is,' Atherton agreed. 'And she's seen me at my worst. That's a comfort.'

'And since she's not glamorous and exciting, you don't have to be on your mettle all the time,' Slider suggested.

Atherton looked hurt. 'That was a bit blunt. You really do think I'm shallow.'

'Spot of irony,' Slider said. 'As it happens, I think she probably is exciting. I mean, look at Joanna.'

'Yes,' Atherton said, accepting the shorthand. There was a silence while he eased round a right-turner who wanted to occupy the whole road, and then he went on. 'When I was wounded, I lost a sort of — integrity. That maniac made a hole in me — literally and figuratively. My shell wasn't whole and perfect any more.'

'Yes,' Slider said. He couldn't have put it into words, but he knew what he meant.

'I'm afraid,' Atherton admitted starkly, 'and I hate it. *Hate* it! I feel as if something's been taken away from me, and I resent it like hell.' He paused, and went on in a different voice, 'And then, I missed her, and I can't afford to cope with that as well as everything else.' He glanced sideways again. 'These days I see you looking at me, wondering if I'm going to make it.'

'I don't —' Slider began, but Atherton stopped him.

'You do, but it's all right; I wonder too.'

'You'll make it,' Slider said, with a great deal more certainty than he felt. He wasn't always sure about himself, let alone his damaged companion.

'But I don't think I can do it on my own. Not any more.'

'Well,' Slider said again, 'she's a nice person.'

Atherton smiled privately at this concluding benediction. His boss might just as well have said, 'You have my blessing to proceed.' Bill had never had much facility in expressing emotions, and with Joanna was having painfully to learn a whole new language. Atherton, on the other hand, had always had all the words, an easy, sparkling stream of them; now he was going to have to learn to put his money where his mouth was.

'But nothing worth having was ever achieved without effort,' he concluded aloud. Slider grunted agreement without questioning of what the comment was apropos.

When they reached the flat, Slider

invited Atherton in for a drink, and finding that they were both hungry, rummaged through the kitchen and offered the old standby bread and cheese. Atherton looked at the bread and the cheese and quickly offered to make them both Welsh rarebit, which he did the proper, painstaking way, melting the cheese in a pan and adding mustard and Worcestershire sauce before pouring it over the toast and grilling it. While all this was going on and Slider sat on the edge of the kitchen table watching, they both sipped a handsome-looking Glenmorangie with a beer chaser, and talked about the case.

'Now that Defreitas has made a complete Jackson Pollock of the evidence,' Atherton said, 'and Eddie's turned out to have an alibi, I suppose it puts Meacher up as prime suspect. There's this story about him chasing some other woman, a rich one. But if Jennifer was about to queer his pitch with some serious money, that's a good enough motive to kill her, if he's really the creep you think he is.'

'But he's got an alibi.'

'Not much of one. The girl would obviously say anything she was told to, but a little judicious — or even judicial — pressure might change that. Effectively, he's not accountable for most of the evening and all of the night.'

Slider shifted restlessly. 'But most of the same objections apply to Meacher as suspect as to anyone else. We're not just trying to find someone to nail this to, we're trying to find out what really happened.'

'Hey,' Atherton said, wounded, 'it's me.'

Slider made a gesture of acknowledgement, and went on thinking aloud. 'There's the problem of the makeup. How would the murderer do the retouching out of doors and in the dark?'

'Maybe that's why it was done clumsily,' Atherton said.

'It wasn't *that* clumsy. Most men couldn't do it that well in a barber's chair under a spotlight.'

'Well, what about in someone's car? You know that most drugs are bought, sold and ingested in cars: it's the new privacy. So why not murder? You'd have interior light to do the making-up by.'

'Well, it's a possibility,' Slider said.

'A bare one, by the tone of your voice,' Atherton complained. 'Here I am thinking my heart out for you —'

'Well, look, if she was smothered without a struggle, she must have been drugged in some way, and how was that to be done?

You don't suddenly produce a pill when you're out for a walk in the country and say, "Here, swallow this." Or even,' he anticipated Atherton's rider, 'sitting in a car.'

'All right, then, maybe it was done indoors,' Atherton said. 'There are other houses in the world than Eddie's. And we don't actually *know* it wasn't at Eddie's. It's just that we've no evidence it was.'

'But then you've got the problem — which applies to any house — of hauling the body out and getting it across to the Rectory, and I can't believe no-one would notice.'

'People don't notice things like anything, all the time, every day of the week,' Atherton pointed out.

Slider shook his head. 'The thing that's really bugging me, I suppose, is that even if no-one noticed at the loading-up end, and even if the Rectory neighbours didn't notice the vehicle driving up and the crunching feet over the gravel, I can't believe all that activity went on on the terrace in the dead of night without the dog barking. That dog's on a hair-trigger.'

Atherton pulled out the grill pan to inspect progress, and pushed it back in to bubble some more. The kitchen was filling with the delicious aroma of roasting cheese, and he kept expecting to feel Oedipus's solid body pressing against his legs in the ritual food gyration. Oedipus was particularly fond of cheese: quite a Cheshire cat, he thought.

'And yet,' Slider continued with a frown, 'that's precisely what did happen. Whoever put the body into the hole, the dog didn't bark in the night.'

'Don't go all Sherlock Holmes on me,' Atherton said. 'Maybe they just didn't hear it. People with yappy dogs can learn to shut out the noise — like people living by a railway not hearing the trains.'

'It isn't exactly a yappy dog. And it's supposed to be a guard dog: would anyone ignore the barking of a guard dog, especially in the night?'

'It's possible they simply didn't hear it,' Atherton said reasonably. 'Mr Dacre said he slept well that night for a change, so presumably he needed the sleep. Maybe he even took something to help him.'

'Mrs Hammond says she's a light sleeper. And she said she didn't sleep well that night. If the dog had barked, surely she would have heard it?'

'People who say they don't sleep actually sleep a lot more than they think — it's a proven fact. It's a peculiar form of vanity, to claim not to sleep,' he diverged. 'As though sleeping were something rather gross and common. Like those nineteenth-century ladies who prided themselves on never eating, and fainted all the time to show how refined they were. In any case,' he reverted robustly, pulling out the grill pan again, '*que voulez vous?* There are only two possibilities, aren't there? Either the dog didn't bark, or they didn't hear it.'

'Some help you are,' Slider said.

They carried the supper through to the sitting room to eat. Atherton made free with Joanna's sound system and put on Brahms' fourth symphony, because that's what the women were playing at Milton Keynes that evening, and he thought it might give them sympathetic vibrations and improve his chances for later.

Slider said, 'If it was Meacher, or anybody else come to that, *why* would he put the body in the hole? It doesn't make sense for anyone other than Eddie Andrews. It's got to be Eddie, even if it can't be.'

Atherton sat with his plate and glass and stretched out his legs. 'Let it go, now. You've got to learn to switch off, or you'll burn yourself out.'

'That's what I've always told you, about women,' Slider said, with a slow smile.

'That's better,' Atherton said approvingly. 'Just forget about it for a few hours. We've probably missed something glaringly obvious, and the subconscious will chuck it out if we leave it alone. You'll wake up in the morning knowing everything from aardvark to zymosis.'

'Tomorrow,' Slider said. 'Oh, Nora, Joanna's going to take my car again.'

Atherton raised his eyebrows. 'Bad move,' he said. 'You know there's a tube strike tomorrow? And some of the buses are probably coming out in sympathy.'

'*Bloody* Nora.' Slider upped the stakes. Of course, that would be why she had to have the car. Why hadn't he remembered?

'There you are,' Atherton said, watching his face, 'counter-irritant. A nice go of toothache to take your mind off your headache.'

The solution to the transport problem turned out to be an early call to the AA while Joanna, having inspected the breadless kitchen cupboards, departed in Slider's car for Henry Wood Hall near enough to the crack of dawn to be able to stop for breakfast somewhere on the way. Slider made a few phone calls and tried to let his mind lie fallow so as to let the back-

413

burner syndrome take effect. He had woken no closer to making sense of the senseless than he had gone to sleep.

The AA man arrived unexpectedly soon, and Slider hurried out to unlock the car for him. He was a young, burly and immensely cheerful man, who when Slider apologised for the early call, said, 'No worries, mate, I'd sooner this than the middle of the night trying to work in the dark.' But his demeanour suggested he'd have been just as cheerful at midnight in December. Slider envied him such a robust disposition.

He tried it first and checked the fuel gauge. 'Just in case,' he said. 'How are you for petrol? Quarter full, that's okay. You'd be surprised how often I get called out and all it is, there's no petrol in the tank. Not just women, either.'

He put up the bonnet of Joanna's Alfa and dived in with enthusiasm, while Slider hung about and looked over his shoulder like an auntie in the kitchen. They were watched through the window of the van by a large mongrel that plainly featured collie and Dobermann amongst its varied ancestors.

'The wife feels happier if I've got him with me, the lonely stretches of road we get called to sometimes,' the patrolman said, in answer to Slider's conversational query. 'He loves it, out and about all the time. I don't approve of leaving a dog shut up in the house all day. It's not fair on them.'

Slider agreed absently. 'Good guard dog, is he?'

'If anyone tried to mess with me or the motor,' the man said elliptically, looking back over his shoulder at the intent face at the window. 'One-man dog, that one,' he added proudly. 'I'm the only person who can do anything with him.'

'Oh?' Slider said, and grew very still, thought taking hold of him. Further conversation went over his head, and he barely even noticed when the engine jumped at last to life, following a delicate mechanical operation, involving a judicious whack on the starter-motor with a hammer.

The AA man slammed the bonnet down and said, 'Well, that'll tide you over for a bit, but I don't promise anything. It could go again any time. You really want to get that starter-motor replaced.'

'I will. Thanks. Thanks a lot. I've really got to dash now, but I'm very grateful to you.'

'S'all right. All part of the job, squire,' the AA man said easily.

Chapter Fifteen

Alf The Sacred

He drove to St Michael Square, deep in
thought. The square was quiet, basking in
the young sunshine at the innocent time of
day when workers have departed, non-
workers are still indoors, and intentions,
good and bad, are only just waking up. He
parked round at the end of the church and
stepped out to stand leaning on the railings,
hoping inspiration would strike. It was cool
in the shadow of the tower, but across from
the churchyard, the odd but mellow façade
of the Old Rectory was warm with sunlight.
Squint up a bit, he thought, and you could
be in a village. A brisk dog, trotting on its
rounds, smiled up at him as it passed; all
that was wanted was the schoolmistress on a
bicycle and the village bobby on his beat.
Not that that was how he remembered his
own village life as a child. Perhaps he had
grown up through a rainy decade, but his
images of childhood in Essex were chiefly of

mud: lanes, yards, fields of it, as far as the eye could see; cows plastered with it, hens sodden with it, wellies clogged with it; football boots weighted with it, welding tired junior legs to a school pitch like the Somme; passing tractors on the road chucking great homicidal gouts of the stuff at your head from between the lugs of their tyres. His mother had waged a lifelong, losing battle to keep the tide of mud from invading the house. Her life, he thought, was the microcosm of the struggle of civilisation: an endless fight to keep out the forces of chaos. It was why he had become a policeman, really — that and the recruiting-sergeant's promise of all the women he could eat.

The evocative clang of a heavy wrought-iron gate was transmitted through the railings to his hand, and he roused himself to see an old man in a flat cap, collarless white shirt with the sleeves rolled up, elderly grey flannel trousers and stout army-surplus boots, just leaving the churchyard from the gate on the side that faced the old Rectory. He held a large metal ring on which a number and variety of keys were hung, and now fumbled for one with which to lock the churchyard gate. Slider went round and accosted him.

The old man turned sharply, but seemed reassured by the look of Slider, and said pleasantly, 'Hello! Where did you pop up from?' while he went on locking the gate.

'I've just parked over there. Detective Inspector Slider.' Slider showed his brief, and the old man inspected it with watery blue eyes, nodded, and then slowly dragged out a handkerchief and blew his nose thoroughly, ending up with several wipes, exploratory sniffs, and a general polishing of the end, before restoring the handkerchief to his trousers.

'I suppose you're looking into this business about Mrs Andrews,' he concluded. 'Shocking! Is that right she was done away with?'

'It seems that way,' Slider said. 'I see you have the keys to the church.'

'Who else should have 'em?' he said, straightening up as though coming to attention. 'Sexton, me. Alf Whitton's the name.' He inspected his palm to see if it was fit for the task, and then offered it to Slider. Slider usually avoided shaking hands with the public, but there was something beguiling about the man and the gesture, and he took the dry, horny palm and shook it briefly. 'Just been sweeping up,' Whitton added, jerking his head towards the church. 'She don't get so dirty this dry weather, but she do get dusty. Mondays I sweep, even when there's not been a service the Sunday; Tuesdays I does the woodwork — dust and polish.'

'There must be a lot of work in keeping a church like this nice,' Slider said sympathetically.

'Oh, there is, there is,' he said eagerly, 'but I don't mind it. I learned all about spit an' polish in the army, and there's a kind of rhythm to cleaning, a knack, if you like. Satisfying, it is, seeing things come up. Brass and silver especially: it's 'ard work, but the results are lovely. There's a brass lectern in there, shape of an eagle. All feathers! Cuh!' He jerked his head and lifted his eyes to demonstrate the difficulties of cleaning brazen birds of prey. 'But it comes up a treat when it's done. I been looking after this 'ere church for forty years, give or take,' he went on, casting an affectionate eye over his shoulder at the grave, grey tower.

'I should think they're lucky to have you,' Slider said warmly.

He looked pleased. 'Sexton of her and St Melitus's, but it's her I like best. Otherwise I wouldn't've taken on the cleaning, not at my age. Used to have a cleaner, up till five year ago, then they said they couldn't afford to pay for one any more. Couldn't *justify* it, they said,' he added, as though it were a particularly nauseating weasel-word — which perhaps it was. 'Well, I couldn't stand to see her get grubby and sad, like I seen so many churches, so I said I'd do it. Keep her lovely, I do, though I says it as shouldn't. But I wouldn't do it for no-one else. I don't clean St Melitus's,' he said sternly, in case Slider got the wrong idea.

'You seem to keep very fit on it,' Slider said.

Whitton jutted his white-bristled chin and slapped himself in the chest. 'Eighty-two come September. How about that?'

'Marvellous!'

'And I still keep the graves, *and* stoke the boiler in winter. Not that that's a job I like. Messy stuff, coke, and I never did like being down the crypt. Reminds me too much of air-raid shelters. Don't like cellars and tunnels and such.'

Where Alf the sacred cleaner ran, through caverns measureless to man, thought Slider. Eighty-two and still shovelling it — they bred 'em tough before the war.

'Wouldn't mind someone younger taking

over the boiler, but where you going to find one?' Alf went on. 'Young people today weren't brought up to service like you and me was. Never think of nothing but themselves.'

'If you've been sexton here all that time, you must know a lot of people hereabouts.'

'Course I do,' he said smartly. 'Know everyone in the square, and the church, all the congregation, the council. Seen 'em come and go. Eight vicars we've had here since I been sexton. It's the trufe! And everyone knows me, what's more. Knew Jennifer Andrews, if that's what you're working up to. Want to have a little chat with me about it do you?'

'Yes, if you don't mind.'

He smacked his lips. 'Can't talk with a dry mouth. Want to come in and have a cup of tea?'

'In?' Slider queried. In the church, did he mean?

'My house,' Whitton said, gesturing across the road.

Slider looked blank. 'You live nearby, do you?'

'Church Cottage, next to the Rectory,' he said patiently, gesturing again.

Now Slider twigged. He meant the small cottage next door on the left of the Old

Rectory. 'You're the missing householder!'

'How's that?'

'We tried to interview everyone in the square, but we never got a reply from your house, so we thought you were away, on holiday or something.'

'Away? I don't go away. Prob'ly wasn't in. I'm not in much — here and there, doing little jobs.'

'We tried in the evening, too.'

'I like to go to the pub of an evening. And even if I'm in, I don't answer the door. Not at night. Never know who it might be.'

'And you don't have a telephone.'

'Never have had,' Whitton said triumphantly. 'Never felt the need.'

'So how do people ever manage to get hold of you?' Slider asked in frustration. 'Suppose someone had an urgent message?'

'Oh, I'm here and there and round about. People know where to find me. You managed all right,' he pointed out.

Slider gave it up, and followed the old man across the road to the cottage. In contrast to the baking day outside, it was dark and cold inside Church Cottage, and smelt strongly of damp and faintly of dog. The door opened directly onto the sitting room, which was dominated by a large fireplace with a fire of logs and paper in it made up ready to light. There was a massive beam over the fireplace, which supported a mess of ornaments, knick-knacks, letters, bills, photographs and assorted small junk, and a door beside it which Slider guessed would conceal the stairs to the upper floor. The low ceiling was also beamed, the plaster between them stained richly ochre by years of smoke — an effect refurbished pubs paid decorators large sums to replicate. For the rest there was a thin and ancient carpet on the floor, two old armchairs covered in imitation leather from the fifties flanking the fire, and a portable television on an aspidistra stand. Under the window was a small table covered by a lace cloth on which stood a birdcage containing a blue budgie. It whistled as they came in, but then fell silent, looking rather depressed. The window was small and heavily draped in nets which kept out most of the light, so Slider was not surprised.

'That's Billy,' Whitton said, noting Slider's look. 'He's company for me, since my old dog died. I'd like another dog, but I haven't got the time to train a puppy, and I don't fancy someone else's leavings.' He chirruped at the bird, but it just sat there glumly, shoulders hunched, like someone waiting for a bus in the rain.

Whitton led the way through the open door on the other side of the fireplace to the kitchen, evidently the only other downstairs room. It was a narrow room, lino-floored and defiantly unreconstructed: an earthenware sink with an enamel drainer and a cold tap, a geyser on the wall above for hot water, one of those 1950s cupboards with the flap in the middle that lets down to make a work surface, and on a home-made shelf beside it an electric kettle and a double gas-ring.

There was also a wooden kitchen table and two chairs, drawn up under the window. Whitton gestured Slider towards it. 'Have a seat, while I put the kettle on. I mostly sit in here in the summer, when I don't have the fire going. It's brighter.'

It was. Slider sat as requested, and looked out through the window at a neat square of garden, gay with flowers. Where the Rectory's plot went all the way down to the railway, Whitton's extended a mere twenty feet, ending in a high fence over the top of which could be seen the walls and roofs of some natty new little one-size-fits-all houses. 'Your bedders look very nice. Are you a keen gardener?' Slider asked, conversationally.

Whitton turned from his kettle activities with a bitter look. 'Used to be. Nothing to be keen *with*, now. Used to go all the way down to the bottom, my garden. Fruit, vegetables, apple and pear trees. Lovely chrysanthemums, I used to grow. Potting shed down the bottom. Greenhouse. And a little bit of a wall I grew figs against. You like figs?'

'Yes.'

'All gone now. Sold the land, they did, for development. Cuh! Call that development? Rabbit hutches! I said to them, I seen that kind of development in a dead bird I found under a hedge. Developed into a maggot farm, it had.'

'They sold your garden without your permission?'

'Belongs to the Church, this cottage. They can do what they want. Oh, I got advice,' he added, seeing Slider's concern. 'I asked Mr Dacre what he thought, and he asked Mr Meacher, the estate-agent man, to look into it for me, but it turned I didn't have any right to use the land. I didn't understand the ins and outs of it, but that was how it was in the Law. Mr Dacre's a proper gentleman. He wouldn't put me wrong.'

It had led very nicely to the subject. 'You've known him for a long time, I suppose?'

'Oh, yes. He's an important person around these parts — practically like the local squire, if you take my meaning. Lived here all his life. His dad bought the Old Rectory from the church when they built the new one in eighteen ninety or thereabouts — that's that big house on the other side of the square, with the bay windows. Course, they've sold that now, too. Vicar's got a new house opp'site St Melitus's. Sell everything in the end, the Church will,' he added gloomily.

'So Mr Dacre was born in the Old Rectory?'

'That's right,' he said, milking the tea. 'Only son, he was, and with his father dying when he was only a boy — died of the Spanish flu, just after the First World War — he come into the house then, so to speak, so he never needed to move away. Three older sisters, he had: they all married and went. Then it was just him and his mother. I remember her — she died in, what, 'thirty-six it must have been.' He put a cup down in front of Slider and sat with his own opposite. 'Real hatchet-faced woman she was! What I'd call a Victorian matron, if you get my drift. Tongue like a razor blade. And everything had to be just so. Even used to tell the rector off — it was a rector we had then. Used to criticise his sermons.' He chuckled at the memory. ' "My husband was a literary figure," she used to say, "so I know what I'm talking about." He was in publishing, Mr Dacre's dad — had his own company. Mr Dacre's a writer, did you know that?'

'Yes, I did,' said Slider.

'I suppose that's why he went in for it. Went to university at Oxford, and then started writing books and everything, and got famous straight off.' He shook his head in wonder at such cleverness. 'Got married straight off, too, to a very pretty young lady, and they had a little boy. 'Thirty-two or '-three, he was born. Gor, Mr Dacre doted on that kid! Frank, his name was.'

'So he's Mrs Hammond's brother?'

'Half-brother. I'll tell you how it was. Terrible sad thing. Mrs Dacre had this message that her dad had been took queer and took to hospital. Winter of nineteen forty, that must've been. Anyway, she went over to see him. They lived in South London,' he added, in the same tone of voice that he might have mentioned Zanzibar or Bogota. 'So she's on her way back when the air-raid siren goes off, and she goes down the tube to shelter. That was the night Balham tube station took a direct hit. A bomb goes right through to the tunnel. Sixty people killed. Terrible.'

'I've read something about it,' Slider said.

'And the worst thing, so Mr Dacre always said to me, was that her dad wasn't even really bad. They thought he was having 'eart-attack, but it turned out to be just his stomach turning him up. He had one of them drastic ulcers. By the time she got there, he was getting dressed to go home. So she needn't've gone.' He shook his head. 'Ironic, Mr Dacre always said it was. He said God must have a funny sense of humour. He used to talk to me a lot when he was on the council. Tell me all sorts of things. People like him think people like me are a safe pair of ears. Truth to tell, I think they think we don't understand half what's said to us.'

Another insight. Slider wondered whether that accounted for his own confidability. 'So Mr Dacre married a second time?'

'That's right. Near on right away it was. Well, he was always an impulsive one. Young Frank got that from him. Anyway, he married a nurse he met at the hospital where they took Mrs Dacre's body. Margery, her name was. Ever such a nice lady, but not glamorous — older than him — very quiet and shy. Not shy, but —' He groped for a word.

'Self-effacing?' Slider hazarded.

'That's it. Like that. I suppose he thought she'd be a good mother for young Frank. Anyway, she was Mrs Hammond's mother. Born in 'forty-two, Mrs Hammond was, so you can see Mr Dacre didn't waste any time.'

'And they called her Frances as well,' Slider mused.

'That's right. It was a bit of a rum do, that was. To tell the truth,' he leaned forward confidentially across the table, 'I think he regretted marrying the second Mrs Dacre because, nice as she was, she wasn't his class, and, like I said, not glamorous. But, well, when a man's in a state like that, it's easy to fall for a nurse. And the uniforms they used to wear in them days, with them big white head-things like nuns —'

'Hard to resist.'

'That's right. But then, of course, when he got her home and woke up, like, from the dream, he was stuck with her. A gentleman like him wouldn't go back on his word, and divorce just wasn't done in them days. And then when she has her baby, it turns out to be a girl — which Mr Dacre's got no use for daughters anyway. So *I* think he named her after young Frank, just to put the second Mrs Dacre in her place.'

Some gentleman, Slider thought. But it was throwing an interesting light on the domestic set-up at the Old Rectory. 'So he was never very fond of Mrs Hammond?'

'I don't think he knew she existed when she was a little kid. Well, her ma kept her quiet, and there was young Frank, you see. He came first in everything. Mind you, he was a smashing kid. Handsome lad, full of fun. Clever, too. Always up to something.' He looked across into Slider's eyes. 'Don't you think sometimes that youngsters like that are marked out to die young? Everything golden about them — too good to last. You know what I mean?'

'Like spring sunshine,' Slider said.

Whitton seemed struck by that. 'That's it. You said it. Just like that. Spring sunshine.' He dreamed a little.

'What happened to him?'

'Smashed himself up on a motorbike. His dad had just bought it for him —

Frank wheedled him into it, because Mr Dacre didn't like the idea. Not because of the danger, but because he didn't want his lad mixing with all them rock-and-rollers and teddy-boys. Then the first time he takes it out — woof. Gone. He was only twenty. I don't think Mr Dacre ever really got over that.'

Another instance of God's funny sense of humour? 'It ought to have made him fonder of the child he had left,' Slider suggested.

'*Ought* to of,' Whitton agreed economically. 'Another cup?'

'If there is.'

'I can always add a bit more water. Well,' he said, heaving himself up, 'after that it was all downhill, as the saying goes. Mr Dacre buried himself in his writing, and Mrs Dacre, Mrs Hammond's mum, and Mrs Hammond, not that she was married then, of course, they looked after him. It was a queer set-up,' he mused, as the kettle came back to the boil. 'You'd have thought they were the housekeeper and the parlourmaid, rather than his wife and daughter. Oh, I never offered you a biscuit.'

'No, thanks, not for me. Tell me about Mrs Hammond getting married.'

'Wait'll I do the tea.' He brought back the refilled cups and sat down again, his face alight with the pleasure of having someone to tell the story to. 'Well,' he began with relish, 'that was a queer thing, too. How it happened was this: one of Mr Dacre's sisters died, and he was the whatjercallit for her will and that.'

'Executor?'

'That's right. Anyway, she had this big house, which Mr Dacre had to sell, and he put it with this posh estate agents, and the person they sent round to deal with it was David Meacher — you know him?'

'Yes, of course. Mrs Andrews worked for him. I've talked to him about her.'

'Course you have. Well, selling the house turns out to be a complicated business, and he's around a lot, and Mr Dacre seems to take a shine to him, and he becomes like a family friend. Wormed his way in, I shouldn't wonder,' Whitton added with disapproval.

'You don't like him?'

'Not for me to like or not like, but he strikes me as smarmy. Anyway, he introduces this friend, Gerald Hammond, that he was at school with, and before you know where you are this Mr Hammond's asking Mr Dacre for his daughter's hand in marriage, which Mr Dacre don't hesitate to say yes.'

'Why did he do that, I wonder?'

'Why? To get her off his hands, o' course. Well, she was pushing thirty by then.'

'I mean, why did Hammond want to marry her? Was he in love?'

'After her money, if you ask me. It must have been a big shock when he found she didn't have any. No, to be fair, she was pretty, but very, well, mousy. Well, you know what she's like now, and she was never any different. Wouldn't say boo. How could she, brought up like she was? Still, I expect Mr Hammond thought Mr Dacre would part with some money for his only daughter, not realising he couldn't care tuppence for her. I do know that later on he asked Mr Dacre to invest some money in his business — Mr Hammond did — and Mr Dacre said no. Quite a row there was about it, Mrs Hammond told me. And it was soon after that that Mr Hammond run off with this young girl to South Africa. Sold the business and took every bit of money, and even sold the house without telling Mrs Hammond. She'd have been homeless with her two little boys, if Mr Dacre hadn't invited her to come back home.'

'That was kind of him.'

'Well, it was really, I suppose. But he hasn't suffered by it, because Mrs Dacre was never a well woman and she was ailing by then, poor thing, so Mrs Hammond was able to take over running the house, and when her mother got really bad, she looked after her as well.'

'Living at the far end of the house,' Slider murmured.

'That's right,' Whitton nodded. 'Her and the boys in the servants' end of the house, and her ma and pa right the other end. And if ever the boys made a noise, or broke anything, or played ball in the garden, there was an almighty row, and poor Mrs Hammond in tears in the kitchen, which I've seen with my own eyes on more than one occasion. But still, she owed everything to her father, and there was nowhere else she could go, never having earned her living in her life. I mean, women like that, they can't get on without a man, can they?'

'No,' said Slider; and he thought briefly, painfully of Irene. Thank God for Ernie Newman — and who'd have thought he would ever say that? But if there were no Ernie in the case, he would have had to support Irene for the rest of her life, whatever the courts said, because she, like Mrs Hammond, had never earned her living. She had been promised as a child that if she was good, she would get married and never have to, and it wasn't her fault that history had overtaken her.

'It was different for her boys, of course. Harry and Jack — nice youngsters, and clever. As soon as they could, they left home.'

'You'd have thought Mr Dacre would be fond of them. His only grandchildren — and they're boys, not girls.'

'Ah, but they're Hammonds, you see, not Dacres. They're not Frank's boys.' He drained his cup, wiped his lips, and sighed. 'You got to feel sorry for Mrs Hammond, really. Her husband gone and her mother gone and now her boys gone, stuck there looking after her father, and he's no company for her. And now he's on the way out, poor gentleman. It just shows you, money can't buy you happiness nor health.'

'I suppose he *is* well off?' Slider asked cautiously.

'Oh, yes, rich as treacle. Well, there's his books, and he had a share in his dad's company. And then there was money the first Mrs Dacre left him, and I heard tell his sister, that he was whatsisname for, she left him a lot. And there's the house, o' course. That must be worth a bit nowadays.'

'And will it all go to Mrs Hammond?'

He shook his head. 'I couldn't tell you on that score. He's never cared for her, and I've never heard she'd been promised anything. But when it comes right down to it, who else is there? I reckon she'll come in for it. For the house, at least, because he's always been keen for it to stay in the family. Hates the idea of selling it.'

'It is a lovely house.'

'D'you think so? Can't see it, myself. If I had that sort o' money, I'd buy a nice modern place. Mind you, some old places I can see the beauty of, though it's not what I'd want. But the Old Rectory — well, it's neither fish nor fowl to my mind. And it's not been a lucky house for Mr Dacre. You wouldn't think he'd be so attached to it. I mean, even his last days are going to be upset with all this business over Mrs Andrews.'

'I gather Mr Dacre didn't like her?'

'Well, he wouldn't. She was common, was Mrs Andrews — not Mr Dacre's sort at all. And thick-skinned. She never knew when she wasn't wanted. You couldn't freeze her out, or give her a hint. I've heard

Mr Dacre at church give her a set-down, real cutting-like, and she's not even known it was one. Took it for a compliment. She thought everyone was mad for her company.'

'She went to the Rectory a lot?'

Whitton assented. 'Sucking up. She always wanted to be in with the nobs. They used to give parties, before Mr Dacre got ill, musical evenings in that big hall, and garden parties in the summer on the terrace, and his posh friends would come. She'd have died to get invited, would Mrs Andrews. That's why she got herself in at the church, because Mr Dacre and Mrs Hammond is both church people, and the vicar and some of the others on the council got invited to the house, and she thought she could get in on their back. And, of course, being Christians, the church couldn't refuse her when she said she wanted to help. Didn't get her invited to parties, but now she thinks she's so well in she just calls round when she likes anyway.'

'Or she did until last Tuesday,' Slider corrected.

He opened his faded eyes in comic alarm. 'Deary me, I was forgetting for a minute! Yes, and her visit there must have

been nigh on the last she ever made anywhere.'

'Her visit there when?' Slider asked.

'Tuesday night. Quarter to midnight,
just after, I see her go in. The quarter
struck as I was coming up the steps from
the crypt. I'd been —'

Slider leaned forward. 'Wait, wait, you're
telling me you saw Jennifer Andrews going
into the Old Rectory last Tuesday night?'

'The night she was murdered. Like I'm
telling you. I was on my way home from
the pub when I stopped off to check everything was locked up, which I always do,
because you can't trust anyone these days.
And then I went down the crypt to check
how much coke we had, because I remembered vicar had give me a leaflet from the
coal merchants saying there was a big dis-
count if we ordered our winter fuel now,
and he asked me to see if there was room
to get any more in, and if there was, to
order it, so I thought as I was there I'd
have a look and then I could order it the
next morning. So then I come up again
and locked the crypt behind me, and as I
turned round I saw Mrs Andrews just skip-
ping across the parking place beside the
house and round to the back door.'

'You're sure it was her?'

438

'Course it was. D'you think I don't know Mrs Andrews after all this time? And I remember thinking the next day when I heard about her being found dead that I must have been one of the last to see her, barring Mrs Hammond and Mr Dacre. And her husband, of course.'

'Her husband?'

'Eddie Andrews, the murdering swine. Well, he must have been the last, if he killed her, mustn't he? But I suppose you don't count that. Poor creature. I didn't like her, but I don't hold with that, not with murdering her.'

Slider thought of all the hours they'd spent trying to trace the woman's footsteps that fatal evening. 'Why didn't you tell us this before?' he asked, with strained patience.

'You never asked,' Whitton said indignantly. 'I thought someone would come and ask me questions, me having known all the people in it, but no-one did until now.'

'No-one could catch you in.'

'Well, they could've come and found me, couldn't they? I'm out and about all day, and anyone could've told you where I was. Anyway,' he went on reasonably, 'I don't see it makes any difference. Mr Dacre and Mrs Hammond will've told you all about it

439

already. I know you've been to see them.'

'Of course,' said Slider. 'There is that.'

Eileen Rogan, the physiotherapist, was an athletic-looking girl, trim of figure, nicely tanned, and with such wonderfully clear skin it looked like exceptionally delicate eggshell china with a light behind it. Her hair, short and dark in a pageboy bob, shone and bounced with health like one of those irritating shampoo ads, and the whites of her eyes were so clean they looked blue. At the sight of her all the late nights, bad food, excesses and bodily neglects of Slider's life coagulated in his veins, rusted up his joints, and withered his brain. He felt like a cross between the Straw Man and the Tin Man. He could feel his face wrinkling and his hair greying as they spoke, like She after the ill-advised second bath.

'I understand you want to know something about Mr Dacre?' Miss Rogan said, preceding Slider into the sitting-room of her little flat in a small modern block in Ealing. She had a noticeable but pleasant Australian accent, and Slider wondered, not for the first time, why so many Antipodeans became physical therapists of one sort or another, from doctors and dentists through to masseurs and sports trainers. Maybe it was the climate: spending so much time out of doors and semi-nude must concentrate the thoughts on the body.

'If you don't mind,' Slider said politely, trying to keep his thoughts off her body. She was wearing a white uniform dress with a broad black elastic belt, like a nurse, but the skirt was short and the neckline low and when she bent to clear a heap of files off an armchair for him he discovered he wasn't as old as he'd thought after all.

'No, I don't mind,' she said, answering him literally, 'but I can't give you too long. I've got to get to a patient, and I expect the roads are terrible this morning, what with the strike and all.'

'They don't seem too bad,' Slider said, sitting. 'I got here from Turnham Green all right.'

Miss Rogan perched on the arm of the chair opposite and folded her arms, a compromise between staying and going which had the, no doubt unintentional, effect of enhancing Slider's view of her legs and her bosom. 'Righty-o, then. What did you want to know about Cyril? I hope you're not intending to upset him? He's a real cantankerous old divil, and he can be a pain in

441

the nick sometimes, but I wouldn't want him disturbed at this late stage.'

'Late stage?'

'He hasn't got long to go,' she said bluntly. 'He's fighting gamely, but it's a losing fight. A few weeks — a couple of months at most.'

'I see,' Slider said. 'And what treatment do you give him?'

'Me personally? Well, I work for the Princess Elizabeth Clinic, which is a private health clinic specialising in the treatment of terminal illnesses, like cancer, which is what Cyril's got. The PEC's philosophy is to adopt a holistic approach to disease and pain management.' This part sounded like a quotation from the brochure. 'As part of that holistic approach I provide physiotherapy, massage and other hands-on treatment. Raising the physical and mental levels of well-being through physical contact can have a big effect on the immune system.' Her eyes widened a little and she dropped into normal speech. 'A lot of old people die, you know, because no one touches them any more. We live in our bodies, and we need to be kind to them.'

'So you give Mr Dacre physiotherapy and massage as part of his treatment?'

'That's right.'

'Always at home?'

'Sometimes at the clinic, when there's equipment there I want to use. He gets his drugs and radiotherapy there, of course, and he comes to see me at the same time. I encourage him to swim to improve his muscle tone — there's a pool at the clinic — and I give him heat treatment there. But I visit him at home twice a week — more, if he's having a bad spell.'

'All that must be pretty expensive,' Slider suggested.

'Not my province,' she said shortly. 'I don't send out the bills.'

'But it's not on the National Health?'

'Oh, no, it's private medicine. A lot of the patients have insurance, of course, but that hardly ever covers everything we do at the PEC.'

'So Mr Dacre must be pretty well off to afford it?'

She shrugged. 'He doesn't look as if he's short of a bob or two, does he, living in that big house? But if you want to know about his financial position, you'd have to speak to the PEC's secretary. She's the one who sends out the bills.'

Slider nodded to that, and said, 'What I wanted to know from you was, how disabled is he really?'

'Cyril? He's not disabled. I told you, he has inoperable cancer.' She looked puzzled, and then her brow cleared. 'Oh, you mean the wheelchair business?'

'Is he able to walk at all?'

'Oh, he can walk all right. I told you, he's not disabled; he's just weak. It's understandable at his age, even without the extra burden of his illness; but I'm sorry to have to say, in his case, he's also lazy. I have to bully him into doing things, or he'd just sit around all day feeling sorry for himself. Probably never get out of bed at all. And his daughter encourages him, I'm afraid. I gather she's always waited on him hand and foot, and that's the last thing he needs now.'

'So he can walk? Get out of his chair unaided?'

'Oh, yes, if he wants to. He can push himself up. He's surprisingly strong in the arms still — I suppose it was all that mountaineering when he was younger. Did you know he used to be a climber?'

'I've seen the photos in the drawing-room.'

'He went on well into his fifties, and even after that he still went hill-walking. He was very active right up until he got ill. He talks about it a lot. I think he resents not being able to do what he used to do, so in a contrary way he kind of revels in doing nothing at all — cutting off his nose to spite his face, you know?'

'Yes, it's understandable,' Slicer nodded.

'And then, I think he likes to keep Mrs Hammond running about after him. It'd probably be better for him not to have her around, in some respects. But of course the stage will come — pretty soon, in fact — where he really can't help himself, and then he'll need her.' She eyed Slider with birdlike curiosity, trying to fathom his thoughts. 'This is something to do with that woman's death, right?'

'Did you ever meet her?'

'What, Jennifer Andrews? Not to say met her, really, but I passed her in the doorway once or twice. Cyril couldn't stand her. I always got an earful when she'd been round to the house. I think she was probably quite good for him in a way — got his circulation going, and took his mind off his troubles for a bit!' She smiled to show this was a joke, revealing even teeth of dazzling whiteness. Teeth, hair, skin, figure — and she did massage as well, Slider thought. She was like an updated version of a Stepford wife. He had always wondered why Ira Levin set such store by housework.

'Does he only use the wheelchair downstairs, or is it taken upstairs for him as well?'

'Oh, he has it by his bed, and comes down in it in the morning. He has a lift — haven't you seen it?' she said. 'Not a stair-lift, the real thing. They installed it years ago when Mrs Dacre was in her last illness. One of the spare bedrooms was turned into a sort of vestibule for it, and it comes out in that room between the front door and the kitchen. That used to be Cyril's study, until he had his desk moved into the dining-room. Well, he likes it better there anyway. He can see everyone go past his window. Nearly everyone comes in round the back, you see.'

'Yes, so I understand. The front door sticks.'

She dimpled at him. 'To tell you the truth, Cyril won't let Mrs Hammond have it fixed. He likes being able to keep an eye on who visits her. He teases her dreadfully, the naughty man.'

'Teases her? About what?'

'Oh, about her husband leaving her, and not being able to keep a man, that sort of thing. And now he's made this joke for himself about her having hundreds of men chasing her, and every time a man comes to the door — the postman, the milkman, anybody at all — he goes on about, "Here's another of your gentlemen followers." It makes her blush, poor thing, because of course she's well past the age for getting married, and she can't like having him keep reminding her that her husband ran off with a girl half his age.'

What a prince the man was, Slider thought.

She stood up, and looked at the smart watch that clasped her slim wrist. 'Well, look, I really do have to go, if that's all the questions you wanted to ask me?'

Slider stood too. 'Just one more,' he said. 'Does Mr Dacre have sleeping pills?'

'No, not as such. He doesn't like the idea. But he does have flunitrazepam for the pain, which has a sedative effect.'

Slider took out his notebook. 'What's the name again?'

'Flunitrazepam. The PEC's using it experimentally to control intractable pain, especially at night, so that the patients can get a good night's sleep. It's not available on the National Health, but some of our people are getting very good results with it.'

Chapter Sixteen

Sick Transport, Glorious Monday

When he got back into the car, he found the traffic suddenly thickened, as though everyone who'd skived off work because of the strike had decided at the same moment to abandon their lie-in. At least the creeping and stopping gave him a chance to use his phone without violating moving-traffic regulations. He dialled Tufty's number, and tried him with the name of the drug Miss Rogan had mentioned.

'Oho!' Tufty bellowed with mighty interest. 'So that's how the milk got into the coconut!'

'Mean something to you?'

'Flunitrazepam, my old banana, is the chemical name for Rohypnol, or in other words, our old friend the Roofie.'

'Oh,' said Slider, enlightened. New friend rather than old friend; and no friend at all, come to that. 'That's not nice.'

'Do you think your victim might have been slipped one?'

'It's possible. The old man had them, who owns the house where she was found. He goes to a private cancer clinic that gives them out.'

'Well, flunitrazepam would certainly do the job.'

'Can you test for it?' Slider asked anxiously.

'Now I know what I'm looking for, I can try,' Tufty said. 'It leaves the bloodstream after thirty-six hours and the urine after seventy-two, but since she died within minutes, there's a good chance we'll be able to detect it. I'll do my best, anyway.'

'Thanks, Tufty,' Slider said. 'Let me know as soon as possible, will you?'

He rang off and sat staring at nothing, remembering what he knew about Rohypnol. It was a tranquilliser ten times stronger than Valium, which induced a trance-like state and mental blackout which could last for up to twelve hours. It had been used by some doctors to treat back pain and insomnia, and was in circulation on the black market in Scotland as a cheap substitute for heroin; but more notoriously, especially in America, had been implicated in date rape, and it was in this context that it had come to Met police attention. The small purple pill was colourless and odourless when dissolved in alcohol, and after about ten to fifteen minutes — or less if the drink was gulped down — the drinker would turn into a helpless zombie without ability to resist and without memory afterwards of what had happened. Memory of events usually returned some days later when the drug had passed out of the system, which made it difficult to prosecute, even if the victim came forward. Many didn't, unable to understand what had happened to them, thinking perhaps they were going mad or hallucinating.

He shivered a little, his mind working on, whether he liked it or not. It was his job to track down the killer, but he didn't like it — he never liked it — when he got close to the answer. He didn't ever want to have to realise about anyone that they were capable of such a monstrous act as murder. And this murder — ! There was something of the hunt in it. He saw Jennifer Andrews on her last day, increasingly frantic, running from place to place — no, not stocktaking, seeking escape. But one by one the earths were stopped, until finally she had gone to ground. No matter that her character had been flawed, her conduct faulty, her motives less than pure; she had still been dug out and killed. How much had she known about her own death? But he didn't want to think about that.

He picked up his phone again and rang Atherton. 'I want you to meet me at the Old Rectory. Park on the other side of the square, though — I want to talk to you first.'

'Have you got something new?' Atherton asked, recognising the tone of voice.

'I'm not sure if it's nuts or not. That's why I want to talk.'

'He needs me! Thank you. Thank you. You've made a young man very happy,' Atherton said, in a tremulous voice.

'Shut up and get going,' said Slider.

Atherton drew up behind him and sprang from his car with something of his old eagerness. Slider pushed open the passenger-side door and he slipped in.

'Why are you driving this old wreck?'

'Because Joanna's got my old wreck. Don't breathe on anything: it's got to get me home tonight.'

'So what's cooking?'

Slider hesitated a moment longer before

plunging in. 'It was the AA man who put me on to it.'

'What, Mr Milne?'

'For once — !' Slider pleaded. 'The dog was the key element. I didn't see it at first, not consciously, but it always bothered me, nagging at the back of my mind. There was something not *right* about it. Look, you said there are only two possibilities: either the dog didn't bark, or they didn't hear it.'

'Succinct, elegantly phrased: sounds like me,' said Atherton.

'But if the murderer was out on the terrace in the small hours, morrissing about with a corpse and a tarpaulin — which we know he must have been — *why* didn't it bark?' Atherton looked at him cannily, trying to read his thoughts. Slider continued, 'The AA man had a dog that he said no-one else could do anything with.'

'A common boast.'

'So here is your starter for ten: name the one person who could have stopped the dog barking during nocturnal corpse-shifting activities.'

Atherton got there. 'Isn't it this time of year your head goes in for servicing?' he said. And then, quizzically, 'You're not kidding me. You are seriously setting up old

Professor Branestawm for murderer?'

'Why not?'

'Because he's about two hundred years old and wheelchair-bound. If he was a car, this car would give him points.'

'Ah, but he's not wheelchair-bound,' Slider said. 'Eileen Rogan, his physiotherapist, says he's weak, not crippled.'

'Oh, that's where you've been!'

'She says he can walk, and he's quite strong in the arms. She even hinted that he could probably do more than he lets on, but likes having his daughter wait on him. Suppose even Eileen Rogan isn't aware of how strong he really is? Suppose in a good cause he's quite strong enough for a one-off operation?'

'But why suppose it?' Atherton countered.

'Because the private clinic he attends prescribes him flunitrazepam tablets for the pain at night. And flunitrazepam is the chemical name for Rohypnol.'

'Ah,' said Atherton. 'Roofies, or how to induce quietus in your date's bare bodkin.'

'Praise God for an intelligent bagman.'

'I do my homework, that's all. Okay, his possession of Roofies is one point to you. Walk me through it. You might start with motive.'

'Cyril Dacre is a clever man, embittered by personal tragedy. Several people have said, or hinted, that he has a warped sense of humour, and I got a little of that impression myself. He has no liking or respect for women, and he particularly hated Jennifer Andrews: a vulgar, attention-grabbing woman who patronised and embarrassed him. He told me she was ripe for the plucking. In the shadow of death himself, inflicting it on someone else may no longer be unthinkable to him; and his mind could well be unbalanced by pain and illness to the point of acting out his thoughts.'

'Could and might butter no parsnips.'

'True, but play the possibility through with me. You know that Jennifer told Defreitas she had one more person to visit?'

'At a quarter to twelve, yes.'

'I have a witness who saw her going into the Old Rectory at that time.'

'You have been busy this morning. Why did she go there?'

'I don't know. For some reason. The question is rather, why didn't Cyril Dacre mention it before?'

'Another point,' Atherton allowed. 'But maybe he didn't see her.'

'Being a regular visitor she goes to the

back door rather than the front, knowing that the front door sticks, and in doing so must pass Cyril Dacre's window. Miss Rogan says he takes a keen interest in all comings and goings — suggested that's why he won't get the front door fixed. I think he saw her pass the window, and was suddenly overcome with the irresistible desire to get rid of this ghastly woman for good. Maybe he was in pain; maybe she waved cheerily as she passed, or blew him a kiss —'

'Whatever. You're winning so far,' Atherton said.

'Frances Hammond is in the kitchen,' Slider continued. 'Coming from the direction of the footpath, Jennifer doesn't pass the kitchen window, so Mrs Hammond doesn't know she's there. Dacre whizzes out in his chair and intercepts Jennifer at the back door. He invites her into the drawing-room, and offers her a drink.'

'Which she accepts because — ?'

'Why wouldn't she? She knows him — why should she refuse? She's been drinking all evening. She likes drink. She likes men's company, even an old man like Cyril. He can be charming when he wants to, and he was celebrated in his heyday; and he's still, presumably, rich. We know she liked rich and eminent people. We also know she was always trying to get in with the Dacre set. She'd probably feel flattered if he showed her attention: I imagine he didn't usually.'

'All right,' Atherton said grudgingly. 'It plays.'

'Like Broadway,' Slider said sternly. He went on, 'It's late and Cyril was about to take a Rohypnol tablet to give himself a night's rest. He slips it instead into Jennifer's whisky or whatever, and chats charmingly until she suddenly goes blah. Now that she's helpless, even in his — putatively — weak state he has no difficulty in smothering her with a cushion.'

'I'll give you this,' Atherton said. 'It makes sense of the drug angle. In his weakened state, he'd need to drug her to be able to smother her, whereas if Eddie — or any other red-blooded male in the throes of sexual jealousy — killed her, you'd expect him to do it on impulse and overcome her with his physical strength. Drugging and smothering is much more like an old man's murder — a calculating, clever old man's murder.'

'That's what I thought,' Slider said unhappily.

'But what about the dog? If the dog's the

key to your theory, do you think it's going to sit by quietly while the murdering goes on?'

'There would be no violence, no struggle. No sound, even. Unless the dog's tuned to alpha waves, it wouldn't even know she'd died. And Dacre's the one person who can shut it up with a glance or a word.'

'I suppose it might not even have been with him at that point. It might have been in the kitchen with Mrs Hammond. Although then you'd have expected it to bark when Jennifer arrived, and alert Mrs H.'

'Dacre usually kept the dog with him. But I'll come back to that. It's later that night that his influence over it becomes crucial,' Slider said, 'because he's got to move the body out to the terrace. That's what I keep coming back to. If the dog had barked in the night, Mrs Hammond would have heard it, because she sleeps over the kitchen and she's a light sleeper. If it didn't bark, it could only be because the person moving around was Cyril Dacre.'

'It's persuasive,' Atherton said. 'All right, retouching the makeup: what was all that about?'

'A ghastly joke, that's all I can think of.'

'I suppose whoever did that would have had to be either thick and earnest, or clever enough to have a diabolical sense of humour and a contempt for his fellow man. This seems to be going quite well, you know. But to go back a step: after the drugging and smothering, there he is with a body in the drawing-room. What's he going to do with it? Wouldn't he have to hide it temporarily in case Frances comes in?'

'I had a thought about that,' Slider said, even more unhappily.

'Tell.'

'When Rohypnol first starts to take effect, the victim becomes mentally helpless, but she still has some ability to move, though slowly and in an uncoordinated way. She can still walk, with assistance — like a drunk.'

'I don't like what you're thinking,' Atherton said.

'I don't like it more than you don't. But suppose Dacre makes her get up and walk to wherever he means to hide her, and smothers her there?'

'Where?'

'What about the dining-room — his study, whatever you want to call it? I doubt whether Mrs Hammond would go in there at that time of night — if at all, without reason. We know the body was left in a sitting position. Suppose he walked her to the next room, sat her on a chair, and smothered her there. That would avoid exciting the dog, which he left in the drawing-room. And then he tied the body to the chair as it was to stop it falling to the floor.'

'Why would he want to do that?'

'Because it would make her easier for him to pick her up later. He might not have the strength to get her up off the floor, but from a sitting position he could get her over his shoulder — or hoist her into his wheelchair and push her to the terrace.'

Atherton now looked unpleasantly disturbed. 'You're making this sound too reasonable. I don't like it. It's nasty.' He thought. 'Why did he put her in the trench, anyway?'

'Again, diabolical sense of humour plus contempt of fellow man. Or perhaps he felt Eddie ought to have controlled Jennifer better, and wanted to punish him too. I don't know. It's only a theory.' The last words had something of plea in them, as if he wanted Atherton to produce some serious flaw for him.

But Atherton only said, 'Yes, and what do you propose to do about it?'

Slider spread his hands helplessly. 'I can't think of anything *to* do, apart from putting it to Cyril Dacre and seeing how he reacts.'

'Phew! Sooner you than me.'

'That's what I wanted to talk to you about.'

Atherton's eyes widened. 'What — now? Me and you — go in there? But I'm a young man! I haven't lived!'

'If he were a younger man, or a well man, we might ask him to come into the factory, and work on him, soften him up over a period of time. But we can't do that. And I don't see that we can do nothing, now that we know she went there late that night. That's the last known sighting of her — and neither of them mentioned it.'

Atherton shrugged. 'Well, that's legit at least. Okay, guv, let's get it over with, then.'

Dacre was in his study, at his desk, which faced the side window, looking onto the gravelled area. Slider and Atherton stopped in front of the window. He seemed to be staring at them, but gave no reaction: so unmoving was his face that for a shaky moment Slider thought perhaps he had died with his eyes open and hadn't been discovered yet. But then Dacre's focus changed, and Slider realised he hadn't been staring at them, but at nothing. Now he registered their presence and made a resigned yes-all-right-come-in gesture to Slider's mimed request.

The back door and the lobby door were both open, and when they stepped through into the hall, Dacre was there, in his wheelchair, with the dog behind him in the dining-room doorway. She watched them warily, but didn't bark. One point to the theory.

'Well, what is it?' Dacre said coldly.

'I'd like to talk to you, sir, if I may,' Slider said. 'This is Detective Sergeant Atherton, by the way. May we come in?'

Dacre looked from him to Atherton, and something happened to his face. It was an almost frightening greying. *He knows we know*, Atherton thought, and for the first time he really believed his guv'nor was right about this. The old man turned his chair away without a word, wheeled himself briskly before them into the drawing-room with the dog padding after.

'Shut the door behind you,' Dacre snapped, turning to face them.

'Is Mrs Hammond in the house?' Slider asked.

'She's in the kitchen. She won't come unless I call her.'

How did he know this was private? Atherton thought. But a man so intelligent would know when the game was up, and wouldn't drag it out. He'd turn over his king — wouldn't he?

'Well? You've questions to ask, I suppose?'

Slider looked for the end of the string. 'What time did you go to bed on Tuesday night, sir?'

'I don't remember,' he said at once.

'What time do you normally go to bed?'

'I don't have a regular bedtime. I am not an infant. I go when I feel like it. You had better tell me why you want to know. It may jog my memory.'

There was nothing for it. Slider said, 'A witness has come forward to say that he saw Jennifer Andrews come to this house on Tuesday night, very late, at a quarter to midnight. He saw her cross the gravel and go round to the back door.'

Slider, who had removed his eyes from the old man's face as he asked the question, saw the phthisical hands tighten on the chair-arms. But Dacre sounded confident as he said, 'Witnesses are frequently mistaken.'

462

'It was someone who knew her — all of you — very well. I don't think he was mistaken. But I wondered, you see, why neither you nor Mrs Hammond had mentioned the visit. Of course, if she came to see Mrs Hammond, and you had already gone up to bed, you wouldn't have seen her pass the window.'

'If she had visited my daughter, she would have said so. Frances is incapable of lying. She hasn't the wit,' he said, his voice cold and dark as the Mindanao Trench. 'Your witness was mistaken, that's all.'

Move the question sideways. 'You have tranquillisers for the pain at night, I understand?' Slider said.

'What the devil business is it of yours?'

'A tranquilliser called Rohypnol, which has rather unusual properties,' Slider went on steadily, and now he looked up from the hands to the face. He saw Dacre draw a sharp, small breath, and in the silence that followed, the dark, intelligent eyes, caged with pain, were occupied with a chain of thought, rapid and unstoppable, like a nuclear reaction.

'Yes,' he said at last, very far away. 'I do.'

'Mrs Andrews didn't struggle when she was smothered to death, so it seems likely she was somehow rendered helpless beforehand. The interesting thing about Rohypnol is —'

'Thank you,' he said, raising his hand like a policeman stopping traffic, 'I know all about Rohypnol. I have read the sensational stories in the press. And do you think I would accept any drug without knowing its exact properties? But you have not found the drug in Mrs Andrews' body.'

'Why do you say that?'

'Because you would have said so if you had. That would be a piece of solid evidence, rather than mere wild conjecture.' He was getting his voice back now; he sounded confident again.

'We are testing for it,' Slider said. 'We haven't had the results yet. But as you say, if the tests are positive —'

'I understand that you are trying to suggest in your clumsy way that *I* killed Jennifer Andrews,' Dacre said impatiently, 'but I can't think of any reason why I should.'

'You told me yourself that you loathed her.'

'I loathe many people. I loathe most people, if it comes to that, but I do not kill them.'

'You haven't the means or opportunity to kill most of them; and they don't thrust

464

themselves on you, invading your very house, as Mrs Andrews did. She was an extreme irritant, I do see that,' Slider added sympathetically. 'I can understand how you might want to be rid of her.'

'In that case, you may as well suspect everyone she ever met. You might perhaps,' he went on, with withering irony, 'consider promoting to the head of your list someone not confined to a wheelchair.'

'Oh, but you aren't,' Slider said gently. 'Miss Rogan says that you are quite capable of standing and walking, and that you are surprisingly strong in the arms — a legacy from your mountaineering days, no doubt.'

His face darkened. 'How dare you discuss my condition with Miss Rogan? That is a private matter, and none of your business.'

'She suspects you may pretend to be weaker than you really are,' Slider went on as if he hadn't spoken. 'And it occurs to me that a mountaineer knows a great deal about how to move a body about in difficult conditions.'

Now Dacre laughed. 'This is most entertaining! Do go on with your work of fiction. I don't know when I've been more diverted.' But to Atherton, the laughter was forced, and there was a blank look about Mr Dacre, like that of someone who has had a bad shock and hasn't yet quite registered it. And if he really was innocent, why wasn't he angry? Atherton would have expected blistering rage. Why, indeed, was he even listening to all this, unless it was to find out how much they really knew?

Slider went on. 'What really started me wondering was the question of the dog.'

'Sheba?' Dacre said in surprise, and the Alsatian lifted her head briefly to look at him, triangular yellow eyes under worried black eyebrows. Then she sighed and lowered her nose again to her paws.

'You see, if Mrs Andrews had been killed elsewhere, as we first thought, and a stranger had carried her body to the terrace and laid it in the trench, the dog would surely have heard and started barking. You said yourself she's a guard dog, and I know from my own experience that when I tried your garage doors, it set her off — and that was in daylight. But if Sheba had barked, Mrs Hammond would have heard her. She's a light sleeper, and sleeps in the room above the kitchen where Sheba is shut at night. And Mrs Hammond says she didn't bark. One thing we know for certain is that the body was put into the trench on the terrace during the night. That leaves us with the question: who could have persuaded the dog to remain silent while all that was going on?'

There was no answer. For a moment there was silence; the bright day outside and the dusty air within equally still. Atherton glanced towards his guv'nor, and saw, with a strange chill, that Slider had thought of something, was pursing a train of thought which must have been triggered by something he had just said or noticed. He was preoccupied; he was no longer looking at Dacre. The urgency of his thoughts was almost palpable to Atherton, and he tried anxiously to work out what it was Bill had thought of, because he had a sense of being left behind in a cold place where he very much didn't want to be.

Then he looked at Dacre. The dying man was etched against the bright window, thin as a Byzantine martyr and with eyes as deep and dark and burning; failing hair making a fuzzy aureole around that thinker's skull. And then Dacre started shaking, his bunched hands, his knees under the tartan rug, his shoulders, his head. Slowly as a cinematic western shoot-out, he moved one hand to his lap, caught at the rug, pulled it away and threw it down, shoved away the foot-rests, put down his feet and stood up. It was terrible and unnatural, like seeing a tree uproot itself and walk. The dog looked up, startled, and then rose, backing away a step, tail and ears down, unsure what reaction was required. Dacre let go the chair-arms and reached equilibrium. Erect and burning, impressive and frightening as a forest fire, he said with quiet triumph, 'You're right, Inspector. I applaud your diligence and persistence. I killed Jennifer Andrews — or rather, I exterminated her! Don't look upon it as murder, if you please, but as a public service. I killed her, and I am ready to take my punishment.'

Slider rose as well, facing him, and the dog began to growl menacingly; and when Atherton, between them, stood up, she jumped at him, barking. Dacre turned his head and fixed her with a look. 'Quiet, Sheba! Lie down!' The dog subsided slowly; but in the moment Dacre was thus occupied, Atherton looked at Slider, and saw that his earlier expression had changed from the taut, preoccupied look of the man on the scent to a look of sadness and defeat.

'Please sit down, Mr Dacre,' Slider said quietly.

Dacre stared a moment, and then lowered himself back into his chair. He did not attempt to replace the rug; his legs inside his trousers were like broomsticks inside a Guy Fawkes effigy. 'Well,' he said, and Atherton could see it cost him an effort to speak, 'what happens now? Am I to be arrested and carted off to the police station?' He met Slider's eyes, and some message passed between them, something almost of pleading from the old man, out of a black depth beyond anything Atherton could imagine. Bottom of the trench, sea-bottom, colder and darker than death.

But Slider had no opportunity to answer, for the door opened and Mrs Hammond was there. She registered the scene and a look of alarm came over her vague, indeterminate face. 'What is it? What's happening? I didn't hear anyone come in.' She came forward, her hands moving nervously. 'Father, what is it? Are you all right?'

'Everything is quite all right, Frances,' Dacre said. 'Don't fuss.'

She went on scanning the room, trying to understand. 'Why is the rug on the floor?'

'I put it there. Be quiet. There is nothing for you to do here,' Dacre said. 'I was merely demonstrating a point to Inspector Slider. And now, having satisfied him on that point, I am going to make a statement, which he will take down to my dictation.' He looked at Slider, trying for hauteur and almost succeeding. 'I imagine that will obviate the need to take me to the cells? As you are aware, I am in no condition to flee the country — or, indeed, this house — and I should prefer not to be locked up for the short time that still remains to me.'

'A statement is all that's required at this stage,' Slider agreed neutrally, dividing his attention between Dacre and his daughter. 'You can make that here as well as anywhere.'

'What are you talking about?' Mrs Hammond was looking bewildered. 'Statement? Father, what's going on? Statement about what?'

Dacre held her eyes. 'A statement about how I killed Jennifer Andrews.'

She whitened. 'No!'

'I told you, Frances, there's nothing to make a fuss about.'

'No, you mustn't!'

'I understand it must be a shock to you, but you know I always disliked the woman. I am perfectly happy to confess to my

470

crime and take what's coming to me. And at my age and in my condition, I have nothing to fear. What can they possibly do to me?'

'No, Father, no!' Her face was collapsing in distress, with the slow inevitability of a demolished factory chimney; almost tumbling in anguish. Her hands were twisting about as though they were trying to burrow into her stomach for shelter; her eyes held her father's pleadingly. 'Oh, no, please!'

'Be quiet, child,' he said, so gently it made Atherton shiver. 'Leave the room now. I wish to be alone with the officers. No! Not a word. Go!'

The command in the voice was so firm it even had the dog on her feet again. Mrs Hammond dragged out a handkerchief and applied it to her face, covered her trembling lips. She was making hoarse noises, a cross between sobs and gasps, and her eyes were everywhere, but she turned away, to obey as she had obeyed all her life.

And Slider said, 'Just a moment.'

His voice was quiet, but Mrs Hammond jerked as if she had been hit across the spine with a heavy stick. She stopped, turning only her face back towards him, so that her eyes showed white like those of a frightened horse.

'Go, Frances,' said Mr Dacre, but the command had gone out of his voice. It sounded much the same, but it was powerless; an empty firework case. 'Inspector, I forbid you to speak to my daughter. I forbid you to trouble her with this. I've told you, I'm ready to make a statement.'

But Slider only looked at the woman. 'Mrs Hammond,' he said, 'I can quite see how, when you realised the enormity of what you'd done, you wanted to cover your tracks, but how could you let us arrest poor Eddie Andrews? How could you let him take the blame for your crime? That was cruel.'

Atherton looked at Slider. *Her?* he thought.

She turned. 'Cruel?' Her face was working horribly, like something trying to escape from under a blanket, and her voice rose as she repeated, *'Cruel?* What do you know about *cruelty?'*

She flung herself at Slider. Atherton moved fast — the reaction of instinct, which later he would remember and be glad about — to try to interpose himself between them. The dog barked like machine-gun fire and jumped at him, teeth not quite making contact, but keeping him back. But as he tried to fend it off, and Mr Dacre shouted at it and him and Slider almost indiscriminately, Atherton saw that Slider was holding Mrs Hammond, not wrestling with her, that she was not trying to kill him, but weeping on his shoulder, in his arms; a big woman, almost as tall as Slider, too big and ungainly easily for him to comfort.

Chapter Seventeen

Ethics Man

When sufficient back-up had arrived, Slider pulled Atherton out of the room, which saved Atherton from having to pull Slider out.

'Are you crazy, or am I?' Atherton asked urgently. 'I'd just like to know.'

Slider hardly noticed. 'Come with me. I need you to witness this.'

'What?' Atherton demanded, but he got no answer.

Slider led the way across the hall to the kitchen. The kitchen door was open, the room was empty, cool in shadow, the window a dazzling rectangle of white light. A cup of tea, half drunk, stood on the table, and a library book lay open and face down on the sagging sofa where Mrs Hammond must have abandoned it when she heard the dog bark. Under the scarred polythene protective, the dust jacket showed a passionate embrace, a woman in red, a man with dark hair and huge shoulders. Here it was: love — authentic, romantic, unfailing, marriage guaranteed; every woman's birthright. What Irene had been promised as a little girl. No, not Irene, this was not the time for that. Frances, woman turned monster, still feeding on the poison, the white refined sugar that warped and rotted.

He crossed the kitchen to the darkest corner and bent over the dog's basket, probing down amongst the hairy blankets. In a moment he straightened up, with the shredded strip of red silk dangling from his fingers, damp with dog saliva. He felt as though, with a very little encouragement, he would be able to cry.

He turned to Atherton. 'Jennifer's scarf,' he said, in a dead voice. 'The one she was wearing the last day, that got lost somewhere between the Meacher house and the grave. I saw the dog chewing it in its basket, but, God help me, I never made the connection until just now.'

Atherton came close and looked. 'Her scarf?'

Slider was looking round. 'Here. She did it here, on this sofa, where she always sits — where she was going to go on sitting, drinking tea and reading romances. My

475

God, what a monster!'

'That pathetic nothing of a woman?'

'She didn't take the dog out that morning, as she said she did. I should have realised from the beginning. I did know something wasn't right about it, but I didn't know what, and of course I never suspected her — a pathetic nothing of a woman, as you say.'

'But what — ?'

'Don't you see? If she'd taken the dog out with her on the terrace that morning, it would have found the body! It would have gone straight to it and barked its head off. But she never said a word about the dog's reaction to the corpse, and neither did Eddie. And the next-door neighbours, who heard her cry out or shout when Eddie arrived, heard no barking. Because the dog wasn't there.'

'But where does that get us? When you said the dog was the key, I thought you meant about the barking in the night.'

'Yes, I did. I was wrong there, too. My God, I made such a stupid, elementary mistake!' he said fretfully. 'And after I'd been warning everyone else — *and* refer-ring to the Christie case. Timothy Evans hanged because no-one entertained for a moment the notion that he might be telling the truth and Christie lying. It was the same with Eddie Andrews and Mrs Hammond. I thought Andrews was trying to distance himself from the trench by saying the work was her idea, but in fact he was telling the truth and *she* was trying to distance *herself.* I should have known the corner of the tarpaulin couldn't have blown back. It was a still night, and the ropes on the corners showed that he was in the habit of tying it down. It was she who turned the tarpaulin back, because she knew what was under it. But from the very beginning I took her as the standard, and everything had to be measured by her truth. Stupid, stupid!'

'Don't beat yourself up. Who would have thought — ?'

'I should have thought.' He looked at Atherton. 'There weren't two possibilities, but three. Either the dog didn't bark, or they didn't hear it — or it did bark, and she was lying.'

'Yes,' said Atherton.

'Mrs Hammond had the same access to the Rohypnol as her father. Jennifer went to see her that night. Mr Dacre must have been already tucked up asleep in his bed, and he slept soundly all night. She gave Jennifer a spiked drink here in the kitchen, and smothered her, probably with one of the cushions from this sofa. At some point in the — not exactly struggle, but let's say transaction — Jennifer's scarf came off and I suspect got lost amongst the cushions. In her distracted state, Mrs Hammond didn't notice it, or its absence; but later the dog nosed it out — she was wearing quite a lot of scent, you remember — and carried it to its basket, where I saw it chewing it. Saw, but didn't see.'

'But what did Mrs H. do about the dog? If Dacre was already in bed, it must have been in the kitchen with her while she was murdering.'

'Yes, of course. The dog was upset, and she couldn't deal with the corpse with it barking and growling, maybe even trying to attack her. She had to drag it out into the passage; but she knew it could get the kitchen door open by lifting the latch — I saw it do it — so she dragged it into the empty storeroom, the first on the left, which had a bolt on the outside. The dog went mad trying to get out — I saw the gouges on the inside of the door, and the empty sacks were ripped where it worried them in its frenzy. But no-one could hear it in there. The room has no window, and those walls are two feet thick.'

'My God, yes. It's the perfect cell.'

'And there the dog stayed all night. It was still in there in the morning when she went out on the terrace to do whatever she meant to do.'

'And what was that?'

'I don't know. There are some things I shall have to ask her, little as I want to. But I think I've worked most of it out.'

'You might let me in on it, then,' Atherton said. 'What did she do with the body? Leave it on the sofa?'

'No, I think she moved it straight away, started dragging or carrying it out as soon as she'd shut the dog in. I don't know what she meant to do with it in the long run, but I think she got it as far as the back lobby and then decided to hide it temporarily in the downstairs loo, perhaps because that was the one room she knew her father would never go in — the door's too narrow for his wheelchair.'

'Oh, my God, and she sat the body on the loo?'

'On the closed seat, and kept it in place by tying it to the down-pipe. Freddie said the ligature had a broad, flat section like a luggage strap, and I saw a long webbing dog-lead in the lobby she could have used.'

'I expect the dog was very much on her

mind,' Atherton remarked.

'Later, when the Mimpriss Estate had gone to bed and there was less chance of anyone passing in the street, she took the body out to the terrace and laid it in the trench. Early in the morning she went back out to do something else with or to the body —'

'What?'

'God, I don't know. Maybe she didn't either. Eddie said she was just standing staring at it, didn't he? Maybe she was frozen with horror and simply couldn't think. But anyway, he interrupted her. He made her call the police, and then sat down with his head in his hands, desperately upset, and that was when she took the chance —'

'To throw Jennifer's bag into the pickup!' Atherton finished triumphantly.

'Yes. Then she had to hurry indoors, because she knew the police were coming and she didn't have long to cover her tracks. She had to let the dog out of the storeroom —'

'Sooner her than me. I don't suppose it was pleased.'

'It was probably exhausted by then. And she had to go and check on her father and make sure he hadn't heard anything.'

'Yes, and wait a minute,' Atherton said, frowning, 'what was all that with the old man? Why did he confess?'

'To save her, of course,' Slider said miserably. 'I think maybe he'd had a suspicion all along. He's an intelligent man, with a trained, academic mind and plenty of time to think; and I remember how quick he was from the beginning to suggest it must have been Eddie who did it, and to tell me Eddie and Jennifer were on bad terms.'

And Slider remembered, too, how he had abruptly stopped himself on that same subject — not happy to be incriminating an innocent man, even though he felt he had to do it. But his suspecting must surely at that point have been only back-of-the-mind stuff, for how could he really, consciously have believed his daughter a murderess?

Atherton said, 'When Mrs Hammond came in, he said he'd been proving a point to you.'

'Yes, proving that he could stand, that he was capable of moving the body. But did you see his legs?'

'Like knitting needles,' Atherton agreed. 'It was a terrible effort for him to get upright.'

'He's got very little time to live. He

wants to take the blame to save her, because it can't matter to him.'

'I thought he had nothing but contempt for her?'

'Perhaps he thought that too, until he saw her in danger. It's surprising how deep the instinct of fatherhood goes.'

He thought of Dacre's burning eyes, and the appeal in them at the end. Caged in his failing body, raging at life — and perhaps suddenly guilty at the way he had always treated his daughter, the one thing left to him that mattered, wealth and repute having proved no barrier to encroaching chaos. That last, furious, noble gesture saddened Slider immeasurably because it was futile. It would not save her, for truth was stronger than the devices of men, as Cyril Dacre, historian, ought above all to have known. The writers of history may lie for their own purposes or of their preju-dice, but the truth has a life of its own, in stones and bricks, in the earth, in artefacts, in the marks it makes on the fabric of the world. An historian, if he is a scholar, and a detective, if he cares about his craft, are very much akin: both study the traces men leave behind them, in order to reveal their actions.

Atherton brought him back from his

thoughts. 'So he struck the manly chest and said, I cannot tell a lie, I did it with my little hatchet. I wish you had taken his statement now. It would have been interesting to see exactly how much he had worked out.'

'He'll have to give a statement anyway. I want you to take that. Now that you know what to look out for, he can't lie to you. But I think probably he won't try, now.'

'No endgame,' Atherton said, remembering his earlier thought.

'Eh?'

'Never mind. What about you? Mrs Hammond?'

'Yes,' Slider sighed. 'I'll do a preliminary here, because we can't take her away until something's been arranged about her father. He can hardly stay here alone. And if he goes, something will have to be done about the dog. It's the devil of a mess,' he concluded gloomily.

'Not your fault, guv. People shouldn't murder people. I wonder why she did it, by the way?'

'Only she can tell us that. But I have an idea,' said Slider, turning back reluctantly towards the place where duty lay.

In Atherton's little bijou back yard — he

called it a garden by virtue of a square of grass so small it didn't even merit a lawnmower and was cut with shears — Slider and Joanna sat on canvas folding chairs and looked at the jasmine climbing over the wall opposite, beyond which the upper windows of the next row of houses peeped Chad-like, only two ten-foot plots away. Everyone was out in their back gardens this evening, and a muted composite of conversation and cutlery noises rose into the air, along with the inevitable barbecue smoke, to mingle with the sound and smell of traffic to which they were so accustomed it was actually an effort to notice it.

'Did you read that bit in the paper,' Joanna said, on the thought, 'about the new research they've done in America on tinnitus? They reckon it's not physical damage that causes it but mental damage. There's background white noise all the time that our brains automatically filter out, but the brains of tinnitus sufferers have forgotten how to edit.'

'Makes sense,' Slider said. 'After all, every copper knows that what you see is not what goes into the eye but what the brain registers. It's the great forensic myth, the infallibility of the eye witness. And then there are the other forms of blindness — like blind prejudice.'

Joanna laid a hand on his knee. 'You got there in the end.'

'By machete-ing my way through Eddie Andrews' life.'

Along the A40 for quite a stretch, between Savoy Circus and Gypsy Corner, the houses had been pulled down to make way for road widening. But the widening had never happened — the scheme shelved, perhaps for ever — and the gardens of the houses remained, isolated, untended, the sad ghosts of a settlement which had come and gone and would soon be forgotten. Eddie Andrews reminded Slider of those gardens, when he had gone to tell him he was no longer suspected of the murder — unkempt and overgrown, not with any temporary absence of care, but with the desperate neglect of the ending of everything. No-one was ever coming back to prune the bare, ten-foot-high roses, trim the privet, pull up the rosebay willowherb flourishing impudently amongst the grasses of the lawn. Eddie's hollow cheeks were sprouting, his hair was a thicket, there were seeds in his eyes, and his clothes seemed ready to migrate from his hunched and shambling shoulders. His world had been destroyed and he would never be put back together again.

'Bill, you've got to stop picking at yourself,' Joanna said reasonably. 'You know you're always low at times like this. In the balance of things it probably didn't make any difference to the man. He might even have been glad of the counter-irritant.'

'You sound like Atherton,' he said, with a grudging smile.

Atherton came out at that moment with two tumblers. 'Nobody sounds like me. I'm unique. A little drinkie for the memsahib?' He handed a man-sized gin and tonic to Joanna. 'And one for my dear old guv'nor, what is covered with laurels.'

'Privet's the highest I rate on this one,' Slider said.

'Do I detect the chafe of sackcloth?' Atherton enquired.

'Are you coming out?' Joanna asked him. 'I want to hear all the details.'

'Not if you want to eat tonight. Bill can tell you. I've heard it.'

'What about Sue?'

'I'll tell her while we stir.'

'Oy!' came a bellow from the kitchen. 'Should it be boiling like this?'

'Coming, Mother!' Atherton trilled.

Joanna tried her drink. 'Crikey, this is strong!' she spluttered.

'Matches the strength of my character,' Atherton said modestly.

She dimpled at him. 'I think you're cute.'

He dimpled back. 'So do I, but what do we know?' And disappeared.

'Now,' said Joanna, turning to her lover. The westering sun lit up the tired lines in his face and the shadows under his eyes. He hadn't been home at all last night. The rest of Monday and the whole of Tuesday had been taken up with interviews, new forensic examinations, writing reports, and sorting out the Dacre-Hammond *équipe*. Joanna had had a call this afternoon to meet Slider and Atherton at the latter's house at around seven for a celebration meal. She had arrived to find Sue already there, but the men hadn't arrived until half past — in Atherton's car. Joanna's beloved wreck was still sitting in St Michael Square: when Atherton had driven Slider there to pick it up, it wouldn't start.

'So, tell me all,' Joanna invited. 'Why did she do it?'

'Love,' Slider said. 'Jealousy. Desperation. All the old candidates. I'd begun to suspect — not the detail, but the general direction. I knew David Meacher had to be involved in some way — he kept popping up everywhere I looked. Jennifer Andrews told her friend that Meacher was dropping her for another woman, a rich woman, who mustn't find out about his other affairs.'

'And that woman was Mrs Hammond?'

'Cyril Dacre's a wealthy man, and he's dying. A few months ago he told Mrs Hammond that he was going to leave her the house and half of everything else, the other half to be divided between her sons. She'd looked after him so long it was only justice — and maybe he'd begun to realise what a rotten life she'd always had. Anyway, at about the same time David Meacher, the good old family friend, started to take a more romantic interest in her.'

'She'd told him about the legacy?'

'It's conjecture. I doubt whether Dacre would have said anything, but Mrs Hammond might easily have let it out. Or Meacher might just have assumed: there was no-one else, after all. The house alone would have been enough to fill him with lust: he had a thing about beautiful real estate; but I gather Dacre was otherwise rich as well. But Mrs Hammond didn't make the connection. When the swine started making love to her, he told her that he'd always admired her and it just happened to be now that his admiration had ripened into love, and she believed him.'

'The need being father to the thought?' Joanna said.

'Perhaps. Probably. However difficult her father was to live with, she must have been frightened at the thought of being left all alone by his death. And Meacher is a smooth, plausible man, and *apparently*,' he put the word in with a large air, 'attractive to women. Anyway, when Meacher started to make delicate approaches to her, she responded with eagerness and gratitude.'

'And most things twinkled after that,' Atherton said, re-emerging. 'Something to soak up the alcohol, children, and stave off the pangs of thingummy.' He put down an ashet bearing slices of French bread toasted and spread with pâté. 'I suspect — though Bill doesn't agree with me — that she'd been in love with him for years, probably ever since her husband left her and Meacher was nice to her.'

'It was Meacher who introduced her rotten husband to her in the first place,' Slider reminded him.

'All the more reason to be grateful. She'd

never have been married at all, otherwise.'

'And marriage is every woman's dream and salvation, is it?' Joanna said indignantly. 'Go away, you horrible, sexist, patronising beast. Get back in the kitchen where you belong.' Atherton smiled at his most sphingine and went away. 'Go on,' she said to Slider. 'More about Meacher.'

'His wife was finally getting fed up with him. All the money in the marriage was hers, and her father had sensibly tied it up so that Meacher couldn't touch it. If she was threatening to pull the plug on him — as she hinted to me — and divorce him, it was going to leave him right up a close.'

'Hence the urgency to woo Mrs Hammond, and shuffle off Mrs Andrews?'

'Quite. Of course, he might have been fed up with Jennifer anyway. I imagine a little of her went a long way. Jennifer, however, wasn't ready to be shuffled. She was desperate to get away from Eddie and wasn't going to be thwarted by a flabby middle-aged nonentity like Mrs Hammond. She tried desperately to get Meacher back, and when he proved adamant, and all her other options failed, she decided to tackle the problem from the other end and put Mrs Hammond off him.'

'That's stupid! Even if she succeeded,

490

how was that going to make him marry her?'

'She was in a panic and a temper and she'd been drinking: I don't suppose she was thinking very clearly. And there was an element of revenge in it, I expect. "Other women" who tell wives usually do it in the hope that the wives will punish the men, since they can't make any impression on the men themselves.'

'Yes, that's true,' Joanna said thoughtfully. 'Have one of these.'

He took one without looking, his mind elsewhere. 'Mrs Hammond was devastated.' He stopped a moment, remembering how she had cried just telling him about it, torn with the desolation of loss and humiliation. 'She'd thought he loved her truly for herself alone.'

'And, of course, like every woman who finds out her man has been two-timing her, she turned her hatred on the other woman. She couldn't hate him, so she blamed Jennifer.'

He didn't want to think about that. It brought it too close to home. 'She'd just come down from settling her father in bed when Jennifer arrived. She'd given him his Rohypnol, and still had the box in her pocket, and she was crossing the hall when

Jennifer came in at the back door. She said she had something important to talk about, so Mrs Hammond took her to the kitchen. Jennifer must have been getting cold feet about it, because she asked for a drink, and Mrs H. fetched her a whisky. Then she spilled the beans. She told Mrs H. that she and Meacher were lovers, that he loved her and had promised to marry her, and that he was only after Mrs H. for her money. She said Meacher had told her he meant to wheedle the money out of Mrs Hammond after her father's death while stringing her along with false promises, which Mrs Hammond was so desperate for a man she would believe. She said she and David had often laughed together about it, and that he had called Mrs Hammond a sad old man-eater.'

'The poor creature,' Joanna said with feeling. 'That Andrews woman deserved —'

'Don't say it,' Slider stopped her. 'It's not true.'

'Metaphorically, I meant.'

'I know what you meant.'

'Go on, then. What happened next?'

'A murderous rage came over Mrs Hammond.' The temper her father had bequeathed her came into its own at last, and for once in her sorry existence she hit back at the forces that had bullied and mocked and subordinated her, taken from her everything pleasant and lovely and left her with nothing but the shucks and the labour. 'It was easy to slip a pill into Jennifer's second whisky. Jennifer went on talking. She was not entirely sober, of course, and I imagine Mrs Hammond's apparent lack of reaction threw her. She must have expected a flare-up of some kind, but of course Mrs H. had spent a lifetime being meek, patient and silent, and her responses were all bottled up inside. Eventually Jennifer went floppy, and Mrs Hammond got up, put one of the cushions over her face and smothered her.'

Just like that, Joanna thought. Slider had stopped, and she didn't prompt him, seeing he had gone away, probably back to the long, frequently interrupted, exhausting and harrowing interview he had conducted with Mrs Hammond. For Joanna, the whole story was just a story: she knew none of the protagonists and they meant nothing to her. But through his distress she could catch a glimpse of the reality behind the words; could feel through him the leading edge of the black, bitter cold of chaos and evil that lay under the surface crust of the world and every now and then broke through. He must be so much stronger than her, Joanna thought, to be able to bear such repeated contact with it and still stay on his feet and sane. At times like these she admired him almost painfully.

Sue stuck her head out of the door. 'Jim says to eat inside. We don't want your responses to the food confused by the smell of other people's barbecues.' They looked at her but didn't move. 'Well, shift then,' she commanded. 'We're just dishing up.'

'What's all this "we"?' Joanna said, getting up. 'From a woman who couldn't burn water . . .'

'We're a team,' she said with dignity. 'He cooks, I taste.'

'How did he ever manage without you?' Joanna marvelled. She held out a hand to Slider, and he took it and got up, and then drew her to him and held her a moment gratefully, resting his head against hers. It felt heavy to her, and she knew how much effort it took him not just to lay it on her shoulder and go to sleep.

A long time later, after a prolonged and mostly merry meal, when they were back at her place and in bed, Joanna was ready for sleep, but felt how the tide had gone out again for him, leaving him wakeful. The talk and the company as well as the food and drink had stimulated him, and she had been glad to see him shake off his sadness and respond. There had been plenty of chat and plenty of laughter to dilute the rest of Mrs Hammond's strange story, as Jim and Bill between them told it to her and Sue.

For all the rest had been Mrs Hammond's story, and Joanna, who had never even seen the house, saw with strange clarity, as though watching a film, her shock and fear at finding herself, as her rage dissolved, alone with the corpse, intruder in her familiar kitchen. She watched Mrs Hammond struggling with the hysterical dog, dragging it out to lock it in the storeroom, hurrying away from its muffled barking and scrabbling, to face that lolling dummy on the sofa, and wonder in spinning terror what she was going to do with it.

The downstairs loo was the immediate and desperate hiding place, just to get the thing out of her sight. Then she had returned to the kitchen and paced up and down for hours, trying to think what to do.

She couldn't leave the body where it was for ever. She considered briefly throwing it onto the railway lines in the hope that a train would run over it and thereby advance a reason for the death. Then she thought of burying it in the garden; but the ground was rock hard after the long drought, and how could she dig a hole big enough and fill it in again, all before Eddie Andrews arrived?

And thinking of Eddie she thought of the hole in the terrace, which he had already dug. It was the right size and shape, and she was sure she could get the body that far. She went back to the cloakroom to look at it again, half fascinated, half horrified, and it was then that she noticed how smudged the makeup was. She fetched Jennifer's handbag and redid Jennifer's face with her own makeup.

'But *why?*' Sue had demanded at that point in the story. 'That was bonkers.'

'Guilt, shame; some confused idea of covering up her traces,' Atherton said. 'You have to realise she was bonkers by that time. But it had the benefit, from her point of view, of reminding her of something that had to be dealt with — Jennifer's handbag left behind on the sofa.'

She took the handbag with her out onto

the terrace and put it down by the wall while she untied the tarpaulin and folded it back. Then she went back for the corpse, hoisted it over her shoulder, and staggered out with it: she was a strong woman, and having nursed her mother and her father, had some experience of handling inert bodies. She put it into the hole, but at the sight of it lying there was overcome with fear and guilt and remorse. As an act of atonement she had straightened the limbs and pulled down the skirt, laying it out decently. Then she had simply knelt there, frozen, unable to think or act.

'But what was she meaning to *do?*' Joanna had asked. 'I mean, Eddie was due to arrive next morning. How was she going to explain it to him?'

'Her idea was to fill the hole in with the stuff that had come out of it,' Atherton had explained, shaking his head in wonder, 'and when Eddie came, tell him they had changed their minds about having the work done and send him away. You see, Eddie had said all along that it wasn't really necessary; she'd insisted out of fear of the terrace falling down, after all the horror stories she'd heard from other people about subsidence. So if she now said she'd changed her mind, there was nothing he could do about it.'

'Now that is bonkers,' Joanna had said. 'Wasn't he supposed to wonder why she'd filled the hole in with her own hands in the middle of the night? Or why there was so much of the filling left when the hole was full?'

'You can't expect someone in her position to think straight,' Atherton said kindly. 'It was the best she could manage in the circumstances. But anyway, when it came to it, she couldn't do it. The thought of throwing earth and rubble into Jennifer's face might have been enticing in life, but was impossible in death. She was still standing there trying to bring herself to the point when Eddie arrived, much too early, and she realised the night was over and her chance had gone.'

The shock of seeing his wife dead, especially after his drunken ravings the night before, had gone to Eddie's legs. He told Mrs Hammond to phone the police, sat down on the wall and put his head in his hands. It was at that point Mrs Hammond had seen the handbag which she had left there, practically under Eddie's feet, and in a panic she had grabbed it and thrown it into his pickup, not to incriminate him, but simply to be rid of it. Eddie was in no state to notice. Mrs Hammond had gone into the house, leaving Eddie with time to think how bad things were going to look for him, and to decide on his feeble story of having been home all evening watching television. And so the stage was set, as Slider had said, 'for the rest of the farce'.

Joanna felt his chest move under her cheek in a sigh, and she pressed herself a little closer for comfort — his and hers, both.

'What will happen now?' she asked, knowing he would still be thinking about it.

'I don't know,' he said. Mrs Hammond was in custody; Dacre had been found a bed in the clinic where he had his treatment, and from his state of collapse it seemed unlikely that he would ever leave it. The problem of the dog had been solved by Alf Whitton, who had willingly taken it into his cottage next door. Sheba had gone with him without a struggle, and he had seemed happy to have a dog about the place again. 'She knows me, she'll be all right with me, poor old girl,' he had said, and Slider had thought it would be a good permanent home for the creature, should such a thing become necessary. The house — that lovely old house he had coveted —

was empty. For centuries it had grown and changed, matured and mellowed harmoniously, sheltering generations of normal, happy families. Now in one short week its peace had been destroyed, perhaps — who could know? — for ever. It was such a terrible, pitiful waste, he thought.

But that was not what Joanna meant, of course. 'Porson thinks the CPS won't go for it,' he said.

'But you've got her confession.'

'They won't go on a confession these days, not after all those overturned sentences. There's got to be good material evidence as well.'

'But you've got — what, the scarf?'

'Can't prove that was Jennifer Andrews'.'

'The fingerprints on the handbag — didn't you say they matched Mrs Hammond's?'

'Yes, but they could have got there any time. Jennifer visited the Old Rectory frequently.'

'What about the traces of makeup on the cushion?'

'That's suggestive, but not enough on its own; and even with the Rohypnol in the bloodstream, we can't prove it was Mrs Hammond gave it to her. The trouble is, you see, that the CPS is judged on results.

If they take a case and don't win it, it's a slap on the wrist for them; too many failures and bang goes their bonus. And they've got budgets — prosecutions are expensive, and Mrs Hammond is low priority, quite apart from the winnability factor. In the old days, when the police conducted their own prosecutions, we'd have a go if we were sure, and if we lost, well, *c'est la guerre*. Now we catch 'em, and the CPS shrugs and let's 'em go.'

'Is that why you're so down?' she enquired delicately.

'No. Not entirely,' he amended. He was silent a moment, and she waited for him. 'So many lives have been ruined. Jennifer, Eddie Andrews, Mrs Hammond; her sons — how will they live with it? Dacre's last days turned into horror. Janice Byrt. Lady Diana.'

'It's not your fault. It's Meacher's, for being a greedy, unprincipled tart. And Jennifer Andrews', for being a spiteful, heartless tart. And Mrs Hammond's —'

'For being what? A put-upon tart?'

'For being a murderess,' Joanna said robustly. 'Nobody made her do it. And it was her who let Eddie Andrews suffer by being wrongly accused, not you. She should have owned up. You don't need to feel sorry for her.'

'I don't — not for that. For the rest of her life, perhaps.' He thought about her reluctantly, and saw, quite separated from the meek and bullied woman of his first acquaintance, the monster in the kitchen — as if they were two different people. The monster had slipped Jennifer Andrews the drug, and then waited for it to take effect before killing her. Waited and watched. That was what horrified him. It had not been the action of an instant, it had been slow, calculated, deliberate; and he couldn't convince himself otherwise than that, at the moment Mrs Hammond had smothered her victim to death, *she had enjoyed it.*

He dragged his mind away from the image, which he knew from experience was going to dog him for a long time. 'Well, she's paying for it now, anyway.' Horror and shame and guilt were her portion. 'And even if it never comes to court, she'll have to live with it for the rest of her life. Her father's dying. Meacher will never speak to her again. Perhaps her sons won't either. She'll never be able to serve on any more church committees. She'll be ostracised — all alone in that house for ever.'

'Well,' Joanna said, 'maybe after all it's

really Gerald Hammond's fault, for leaving her in the first place for a younger woman.'

'Oy,' he protested.

'You asked for it. Listen to me, my darling dingbat, I think you are wonderful: clever, resourceful, thoroughly professional, honest, full of integrity; and kind and tender-hearted into the bargain. I am very proud of you — and very proud to be here in bed with you, too.'

'Really?' he said, almost shyly.

'One thing you can be absolutely sure of is that I'm here because I want to be.'

'It's your bed.'

'Don't nitpick. All right, you're here because I want you to be. I'm trying to tell you that I love you.'

'Tell me, then. Don't let me stop you.'

'I love you, Inspector.'

'I love you, too.' He kissed her, long and thoroughly, and then settled again with her head on his shoulder. 'Are we going to be all right, do you think?'

'What, you and me? It should be me asking you that. Have you really settled things with Irene?'

'I think so. I hope so. Of course, there will always be problems. And I'm going to be pretty tapped until the children leave school.'

She didn't say anything to that. Pretty tapped was putting it mildly, if the experience of various of her divorced musician friends was anything to go by. And that meant she would be tapped too. It wasn't that she had wanted him for his money — fat lot of use that would ever have been! — but her life as a self-employed musician was doubly precarious: she might fail, or the work might fail. Was it unreasonable or base of her to have hoped that if ever she did get together with a man, he would provide a little fall-back security for her? Setting aside accident and the various physical ills that attacked violinists, and provided she had no breakdown of nerves or temperament, she could go on playing the fiddle to orchestral standard until and perhaps after retirement age; but with new young musicians pouring out of the colleges every year, and rampant gerontophobia attacking promoters and managements alike, would anyone go on employing her? Just a little security in an insecure world was all she had hoped for; but it seemed that was not to be. She would have to provide the fall-back position for him instead, and try not to feel resentful of the wife and children she would be indirectly supporting.

Well, that was the way the bones had fallen. Ain't nothin' but weery loads, honey. He was here, that was the important thing, warm and alive and wrapped around her in her bed, and that was worth the price. She could feel he had relaxed now: his breathing had steadied, and she thought he was falling asleep. But then he said suddenly, diffidently, and in a perfectly wakeful voice, 'Should we get married, do you think?'

That was one out of left field, if you like! 'Are you in a position to ask me, sir?' she said, temporizing.

'Well, I will be, one day. When I am, if I ask you, do you think you'll say yes?'

She started to smile, unseen in the darkness. 'That's a hypotheoretical question, as your Mr Porson would say.'

'I wasn't thinking of asking him,' Slider assured her.